Beauchamp Hall

By Danielle Steel

BEAUCHAMP HALL · IN HIS FATHER'S FOOTSTEPS · THE GOOD FIGHT
THE CAST · ACCIDENTAL HEROES · FALL FROM GRACE · PAST PERFECT
FAIRYTALE · THE RIGHT TIME · THE DUCHESS · AGAINST ALL ODDS
DANGEROUS GAMES · THE MISTRESS · THE AWARD · RUSHING WATERS
MAGIC · THE APARTMENT · PROPERTY OF A NOBLEWOMAN · BLUE
PRECIOUS GIFTS · UNDERCOVER · COUNTRY · PRODIGAL SON · PEGASUS
A PERFECT LIFE · POWER PLAY · WINNERS · FIRST SIGHT
UNTIL THE END OF TIME · THE SINS OF THE MOTHER · FRIENDS FOREVER
BETRAYAL · HOTEL VENDÔME · HAPPY BIRTHDAY · 44 CHARLES STREET
LEGACY · FAMILY TIES · BIG GIRL · SOUTHERN LIGHTS
MATTERS OF THE HEART · ONE DAY AT A TIME · A GOOD WOMAN
ROGUE · HONOR THYSELF · AMAZING GRACE · BUNGALOW 2 · SISTERS
H.R.H. · COMING OUT · THE HOUSE · TOXIC BACHELORS · MIRACLE
IMPOSSIBLE · ECHOES · SECOND CHANCE · RANSOM · SAFE HARBOUR
JOHNNY ANGEL · DATING GAME · ANSWERED PRAYERS
SUNSET IN ST. TROPEZ · THE COTTAGE · THE KISS · LEAP OF FAITH
LONE EAGLE · JOURNEY · THE HOUSE ON HOPE STREET · THE WEDDING
IRRESISTIBLE FORCES · GRANNY DAN · BITTERSWEET · MIRROR IMAGE
THE KLONE AND I · THE LONG ROAD HOME · THE GHOST
SPECIAL DELIVERY · THE RANCH · SILENT HONOR · MALICE
FIVE DAYS IN PARIS · LIGHTNING · WINGS · THE GIFT · ACCIDENT
VANISHED · MIXED BLESSINGS · JEWELS · NO GREATER LOVE
HEARTBEAT · MESSAGE FROM NAM · DADDY · STAR · ZOYA
KALEIDOSCOPE · FINE THINGS · WANDERLUST SECRETS · FAMILY ALBUM
FULL CIRCLE · CHANGES · THURSTON HOUSE · CROSSINGS
ONCE IN A LIFETIME · A PERFECT STRANGER · REMEMBRANCE
PALOMINO · LOVE: *POEMS* · THE RING · LOVING · TO LOVE AGAIN
SUMMER'S END · SEASON OF PASSION · THE PROMISE
NOW AND FOREVER · PASSION'S PROMISE · GOING HOME

Nonfiction

PURE JOY: *The Dogs We Love*
A GIFT OF HOPE: *Helping the Homeless*
HIS BRIGHT LIGHT: *The Story of Nick Traina*

For Children

PRETTY MINNIE IN PARIS
PRETTY MINNIE IN HOLLYWOOD

DANIELLE STEEL

BEAUCHAMP HALL

A Novel

Delacorte Press | New York

Published in the United States by Delacorte Press, an imprint of Random House, a division of Penguin Random House LLC, New York.

DELACORTE PRESS and the HOUSE colophon are registered trademarks of Penguin Random House LLC.

LIBRARY OF CONGRESS CATALOGING-IN-PUBLICATION DATA

Names: Steel, Danielle, author.
Title: Beauchamp Hall : a novel / Danielle Steel.
Description: New York : Delacorte Press, [2018]
Identifiers: LCCN 2018022558| ISBN 9780399179297 (Hardcover) |
ISBN 9780399179303 (Ebook)
Subjects: LCSH: Television—Production and direction—Fiction. |
Interpersonal relations—Fiction. | BISAC: FICTION / Contemporary
Women. | FICTION / Sagas. | FICTION / Romance / Contemporary. |
FICTION / Family Life. | GSAFD: Love stories.
Classification: LCC PS3569.T33828 B43 2018 | DDC 813/.54—dc23
LC record available at https://lccn.loc.gov/2018022558

Printed in the United States of America on acid-free paper

randomhousebooks.com

2 4 6 8 9 7 5 3 1

First Edition

Book design by Virginia Norey

To my wonderful children,
Beatrix, Trevor, Todd, Nick,
Samantha, Victoria, Vanessa,
Maxx, and Zara,

May you always have the courage
to pursue your dreams,
and may all your dreams
come true!

I love you with all my heart and love,

Mom/d.s.

Beauchamp Hall

Chapter One

Winona Farmington opened one eye and saw through the window the white wonderland she woke up to for most of the winter in Beecher, Michigan. It was a small town, almost two hours north of Detroit, with a population of ten thousand. Beecher's main claim to fame was that it had been hit by the tenth deadliest tornado in U.S. history in the 1950s, long before Winnie was born. Nothing much had happened there since.

The other side of her double bed was cold, which meant that Rob had gotten up at least an hour before, and left for the meat processing plant where he worked. She guessed even before she glanced out the window that he hadn't bothered to shovel after last night's snow. The house she lived in had been her mother's, and she owned it with her sister, Marje. Marje was already married with kids when their mother died, and she and Erik owned their own house, so Winnie stayed in the family house and they agreed that if they ever sold it, they'd split the proceeds equally. But for now at least, Marje didn't need the money. Her husband owned a busy plumbing company, and the house was a good investment and likely to increase in value, so she'd never asked Winnie to sell it.

Rob stayed with her almost every night. He had his own apartment, but rarely went there except when they had a fight, or if he stayed out too late and got too drunk when he went out with the boys and didn't want to hear Winnie complain about it the next morning. The rest of the time he slept at Winnie's, did no repairs, felt no great attachment to the place, and only helped her with something minor when she asked him. He kept some clothes in her closet, but nothing too personal, and none of his favorite items to wear.

Winnie had once escaped Beecher to attend the University of Michigan in Ann Arbor, and had loved it for the three years she'd been there. She had big dreams then, and wanted to work in publishing in New York after she graduated. She'd even visited the city a couple of times with her roommates and loved it, but then her mother got sick at the end of junior year, and by the end of the summer, it looked as if she only had a few months to live. Winnie didn't want to miss being with her mother for her final days. They'd always been close, particularly after Marje moved out after she graduated from high school when Winnie was eight. She had her mother to herself from then on, and their time together was precious. Her mother had shared with her her passion for books, the delight of Jane Austen, the Brontë sisters, her favorite authors, biographies of famous people, history, and current novels.

Winnie took the first semester of senior year off to be with her. But she was no better by Christmas, and Winnie took spring semester off as well to nurse her. It had been hard to come home to a small, quiet town, where nothing ever happened, after the excitement of the university. Coming back to Beecher was like returning to her childhood, and her whole focus was on her mother. She had no life of her own. Her friends had married right out of high school, or gone to Detroit to find better jobs than they could find in Beecher. A few had gone to college, but not many. Some even had babies by then, and Winnie suddenly had nothing in common with them. She was busy with her mother's care.

It was never spoken, but Marje simply assumed that Winnie would be there for their mother. She had a husband and a child by then and made it clear she had no time. Winnie was single, still in college, and Marje saw no reason why Winnie's plans couldn't be deferred, and her dreams put on the back burner. Winnie was the obvious choice of caretaker, and she didn't want to let her mother down. She had always given up so much for them. And Winnie didn't want to abandon her mother in her final months. She loved her and wanted to spend as much time with her as she could.

Miraculously, and despite the doctors' dire predictions, her mother had hung on for seven years, and even rallied several times, but never long enough for Winnie to leave again. She fought a noble battle, and finally died when Winnie was twenty-seven. By then it seemed too late to go back to college. She had a job, a house, a life, and New York and her dreams seemed as if they were on another planet. She was working as a cashier at a restaurant, and got a better job at the local printing company after that. She met Rob four months after her mother died, and the time had drifted by like a river from then on, carrying her along with it. She didn't need a college degree for the job she had. Her own natural organizational skills and common sense were enough.

It was hard to believe she and Rob had been dating for eleven years. She wasn't madly in love with him, but he was familiar and comfortable. They never talked about marriage or the future, they lived in the present, had dinner together on most nights, went to the movies, bowling with friends sometimes. It wasn't what she really wanted, but there was no one else more interesting around, and suddenly she slipped from twenty-seven to twenty-nine, then turned thirty at dinner one evening with Marje, Erik, and Rob. Then just as quickly she was thirty-two and then thirty-five. They'd been together for ten years when she turned thirty-seven. And now she was thirty-eight and couldn't figure out where the years had gone. Eleven of them, with Marje reminding her constantly that she needed to get married and start having kids before it was too late. She conveniently forgot that Winnie had spent seven years, crucial years, taking care of their mother, while Marje claimed she was too busy to help. Winnie wasn't angry about it, but it was a fact of her life. She had sacrificed a big chunk of time, which she'd never get back.

She couldn't see herself having kids with Rob either, and he wasn't eager for kids or marriage. He was thirty-nine, and most of his friends were getting divorced after fifteen and twenty years of marriage. Marje and Erik had a good marriage and seemed happy enough. She knew her sister had had at least one affair, maybe two, which Marje had never admitted to, but Beecher was small, people talked, and Winnie had guessed. She didn't know if Erik knew or not. He was a good breadwinner and a terrific father who coached Little League for their two boys. Winnie couldn't imagine Rob doing that. He had nieces and nephews of his own who didn't interest him much, and he referred to all of them as the "rug rats."

Winnie had read in *Cosmopolitan* magazine once that women couldn't afford dead-end relationships after the age of twenty-eight, or they ran the risk of getting stuck in them for years, and missing opportunities for marriage and children, possibly until too late to have them. The magazine had warned that you turn forty before you know it. Her mom had always cautioned her to try to find the right man and settle down before the bloom was off the rose. She wasn't there yet, but she was getting close, with a man who didn't set her heart on fire, took her for granted most of the time, and never told her he loved her. It wasn't exactly a dead-end relationship, it was more of an open-ended one that just kept limping forward through the years without arriving anywhere. She wondered if he would marry her if she made a fuss about it, but she didn't because she wasn't sure how she felt about it herself. It was a no-frills relationship: a box of candy on Valentine's Day if he remembered, and he almost always forgot her birthday but would take her out to dinner a few days later, if he had time. She couldn't see the point of getting married, unless they wanted kids, and they didn't. She wasn't ready to have babies, she wanted to figure out what she envisioned for her future first.

"Well, you'd better figure it out pretty damn soon," her sister scolded her. "Or you'll wake up one day and be forty-five or fifty, and it'll be too late, for kids anyway. It happens faster than you think." Marje was ten years older than Winnie.

"I'm only thirty-eight," Winnie reminded her.

"Yeah, and it seems like just last week you were twenty-eight. You won't be young forever, Win." Marje always liked reminding Winnie that she was getting older, it made her feel more comfortable about being middle-aged herself. It had taken Marje and Erik a long time to get pregnant, and their boys were now fourteen and seventeen. They were good kids, who had no ambition to leave Beecher. Erik expected both of them to come to work with him at his plumbing company someday, and neither of them objected. They already helped out there after school. The company was a good moneymaker, and neither boy was planning to go to college since their parents hadn't. Winnie's three years at Michigan, as an English major with a creative writing minor, were considered an aberration for her family. She'd gone to college before her nephews were even born, so she wasn't an example they could relate to, and she had done nothing special with her life.

She kept herself busy with the things she loved to do. She still read voraciously and was first on the list at the library for every bestseller that came out. Her mother had been a volunteer at the town library on the weekends and instilled in her a love of books. Winnie wrote short stories from time to time, and had done well in her writing classes in college. And when her mother had gotten too sick to continue working, Winnie had taken over one of her favorite duties. She read stories to children every Saturday morning. It was also a volunteer job and she loved it. Her mother had been "The Story Lady" to the local children, and Winnie happily stepped into her shoes. She had done it at first to help her mother, who didn't want to disappoint the children who expected her to be there on Saturdays. It gave Winnie a chance to share the gifts her mother had given her with the children. She introduced them to "The Red Shoes," *Charlotte's Web, Stuart Little, The Little Prince, The Secret Garden, Little Women,* and Nancy Drew for the slightly older girls. The children loved her and Winnie got to read her favorite childhood books again. She had a gift with the children, like her mother had, although she didn't think so. Marje always said the books their mother read to her had bored her, while Winnie devoured them, much to their mother's delight. Every Saturday morning, Winnie spent two hours at the library, and was "The Story Lady," carrying on her mother's tradition and following in her footsteps. It was Winnie's only contact with kids, other than her two nephews, who were as uninterested in books as their mother.

Winnie's other passion had always been horses, ever since she was a little girl. She'd had a chance to ride at a friend's father's farm, and had had a few lessons. She was a decent rider and her friend's father said she was a natural. She liked to ride, but what she liked best was watching them. She had an instinctive sense for what a horse seemed to be thinking or feeling. She had walked into the corral once where they were keeping a horse that had been mistreated before they bought him. No one had been able to ride him, he was wild-eyed and terrified, bucked off anyone who rode him, and kicked anyone who came near. The men at the stable said he was hopeless and they were planning to sell him again, or worse. Winnie felt so sorry for the horse that she let herself into the corral where he stood alone. She spoke softly to him, as he eyed her in terror but didn't move. He let her stroke him, and pawed the ground next to her, as one of the men watched, afraid to call out to her to stand back, stunned by what she was doing.

In time, Winnie was able to ride him, bareback with only a bridle. They called her "the horse whisperer" after that. She had a talent for taming abused horses, and people in Beecher knew it, and called on her once in a while to help them out. As far as they were concerned, she had a gift. She didn't get a chance to use it often, but it was there. It was as if she could get into a horse's mind and still its fears. They trusted her, and calmed down whenever she was there.

Winnie peeled off her flannel pajamas and got into the shower. She had a long, lean body, in contrast to Rob's heavyset frame with a paunch. He liked drinking beer when he came home from work. Marje had put on weight, and was a different body type from Winnie, who had always been tall and slim. Winnie had dark hair, pale blue eyes, and creamy skin. With better clothes and somewhere to wear them, she would have been pretty. Their mother had been, though she had let herself go once she was widowed at thirty-three. Her husband had died in a hunting accident. Marje remembered him slightly, Winnie didn't. Marje looked more like him, sturdy and rugged, with a tendency to put on weight after she had her kids. She envied Winnie's slim figure, but ate too much of what she cooked for her family to lose the weight she'd gained. She'd been the prom queen in high school, but looked ten years older than she was while Winnie looked younger than her age. Winnie had never been a prom queen and didn't care. She was always lost in the books she read.

While drying her hair, Winnie looked out the window again, trying to assess how long it would take her to shovel the driveway. She did it nearly every day since there was new snow almost every night this time of year. Rob could have, before he left for work, but never did. When she asked him to, he reminded her that it wasn't his house and that was why he parked his truck in the street, and suggested she do the same.

She made a bowl of instant oatmeal and had a cup of coffee, bundled up in her parka and snow boots, grabbed the shovel from the garage, put on gloves, and went to work on the driveway. It took her half an hour to get the snow pushed aside and packed down enough to drive over it in her SUV, but she was only ten minutes late when she got to the printing company where she worked as the production manager. She kept all the big projects organized and on track. She had exceptional organizational skills, and thanks to her, they met all their deadlines. It wasn't a creative job, but vital for the smooth running of the business, and she did it well.

Hamm Winslow, her boss, came out of his office and glared at her. She hated the job, and her boss, but it was decent money. He owned the printing company, and had been her boss for the last ten years. Her best friend, Barb, worked there too. She had a more menial job than Winnie, but was good with layouts, and very visual.

"Nice of you to come in before lunchtime," he said snidely. He always had something unpleasant to say, and had no respect for his employees, or anyone for that matter. He was a miserable person.

"Sorry, my driveway was iced up," she said blandly.

"Whose isn't? You expected to wake up in Hawaii, maybe? Get up earlier, don't come in here late again. Got it?" He was even nastier to the women who worked for him than the men, and he got away with it.

"Sorry." He was always angry and complaining about something.

Nothing was ever done fast enough or well enough for him, and he took pleasure in pointing out publicly the mistakes they made. "He's in a great mood," Winnie commented under her breath as she slipped into her seat at the desk next to Barb's. They'd gone to middle school and high school together, and Barb had gone to junior college and got her two-year associate's degree, which didn't seem to make much difference. She'd been dating Pete for four years, they'd gotten engaged a few months before, and were planning to get married next summer. Her future husband was a dentist and a nice guy. She spent all her spare time now planning the wedding. They were going to have the reception at the local hotel. Barb wanted to work in his office after they were married and quit the job she had, which would leave Winnie to face the ogre alone. She wasn't looking forward to it.

"Somebody screwed up a big order for the bank," Barb whispered to her. "You should have heard him yelling ten minutes ago."

"Glad I missed that," Winnie whispered back, shot a smile at Barb, and turned on her computer. It felt just like high school, and middle school before that, when they sat next to each other in class. Barb opened a drawer and pointed to three bridal magazines in it and Winnie laughed.

"I'm throwing the bouquet at you, you know. You'd better be ready to catch it," Barb said, smiling.

"I'll be sure to duck," Winnie said, checking on an order she had on her screen. It wasn't ready yet, and they were getting close to deadline. She was going to get on the production department about it immediately. Hamm never realized how vital her services were to him, or never showed it if he did. He never praised her or thanked her.

12

"Rob is a great guy, you should marry him. It's time, Win," Barb said as a follow-up to her comment about the bouquet.

"Who says?" she said, looking unconcerned.

"We're getting old!"

"At thirty-eight? You sound like my sister. She got married right out of high school. Thank God we didn't do that. She could be a grandmother by now, for God's sake. Now there's a scary thought."

"You'll be old enough to be one by the time you start having kids, if you don't hurry up." There was nothing else to do in Beecher except marry, have kids, go bowling, and play softball in the summer. She didn't say it, but Winnie wanted more than that, much more. Barb had been engaged once before, after years of dating the same guy, and it hadn't worked out. He'd cheated on her constantly. Now she was ready to settle down, and in a hurry to have babies. Winnie wasn't. "Who are you waiting for? Bradley Cooper? Send him a map. You've got everything you need right now." That wasn't how Winnie saw it, but she didn't say it. She didn't know what she wanted, but she knew this wasn't it, working for Hamm Winslow for the rest of her life. And she wasn't sure Rob was it either. After eleven years, she knew things weren't going to get any better than they were now. Their relationship was lackluster at best, but not bad enough to walk away from either. It wasn't exciting, or romantic. Rob said only women, and men with low testosterone, were romantic and liked all that mushy crap. That was one way to look at it. She didn't expect him to throw roses at her feet, but a little more attention might be nice. Like shoveling the driveway for her once in a while, so she wouldn't be late for work and didn't have to start the day cold and tired. He could have done at least that for her, particularly since he slept there most nights. He bought groceries occasionally, which he thought was a big deal. He always said she owned the house after all, and she wasn't paying rent, so she could afford to pay for her own food. There was nothing gallant about Rob.

Both women got busy at work then, Winnie went to push the production department. At the end of the day, Barb turned to her with a question.

"How about dinner at my place tonight? Pete is going to a dental conference in Detroit."

"I'm having dinner at my sister's," Winnie said with a sigh.

"That should be fun. Not."

"Yeah, but she makes a big fuss about it when I don't see her for a while. She claims the boys miss me. I know they don't. They don't even talk to me when I'm there. I wouldn't have at their age either."

"Have a good time," Barb said with a smirk, and they both left work and got in their cars. It was already dark, bitter cold, and the roads were icy. But it was only two miles to Marje and Erik's house and Winnie was a careful driver. She let herself in the back door when she got there, and the boys, Jimmy and Adam, were watching TV in the basement playroom. You could hear it all the way up to the front door. And as usual, the house was a mess. No one ever cared. Marje's strong suit was not keeping house, and she made no apology for it. Erik was used to it and didn't seem to see it. Whenever the mess got to him, he cleaned it up himself.

She found Marje in the kitchen, getting dinner ready. It was pot roast, which seemed like a hearty meal for a cold night. Her sister was a good cook, and her family were all big eaters, Winnie wasn't, but it smelled good anyway. Marje was lucky, she hadn't had a job in years. She was a stay-at-home mom, thanks to Erik's business, and she got a new car every two years. She drove a Cadillac Escalade, which was a lot nicer than Winnie's six-year-old SUV.

"How was work?" Marje asked, as she checked on the pot roast and smiled at Winnie. They were very different, but there was a sisterly bond between them. Marje blamed their mother for encouraging Winnie to be a dreamer. Marje had made fun of her when Winnie had written a paper once in high school about why Mr. Darcy from *Pride and Prejudice* was her favorite hero of all time and she wanted to marry a man like him. Winnie loved stories from another century, preferably set in England, which her sister thought was ridiculous. Marje loved watching reality shows, and still never read a book. Their mother had given up trying to encourage Marje to read in her teens, and shared her love of books with her younger daughter.

"Work was okay," Winnie answered. "Hamm is such a jerk. He's not happy unless he's beating someone up and humiliating them in front of everyone else. It gets pretty old." But they both knew the money was good, and Winnie had seniority now. She didn't want to start over somewhere else, which was part of what kept her with Rob too. What if she never met anyone and never had another date? It was easier to stick with "the devil she knew," at work and with Rob.

They talked for a few minutes about Erik and the kids while Winnie set the table and Marje slid into her favorite subject.

"So what's happening with you and Rob?"

"Nothing. Don't start that, please. We both go to work, he comes over at night, we fall asleep, and go back to work the next day."

"Sounds very exotic," Marje said, "and a lot like marriage. You've had years of practice. You might as well just do it one of these days."

"Why are you so hot for me to get married?" It always annoyed her. It was the only thing they ever talked about.

"I don't want your life to pass you by. Trust me, at your age it starts to fly. I don't want you to miss it."

"I'm not missing anything. I'm happy."

"Really? You don't like your job, your boss is a horse's ass, you're not crazy about your boyfriend, and what else is there in your life?"

"What's in your life?" Winnie volleyed back. "Erik and the kids. That's no more exciting than mine."

"It suits me," Marje said, and Winnie knew it did. "You've always been such a dreamer, I'm just afraid you're going to dream your life away, waiting for some kind of magic to happen. There's no magic, Winnie. This is all we get." It sounded sad to Winnie.

"You mean I don't get to be Cinderella when I grow up? Mom always said I could be anything I wanted to be. That's why I went to college and wanted a job in New York." It would have been so much more than what she had here.

"Well, that didn't happen, so you've got to work with what you've got. 'Bloom where you're planted,' as they say." That was very philosophical for Marje, and Winnie smiled.

"Very profound. Don't I look like I'm blooming?" she teased her sister. She knew Marje meant well, or thought she did, although she could be a pain in the neck at times. And there was a wide chasm between them. They were so different and always had been. That hadn't changed.

"Actually," Marje said, narrowing her eyes to study her, "you look depressed. Why don't you get highlights or something, or change your hair color? Rob might like it." It was always about Rob and what might make him propose. Marje had dyed blond hair with three inches of dark roots. Winnie's was her natural dark brown, almost black, color. Their mother used to say she looked like Snow White.

"He likes me the way I am," Winnie argued. "And I'm not depressed. I accept my life as it is." But she thought about what she'd said again on the way home. Did she accept her life? Had she made her peace with it? Did she still want more? Did she have a right to it? She was no longer sure. Dinner at her sister's had been the way it always was, always the same conversation between the adults, about work or the kids, brief chaos when the boys joined them at the table, and then Winnie went home to her empty house. Rob was bowling with friends that night.

She turned on the lights when she got home and sat in front of the fireplace in the living room for a few minutes. She remembered when she used to sit there with her mother, in the last years of her life, talking about the books they read, and the dreams the stories spawned. She still thought she was going back to college in those days, but they never talked about that because it would only happen after her mother was dead. And then she didn't go back anyway.

She heard the front door open behind her and turned to see Rob walk in and shake the snow off his boots. He was a big, burly guy with lumberjack looks, and didn't talk a lot. His family was originally from Norway, and there was a raw, hearty look to him. She had expected him to come home later, he usually did.

"You're home early." She smiled at him. "I just got home from Marje and Erik's."

He went to get a beer, popped it open and took a sip, and sat down on the couch next to her with the can in his hand. "Everyone was tired tonight, and two of the guys were sick. We called it a night early, and went to Murphy's Bar for a while." She could smell it on his breath. He wasn't an alcoholic, but he drank a lot. He said it was the Scandinavian in him. Her brother-in-law drank just as much. Most of the women she knew didn't. "What are you doing in here?" He looked around the room they never sat in. They either sat in the kitchen or her bedroom. There was an old-lady quality to the living room. She hadn't changed anything since her mother died. It was full of her mother's things, and some antiques she'd inherited from her grandmother. Winnie kept the room as a kind of shrine.

"I was just thinking of my mom when I got home, and the books we used to read. At the end, I used to read aloud to her. *Rebecca* was one of her favorites." She didn't know why she was telling Rob, she knew he didn't care. Just the thought of reading a book put him to sleep.

"That sounds maudlin," he said matter-of-factly, chugged his beer, and got up. "I'm beat. I'm going to bed."

She turned off the lights and followed him upstairs. He turned on the TV in her bedroom, dropped his clothes on the floor, and climbed into bed while she took a shower, in case he wanted to make love. Their sex life was pretty good, despite his lack of romantic sensibilities. He was great in bed when he was in the right mood. It had been part of the glue that held them for the last eleven years, the strongest thing between them.

She started talking to him when she got out of the shower, and he didn't answer. She walked into the bedroom, and he was sound asleep on his back, snoring loudly. The beers on his bowling night had caught up with him. She looked at him for a moment, put on her pajamas, and tiptoed downstairs to her mother's bookcase. She knew exactly where the book was that she wanted, she hadn't read it in years. *Jane Eyre.* She ran back upstairs with it and got into bed, smiling as she held it. It was like a visit with her mother, and a trip back in time, as she opened the familiar book. There was always something comforting about holding her mother's books. She loved the familiar feel and smell of them. The pages were yellowed, and it was like meeting up with an old friend as she began reading, and Rob continued to snore next to her. She knew that when she woke up in the morning, he'd be gone again, and he wouldn't have shoveled the driveway for her if it snowed during the night. Nothing was ever going to change. But as she read the book her mother had given her as a young girl, nothing around her mattered, and her real life faded away. That was one of the best things about reading, she could just disappear and forget everything she didn't like about her life.

Chapter Two

The printing business where Winnie worked was always busy in December, with calendars and Christmas cards, and end-of-the-year reports to deliver. They could hardly keep up and Winnie and Barb had to work late almost every night. Winnie was planning to spend Christmas Eve and Christmas Day with Marje and Erik and their boys as she always did. And Rob went to relatives in Detroit. They never spent Christmas together. His mother was in a nursing home in Detroit. Winnie had never met her. She had Alzheimer's so there wasn't much point. He'd never invited her to meet his other relatives. They didn't have that kind of relationship, he said. With the exception of his bowling league, they spent most of their time together alone, in a kind of bubble suspended in time. She had promised to make dinner for him the night before Christmas Eve, and hurried home from work to do it. He brought venison he'd shot with a friend. Winnie cooked it from a recipe she found on the Internet, and it was delicious. Rob was impressed. She had poured him a glass of red wine with dinner, and he said he'd rather stick with beer.

"That was a damn fine meal," he said, smiling at her. "I didn't think you could cook like that."

"Neither did I. The recipe was easy."

"What are you doing for Christmas?" he asked, as though he expected it to be different.

"I'll be with Marje as usual, same as every year." The holidays always made her miss her mother, but she didn't want to tell him that. He wasn't the kind of man you exposed your soft side to. It would have made him uncomfortable, and Winnie feel too vulnerable.

"Well, save New Year's Eve for me. We can go to Murphy's for dinner, and hang out till midnight, and then come back here." It was his favorite bar, and she knew he'd spend half the evening shooting pool with his pals who hung out there too. She had nothing else to do. They'd been going to Murphy's on New Year's for eleven years. Her life with him was one long déjà vu, but she never met other single men.

She brought out her presents for him then, a heavy cobalt-blue sweater, a black knit cap, and some thermal gloves with a heated panel that you could put in the microwave to warm them up. He said he really liked them. The sweater fit him perfectly, the hat was warm, and he said the gloves were great.

"They'll keep your hands warm while you shovel my driveway," she teased him, and he grinned.

"Then I guess I should have gotten a pair for you," he shot back at her, and then went out to his truck to get his gift for her. It was a medium-sized box in silver Christmas paper with red ribbon. She opened it and found another sweater. He gave her one every year, this year's was yellow, and when she took it out of the box, she saw that there was a black lace G-string in the box too. He loved seeing her in sexy underwear and bought it for her himself, since she never did. "Why don't you put it on and show me," he said. She reached for the sweater, surprised he wanted to see it, and he stopped her and handed her the G-string. "Not the sweater," he said, laughing at her with a lustful look. There was something about the underwear he gave her that always made her feel cheap. It usually had rhinestones on it, or tassels, or an arrow pointing toward the crotch, but to keep him happy, she disappeared and came back wearing it with the sweater she'd had on, and high heels.

"Come on, baby, take off the sweater." He was leering at the G-string, and with her long legs, she looked sensational in it. She peeled off the sweater, pretending to strip for him, and she was wearing a black lace bra that almost matched the lace G-string. "Now that's more like it!" He grabbed her as soon as she got near him, and lifted her off the ground in his powerful arms and laid her on the couch. He had his own clothes off and was on top of her immediately, making deep guttural sounds. Everything about him was familiar to her. He was an adept lover and knew what she liked best, but there was nothing tender about his lovemaking. He was too aroused by the thong he had given her to wait for long, and he came with a shudder and a fierce shout, then lay still on top of her.

"God, I love you in that underwear," he said, as she looked up at him. It always had the same effect on him. The gift was more for himself than for her, but she always went along with it. She knew it meant a lot to him. They went upstairs then and made love again, and it reminded her why she stayed with him. She couldn't imagine the sex being as good with anyone else, and finally, exhausted and happy, he rolled over and fell asleep. She got up, put a bathrobe on, and went downstairs to clean up the kitchen. She picked up the G-string from the living room floor and put it in her bathrobe pocket, and then went back upstairs and slid into bed next to him. She knew there should have been something more with him, but there wasn't, just hot sex when she wore the right underwear and a warm body in her bed. He still hadn't told her he loved her. He never did. And when she woke up in the morning, he was gone. He hadn't stayed to wish her a merry Christmas, or left a note to say so. He figured he had given her his best gift the night before, on the couch and in her bed. She knew it was all he had to give and all she'd ever get from him, other than a sweater once a year and sexy underwear.

She shoveled the light snow from her driveway and left for work. Everyone was in a festive mood. Their office party was set for noon, with a buffet from an Italian restaurant, and after lunch, they could all leave. The office would be closed for a week. No one needed to have anything printed between Christmas and New Year's Day. Even Hamm, the original Scrooge, was willing to give them the week off.

"Did you bring your present for the game?" Barb whispered to her, as she took hers out of her desk right before lunch. The whole office played the white elephant game every year. Each employee bought a gift that cost roughly twenty dollars, wrapped it anonymously, and put it in a pile. They all drew numbers and took turns in order picking a gift. The other employees could steal any gift they wanted twice, from whoever picked it, and after that they were safe and could keep the gift they had. And the person a gift was stolen from would get another turn. It usually led to jovial screams of protest as a gift someone wanted was taken, and shouts of victory when someone else got to keep it or stole it back. Some of the gifts were really fun, most weren't. Winnie thought that she should put Rob's Christmas G-string in the game one year. She was tired of getting them, but she had bought something respectable for the game, a good-looking cheese platter someone could use over the holidays. There were bottles of wine, and an assortment of odd-shaped gifts people were eyeing, trying to guess what they were.

"Of course I brought a gift," she said to Barb, went out to her car to get it, and put it in with the others. "I never get lucky with this game," she said to Barb in a whisper as they each picked a number. "I've gotten a set of coasters three years in a row, and I never have guests over. I've had a jeweled tissue box, a leatherette pencil cup, and a pair of mittens with reindeer on them."

"I hope you get mine," Barb whispered, and pointed to where it was. "Trust me, you'll love it." Winnie smiled at how excited she was, and indicated which one was hers.

The game had begun and their coworkers were already stealing bottles of wine from each other by then, and a bottle of vodka. There was a nice-looking plaid shirt, three pairs of wool socks, a wool hat that looked like a polar bear, an Italian cookbook, a pair of light-up Christmas earrings that three of the women wanted and kept stealing. The game started getting loud and boisterous halfway through. Barb got Winnie's cheese platter and loved it, someone else stole it, and she got it back, and Winnie decided to trust her and picked Barb's gift, opened it and found two DVD sets of a TV series she'd heard of and never seen. The actors in the photograph were wearing clothes from the 1920s, there was a castle in the background, and it was set in England. The series had been a big hit and was still on TV. Barb had given her the first two seasons, and knew from veiled inquiries that Winnie had never seen it.

"You're going to love it," Barb promised her. "They're in their sixth season now." It was called *Beauchamp Hall,* which Barb said the British pronounced "Beecham," and was about a fancy family. Winnie was a little disappointed, she never watched TV, and would rather read a book, which was why she'd never seen it. She hoped someone would steal it from her, so she could pick something else, but no one did. The game ended, and Barb clutched the cheese platter, saying Pete would love it. Winnie put the DVDs in her purse and told Barb that she was thrilled and could hardly wait to see the show, which wasn't true.

They all enjoyed the buffet lunch of lasagna and pesto ravioli after that. They'd been allowed to drink wine to go with it since the office was closing after lunch. Hamm was feeling very expansive, and even gave Winnie a flirtatious look after a glass of wine. Everyone was careful not to drink too much since they had to drive home on snowy roads. There was eggnog without alcohol too, and Winnie opted for that. Barb had two glasses of wine since Pete was picking her up.

"What did Rob give you for Christmas?" she asked Winnie as they ate tiramisu for dessert.

"A yellow sweater and black lace underwear. He gives me the underwear every year, it's for him."

"I wish Pete would give me something like that," she said, giggling.

"It gets old after a while."

"Well, I know what you'll be doing on Christmas night," Barb said with a gleeful look.

"No, he's visiting his relatives in Detroit like he does every year. And staying to see friends afterwards. And he's going to visit his mother in the nursing home there. Besides, we did that last night," she replied, laughing at her friend's comment, and Barb shook her head.

"No! I meant you were going to watch the DVDs of *Beauchamp Hall*. You've got to watch it, Winnie. The way you love period stories, you're going to die. The costumes are gorgeous and the characters are fantastic. And they shoot it in a real castle in England, I forgot what it's called."

"Oh . . . of course . . . I'll watch it before we come back to work," Winnie promised, feeling as though she'd been given homework. She'd never gotten involved in watching a series, and for some reason the idea didn't appeal to her. But she didn't want to offend her friend, and now she felt she had to see it. She wished again that someone had stolen it from her. Another set of coasters would have been better.

"You have to call me the minute you've seen it. I want to know what you think," Barb insisted. "Believe me, you'll be hooked after the first episode. They're starting to shoot the seventh season now in England. Pete loves it too." Winnie knew one thing was sure, she wouldn't be watching it with Rob, he'd have a fit and laugh her out of the room.

"What are you giving Pete for Christmas, by the way?"

"An espresso machine. It's what he said he wanted. He's giving me a really fancy new Cuisinart. I already know. I saw it in his car." She looked faintly disappointed. "What did you give Rob?"

"We have a sweater exchange every year. And I gave him heated gloves so he could shovel my driveway. He didn't take the hint."

Pete came to pick her up, as expected, and the two women hugged and wished each other a merry Christmas, and agreed to talk during the week. Barb made Winnie promise she'd watch the DVDs as soon as she could. They were in her purse and she forgot about them when she got home. She picked up *Jane Eyre* for a while, and then dressed for dinner at her sister's, and put her gifts for them in her car. She had autographed basketballs from the Detroit Pistons for both boys. She had bought a dress that Marje had said she wanted that she got on the Internet, and the same heated gloves for Erik that she'd gotten for Rob, since Erik did shovel their driveway.

She arrived just as Marje was putting the finishing touches on dinner, and the Christmas tree was lit. Winnie had a small one at her house, which Rob said was silly, since she didn't have kids and it just made a mess. But it smelled delicious and Winnie loved having a tree every year, even if it wasn't big. The one at her sister's house touched the ceiling, with an angel on top that had been their mother's and reminded them both of their childhood. Winnie had agreed to let her have it, since Marje had kids.

Erik served her a glass of spiked eggnog, and then they sat down to dinner. Marje had made turkey and it was delicious, and they all had second helpings of the stuffing until it ran out. It was the perfect Christmas meal. Afterwards they sat in the living room, listening to Christmas carols and opening their gifts. After they got their basketballs, the boys went downstairs to the playroom to play video games. Their parents had bought them a new, bigger flat screen TV. Marje had given Winnie a new pair of red Uggs, which she always wore around the house on cold nights. Marje gave her a pair every year. Like the sweater from Rob, it wasn't a surprise. But Marje loved her dress from Winnie. Marje always said she didn't have time to shop and didn't enjoy it anyway.

It was a cozy family Christmas. They asked where Rob was, and she said he was in Detroit with his relatives, as always, and would be back later in the week. At midnight they all went to mass. She got home at one-thirty in the morning and slipped into bed, thinking about Rob. He hadn't called her, but she thought he might on Christmas Day. He didn't like holidays as much as she did, and didn't always call her. He thought holidays were for families and married couples, not for people who were just dating. After eleven years, she was just a "date," but he wasn't much more than that to her. And as she thought about it, she fell asleep.

Winnie woke up to bright sun on the snow on Christmas Day. It looked like a Christmas card. She lay in bed reading for a while, and dressed in time for lunch at her sister's, which was casual and would be a meal of leftovers from the night before. Erik and the boys would watch football on TV all day. It gave the two sisters time to talk.

"Have you heard from Rob?" Marje asked with interest and Winnie shook her head.

"I don't expect to. He's not big on holidays, and he's probably busy with his family, or his mother at the nursing home." He was good about that, which Marje always said was a good sign, but of what?

"How depressing," Marje said sympathetically.

"Yes, it is. He doesn't talk about it much. He says she doesn't recognize him anymore. He goes a few times a year, but she has no idea who he is."

"The poor guy needs a family," she said meaningfully and Winnie laughed. Her sister was never subtle.

"He has one, and so do I. You're all I need, big sister," she said warmly.

"That would be pathetic. Don't you want to be more than just Aunt Winnie? Don't you want to be a mom one day?"

"To be honest, I'm not sure," she said seriously. "I've been thinking about it. Maybe I'm just not the marrying kind, or meant to have kids." She enjoyed the children at the library for two hours a week but never longed to have her own, at least not yet.

"What would you do for the rest of your life without children?" Marje couldn't imagine it. Erik and the boys were her whole life and her job.

"Maybe I'd be happy. I'd still like to do some writing one day. I always wanted to do that after college, but I never got the chance. I'd love to try, short stories like I used to write, or something." She had published several in a magazine in college, and their mother was very proud.

"Mom always said your stories were good." Marje had never read them.

"She was prejudiced." Winnie laughed. But their mother was also well-read and intelligent, even though she hadn't gone to college.

She had inspired Winnie and encouraged her to write. It had just never happened, except in her creative writing classes, which didn't really count.

At the end of the day, Marje switched on one of the reality shows she loved, and Winnie watched it with her. It was a group of housewives in Las Vegas, who all looked like hookers, had set up a Christmas meal together, and were joined by their husbands at the end of the show. The men looked like gangsters and the women were squeezed into tight, sexy dresses with big hairdos, too much makeup, and tons of jewels. The dining room the show was shot in looked like a bordello. Winnie was mesmerized and couldn't believe what she was seeing, and Marje was glued to it with delight. She told Winnie which ones were her favorite women on the show.

"You watch this regularly?" She was amazed.

"I never miss a show. Today is their Christmas special." Winnie couldn't imagine watching it again, or caring about the women involved, but Marje felt as though they were her friends. And she said the dress Winnie had given her that she had wanted was vaguely inspired by the women on the show. Winnie had already noticed that all of them looked as though they had breast implants, their breasts were huge, and their lips were puffed up with collagen. Nothing about them was real.

At the end of the show, Winnie got up to leave. She went downstairs to see Erik and the boys, thank them for her gift, and wish them a merry Christmas again, then she hugged her sister. It was snowing outside again, and she wanted to get home before it got too deep.

When she got home, she made herself a cup of tea and sat in her kitchen, watching the snow falling. Rob called her from Detroit.

"How was your Christmas?" he asked her.

"Really nice with Marje and Erik and the kids. What about yours?"

"It was great. We went to a bar to shoot pool for a while last night, then we came home. I haven't stopped eating since I got here."

"How's your mom?" she asked carefully, not wanting to upset him.

"I'm seeing her tomorrow. She doesn't know it's Christmas anyway." But what if she did, even if she didn't recognize him? It seemed so sad to her. "We're going out for dinner tonight with some cousins I haven't seen in years. They're here from Miami." It all sounded foreign to her, since she didn't know any of the people. He only had one brother and he hadn't seen him in years. The people he visited in Detroit were aunts and uncles and cousins, but Winnie could never keep any of it straight. "I'll see you when I get back. You'll have to model your Christmas gift for me again." She wasn't sure why, but he made her feel cheap when he said it, like a hooker he was hiring for the night. She loved having sex with him, but not by masquerading as a stripper, or pretending to be a whore, even if just for him. She didn't answer and changed the subject.

"I hope you have a great dinner," she said vaguely.

"What are you doing tonight?"

"Going to bed, I'm exhausted. Too much food, and I was up late last night after church. I'll probably read in bed."

"My cousin gave me a couple of great porn films for Christmas. We'll watch them when I come home." His saying it made her think of the DVDs she'd won in the white elephant game. She hated porn films and didn't want to see any more of his. But Rob loved them, they aroused him, and he always wanted to have sex with her while they were watching, imitating what was happening on the screen.

She avoided watching them with him whenever she could. There were still things about him that gave her the creeps, even after eleven years. At least he wasn't addicted to porn, but he liked it a lot. She had let him know as often as possible that it wasn't her thing. Rob was more about sex than about love. He was good at sex, but love wasn't in his repertoire. "See you when I get back, Win," he said and they hung up. No *I love you,* no *Merry Christmas*. Same old Rob.

She went up to her bedroom then, got into bed and reached for the copy of *Jane Eyre* on her night table, and remembered the DVDs again. She had no interest in them, but thought that if she watched one, she could fake it to Barb about the other ones when she asked her. She decided to get it over with. She had nothing else to do that night. She looked at the boxes when she took them out of her purse. Each season had eight episodes that were each an hour long, and a two-hour Christmas special at the end. Barb had given her two seasons. Twenty hours of TV, way too much, but if she watched an episode or two, maybe Barb wouldn't care about the rest.

She dutifully got the first disc out, and put it in the DVD player attached to the TV in her room. It was Rob's. He had brought it over so he could watch porn videos with her. She dreaded it when he came over with a new one, and she tried to find an excuse not to see it: tired, sick, headache, busy, early day tomorrow. Sometimes he couldn't be put off, but she always tried.

The screen sprang to life with the first season of *Beauchamp Hall,* and she hopped into bed, pulled up the covers, and turned off the light as the first episode began. She was struck by the beautiful costumes, all historically accurate, and the incredible décor inside the castle, with enormous paintings and elegant antiques. It had an *Up-*

stairs Downstairs feel to it, with a fleet of servants, and a family composed of all the important players on the show. Three of them were famous actresses, several of the men looked familiar to her, even though it was an English production, but she had seen them in movies. And the manners and mores of the players were authentic to the period. It was everything she loved about English books and movies. The behavior of each actor was exquisite, the performances flawless, the dialogue brilliantly written, the story engaging, the characters perfectly defined in their roles as good or bad people. Their position in the world was clear, bound by tradition, whether noblemen or servants. It was an absolutely gorgeous show, as she got engrossed in the story for the first time. Predictably, by the end of the hour, several of the storylines were left hanging, and she wanted to see how they turned out, so she watched another hour. And a third one after that. She had to put another disc in for the next two episodes. At the end of it she had binge-watched five hours of *Beauchamp Hall,* and she wanted to watch more. But it was midnight by then. She looked at her watch, and like a naughty child past curfew, with no parental supervision, she grabbed another disc, put it in, pressed Play, and watched the intricate stories unravel. She was in love with the characters by then, and fascinated by the castle, the family, and the staff. It was a perfect replica of English aristocracy in the 1920s, when grandeur, opulence, and the upper class still prevailed. She felt as though she had been pulled into a different world, where her own life ceased to matter, only theirs did.

It was two in the morning when the third disc finished, and she still had another episode and the two-hour Christmas special to go, and she decided to watch them in the morning. She could hardly wait to wake up and see more. It was snowing hard and had been all night, and she hoped she'd get snowed in so she could watch the rest. She didn't have to go to work all week. She wanted to savor it and enjoy each moment of the story, and the costumes and the sets, but once she started, she couldn't stop. It was exactly as Barb had said. It was totally addictive, and she had had a fantastic evening watching it all alone.

She woke up the next morning and watched the rest of the first season, and the cast felt like old friends by now. It was lunchtime when she stopped. She ran downstairs to the kitchen, grabbed something to eat, and went back upstairs and started the second season, which was even more exciting than the first one.

She spent another three hours watching it in bed, and it was dark when she finally got up, and had another seven hours left to enjoy. She took a shower, put on fresh pajamas, and watched another four hours that night, and woke up again the next day to watch the last three hours of season two, and felt bereft when it ended. It was as though she had lost her best friends, and had been exiled from their magical land. She watched two of her favorite episodes for a second time that night. She had spent two full days and nights, and Christmas night, watching *Beauchamp Hall,* and as Barb predicted, she was totally hooked.

She called Barb that night. "What did you do to me?" she said when Barb answered.

"What do you mean?"

"It's like a drug! I can't stop! I've just spent two days in bed watching it, and all I want is more."

"Well, there are four more seasons for you to watch, including the one playing in England now. And they're filming the seventh season as we speak, or they will be, starting next week. You can order the others that have already been shown on the Internet. I'm exactly like you. I binge-watch it when I get it. And Pete is just as bad. We love it."

"The castle is incredible. Is it really like that in real life?"

"Haversham Castle. Apparently it is. It's owned by a British marquess, and he lives there with his sister, a lady, but he owns it because of the laws in England, which give the land and the title to the oldest son, and traditionally no one else inherits anything. They looked pretty cool in the article I read, they're about our age or a little older. The show saved them from losing the castle apparently, they were out of money, and they make a fortune from renting it for the show. The whole town gets involved and watches them film it."

"The man who writes the show must be brilliant," Winnie said with open admiration.

"It's his first big success. It's a huge hit over there. I knew you'd love it, Win. I'm so glad you watched it."

"It's the best Christmas gift I got. I've never been addicted to a TV show before."

"Neither was I, until *Beauchamp*." Barb sounded thrilled that Winnie loved it.

"I'm going to order the other seasons tonight." She went straight to her computer after she hung up, and ordered them all. The sixth season wasn't available yet, since it was still playing in England, but she put in an advance order, which she'd have in four weeks. She had three more seasons to look forward to for now, as soon as they arrived. She could hardly wait.

She had just pressed the send button with her order when Rob called her.

"Hi, I just got back. What are you up to? I missed you." It was nice to hear that and surprising coming from him, he rarely admitted it.

"I've been in bed watching DVDs for the last two days. The ones I won in the elephant game at work. It's a fantastic show."

"I've got a pretty fantastic show for you too. Can I come over?" He usually didn't ask, he just showed up.

"Sure. I don't have anything to eat in the fridge, I haven't been to the grocery store in days. I couldn't tear myself away from the TV."

"I'll pick up something on the way," he said, and walked in half an hour later with a pizza box. He bounded up the stairs after he left it in the kitchen, walked across the room to her bed, and kissed her hard. She'd been watching an episode from season one again, and enjoyed it just as much the second time. "What's that?" He noticed it on the screen, and looked unimpressed by the costumes and the main drawing room of the castle.

"The show I told you about." She smiled.

"Never mind that." He ejected it and tossed it on the dresser, took a DVD case out of his pocket, put a disc in, and hit Play. And within seconds she could see what it was, the porn film his cousin had given him, and it was one of the roughest ones he'd brought over yet. She looked at it, uncomfortable at how extreme it was, and it was a shocking switch from the genteel show she'd been watching for three days. Before she could comment, he tore off his clothes and grabbed her, and started re-enacting what they were doing on the screen, trying to force his fist inside her, until she pulled away and made him stop.

"What's wrong?" He looked annoyed and was violently aroused.

"That's kind of a rough hello, isn't it?" She was unhappy about how brutal he wanted to be. There was nothing loving about it, it was the rawest kind of sex.

"Since when did you get so prissy? Come on, babe, I missed you. I've been thinking about this for three days."

"I missed you too. How about we just make love, that works pretty well for us. We don't need to play porn games. Those guys are pros." She wasn't prudish, but there was something disgusting about it, and she didn't want to participate. But he wanted more than just making love. He looked angry as he grabbed her again, and made love to her more roughly than he usually did. It frightened her a little, and wasn't fun for her. But he came like a rocket, and within minutes wanted to make love again. He had come home starving to the point of being crazed. And after the second time, she wanted him to stop for a while.

"What's wrong with you? Most women would beg for a guy who can make love to them like that. I've got the cock of a twenty-year-old." *But a heart of stone,* she wanted to say.

"I like it better when you're more tender and sensual."

"I like it better this way," he said angrily. "I'm not gay." He looked furious.

"You don't have to be gay to be gentle, Rob," she said quietly. She didn't like his homecoming style at all. And out of the blue, she suddenly wanted to ask him a question. "Are you in love with me, Rob?" It broadsided him completely and he didn't answer for a minute.

"What the hell have you been watching on TV while I was gone? *Desperate Housewives*? What kind of question is that?"

"An honest one. You never say it. Do you love me?"

"What do you expect, for me to throw flowers at you or burst into song? Sure I love you. Do you think I could make love to you like that, if I didn't? That's how men express love."

"No, that's how men express lust. That's different."

"I love your body," he said, ignoring what she said. "I like being with you. We've been together for eleven years. That must mean something." It could also mean habit, fear of loneliness and of being alone. They had great sex, but all of a sudden she wondered what else they had, and what he felt for her. And even what she felt for him. The love interests on *Beauchamp Hall* were so intelligently expressed, the characters really cared about each other, and despite their upper-crust manners, they fell in love and found elegant ways to demonstrate it, nothing like the porn film he wanted her to re-enact. She felt violated by everything he had done that night.

"Eleven years together means a lot. I just wonder what we're doing sometimes."

"We're having great sex. Unless you want to go all virginal on me now."

"I don't just want to be made love to, I want to be loved and respected too."

"Oh, for chrissake," he said, leaping out of bed, and pulling on his clothes. "I don't know what you've been watching since I've been gone. *Little House on the Prairie* or *The Sound of Music*. I'm not a kid, Win. I'm a man. And this is how I am. If you don't like it, then maybe we need to think about this. I'm going home. Call me when you're normal and ready to act like an adult again."

"I don't need to act like a whore to be an adult, Rob. I'm a woman and a human being. I'm not some hooker in a Tijuana bar."

"And I'm not some namby-pamby guy who wants to beg you to have sex like a fifteen-year-old. You know what I like, and how I like it."

"I don't like watching porn with you," she said bluntly, "or how it makes you act."

"And here I just told my cousin you're a great woman and will do anything I want."

"Actually, I won't," she said firmly. "Is that what you like about me?" She looked shocked.

"I don't like how you're acting now. I can tell you that." And with that, he stormed out of the room, thundered down the stairs, and slammed the front door behind him. She could hear his truck start a minute later, and then drive away.

Shaking at everything that had been said, she rescued the DVD of *Beauchamp Hall* where he had tossed it, took his out, and put the *Beauchamp* disc back in, pressed Play, and climbed back into bed. Within a few minutes, she felt calm again, and as though she had entered a world of noble gentlemen and ladies, people who knew how to behave and how to treat those they loved. She watched three episodes in a row, and felt as if all was right with the world again. And she had the answer to her question. Rob was not in love with her. It hit her like lightning. And she was not in love with him.

Chapter Three

Rob didn't call her for three days after the night he came home from Detroit. She didn't call him either. She didn't like the way he had treated her, and her realization that he didn't love her and her own doubts about loving him had shaken her. They were great sexual partners, but not much else. They had no common interests, no shared friends, except for a few of the men in his bowling league. They went to work, came home, slept in the same bed on most nights, and made love when he felt like it. She realized suddenly that he hardly talked to her, and it had taken her eleven years to notice. For years, she had told herself that all men behaved like that. But what if they didn't? The men on *Beauchamp Hall* didn't, but it was a TV show, and set nearly a century earlier. And Erik respected her sister, although she knew their marriage wasn't exciting, and she knew that her sister had had an affair he probably didn't know about a few years back, but she'd stayed with Erik.

What did she have with Rob, other than predictably efficient sex?

She wanted more, she wanted real conversation, someone to take walks with, to share good times, and to learn things from each other. She wanted what the players at *Beauchamp Hall* had, but that was a fantasy and she knew it. Now she was dissatisfied with her life and a man who wanted to re-enact a porn video with her, who said he loved her body, but not much else. She wondered if he even knew her, or asked himself if he did, or cared. She would have talked to Barb or Marje about it, but she knew she'd sound crazy if she told them she wanted her life to resemble a TV show. Marje especially would have gone nuts over that and accused her of being even worse than a dreamer.

Rob called her the morning of New Year's Eve. She'd been watching season one of *Beauchamp Hall* again, and assumed she'd be watching it that night if Rob didn't call or take her out, and that was beginning to look like a serious possibility. She wondered if it was over between them and didn't want to ask.

"So, are we going out tonight?" He sounded awkward.

"Do you want to?" she asked cautiously.

"Yeah, I do. I don't know what got into you the other night, but let's forget about it, and have a nice time at Murphy's like we always do." She had just watched the Christmas special from the first season with everyone in white tie and tails on New Year's Eve, as they danced around the ballroom. The reality of her own life was laughable compared to that, but it was also almost a hundred years later, and even in British aristocratic circles the world had changed dramatically since then. She would be spending New Year's Eve watching her boyfriend play pool at his favorite bar, drinking beer instead of champagne. And she'd been spending New Year's Eve with him that way for eleven years. "I'll come pick you up at seven. I have some things to do before that."

"That would be nice," she said, sounding subdued. Despite her epiphany, she wasn't ready to end it with him yet, and not on New Year's Eve. That was more drama than she wanted with him. She wanted to be sure of what she felt for him, or didn't, before she reacted to it.

She was wearing jeans when he picked her up. There was no point wearing anything else. No one at the bar would be dressed up. A few of the younger girls might be wearing halter tops, but she felt stupid wearing one in the dead of winter, and freezing in the drafty bar all night. Instead, she wore the yellow sweater he'd given her for Christmas, and he looked pleased when he saw it.

"You wearing the thong I gave you too?" he whispered in her ear when he kissed her, and she laughed.

"No, I'm not."

"You can put it on for me later, to start the year off right." She didn't comment, and they drove to the bar in his truck. He started playing pool with his friends as soon as they arrived, and they had burgers at the bar around ten o'clock. He started another pool game half an hour later. At midnight, he was winning, and she walked over to him, tapped him on the shoulder and kissed him at the stroke of twelve, while his friends hooted and whistled. Then she went back to sit at the bar, and he went back to the game. She found herself wishing that she were at home watching *Beauchamp Hall*. She was living vicariously through the actors and the show. Their dialogue was so perfect. They said everything she would have wanted them to say. Even their hair looked impeccable in the style of the period, their

jewelry, their clothes, their manners, the way they moved and behaved and reacted to each other. The restraint they used when dealing with difficult situations. She watched it at every opportunity, it
had Winnie in its thrall. It had become her guilty pleasure. She was
already depressed that in two days she had to go back to work, and
wouldn't have much time to watch it anymore. It had been perfect in
the past few days, because Rob was working and she wasn't, so she
sat at home in her pajamas all day and watched it. But in two days
that had to end.

Rob drank too much beer that night, while playing pool, and Winnie had two beers early in the evening, and had eaten since. She was
totally sober at 2:00 A.M. when they went home, so she drove his
truck, and she had to help him into the house.

"Come on, baby . . . put the G-string on for me. . . ." He was stag-
gering and slurring. He leaned on her heavily and she could barely
get him up the stairs, and the minute he hit the bed with all his
clothes on, he passed out.

He woke up at eleven o'clock on New Year's Day with a pounding
headache, and went downstairs to find her. She was sitting in the
kitchen, watching an episode of *Beauchamp Hall* on her computer,
when he walked into the kitchen and sat down.

"Not that crap again. Why are you watching that? I can't even
understand what they're saying." She turned it off so it wouldn't
bother him, and poured him a cup of coffee. "I won a lot of money
last night," he said, looking pleased. "I had a great time." She nodded. She hadn't, but didn't want to complain. It was no different
from all the other New Year's Eves they'd spent there since they
met, and she'd put up with it before. She knew he wouldn't under-

stand why something had changed. She wasn't sure she understood it either.

He went back to his place after she cooked him breakfast. He said he was going to meet up with some of the guys, and would be back that night.

Barb called. Pete had some work to do in the office, and she came over to watch two episodes of *Beauchamp Hall* with Winnie. They had just finished the last episode they'd been planning to watch when Rob came home early and saw Barb in leggings and a tight exercise top that showed off her figure. He looked her over with a practiced eye, as though Winnie weren't there. Winnie pretended not to notice, and Barb said she'd see her at work tomorrow and left.

"She's hot," Rob commented when the door closed behind her. She had a good figure, but always complained about her big breasts and what an encumbrance they were.

"She's getting married next summer," Winnie said, putting the DVD away.

"To the dentist?" Winnie nodded. "He's a wimp. She deserves better than that."

"He's good to her," Winnie said and walked to the kitchen to cook dinner, and Rob followed her.

"Are you okay?" he asked and she nodded. "You're acting weird these days."

"I'm trying to figure some things out." She didn't look at him as she said it.

"About us?" He could sense that something was different, but he didn't know what or why, and neither did she.

"Maybe."

"Maybe what you need to figure out is why you watch that stupid show all the time. I think it's making you a little crazy." She wondered if it were true. Suddenly she wanted to be with the people on the show, and live among them, as though they were real and not actors speaking lines someone had written for them. She was starting to believe it was real. Maybe Rob was right. She felt as if she might be losing her grip on reality. And her own life seemed off-kilter. Rob was part of it. The relationship they'd had for eleven years didn't seem like enough compared to what she was seeing on the show, but the universe of *Beauchamp Hall* didn't exist. Yet her life seemed so inadequate compared to it. Even the servants seemed more eloquent and more polished than Rob, who acted like a boor most of the time.

She didn't say anything to him about it. They ate dinner without talking, went to bed afterwards, made love without his putting any exotic demands on her, and he fell asleep five minutes later. When she woke up in the morning, he had left for work. She managed to shovel the driveway after the night's fresh snow and get to work on time. Winnie looked serious when she sat down at her desk. Barb didn't say anything for the first half hour and then looked at her intensely.

"Are you okay? Something wrong?"

"I don't know. All of a sudden, my life doesn't fit, like it shrank in the wash or something."

"Uh oh, sounds like *Beauchamp*-itis to me." Winnie smiled at what she said. It felt that way to her too. "You know they're just actors, right? They're not real people. They don't live at the castle. And they're not waiting for you to show up."

"Yeah, I know," Winnie said sadly. "But everything used to be so great back then. So elegant, so polite, so right. It puts a whole new perspective on my life."

"It's a fantasy," Barb reminded her. "We'd all like to live like that, but even those people don't anymore. They all lost their money, and they look like you and me. There are not many grand lords and ladies around these days. How are things going with Rob?"

"Not so good," Winnie said. "We had a couple of bad fights last week. He gets a little crazy sometimes. I don't think he loves me, Barb. I'm some kind of sex object to him. And what's worse, I'm not sure I love him either. We just stay together out of habit, and because we have nothing else to do. I asked him if he loved me a few days ago, and he told me he loves my body. I think all he wants is sex most of the time. I don't think he even knows who I am, or cares." Barb looked surprised to hear it.

"Do you know who you are?" Barb asked her pointedly.

"I thought I did. Now I'm not so sure." It had been troubling her a lot lately.

"Because of *Beauchamp*?" she asked, worried about her.

"No, because of everything else. What am I doing with a guy who never talks to me?"

"He's hot," Barb said admiringly. She liked his looks, and he emanated a kind of virile sex appeal that had always seemed attractive to Winnie too. But now he seemed like a Neanderthal at times, compared to the aristocrats on *Beauchamp Hall*. And he'd been acting like a sex addict recently.

"He says the same thing about you, that you're hot," Winnie told her with a look of surprise.

"It's the breasts," Barb said, looking embarrassed. She had hated them all her life but was scared of having a breast reduction, and couldn't afford one anyway. "Guys want to meet them before they even want to meet me. They have an identity of their own because they're so damn big. They think I'm the goddess of fertility or something, except for Pete. He loves me, not just my tits."

"Rob acts like I'm a hooker he picked up in a bar somewhere and kept around for eleven years. It freaks me out sometimes. And scares me. He thinks it proves he loves me because he wants to have sex with me all the time. All it proves is that he's a horny guy."

"There are worse things." Barb looked anxious.

"I don't think I'm a person to him," Winnie said. "I'm just a piece of ass. And I'm not even sure what he is to me."

"Have you said all this to him?" Barb looked concerned. Winnie was being so intense, which was unlike her. She always went with the flow, even with Rob. But now she was questioning everything.

"I've said some of it. But I still need to figure it out for myself. Maybe we're the wrong people for each other."

"After eleven years?"

"Could be. Maybe this is all we'll ever be. A guy who sleeps over at my place because my house is bigger than his apartment, and he can get laid before he falls asleep at night, if he's in the mood."

"That's a little harsh, don't you think? He cares about you a lot more than that."

"I'm not so sure. Now he thinks I'm weird because I'm watching the show. He wants to watch hard-core porn and that seems normal to him. He thinks I'm a freak."

"He's into porn?" Barb looked surprised, as Winnie nodded.

"The worse it is, the better he likes it. He wants me to try every-thing they do. We had a fight about it when he came back from De-troit after Christmas. I don't think a man who loves me would ask me to do some of those things. It's demeaning. I don't know. All of a sudden everything feels wrong about us. Maybe it's some kind of midlife crisis for both of us." She was being earnest about it and Barb didn't know what to say.

"Pete would have a heart attack if I put a porn video on. He's pretty straightlaced." She sounded disappointed as she said it.

"It's better that way, believe me," Winnie said with feeling. "I feel like a cheap trick with some of the things he wants me to do."

"I feel like the Virgin Mary with Pete. He thinks I'm some kind of saint."

"Aren't you?" Winnie teased her. She knew Barb's history and all of her secrets since high school. There had been a number of men other than the two she'd been engaged to.

"It's probably better if he believes that, instead of the truth. I was pretty wild for a while after high school. He doesn't need to know that. He keeps referring to me as the future mother of his children. A little porn might do him some good. His maternal grandfather is a minister."

"I guess nobody's ever happy with what they've got. I just want to figure out what Rob and I feel for each other, after eleven years."

"Maybe he'd respect you more if you got married."

"I don't think that's the issue. Honestly, I don't know what the issue is. Maybe we're just bored with each other, and he needs the porn to spice it up. But if that's true, where will we be in ten or twenty years? Cheating on each other? I don't want that either. And

I'm not going to marry someone to make him respect me, if he doesn't already."

"Have you ever cheated on him?" Barb was curious.

"Never. If I want to cheat on him, I'll break up with him. What's the point of staying with him if I want someone else?" Barb nodded, thinking about it, and didn't comment for a minute.

"I guess that's true," Barb admitted. It reminded Winnie of her sister, who had cheated on Erik, but their marriage seemed to be solid in spite of it. And maybe Erik cheated on her too. Relationships were so damn complicated. And getting married seemed so extreme. She wondered if she ever would.

"Do you ever feel trapped here?" Winnie asked her then.

"I never think about it. We grew up here. It's home." She'd never wanted to move away from Beecher, and had always had smaller dreams than Winnie. Getting married was enough for her.

"All I wanted when I went to college was to leave and never come back. I couldn't when my mom was sick, and then I gave up on the idea," Winnie confessed wistfully. "Sometimes now I think about it again. New York, even Chicago. Wouldn't that be exciting?" Barb shook her head.

"No, it would scare the hell out of me. I wouldn't last in New York for a week, or Chicago, or Detroit. What would I do there? I don't know anybody. I'd be terrified to walk down the street." Winnie still loved the thought of it, even though she knew she'd never do it. Rob was more like Barb and her sister. His universe was defined by Beecher. It was all they'd ever known, and they didn't want anything else. If Winnie could have flown away on eagle wings, she would have in an instant.

"I think about it now again when I'm watching *Beauchamp*. I'd give anything to turn the clock back and be part of that world."

"It's just a TV show, Win. It seems real, but it isn't."

"I wish I could write something that seems that real." She was full of dreams suddenly, about places and things and people, and the writing she used to love doing. The series she'd been watching had ripped the lid right off the tiny tin can of a world she'd been living in, and now nothing seemed to fit. Everything in Beecher felt too small for her. The show had changed her, just in the space of a week. She felt as though she had come loose from her moorings. It was exhilarating and terrifying all at the same time. Something was happening to her, she didn't know what it was yet, but she hoped it was something good.

Chapter Four

In February, they hired a new girl named Elise at the office, and neither Winnie nor Barb liked her. She was spectacular-looking, with a sensual body, and wore low-cut, tight clothes and miniskirts that showed off her legs. She was twenty-one. She had been hired for one of their lowest positions, as a girl Friday and assistant to everyone, before they assigned her to any one department. They needed to know her strengths first. Winnie could always use a spare pair of hands in her overworked production department, and Barb was working on layouts. The office manager started Elise off with taking orders for business cards, and the men who came in to order them were nearly rendered speechless by her looks. Hamm had her in his office constantly, giving her projects. She had spent a year in Detroit as a trade model, but said she didn't like it, and had come home. This was the first office job she'd ever had, and she mixed up the orders she took several times.

"Hamm looks like he's going to have a stroke every time he talks to her. He gets all red in the face," Winnie commented, and Barb laughed.

"Bad luck for him, the blood is rushing to his face instead of somewhere else," Barb said in an acid tone. The girl was getting on their nerves. Whatever she did wrong, Hamm was willing to forgive, while he was merciless with everyone else. He was clearly dazzled by Elise's youth and beauty.

A month later, whenever the new girl talked to Hamm, she practically pressed her body up against him, and Winnie noticed his hand resting on her shapely bottom and that Elise didn't move away. She knew who had the power and was milking it for all it was worth.

"I think she's sleeping with him," Winnie whispered to Barb one day, after watching her with Hamm again. There was something different about the way they talked to each other, and Hamm looked possessive whenever any man came too close to her.

"Don't be ridiculous. She's twenty-one years old, he's fifty-eight. And his wife would kill him if you're right."

"I'm sure she doesn't know. How's the wedding coming, by the way?" They were supposed to go to Flint to look for bridesmaids' dresses, but neither of them had had time yet, and the weather had been terrible since Christmas.

Things had been limping along with Rob since New Year's, but they hadn't had any major showdowns since then. He had finally backed down and stopped pushing her to watch porn with him, which was a relief. Whenever Winnie had time to herself, she watched the subsequent seasons of *Beauchamp Hall*. It just got better year by year, and the sixth season was the best one yet when she got it. She'd offered to lend them to Marje but she wasn't interested. She still preferred her reality shows. Rob had stopped bugging her about that too. They were no closer than they'd been before, but things were peaceful again, and he worked late several nights a week. When he did, he usually got to her house exhausted and went right to sleep. He said he was in line for a promotion and was working hard to get it, so their sex life no longer took precedence. At least until he got the promotion, Winnie assumed. He had a strong sex drive and needed sex constantly.

In April, there was an opening at the printing company. One of the senior women, in a technical position doing their digital artwork and graphic design, decided to retire, which created a vacancy that only a few people in the office could fill. The position was filled internally within a week, which left a managerial position open that Winnie was qualified for. It would have officially made her their production director, with a higher salary, a title, and an office. She was in direct competition with two of the men in the office for the job, but Barb was sure Winnie was going to get it. She'd been there longer, she had ten years' experience, and was so good at her job. She could have run the whole place if she had to. Neither of the men who wanted the position had been there for as long as she had. Thinking about it was exciting for Winnie, and the higher salary would be nice to have. She had saved a fair amount of money over the years, but the promotion would make a real difference to her. She talked to Marje and Erik, who were sure she'd get it too. She had even started dreaming that if she got the job, she'd make enough money to do some traveling.

The position sat open for three weeks, while Hamm said he was moving some people around in key positions, and an announcement would be made soon.

He finally broke the news to them on a Monday morning. Hamm gathered everyone around in the main room where they all sat. Winnie was disappointed because Barb was out sick with the flu, and she would have liked to be with her to hear the news. Barb had sent her a few texts that morning about how sick she was. Winnie tried to stay calm while Hamm made a short speech, and she noticed both of her male competitors looking smug. A minute later, he announced that each of the men had been made head of a department, which had taken some reorganizing. And he still hadn't announced who had gotten the position they'd all been angling for as production director. But the two men being given other jobs left only Winnie as a possibility for the position so the conclusion was obvious. With both men out of the running, only Winnie had the organizational skills to run production and finally get credit for it, which she never did, even if she was already doing the job and had been for years. She was starting to smile broadly when he made the announcement.

"And I'm very proud to share with you that Elise Borden is our new director of production. In the two months she's been with us, she has demonstrated her outstanding abilities." Winnie knew that Hamm thought the production department ran itself. Elise was beaming at Hamm, and Winnie's mouth nearly fell open as she stared at them both. What he had said just wasn't possible. Elise was twenty-one years old and a total airhead. What was Hamm thinking? But it certainly confirmed that he was sleeping with her. This made her Winnie's boss. Winnie would be reporting to her now. Hamm thought Winnie could do the job while Elise got credit for it.

Everyone went back to their desks a few minutes later, murmuring softly about Elise's miraculous promotion, and Winnie drifted back to hers with her ears ringing, as though an explosion had gone off in her head. After ten years, she had been passed over for a girl with no experience who had been there for less than two months. It was a massive slap in the face and humiliation. She sat stewing at her desk for the rest of the morning, and sent a slew of texts to Barb. Barb didn't answer, and then finally responded and said it was insane and she'd call Winnie later. She was feeling too shaken to want to talk about it anyway. Tears stung Winnie's eyes, and by lunchtime, she was so agitated that she walked into Hamm's office. Elise was moving her boxes and papers into her new office at the same time.

"What is it?" Hamm snapped at her the minute he saw Winnie come through the doorway. She thought he looked embarrassed but wasn't sure.

"Can I talk to you for a minute?" It was a question he dreaded and never good news, especially now. He knew that Winnie's request could only be about Elise's new job. The whole office was buzzing with it.

"I'm leaving for a lunch meeting in five minutes, you'll have to make it quick," Hamm said vaguely. She was sure that the lunch was with Elise to celebrate her new position. Hamm beamed every time he laid eyes on her, he was ridiculously obvious.

"I'll be quick," Winnie promised as she closed the door behind her. She didn't want anyone else to hear what she had to say, least of all Elise. She knew that if Barb had been there, she'd have kept her from walking into his office, but she wasn't, and nothing was going to stop her now. "What exactly just happened out there? Elise has been here for five minutes, I've been here for ten years. Is this some kind of joke? Or do you have to sleep with the boss to get ahead?" His face blushed purple, and he looked like he wanted to strangle Winnie on the spot. "If that's the way it works now, I never got that memo. It would have been nice to know, although the whole office has figured it out."

"She's had training in production," he said in a choked voice, lying about it shamelessly. "And if you had gotten the memo, Winnie, what would you have done about it?" He challenged her. He had never liked her and it showed.

"Actually, nothing. I don't give blow jobs under the boss's desk. But if that's the way it is now, I wouldn't have bothered to stick around for ten years or wait for a promotion you weren't going to give me. I just got screwed royally."

"Maybe if you were a little more 'cooperative,'" he said, with emphasis on the last word and a wicked look in his eye, "if you get my drift, maybe you would have gotten promoted before she did. She's a hell of a bright girl, and she knows what she has to do to get ahead." Winnie couldn't believe he'd said that to her, and made it quite so clear.

"What happens when your wife finds out?"

"I don't know what you're talking about. But in today's world, some women know what they have to do to get promoted and some don't." She had made him so furious because she had flushed him out.

"Damn, how could I have been so confused for all these years? I thought this was a printing business. I must have read the sign wrong. It turns out it's a prostitution ring." He looked like he was going to have a heart attack when she said it, and there was a vein throbbing on the side of his head. "I don't turn tricks with my boss,

Hamm, even for a promotion I deserve. I don't need the job that badly. I guess she does. She's young. Someone else will offer her a bigger job for doing the same thing, and you'll look like an idiot. And by the way, I quit." With that, she pulled the door open and walked out. She went straight to her desk, put a few things she had on it in her purse, didn't bother to open or empty the drawers, got her coat, and walked out. She saw Hamm scurry into Elise's office before she left. He closed the door to talk to her with a worried look, and Winnie knew he must have been scared stiff she would file a discrimination suit, but she wasn't going to stoop to that. He was a pig, he always had been, just a bigger one than she'd thought. She felt sorry for Barb having to go back to work there, but she was going to quit and go to work for Pete anyway, after they were married.

Winnie wondered how long it would take Hamm to figure out what he'd just lost. Production would slow down to a halt without her, and no matter what her title, or his claims, Elise had no idea how to do the job. And there was no one to take over Winnie's job and make Elise look good in her new position.

Winnie couldn't remember ever being so angry in her life. She had gotten passed over for the girl he was sleeping with. It was so pathetic she couldn't believe he'd done that to her. She was going to text Barb and tell her she'd quit, but she wanted to go home first. She needed to cool off. She didn't even think about what she was going to do next when she quit. She was incredibly well organized, great at what she did, but there weren't many options for her talents in Beecher, Michigan. It was almost as if fate had forced her out of a job she shouldn't have stayed in anyway. But now what? She had no idea.

She parked her car in the driveway, and almost forgot to turn the ignition off. She was surprised when she noticed Rob's truck parked in the street. She figured he'd forgotten something and had come to pick it up, or maybe he was sick. She unlocked the door and walked in. The house was quiet, and she wondered if he was in bed asleep. She wanted to tell him all about what had happened, and ran up the stairs to check the bedroom and stopped dead in the doorway when she saw him. She almost choked when she took in the whole scene. Barb was tied to the bed by her hands with ropes, while Rob was performing oral sex on her, and one of his favorite porn movies was playing on the TV. Barb screamed when she saw Winnie, and struggled against the ropes, Rob thought she was writhing in ecstasy, doubled his energies, and Winnie was behind him so he couldn't see her and she didn't make a sound. She was too stunned to speak. Barb couldn't stop screaming, and Winnie felt as though someone had just ripped out her guts. It was the perfect follow-up to one of the worst days of her life.

"Are you two fucking kidding me? What the hell is going on here?" she said when she caught her breath. Rob's whole body went rigid when he heard her voice. He turned to look at her and groaned, as Barb burst into tears and continued to struggle against the ropes around her wrists. He untied her with shaking hands, and stood up to face Winnie, with his penis in full erection, as Barb jumped off the bed and ran past them to lock herself in the bathroom, sobbing hysterically.

"Winnie, please, this isn't what it looks like." It was the oldest lie in the world.

"I can't believe you just said that," she said, pointing at his penis.

"What are you doing? Giving her CPR? Of course it's what it looks like. How long have you been sleeping with my best friend?" She was shaking from head to foot.

"It just happened a few times, I swear, it doesn't mean anything to either of us. We were just having fun. Pete's a dud in bed."

"Apparently I don't mean anything to either of you. Get out of my house." Barb was out of the bathroom by then with her clothes on, still crying, and Winnie was trembling as she looked at them. She couldn't believe she was still standing and could talk. She was in shock. And she realized that they had probably used her house because his apartment was such a dump and Barb lived with Pete. If they'd gone to a hotel someone might have seen them and squealed. Winnie's house was so much nicer, and familiar to both of them. It had proved to be a disastrous choice.

"For God's sake, please don't tell Pete," Barb begged her. "He'll cancel the wedding. He won't understand." She was sobbing, pleading for mercy as Winnie looked at her in disbelief.

"Are you serious? You're planning to marry him anyway? After this? The two of you are really pigs," she said, looking at Rob.

"I love Pete," she cried miserably, as Rob pulled his jeans on.

"And you're doing this to him? You both make me sick. Now get out, and take your video with you. I don't ever want to lay eyes on either of you again."

Rob didn't try to stay to argue with Winnie. He knew better. She looked as though she was ready to kill someone. And Barb was so hysterical he wanted to get her out of the house before anything else happened. The scene had been bad enough. Barb had sworn to Rob that Winnie would never come home for lunch. They had done this before, several times, and pulled it off. This time they didn't. He wanted to give Winnie time to cool off.

Winnie's legs were shaking so badly after they left that she had to sit down for a minute, and then leapt to her feet at the sight of the ropes still tied to her bed. She went over and pulled them off, grabbed her sheets and blanket off the bed, and ran downstairs to put them in the washing machine. She didn't care if she ruined the blanket. She wanted to throw it all away. She was so upset she didn't know what to do. She turned on the washing machine, and a minute later she left the house and drove to her sister's, sobbing all the way. The floodgates had been opened and she couldn't stop crying as she jumped out of her car at Marje's and ran through the front door. Marje was sitting in her living room, watching one of her reality shows on TV. It was all she did every day until the kids came home from school.

"My God, what happened to you?" She got to her feet as soon as she saw Winnie, who was crying so hard she couldn't speak coherently. Marje tried to calm her down, but it was a full five minutes before Winnie could say anything.

"I've had a terrible day," Winnie said, sounding like a little kid again, and it reminded Marje of when Winnie was five and she was fifteen.

"I figured that much out. Tell me what happened," Marje said soothingly.

"I quit my job," she said, hiccupping through sobs. She told her about the promotion she didn't get and what she'd said to Hamm Winslow in his office when she quit. Marje smiled as she listened.

"Well, he won't forget you in a hurry, and the place will probably fall apart without you. I'd probably have done the same thing. What an asshole."

"Then I went home," she started to cry again. "Rob's truck was outside." Marje got a bad feeling as she said it, and suspected the story was about to get a lot worse. "I went upstairs to look for him." She described the scene in her bedroom when she walked in, and her sister winced.

"Oh, Jesus." She told her about the ropes and all of it. "What a couple of idiots. That was a rotten thing to do. I'm sorry, Winnie." She put her arms around her while Winnie cried.

"I don't think I'm even in love with him. I've been trying to figure it out. But we're still together and she's been my best friend since we were kids. I can't believe she'd do that to me." The memory of what she'd seen made her feel sick. She'd never been betrayed by a woman friend. It cut her to the quick, even more than Rob doing it.

"They're both shits," Marje said with a look of fury, and then looked more seriously at her sister. "This isn't your fault, Win, but maybe because neither of you ever made a real commitment to each other after all this time, he thought he was a free agent."

"He never wanted to get married either. It didn't feel right to me. I couldn't see myself with him for the rest of my life, but it was never bad enough to leave. I just thought we'd hang out together for a while, and then suddenly eleven years had gone by, and we never made a decision. We talked about it after Christmas. I think it's all about sex with him." Marje nodded. It sounded that way.

"I thought he was better than that."

"He isn't," Winnie said sadly. "And I've been so stupid to spend all these years with him. Now I'm too old to find someone, and I'll be alone for the rest of my life." It felt like a tragedy, and Marje smiled as she listened to her.

"Thirty-eight is not exactly the end of the road. You need some time to get over this." They walked to the kitchen together, and Marje poured a glass of water and handed it to her. Winnie's hand was shaking when she took it. She needed a job now too, but what Rob and Barb had done had overshadowed her quitting. "Why don't you stay here tonight?" Winnie thought about it and shook her head.

"I want to go home. I put the sheets in the washing machine before I left. I never want to see either of them again." Marje nodded. "I never thought Barb would do something so low. Our friendship means nothing to her. And she still wants to marry Pete." She already had a dozen text messages from Barb by then and opened none of them.

Winnie stayed until the boys came home from school. They were surprised to see her there.

"What are you doing here, Aunt Win?" her younger nephew Adam asked her.

"Visiting your mom," she said vaguely and left a few minutes later to go back to the scene of Rob and Barb's crime and stupidity. Barb had kept sending her texts every few minutes that afternoon, begging for forgiveness, and pleading with her not to tell Pete. She'd finally read a few of them and erased the rest, unread. Rob had left her a long, rambling message about how it didn't mean anything, it was just fun and games, how sorry he was, and could he come to see her that night. She didn't answer either of them, and she took the clothes Rob had left in her closet and threw them in the garbage can outside.

She made her bed with clean sheets and an old blanket of her mother's and lay down and felt like she couldn't breathe, remembering what had gone on there hours before. She hated even being in the room. Then she noticed one of her *Beauchamp* DVDs sitting next to the TV where Rob must have put it. He had taken his porn video with him. She got up and put *Beauchamp Hall* in the DVD player, and hit Play on the remote control. It was comforting just hearing the familiar voices, like friends in the room. She didn't try to follow the story, she just stared at the TV and started crying again. It had been a clean sweep, her job, her boyfriend, and her best friend, all gone in one day. It was Barb who mattered to her most. There was no one left now in her life except her sister. She had no idea what to do next or where to start. Her whole life had come down around her. Ten years at her job, the promotion she should have gotten given to the girl who was sleeping with the boss, eleven years with Rob up in smoke, and her childhood friend's ultimate betrayal. She lay staring at the TV screen and cried herself to sleep.

Chapter Five

For the next two weeks, Winnie drifted between her house and her sister's, feeling dazed and numb. Most of the time, she was at her own house, and put one of the *Beauchamp Hall* DVDs in the machine, as a sort of background music for her fallen life. She had called the library and taken a leave from her volunteer job as "The Story Lady" and told them she was sick. She didn't want to do anything and couldn't face the children either, not for now anyway, until she regained her balance. She was nowhere near that yet.

She had no idea what to do next. She knew there was a position at the front desk of the hotel. She'd seen in the newspaper that an insurance broker needed a new assistant, and the local mortuary needed a hostess to greet the mourners. It was all so depressing, although working at a printing company hadn't been a dream job either. There weren't many opportunities in Beecher, and she didn't want to commute two hours each way to Detroit and back, nor move there. And she felt too old now to move to Chicago or New York to try to start over. It seemed as though her life had come to a full stop.

Rob was still sending her text messages saying he wanted to see her. He had even shown up at the house late one night. She'd had the locks changed the day after she'd found him in bed with Barb, and when he came by, Winnie didn't answer the door. She responded to nothing he sent. She was finished with him, mourning the lost years more than the man. He wasn't a loving person and hadn't treated her well, with kindness or respect. She saw that now, more clearly every day.

Barb had written her a long letter, trying to explain everything. She said that she thought Winnie didn't really care about Rob, so it didn't matter. They got together just for sex, and some fun. Winnie thought it was pathetic, and even more so because she was about to marry another man, who in fact bored her and didn't excite her in bed, but could pay the bills and drove a Porsche. Barb liked the idea of being a dentist's wife, but she was much more attracted to Rob, who only wanted to have sex with her. They were partners in porn. Winnie didn't bother to answer her. The bond between them had been severed and Winnie never wanted to see her again. She was grateful to Barb for introducing her to *Beauchamp Hall,* but that was it. After what had happened, it was clear that their nearly thirty-year friendship was over. Winnie had nothing to say to Barb and didn't respond.

Winnie kept trying to figure out what she was really feeling. In quiet moments, she realized that she wasn't heartbroken over Rob, but her trust was shattered by all of them. Her boss, her boyfriend, and her best friend had betrayed her, and she felt as though she'd hit a wall. She had enough money saved so that she wouldn't have to work for several months, and some money her mother had left her, which she had never touched. She wasn't financially desperate but she felt as though someone had pulled the plug on her life. She could barely get out of bed.

"You can't sit brooding in your house with the TV on forever," Marje told her. Erik had offered her a job as an assistant office manager at his plumbing company, but he didn't need her and was doing it as a favor, and she didn't want that either. There was a bookstore in town that didn't do a lot of business, several restaurants, some motels, a computer store, a realtor, and a smaller printing firm than Winslow's, which would have been happy to have her, and she was well trained for the job. But that didn't interest her either. None of it did.

"I feel like I'm having some kind of out-of-body experience," she tried to explain to her sister, "where I'm looking down at myself. It's like I'm swimming underwater. Everything is happening in slow motion. I think I'm drowning, and most of the time I don't even care."

"You're entitled to feel sorry for yourself," Marje said gently, "but at some point you have to come up for air." Winnie nodded, went home after that, flipped on the DVD player again, and hit the remote, without looking at the screen. She was surprised when she glanced at the TV and saw the same familiar faces, with the actors not in their costumes, and some of their accents slightly different and not quite so upper crust as on the show. She had accidentally clicked on the icon for "Extra Scenes" and "The Making of *Beauchamp Hall*."

She was about to turn it off, and go back to the episodes she knew almost by heart now, and then stopped when she saw one of the actors walking through the town where the show was shot, with the castle in the background. It was quaint, with little cottages and old-fashioned storefronts, with smiling people walking along and waving to the actor who was explaining how much he had come to love the village, his fellow actors, and the show. "This is home to me now," he said, "we've all been here for six years. We go home for a while during the hiatus between seasons, but most of us can't wait to come back. We love this place, and they love us." The camera showed the smiling villagers again, looking warmly at the actor who played one of the main heroes on the show. Winnie smiled. It gave her a warm feeling, just looking at the village and the castle that felt like home to her now too. The show had given her a rich fantasy life that kept her from getting even more depressed about her own. And as the segment ended, she sat staring at the dark screen and suddenly knew what she wanted to do. She had the time, enough money to drift for a while, and no reason to stay in Beecher right now, except to find another job that she'd probably hate. And she didn't want to run into Barb or Rob, which was so easy to do in a small town. She was afraid to see them whenever she left her house, even to buy food, so she went to the store at odd hours to avoid them.

With trembling hands, she called the airline and made a list of things she had to do, then went to the bank, and withdrew money. She didn't need too much cash, she had credit cards and no debt on them or unpaid bills. She checked her savings, and if she was careful she'd be able to coast for several months. She had never done anything crazy in her life, and she knew she was about to. But she had no husband, no children, no job now, no man, nothing to tie her

down. She was as free as the wind, and as she thought about it, she could feel herself moving quickly toward the surface. She wasn't drowning anymore. She was swimming with long, clean strokes toward where she wanted to go.

She drove to the passport office in Detroit, and with her ticket booked, they promised her a passport the next day. She had to come back for it, but she was determined to get everything done.

She went to Marje's when she got back, and burst through the front door. The boys were doing homework and Marje was getting dinner started. She looked up in surprise when she saw Winnie smiling at her. She looked like a different woman from the one who had left, deeply dejected, hours before.

"You look like you won the lottery." Marje smiled at her.

"I think I did. I know what I'm going to do."

"Does it involve a gun and any of the people who screwed you over?"

"Better than that. I'm going to England."

"England?" Marje looked startled. "What for?"

"To have some fun. I'm going to North Norfolk, to a village called Burnham Market. It's a three-hour drive north of London, or two hours by train. It's supposed to be a lovely place, full of history, and I want to look around. It's where they film *Beauchamp Hall*. I have the time right now, and I'll never get to do it again. I just want to see it, and breathe the air there. There are supposed to be beautiful beaches too." Marje looked a little puzzled. Winnie looked as if she might be high on something, and Marje wondered if her sister was drunk.

"Have you been drinking?"

Winnie shook her head. "I know it sounds crazy, but I love that show. If you could meet the housewives on your Las Vegas reality show, would you do it?"

"Maybe. If they came here. I can't see myself going to hang out in Las Vegas, or stalk them," she said, worried about her sister. Winnie was euphoric.

"You have a husband and kids, I don't. I have nothing here right now." Marje stared at her. "Except you, of course," she added. "But you have a life here, I don't."

"And after you've seen it, then what?"

"I don't know. I'll figure it out. I don't need to work for a few months. I have to do it, Marje. I feel it in my gut. It's one of those things I have to get out of my system."

"It's just a TV series, you know," Marje reminded her. "Sooner or later you have to come back here to reality." But she was going nowhere for the moment, moving from her bed to the couch in her living room, living like a shut-in, and crying all the time. For the first time in two weeks, she was smiling and looked excited and alive again. Marje wondered if maybe it would do her good. "When do you want to go?"

Winnie took a breath. "Day after tomorrow. I got a good rate on a flight to London. I'm going to stay there for two days. I've never been there before, and then I'll head to Burnham Market. It looks like a really charming place. There's a house called Holkham Hall nearby, it was built in the eighteenth century, and is one of the grandest homes in England. I want to take a tour there. And Haversham Castle, where they film *Beauchamp Hall,* is even more fabulous. I want to visit them both. There's a lot of interesting history in the area, and they let the locals watch the outdoor filming of the show." She had seen it on the DVDs, and everyone looked happy to be part of it. She wanted to be there too. She'd been reading descriptions of the village and couldn't wait to see it, with quaint shops and antique stores, and a thirteenth-century church. The year-round population of the village was less than a thousand people. It was a small and very appealing place. "I know it sounds crazy, but it's what I want to do." She sounded like a kid, not a thirty-eight-year-old woman whose life had been hanging in limbo for years, and had totally fallen apart two weeks before. Marje wondered if it was what she needed to get her going again and to find someone decent to settle down with this time when she came home.

"It does sound crazy," Marje agreed with her, smiling at the unbridled joy in her sister's eyes. "You don't need my permission. If you can afford it, go. Then come back and get serious about finding a job and a new guy. Just don't stay in England, please. I'd miss you too much."

"I won't stay. I just want to see where they do the show. I dream about it at night."

Marje nodded. "Do you want to stay for dinner?"

"I have to go home and pack. Will you check on the house for me?" Marje nodded. It had all happened so suddenly, it didn't seem real to her yet. But Winnie's life had fallen apart just as quickly, in the space of an hour, and that didn't seem real to her yet either. Now she was leaving, and starting to feel in charge again. "I'll come back and see you tomorrow after I pick up my passport. I have a lot to do before I go."

By the next day, in her usual competent way, she had everything organized. Her bags were packed, her passport in her purse, her bills were paid, and everything was put away neatly. She felt like herself again, or on the way to it. She had put her *Beauchamp* DVDs in her suitcase, although she wasn't sure why, and took a copy of *Pride and Prejudice* to read on the plane. She was taking mostly jeans and a couple of skirts and casual clothes, hiking boots, a pair of sneakers, one nice dress she was sure she'd never use, just in case, comfortable flat shoes, and a pair of high heels. She was going to wear a coat, since the weather in England was still chilly. She had everything she needed, and she felt ready to go. In her mind, she had already left when she went to Marje's for dinner that night, and afterwards said goodbye to her, Erik, and Adam and Jimmy.

"Maybe you'll bring back an English guy!" her brother-in-law teased her. "And don't forget you have a job with me if you want it when you come home." Working as an assistant office manager at a plumbing company wasn't her dream job, but she was grateful for the kindness of his sympathy offer and thanked him.

"Take care of yourself, don't do anything stupid or crazy," Marje told her as they hugged for a last time. She felt as though she were sending a child off to school, but Winnie would always be her baby sister, no matter how old she was.

"I promise, I'll text you. We can FaceTime or Skype."

"Let me know if you see any big stars on the set," Marje said, smiling at her. "Take care of yourself, Win. I love you." Winnie nodded, with tears in her eyes, and then made a dash for her car, sitting in their driveway. She knew that if she stayed a minute longer, she'd be sobbing in her sister's arms, and she didn't want anything to stop her from going. Marje was still waving with the brightly lit house behind

her, as Winnie drove away. She was back at her own house five minutes later, and saw on her message machine at home that Rob had
called again, since she'd blocked him on her cellphone. She erased
his message without listening to it, looked around her house, and
went upstairs to bed. She had to get up at 5:00 A.M.

Winnie woke up before the alarm went off. It was still dark outside,
and there were light snow flurries in the air, although it was May.
They often had late snows at that time of year. She had left her bags
in the front hall the night before. She had one suitcase, a rolling bag,
and a backpack. She was too excited to have breakfast, and called for
a taxi to take her to the bus depot, to go to Detroit. She was due to
arrive in Detroit at eight-thirty, and would then take another bus to
the airport. She had a short hop to Chicago, a brief layover at O'Hare,
and then a direct flight to London leaving at 2:00 P.M. That would
take eight hours and land her in London at 3:00 A.M. local time. She
had booked two nights at a hotel in London she'd found on the Internet, the Westminster Hotel. She was going to spend two days exploring the London sights she had read about for years and never seen.
The Tower of London, Buckingham Palace for the Changing of the
Guard, the Victoria and Albert Museum, the Tate galleries, Hyde
Park, Madame Tussauds wax museum. She wanted to at least have a
drink at Rules, the oldest restaurant in London. She had seen it on
the show. She wanted to visit everything, and drink it all in, although
she hadn't given herself much time. She was eager to get to Burnham
Market, and she could always come back to London if she wanted to,
or cover more of the tourist sights on her way home. She had an

open ticket for the trip back since she didn't want to limit her stay in England. She wanted to be there for as long as she was happy, or until her money ran out, but that wasn't likely to happen for quite a while. She didn't travel extravagantly, and she had the luxury of time, to go where she pleased and do whatever she wished.

Marje texted her while she was on the runway, as she was about to turn off her phone before they took off on the flight to London. "Have a ball, little sis. Make every minute count. I love you, Marje." There were tears in Winnie's eyes when she read it, and she shot back, "I love you too. Be back soon. All my love, Win." And then she had to turn off her phone. It felt crazy to think that she was thirty-eight years old and had never done anything like this before. The years had sped by her, and suddenly she felt young and free again. She was almost glad that Rob had caused their relationship to end. She would never have had the guts to do it otherwise and their relationship would have dragged on for years. Instead he had shot her out of a cannon with Barb's help, into the chance to follow her dreams. It wasn't all bad after all, although it had been a shocking way to get where she wanted to be. But all of that was behind her now. And there were good times ahead, she told herself, as the plane took off.

She slept on the flight and woke up when they announced that they were about to land at Heathrow. There was a light mist when they touched the ground. And she went through customs and immigration easily, managed her own bags, and treated herself to a taxi to her hotel. She texted Marje from the taxi to say she had arrived safely.

They arrived at 4:00 A.M., as she had warned the hotel she would. She had a small plain room overlooking a narrow ugly street in a seemingly safe commercial district, with a lot of shops and restaurants around. It was in the Bayswater section of London, and the price was right. It wouldn't strain her budget to stay there, and she would be out of her room most of the time anyway. She fell into bed shortly after she got there, and woke up at nine-thirty local time with sunlight streaming through the window. And an hour later, she was outside, with a map she'd gotten at the hotel in her hand, and started on her blitz tour of London. She took double-decker buses, and the Underground, which got her very efficiently to everywhere she wanted to go.

She started at the Tower of London, visiting the dungeons, and saw an amazing exhibit of the queen's jewels. From there she went to Westminster Abbey to see where kings and queens had been crowned for centuries, and stood at the gates of Buckingham Palace, fascinated by the idea that the Queen of England was somewhere inside. She walked around the Tate Modern for several hours, took a walk in Hyde Park, and got to Rules for a drink as she'd promised herself. And by the time she got back to her hotel, she was exhausted but thrilled by everything she'd seen, and happy she had managed to do so much, moving quickly from place to place. She'd bought some fish and chips on the way back to the hotel, and ate it in her room. Afterwards, she took a bath, went to bed, and passed out almost the minute her head hit the pillow.

The next morning at ten o'clock, she started all over again, and had an equally successful day. She saw Parliament and Trafalgar Square, went to the British Museum, and rode on more double-decker buses. By that night, she had covered all the high points on her list. And she loved watching the people bustling everywhere. She had gone to New York a few times when she was in college, and the electricity and energy of London seemed similar to her, but with a lot more history at hand. People were busy, rushing, and she was mesmerized by all of it. She felt alive just being there. But she was looking forward to the peaceful atmosphere of the country village she was going to, the quaint surroundings, the elegance of the castle, and the excitement of the show. She could hardly wait.

She was up at six o'clock on her third morning in London. She got a cab to King's Cross Station at seven, and had breakfast. It didn't bother her at all to be traveling alone. The whole experience was an adventure, and she had managed London without a problem, despite noise, people rushing around her, cars on the wrong side of the road, and an unfamiliar city.

Burnham Market was going to be a great deal easier. The train left at eight-thirty, and the trip would take two hours through the British countryside to the town of King's Lynn. It looked beautiful and peaceful as she watched it drift by, and once they were well out of London, she saw cows and sheep, farms, rolling hills, and the brilliant green of new grass. Her heart pounded for a minute as they entered the station. Winnie had been told that the original King's Lynn station had been closed since the 1950s and housed an antique store now and some other shops. It was used in the series, and she wanted to visit it while she was there.

For an instant, she had an odd feeling that she had been here before and she was coming home. She was smiling when she got off the train, and the stationmaster touched his hat and smiled back.

There was an elderly man in a tweed cap standing next to a battered taxi, and Winnie walked over to him with her bags. She had taken a chance on her accommodations and wanted to check out the options when she arrived. She had read on the Internet that the best hotel in town was The Hoste, a fairly fancy inn on the green, but for the sake of her budget and local charm, she wanted to stay at a simple B and B. The cab driver agreed to take her to Burnham Market, which he said was thirty minutes away. Once in the car with him, she asked him politely, as they drove past farms and the lush green countryside, "Could you suggest a good B and B where I could stay, close to the center of town?"

"So you can see them film the show?" He smiled. He'd had lots of requests like this in the last six years, and he'd even driven many of the actors from time to time.

"Yes, I guess that's right," she admitted, looking a little sheepish. She felt like a combination groupie/tourist, and in fact she was both, although she hadn't thought of it that way before.

"I know just the place. Prudence Flannagan, you'll love it." Half an hour later, after seeing cows and pigs and horses along their route on a narrow country road, she saw the village up ahead. There were charming cottages and stone houses, with rose gardens in front and picket fences. And in the distance, but not too far away, she saw Haversham Castle in all its dignified nobility, and she recognized it immediately. "You know what that is, of course." The driver smiled at her in the rearview mirror and she smiled and nodded. "The Marquess of Haversham and his sister, Lady Beatrice, still live there. They're nice people, a little odd like all of their kind, but the show saved them. They were about to lose the castle, couldn't afford to keep it, but the show changed all that. They must be rolling in money now, for what they get paid to let it to the show. The Havershams are good to the people of the village, though. My grandfather was one of their great-grandfather's tenant farmers. He always spoke well of the family. Everything's changed, of course, since then. But the show reminds everyone of how it used to be. We like that around here, and the show gives lots of jobs to the locals. It's been good for all of us. It brings people like you here, aside from summer visitors." He smiled broadly as he stopped the car in front of a neat stone cottage that looked like something in a fairy tale, with crisp white curtains in the windows. "There's Prudence now," he said, as a small round woman stepped out into the road, and wiped her hands on her apron. She looked like the fairy godmother in Cinderella, and she smiled at the driver who had brought Winnie to her.

"Morning, Josiah. Fine weather."

"Indeed it is." He turned to indicate Winnie as she got out of the cab. "I brought you a guest from America. She's here to watch the show." Prudence Flannagan smiled at the mention of it, and looked warmly at Winnie.

"Welcome, come in and take a look around and see if it suits you." Winnie stepped into the cottage as Josiah unloaded her bags and left them standing outside, as he waited to be paid. There was a delicious smell of fresh bread in the oven, and something bubbling on the stove that looked like stew as she walked through the kitchen. There was a cozy front parlor, a small dining room, and a back garden. The ceilings were low, and the staircase old-fashioned, she noticed as she went upstairs to view the three bedrooms reserved for guests, in addition to Prudence's. All three bedrooms were small and cheery, with flowered chintzes at the windows and on the beds that Prudence had made herself. Two of the rooms shared a bath, and one had its own, and all three were vacant at the moment.

"You can have your pick," she said cheerfully, as Winnie went from room to room. "I imagine you'll want your own bath. Americans always do." Winnie nodded agreement, and was delighted with the accommodations. "You can do whatever you like, except smoke in the rooms. But you can smoke in the garden. Breakfast is included in the price of the room, and I serve dinner every night if you want it, for a small extra fee. I can give you a better rate week by week or month by month, if you decide to stay. Most people do if they can, once they get here. I'll do laundry for you if you like, at no extra charge. It's no trouble. I have to do it for the house anyway."

It was an ideal situation, and Winnie asked for the room with its own bath. She could see the town square and Haversham Castle from her window, and the price was ridiculously low. A week's rent was barely more than the price of a good dinner at home. Prudence Flannagan wasn't taking advantage of the tourists brought in by the show. She said she got plenty of business, and the house was full most of the time. All three guests had just left the day before, and she had three more arriving that week, one from Italy and two from Germany. The show was aired all over Europe, and popular in every country where it was shown.

Josiah brought Winnie's bags upstairs for her, and she tipped him handsomely for his kindness and for bringing her to Mrs. Flannagan's B and B. She felt as though she were visiting an aunt, or someone's grandmother. And it occurred to her that her mother would have loved this. It was so perfectly English, and old-fashioned and cozy. She couldn't imagine being lonely here.

She unpacked in her room, and came down a short time later, as Mrs. Flannagan took her freshly baked bread out of the oven, and there was a plate of scones with clotted cream and strawberry jam sitting on the table.

"Help yourself, dear," she said with a wink at Winnie. "You'll be doing me a favor if you do. If you don't eat them, I will." She patted her hips as she said it. Winnie put a scone on a plate with the clotted cream and jam and the first bite melted in her mouth.

"Oh, that's delicious," Winnie said, smiling.

"Thank you. If you want to watch them filming, they shoot outdoors most mornings, and at the end of the day. They do the studio shots indoors in the middle of the day and at night."

"I'd like to watch them film outside," Winnie said hopefully.

"Of course. They're very friendly and congenial about it. They don't seem to mind at all, you have to stand behind barriers they set up, but they let people get very close. You have to stay quiet, though."

"I'm addicted to the show," Winnie confessed, as she finished the scone and helped herself to another.

"We all are, the whole world is. People come from all over to see it. No one knew we were here until the show came on. You should take a tour of Haversham Castle too. There are parts they don't use for the show, and they'll take you through them. And then there are the family quarters. There are only two of them now. His Lordship the Marquess, and his sister. Their parents died quite a long time ago. The marquess inherited his title and the estate when he was barely twenty, and his sister is a year or two younger. That was more than twenty years ago now." Listening to her was like watching the show, and Winnie loved it. "They haven't changed much in the castle. They couldn't afford to. They have titles and a beautiful castle, but had no money to maintain it. The show changed all that, and now the producers don't want them to modernize anything. It works for the show as it is."

She seemed to know all about it, and Winnie set out on foot a few minutes later, to explore the village. She walked around the village green, soaking up the sunshine, and walked into the little shops. There were several pubs that she didn't venture into, and the restaurants in town were supposed to be excellent. She was on her way back to the cottage several hours later, when she saw cameras on rolling platforms appear, barriers set up, a cluster of people in period costumes, makeup artists and hairdressers and a flock of assistants, and she realized they were going to start filming. She stood under a tree, behind the barrier, and watched them for two hours. This was what she had come for, and as they put tape on the ground to mark where the actors would stand, she saw the two stars walking toward her, talking seriously, and then repeating it again and again. The actress was wearing a beautiful hat and an embroidered Chinese coat of the period, and the actor looked dashing. Winnie's heart pounded as she watched them, and there was silence all around. Then the whole group walked back to the castle after the scene was shot, and the two stars were talking and laughing and looked like they were teasing each other. She swatted him with her elegant hat, and they waved at their fans as they walked by, while the locals cheered them. They were gone in a minute and Winnie looked awestruck as she walked into Mrs. Flannagan's kitchen.

"I just saw them shoot a scene!" she said, still amazed by it, and Mrs. Flannagan laughed. They did it almost every day, and the townspeople were used to it.

"Welcome to *Beauchamp Hall,* my dear," she said warmly, and Winnie ran up the stairs to her room, feeling as though she had died and gone to Heaven. This was just what she had wanted when she decided to come, and what she had dreamed of. It was perfect.

Chapter Six

Winnie watched another scene being shot early the next morning when she went for a walk before breakfast. The actors were different this time, some of the younger stars, and the father on the show was with them. She recognized them all and stood rapt until they finished shooting. She couldn't imagine getting tired of it or becoming blasé about it. It was magical watching them.

After breakfast, she walked up to the castle, and waited for a tour of the parts they showed visitors. The history of the place was fascinating. Its heyday of opulence and luxury had been in the nineteenth and earlier part of the twentieth century. The family had had serious reverses after the Crash of 1929. Changing times had continued to diminish their fortune after the Second World War, and by the 1960s they were in serious trouble, but had managed to hang on to the castle and estate by selling works of art, valuable objects like Fabergé boxes, or the occasional investment that did well. The days of armies of servants like on the show, grandeur, and unlimited funds had ended some ninety years before. And parts of the castle showed it and were in need of repair. The days of the castle's occupation by the Haversham family went almost all the way back to the Norman Conquest, and many of the crowned heads of Europe had stayed there. Queen Victoria and Prince Albert had visited the family frequently, so had King George VI, and Queen Elizabeth II was the godmother of Lady Beatrice, the current marquess's sister. There was no question of their noble birth or importance in the British aristocracy, and some of the rooms of the castle and their contents were magnificent. The tour guide explained that the parts of the castle being used to film the show were the most beautiful, and were not on the tour at the moment as they were in use for filming on a daily basis. Learning about it was fascinating and Winnie bought a book about the family and the castle on the way out.

She asked the guide if one could watch filming inside the castle and was told with a smile that you had to know someone in the cast or the producers to do that, but she said that the actors were frequently seen around the village, and the outdoor shots were easy to see happening, and all observers were welcome.

After the tour, Winnie looked around for a place to have a cup of tea and noticed a bright yellow food truck parked in a corner of the main square. She wandered over to it. A man about her own age was handing out tea and coffee, and selling sandwiches and pastries to visitors and locals. He smiled at her, and she asked for a cup of Earl Grey tea, and he handed it to her. As soon as she paid him and thanked him and he heard her speak, his smile grew wider.

"American?" She nodded. "Came to see the show being filmed?"

She nodded again. "You know, they hire extras right off the street. We've all been in it at some point. You should get on the list, it's fun, and you probably don't need a work permit for a day of occasional labor. You don't have to do anything, just stand there looking like a villager in whatever costume they put you in. They pay you something for it, not much, but I do it for the amusement and to see the actors. You might enjoy it."

"I'm sure I would." She looked interested by what he was saying. "Where do I sign up?"

"Just watch where they're shooting at the end of the day. They often walk around asking for extras. They sign them up for the next day. One of the assistants will have the list, you'll see it."

"Thank you, I'll watch for it." She smiled at him.

"My name is Rupert, by the way." He reached out of his food truck and shook her hand.

"Winnie," she supplied, still smiling.

"Where are you from?" He was curious about her, and he thought she was a pretty woman.

"A small town, north of Detroit, Michigan. It's very cold there."

He grinned. "It's not tropical here either. How long are you staying?"

"I haven't decided. I'm free for a while." He nodded and then got busy with other customers, so she walked down one of the narrow streets she hadn't explored yet, and the truck was gone when she got back.

She didn't see anyone making lists of extras for the next two days, and then on the third day she saw a young man doing exactly what

Rupert had described, asking for volunteers as extras and jotting down names as people put up their hands. Winnie approached and put up her hand so the assistant would see it.

"Name?" he asked her quickly.

"Winona Farmington."

"Great, thanks." And when he had as many as he needed, he told them to come to the main entrance of the castle at seven the next morning, and they'd be given costumes. He warned them all not to wear jewelry or modern watches, and he told them that they would receive a small token amount, paid in cash.

Winnie could hardly wait as she went back to the cottage, and told Mrs. Flannagan as soon as she walked in.

"Good for you!" she congratulated her. "Maybe they'll discover you and you'll become famous like Marilyn Monroe." Winnie laughed at the comparison.

"I don't think so, but it sounds like fun."

"It is," she admitted. "I've done it myself. It takes a lot of time, though, they keep you standing around for hours while they shoot the scenes again and again. I'm too busy here to do it more than every now and then. I was an extra in Lady Charlotte's wedding scene as the carriage drove her and Lord Hamish away." Winnie had watched the wedding repeatedly and knew the scene she meant. "But you have the time, you'll enjoy it," Prudence added.

The German guests had arrived that morning, they were a young couple and avid fans of the show, as was a young Italian man, who said he was writing an article about it. The other guests were quiet and kept to themselves, and spent as much time exploring the town as she did, so she didn't see them often. The B and B was very well run, and immaculately clean. All the guests loved it.

The next morning, Winnie walked up to the main entrance of the castle, wearing no watch or jewelry, and lined up with about sixty or seventy people. They were going to be a crowd at a church fair, and Winnie loved the coat, hat, dress, and shoes they had for her. A makeup artist gave her a cursory once-over with blush and powder, and two hours later they were taken by bus to the local church where tents were set up, pens with live animals in them, and food stalls, and the crowd was to wander around enjoying themselves as the actors played out the scene in the foreground. Winnie saw three of her favorite actors appear and one of them smiled at her. She felt like a schoolgirl after he did, and she chatted with the other extras between scenes. They were all locals, except for her, and they were impressed that she had come from so far away. She had a great time with all of them. They were given lunch from a giant food truck, and sent home with a little cash for each at the end of the day. The pay was very little, but she didn't care.

"Did you have fun?" Mrs. Flannagan asked her when she got back, she could see that she had, Winnie's eyes were dancing. She had sent Marje a text that she'd been an extra on the show that day. And her sister had teased her that she would become famous.

"I had a ball," Winnie said and went up to her room, smiling. It was the most fun she'd had in years. She went for a walk that night after dinner, and saw two of the major actors taking a stroll and talking earnestly. She would have loved to say hello to them, but didn't dare.

And the next day, at the pharmacy, she saw a beautiful woman with long blond hair speaking to the pharmacist. Winnie recognized her from a photograph in the book she'd bought. It was Lady Beatrice Haversham, the sister of the marquess who owned the castle. The book had explained the rights of primogeniture, which dictated that the current marquess had inherited everything, the castle and the entire estate, along with his title. But being a modern man, he had given the dower house and a portion of the estate, with some of the old tenant farms, to his sister, so she would have a home there forever, and was a part owner of the estate. In earlier times, she would have inherited nothing. Lady Beatrice turned and smiled at Winnie warmly, as though she knew her.

"Sorry to be taking so long," she apologized. "My brother always sends me with a ridiculous list, for vitamins, plasters, headache medicine, he's hopeless!" Winnie smiled at the British pronunciation of "vitamins," and had learned that "plasters" were bandages for small cuts.

"It's fine, I'm not in a hurry," she assured her, and then she couldn't help saying something about the book she was finding fascinating. "I'm really enjoying the book about your home and family," Winnie said cautiously, not sure how she'd take it, and the beautiful aristocrat smiled broadly at her, since she'd written the book.

"How nice of you. That sort of thing is so embarrassing, and of course there are all sorts of idiotic stories in it that make one's relatives look ridiculous, but it helps sell the book, and one has to do something to make money," she said with a smile. "Are you here to watch the series being filmed?"

Winnie nodded. "I am. I love the show, it was sort of a dream to come here. I just decided to do it." There was something so genuine about the way she said it that it touched Lady Beatrice.

"Well, thank God for people like you, you keep a roof over our heads. I do love the show myself. I sit and watch it for hours, and my brother tells me how stupid I am. But the writer is brilliant and quite creative, and it's not all based on us. In fact, most of it isn't. He just used the house and a bit of our family history for inspiration. The *Beauchamp Hall* family are far more interesting than we are. Our parents were quite dull actually, and I don't think my grandfather spoke more than once or twice in his lifetime. Although my grandmother was a bit naughty, quite a few indiscretions, I'm afraid, but she was very beautiful and my grandfather was very boring. And all my brother ever does is play with his cars, he's more or less a mechanic. It's his only activity, other than shooting, riding, and playing with his dogs. And I have no talents whatsoever." She was modest and funny, and Winnie thought she was utterly enchanting. There was nothing pretentious about her, and she had no trouble laughing at herself.

"I have no talents either," Winnie said simply. "I wish I could write something like *Beauchamp Hall*."

"So do I!" Lady Beatrice said enthusiastically. "Think of the pots of money we'd make." The two women were laughing like old friends when the pharmacist handed Lady Beatrice an enormous bag across the counter. "See what I mean?" She turned to Winnie. "All for my brother. He's a dreadful hypochondriac. He needs to marry a nurse really. Or a doctor." She smiled at Winnie again as she walked past her. "Enjoy your stay here. And thank you for buying the book! We need it to fix the roof, it leaks dreadfully!" She waved and then hurried out of the shop, and Winnie turned to the pharmacist, a bit stunned by the encounter.

"What a nice person," she commented and the pharmacist agreed with her.

"She's a good woman. Her brother is very pleasant too, very handsome, but a bit eccentric, I think. Neither of them has ever been married," she volunteered, then took care of what Winnie requested and handed it to her. When she left the pharmacy, she saw Lady Beatrice being driven away by a good-looking man with dark hair in an old Jaguar. He took off at full speed. They were both about Winnie's age. And they were laughing as he drove back toward the castle.

Winnie spent the rest of the day exploring the village again. She had a nice lunch on her own in a little tea room, and went back to the cottage late in the day. Mrs. Flannagan said she'd had a message from the casting department of the show. They needed extras again and wanted to know if she was available. She called the number back, and told them she'd love to do it. She had to be at the set this time at 6:00 A.M., for a hospital scene. She was going to be one of the nurses rushing up and down a hallway. It sounded like fun to Winnie.

By six-thirty the next morning, she was wearing a nurse's uniform of the period, her hair was crimped in neat waves beneath her cap, and tied up in a little bun. She was fascinated to notice a prim little man watching every scene. Someone explained to her that he was their "manners coach," the person who corrected them about how women sat and walked and spoke at the time, and on what men could and couldn't do. He gave the look of the show accurate historical authenticity, in terms of the mores of the era, along with a historical consultant. The two men conferred constantly, and advised the cast.

In the scene Winnie was in, she brought a lunch tray in for one of the main actors, and when she set it down in front of him for the fourth time, and murmured, "Your lunch, Your Lordship," he whispered to her.

"Can I have you for lunch?" he asked sotto voce with a look of innocence, his lips barely moving. She burst out laughing, and they had to shoot the scene again. Afterwards he apologized to her. "Sorry, I couldn't resist. You look gorgeous in that uniform."

"Thank you," she said and could feel herself blushing. He didn't pursue it any further, but it was a nice compliment, and the next day she saw Rupert and his food truck in the square and went over to talk to him.

"Thank you for telling me about signing up as an extra, I've done it twice since I saw you. It's so much fun." He laughed and handed her the tea she had ordered.

"We've all done it. So how are you settling in?" He acted as though she'd moved there, and she almost felt that way too. She had no desire to leave anytime soon. Everyone had been so welcoming. She had Skyped with Marje several times and told her all about it. She'd told her that now she had to watch the show so she could see her baby sister on TV in the church fair scene and in a nurse's uniform at the hospital. "You ought to apply for a job on the set," Rupert suggested.

"I don't think I can work here," Winnie said, looking pensive. "I'm sure I'd need a work visa."

"They can get you one if they want to. If you're going to stay here long enough, it might be good to work there, unless you're a lady of leisure," he said hesitantly. Winnie smiled at him.

"I'm definitely not that. I'm between jobs at the moment. But I wasn't planning to work for a while."

"They might not have anything. You could put yourself on a list and if something comes up, they'll call you." He was very helpful once again, and the idea appealed to her enormously. She thought about it for a few days. She'd been in Burnham Market for a week by then, and it was starting to feel like home. The Italian and German guests had left the cottage, and been replaced by two French couples who were traveling together. The town had definitely become a destination for people who loved the show, and wanted to see where it was made and get a closer look at the cast. She had caught another look at Lady Beatrice too, but didn't speak to her this time. She was driving down the high street in a banged-up old Fiat 500.

After Winnie had been there for two weeks, she screwed up her courage and walked up to the castle, asked for the HR office on the set, gave them her details and how to contact her, and handed them her CV. They explained that with no experience working on the set of a TV show, and no work permit, only the most menial jobs would be open to her. They could hire people like her for the lowest possible salary, sometimes on a part-time basis. For a better job, she'd need a work permit and the union would get involved.

"I don't mind what I do," she said easily, and meant it. For the thrill of working on the set, she would have done almost anything. She really had become a groupie, she told herself, and said as much when she wrote to Marje again. She deleted two more emails from Barb without opening them. Rob had finally stopped calling and texting her. He had obviously moved on. She felt relieved, mostly.

She got a chance to be an extra again, and a week later she was shocked when she got a call to come in and interview for a job. They didn't say what it was on the phone, and she knew it could only be a minor job, but any opportunity to hang around on the set was a thrill to her. She could watch them film the indoor scenes that way.

She wore a short navy skirt and white blouse with sandals when she went for the interview, and she saw a different HR person than she had the first time, and had to explain her job experience again. The woman hesitated, and then finally said that they needed an errand girl on the set. They'd had one and just lost her. She said the position was very poorly paid and was such a minor job that they paid for it out of their petty cash budget rather than payroll, which would have been more complicated. It was perfect for Winnie, because she didn't need a work permit that way. The HR woman warned her that she was not to be overly personal with the stars of the show, nor intrusive, she was not to ask anyone on the set for autographs and she was basically expected to do whatever they asked her for, within reason, as long as it wasn't illegal or dangerous. She was there to make everyone's life easier and spare them from doing menial tasks themselves. She was what was commonly called a gofer in the States. It was a job she would have been offended by at home, and was delighted to have on the set of *Beauchamp Hall*. She was told which production assistant to report to and that her work hours would be decided on, as well as what days they needed her. The woman warned Winnie that the hours could be long if they had night shoots, or a shooting day went to overtime. Winnie had nothing else to do and she couldn't wait to start.

She wandered around the various sets they used after the meeting, some of them were replicas of rooms in the house, and she finally found the assistant she was looking for in the library, setting up a shot and piling books on the floor. She looked up when Winnie walked in, and Winnie thought her new boss looked about fourteen years old.

"Hi, I'm Winnie Farmington, I'm your new gofer," she said without ceremony, and the young red-haired girl looked surprised. She had a face full of freckles and her hair was in braids, which made her look even younger. She was wearing overalls and clogs.

"Aren't you kind of old to be a gofer?" the girl said bluntly. Her name was Zoe. Winnie smiled at what she'd said.

"I probably am, but I'm here for a while and I wanted a job, and this is about all I can do here, so here I am."

"What are you in real life?"

"I worked at a printing company in the U.S. for ten years. Not very exciting, but I'm very good at being organized and getting things done." It seemed like a small skill to show for ten years of work and was hard to explain.

"How are you with putting books all over the floor so it looks like someone had a fit and threw them? Our set dresser is sick today, so I got stuck with it," Zoe asked hopefully, wanting to reassign the task.

"No problem." Winnie started pulling books off shelves and placing them in haphazard piles. It took her five minutes to do it, and Zoe had her get everyone's lunch orders, and then bring them back

from the commissary truck. There were dozens of assistants of varying kinds, as well as hairdressers, makeup artists, stylists, costumers,
seamstresses, four people just to deal with the hats, five who worked
on the wigs for the entire cast. And all kinds of technical people, for
sound and light, mixers for the music. It was interesting to learn
what everyone did. Bringing back lunch on a rolling cart was a good
way to see all their faces, and write down their names, although she
knew she'd never remember them all. In the end, she had brought
lunch back for forty people, and only a few stuck out. The stars were
served lunch in their trailers, or they could go to the commissary
truck. The people she'd gotten lunch for preferred to eat on the set,
and a particularly tall young man thanked her, and asked if he could
have a second sandwich, so she went back and got him another one.
He was a sound technician, and his name was Nigel. He thanked her
when she handed him the second sandwich and she saw him staring
at her as she walked away.

The day flew by doing small assignments for everyone whenever
she was asked. She got to watch a scene being shot, but most of the
time she was too busy, looking for some object that was lost, or track-
ing down another one, or satisfying someone's whim for candy, or a
sweater, or a pair of socks, or softer towels, better tissue, their favorite mineral water, or the kind of toilet paper they liked. She was a
combination requisition officer/magician, and she managed to find
everything they asked for, and even walked the dog of one of the
stars. It was a Jack Russell that tried to bite her the minute she was
out of her mistress's sight. But Winnie didn't mention it when she
brought her back. Zoe let her leave at seven-thirty when all the actors were off the set, and Winnie was surprised by how tired she was

when she walked back to the cottage. She'd been on her feet, and running, for eleven hours. The day had been kind of a treasure hunt, without a map.

"How was your day?" Mrs. Flannagan asked her when she walked in.

"Fun. I don't think I sat down all day. They all want special stuff, and expect me to find it, or invent it out of thin air. But actually, it's kind of challenging in a menial way." She'd also had to find an unusual kind of hypoallergenic lip balm, and a special kind of surgical glue for one of the makeup artists, who was pulling up one of the older actresses' face with elastics under her wig. She had learned some of the tricks of the trade, just watching what they did all day. There was a lot of artifice involved. This was show biz!

Winnie sat down in the kitchen, and was almost too tired to eat Mrs. Flannagan's shepherd's pie, but she made the effort to please her. And then she went to bed right after dinner, and woke up with a start at 6:00 A.M. She had to be back on the set at seven, and this time she put a little kit together, with needles, thread, safety pins, two kinds of tape, super glue, several colored rubber bands. They were the things everyone seemed to ask for most. She even took a spot remover from her own travel kit. And this time she wore jeans and running shoes, which seemed more appropriate to the job, and a T-shirt and sweater. It was a sunny day, but there was still a chill in the air.

She dealt with most of the same people and a few new faces and the same sound technician asked her for two sandwiches again, and he smiled broadly when he saw her.

"We haven't run you off yet?"

"No, I'm enjoying it," she said honestly, as she sank down on a stool to rest for two minutes before they asked her for something else. They just looked at her and thought of things they needed or had to have.

"How'd you end up here?" Nigel was curious about her. "You're from the States, right?"

She nodded. "Michigan. Beecher, Michigan, home of record-breaking tornadoes, and not much else."

"I'm from Leighton Buzzard," he supplied, although she had no idea where it was. "It's near London."

"You didn't answer my question," he prodded her. "Why here?"

"Because I love the show. I quit my job and I had nothing else to do, so I thought I'd check it out. And now I have a job. It's worked out pretty well, so far."

"Lucky for us," he said with a smile and went back to work. He was doing a sound check of the mikes before the next scene. A minute later, Zoe called her away, and asked her to walk the Jack Russell again. It was the only part of the job she didn't like. She was a nasty little thing and she barked the minute she saw Winnie coming, and snarled when Winnie reached down to pet her.

The time flew by and each day was different. Everyone seemed to like her. Some more than others. Nigel was constantly finding excuses to talk to her.

They all had the weekend off, and as she was getting ready to leave, he wandered over. "Can I interest you in dinner tonight or tomorrow?" He looked nervous as he asked her. He was sure she'd turn him down. She was a pretty woman, and he figured she probably had a dozen men pounding on her door, or maybe one she already lived with. He had noticed that she didn't wear a wedding band, which he took as a hopeful sign. Winnie hesitated when he asked her. She hadn't thought about dating anyone so soon after Rob. But Nigel didn't seem like a serious threat, and she thought they could just be pals.

"Sure," she responded, and thanked him. "How about tonight?" She was thinking about renting a car and exploring the countryside on Saturday.

"Sounds great. Where do you live? I'll pick you up." She told him, and he said he knew where it was, and said he would fetch her in his chariot at eight o'clock, which was only an hour away. She barely had time to change. But she put on a skirt instead of jeans, and nicer shoes with little heels.

Nigel arrived promptly in a battered Jeep, and she hopped in next to him. He took her to a Vietnamese restaurant he had discovered, where he said the food was very good.

"All right. So tell me everything. Husbands, kids, why you came here, brothers, sisters," he asked her at dinner.

She smiled at the question. "That's easy, no husbands, no kids, no brothers, one sister. I quit a job and broke up with my boyfriend of eleven years, all on the same day, and now here I am." She made it sound easy, but it wasn't. She didn't mention Barb. It still hurt too much. And she still missed Rob at times. He was familiar, but she didn't want to think about him after what he'd done.

"That is simple. I've got four siblings, no wife, no girlfriend, and a black Lab named Jocko my brother takes care of when I'm away. I'm the only one in my family not married, so they think I'm weird. And I'm not gay."

"Then why aren't you married?" she asked him.

"I'm a nomad, always working on a show or a movie. No time for girls." He grinned. "And it's a temporary life. Working on shows is like being in the merchant marine. I'm always shipping out some-where. And I always seem to get shows that go on location a lot. This one's pretty tame. But you never know how long it will last."

"Six years sounds pretty good to me," she said, after they ordered dinner.

"They can cancel a show anytime. The show gets stale, or they want to leave on a high note. Or three of the stars want to leave and it falls apart. You never know what's going to happen." She had never thought of that, and hoped that *Beauchamp* never fell apart. She'd be crushed. "You move around a lot in this business."

"Sounds good to me," she said, thinking about it. She liked Nigel. He seemed like a nice guy. He was easy to talk to and wasn't full of himself. "I've been sitting at the same desk for ten years. That gets pretty old."

"Is that why you quit? So you could come here?"

"No, I got passed over for a promotion I should have gotten, and I got pissed."

"And the boyfriend?" He wanted to know all about her. There was something about her that he liked. She had spirit, but just enough. She didn't seem like one of those pushy women who wanted to com-pete with a man all the time, or that was the impression she gave him. There was a gentleness to her, but she had her own ideas. She hesitated before she answered his question, and then decided to be honest. It was simpler.

"I walked in on him having sex with my best friend. In my bed."

"Ah, a true gentleman. Classic. So you came here?" She nodded.

"It was a spur-of-the-moment decision, and a dream come true. I always wanted to get out of my hometown. And I did, for college, but then my mother got sick, so I went back. I nursed her for seven years, and after she died, it seemed too late to leave, so I stayed."

"And you're thirty-two? . . . four . . . five?"

"Thank you! Thirty-eight." She smiled.

"I beat you. I'm thirty-nine. I had one of those walk-in-on-them experiences too, about ten years ago. Also with my best friend. I think it's a pretty standard gig. I was very upset. They got married, and have a house full of kids now. I never forgave them for it, though." A pained and still-angry look flitted across his eyes, and then disappeared.

"I don't think I will forgive them either. It's an unforgettable experience. She was tied to my bed."

"Exotic." She didn't tell him about the porn.

Their dinner came then and it was delicious. The conversation was easy and light, and he drove her back to Mrs. Flannagan's afterwards. They talked about a lot of the movies he had worked on, there were some big ones, with big-name stars.

"I had a really lovely time, Nigel, thank you," she said as she got out.

"What are you doing tomorrow? We may not get another day off for a long time." She told him about her plan to rent a car, and explore the surrounding area. "Why don't you let me drive you? I've been here for four years and know it pretty well." He looked hopeful and she liked the idea.

"That would be great."

"I'll pick you up at ten. Bring a bathing suit. There are some nice beaches around here." She had thrown a bathing suit into her suitcase at the last minute, in case she stayed at a hotel with a pool. She nodded, and waved as she went inside and walked upstairs to her room, thinking about him. She hadn't thought she wanted to date yet, and didn't think it would come up while she was here. But she had enjoyed the evening with Nigel. And he seemed like just what she needed right now. A friendly, pleasant person with no strings attached, no agenda, and no complications. He seemed like an easygoing guy.

Chapter Seven

Nigel and Winnie spent Saturday cruising around in his Jeep. They drove to a monastery he knew, which was a spectacular building he wanted to show her, and from there they went to a beach, and went swimming. They lay on the sand afterwards talking, watching children wade into the water and picnic with their parents. They had lunch at a nearby inn, and ate sausages called "bangers," then drove around some more. They talked a lot about their childhoods, their families, and their dreams. She loved his openness and kindness and how different he was from Rob.

Nigel wanted to have his own sound business one day, and Winnie said how much she had wanted to move to New York, before her mother got sick. He had her back to Burnham by 6:00 P.M. Her reason for leaving him early wasn't glamorous but honest, she had laundry to do that night. She was too busy to do it when she was working, and she didn't want to take advantage of Mrs. Flannagan, although she was a good sport about it, and was always offering to help.

They were both in good spirits and had enjoyed each other's company and the relaxing day, and they both reluctantly turned their phones back on, as they approached the cottage. They had agreed to turn them off all day, so no one could intrude on them. As soon as Nigel turned his on, he had a slew of messages, texts, and voice mails. He listened to a few of them, and looked at Winnie in shocked dismay.

"Something wrong?" she asked, and he nodded.

"Very much so. It's Tom White." He turned to her with a stricken look and tears in his eyes. "He went riding today with some of the cast." Winnie knew he was an avid rider from what she'd read about him. He even rode in a fancy hunt regularly. "He had an accident, and was killed an hour ago. He broke his neck." Nigel said he knew Tom had a daughter in London. She had visited him on the set. Tom White was one of the more important members of the cast, with a dedicated following. But aside from that, he was a nice human being, and only forty-six years old. Winnie stared at Nigel for a moment, trying to absorb what he'd just said. They'd been driving around having a good time all day, and Tom White was dead. "I'll call the producer after I drop you off. This is going to throw them into a tizzy," Nigel said, looking distracted and anxious.

"What'll they do about the show?" Winnie asked him. It seemed unimportant in the scheme of life, but would matter to the producer.

"They have to write him out, but there's no way to prepare the viewers in a case like this. There will be a reaction from his fans to whatever scenario they come up with, and the ratings will suffer." But his daughter would suffer more. They were both somber when they left each other, and Mrs. Flannagan had just learned of it too.

She'd heard it on the radio. And someone had told her that reporters were already gathering at the hospital and the castle to interview members of the cast and production team, and photograph grieving people who knew him.

"That's really so sad," Mrs. Flannagan commented to Winnie before she went upstairs. He was one of the actors she liked best on the show. He was also one of the most likable members of the fictional Beauchamp family.

The atmosphere was funereal on the set the next day. An announcement was made to the entire crew, management, and all the stars. Matthew Stevens, the originator and writer of the show, went into seclusion, to try to write Tom out and find a solution for the storyline. It wasn't easy and there were other scenes they'd have to reshoot without him.

Tom's body was being sent to his family in Hertfordshire, and there was to be a memorial service for the cast and crew organized by Michael Waterman, the executive producer, in two days. Tom's death was bound to sink everyone's spirits for a while. He had been on the show since the beginning and it was a huge loss, personally and for the show. He was a lovely person and added a strong element to the show.

By the end of the day, Matthew was still struggling to make the changes he had to, when the executive producer walked into the office he used in the castle, and sat down heavily across from him.

"Not good news," Michael said as Matthew dreaded what would come next. "Miranda Charles wants to leave the show. Apparently, she's been waiting to tell us, and she thought she should do it now, with Tom gone, while you're working on new storylines." He rolled his eyes as he said it. Her timing was atrocious. It was always all about her. "She's had an offer to do a play." It was what they both hated about their jobs, the unpredictability of actors. They'd had losses before, but never as big as this, and not two at a time. It could kill the show. The viewers needed to be weaned gently from characters they loved, not brutally like this. Both men knew the ratings would drop as a result. It couldn't be helped about Tom White, but Miranda was pure self-indulgence. She was a total narcissist.

"Oh shit," Matthew said grimly. "Should we let her go or fight her on it?" They could hold her to her contract, but she'd punish them for it.

"I hate hostages," Michael Waterman said. "They make one's life miserable every way they can. Do you think the show would survive our losing both of them at once?" He looked seriously worried.

"I'll do my best with the writing. But it's hard to predict how attached the viewers are to them." It was going to affect every script for a long time. Matthew took his computer home with him that night, and worked intensely for several days, considering the options for new plot lines, and new characters to complete the cast without Tom, and now Miranda. Everyone else went to the memorial service and Matthew slipped in at the last minute. The press was there en masse. Winnie saw Lady Beatrice and her brother, but Winnie was too far away in a rear pew for the owner of the castle to notice her. It was particularly moving with Tom's daughter there, sobbing in his ex-wife's arms. It brought things into sharp focus for everyone how short life was, and how everything could change in the blink of an eye.

The set was very quiet after that, and all the actors and crew subdued.

They let Miranda out of her contract, after some heavy pressure from her agent, and intense negotiation. Someone leaked it to the press who predicted that without two of its strongest actors and biggest stars, the show would flounder in six months and not survive. But nothing they had said had convinced Miranda to stay, and she didn't want to work without Tom. She was desperate to do the play, which everyone thought was poor judgment on her part, and a bad career move.

Michael and Matthew had tried to tell her that, historically, actors who had big roles in successful series and left to do other projects, seeking greater stardom, had never done as well, and often faded from sight. The show had taken Miranda to another level of fame in the past two years, and she refused to believe that she might vanish without a trace without it, and insisted they were wrong.

It took Matthew two weeks to come up with some storylines and scripts that were plausible, exciting, worked to replace them both, and created new characters to fill the void. Miranda was leaving the show in July, which wasn't far away.

"I told you everything can change overnight," Nigel reminded Winnie when they had dinner again. They'd had no time together since Tom's death. Too much was going on.

"Do you think it will hurt the show too badly to lose both of them?" She was worried about it, she didn't want anything to damage the show irreparably or get it canceled.

"It won't help it, but Matthew is clever. It happened three years ago, if you recall. He had to kill two characters. Their contracts were up. They wanted too much money, and it turned into a standoff. The show was actually better after they left, which no one expected." It was always hard to predict how the public would react to characters leaving the show.

It had been a stressful two weeks for everyone, and Tom's death had cast a pall over the set.

A few days later when they had a Sunday off, and she was out walking around town, Winnie stumbled onto a surprise. It was a tiny cottage not far from Mrs. Flannagan's, with a FOR RENT sign out front. It looked like a dollhouse and Winnie fell in love with it on sight. She told Nigel about it the next day.

"Are you thinking of getting your own place here?" He looked pleased and surprised. He hadn't expected her to do that and stick around.

"I wasn't, but I love it here. I have nothing to go back to now, and hopefully *Beauchamp* will run for a long time. And if it doesn't, I can always sublet the cottage or try to get out of the lease. If I do stay, HR said they can try to get me a special work visa. The authorities have been very sympathetic to the show. I guess I'll do that if I rent a house here." He loved the idea, and so did she. Nothing had gone forward with them, despite the pleasant time they spent together. She was still feeling gun-shy after Rob, and Nigel sensed that and didn't want to rush her, but her wanting to rent a cottage seemed like a good sign, and if she got a work visa, better yet. Their producers had powerful connections, and were willing to use them for the show.

"Why don't we look at the cottage together after work?" he suggested, and she agreed. She called the number on the sign and made an appointment to see it. And Nigel drove her there after work. He had to duck his head to get through the doorway, but the little jewel box of a cottage was as pretty inside as out. It had been freshly painted and was furnished with just enough furniture to live comfortably. She would only need a few things she could find in town to make it homey and really attractive. It was big enough for one person or a couple, and the rent was very modest. She could easily afford it. She was making a minimal salary now, so she had some money coming in, along with her savings at home. She told the realtor she would think about it that night. And just as she had when she decided to come to England, everything about it felt right. She called back in the morning and said she'd take it. She told Nigel when she got to work, and he looked thrilled. She told Mrs. Flannagan that night. And she had asked HR to try for the special visa. She wanted to stay with the show. They promised to do all they could to help her.

"I'm going to miss you," Mrs. Flannagan said sadly. Winnie was good company and she loved talking to her when Winnie came home at night.

"I will miss you too," Winnie said gently, "but I'll come to visit. We can have dinner together, just like we do now."

Winnie moved into the little jewel box the following weekend with Nigel's help, and afterwards, they went shopping for what she was missing.

She was washing a new set of glasses and a set of plates when he came up behind her and put his arms around her, and he felt her hesitate. He turned her around to face him, set down the glass she had in her hand, and looked her in the eye, with a serious, loving look.

"Is it too soon, Winnie?" he asked gently. She wasn't sure if it was. She just didn't know if she was ready to have a man in her life again, or when she'd ever want one. She didn't know how long she'd be staying, and the years with Rob seemed like such a waste. She didn't want to do that again with a relationship that went nowhere. But she had just rented a house, so she obviously wasn't going anywhere soon.

"I don't know what I'm doing, Nigel. I don't want anyone to get hurt," she said in a voice raw with emotion, and held him tightly. He bent to kiss her and she didn't resist. She wanted him, but she was scared, and she didn't know what the future held for either of them.

"We don't have to make any big decisions," he said softly. "We're just two people who care about each other. We don't have to know what the future holds. You never know that in the beginning. Look at Tom White."

"That's how I got to be thirty-eight years old with the wrong man," she said sadly. But Nigel didn't feel wrong to her, any more than coming to England had been, or renting the cottage. He wasn't Rob, he was a good man, and she could tell that he cared about her. And as he kissed her again, she could feel the passion mount in both of them, and they couldn't stop kissing and fondling each other. She unzipped his jeans ever so slowly, and he pulled off her blouse. And suddenly they were wrapped around each other, and she could barely breathe she wanted him so much, as he led her toward the bedroom, and they fell onto the bed she had just made with new sheets.

Their clothes were off seconds later, and he was making love to her, and it felt clean and right and honest, and just what they both needed. He had wanted her since the first moment he'd seen her. She

forgot everything else while he made love to her, and she used everything she'd learned with Rob to please him. But it felt different this
time, and right. It wasn't just sex. They genuinely had feelings for
each other, even though the future was uncertain.

They lay breathless on the bed afterwards, as he ran gentle fingers
down her spine and gave her shivers.

"You're an amazing lover," he whispered to her, "I'm falling in love
with you . . . no, that's not true. I've already fallen." She kissed him,
and wouldn't let him leave her, and a few minutes later they were
making love again.

He stayed with her that night, and she had no regrets. He was part
of the dream she had followed to England, and a new life had begun
for both of them. For Winnie, it was long overdue.

They went to work together the next day, and she felt shy and
mildly embarrassed, and wondered if their coworkers would notice
something different about them. You could always tell when people
were intimate. There was no hiding it. But they walked into the
building separately and went about their jobs, and didn't see each
other until noon. He melted when he saw her and smiled immediately.

"I want you," he whispered to her longingly, as she handed him
the sandwich she had gotten him. "I wish we had time to go home
for lunch."

"Me too. We'll make up for it tonight," she whispered to him and
went back to work.

As she went about her job that afternoon, Winnie was thinking
about her sister. She had given her the change of address when she
left Mrs. Flannagan's B and B, but hadn't told Marje she had rented

a house, and was applying for a special visa. She knew it would panic her, and make her think Winnie was never coming home. And she hadn't decided that. She just liked having a house of her own here, and being able to stay as long as she wanted.

When Winnie gave her the new address, Marje had texted her. "You changed B and Bs? I thought you liked the other one so much?" To which Winnie had responded, "This is better. I found it by accident while taking a walk." She hadn't told her about Nigel either. For the first time, she had people and places in her life that no one knew about. She didn't want to upset her family, but being here was something she knew she needed to do for herself. She had lived her life for others for so long, her mother, Marje, Rob, Hamm Winslow. It was her turn now.

She was still thinking about it, when one of the production assistants asked her to take a manila envelope to Elizabeth Cornette, the most important actress in the show, and biggest star. The production assistant whispered to her discreetly that it was a piece of jewelry that Cartier was lending her. It was valuable and the instructions were to place the package directly into her hands. Winnie had every intention of following the PA's directions, and knocked firmly on the door of the actress's trailer when she got there. She could hear voices inside, but no one answered. Clutching the package to her, she knocked louder until she heard the actress's voice.

"Who is it?" Winnie could hear a man's voice inside too.

"Winnie Farmington, Miss Cornette. I have an important package for you," she said clearly through the door. She didn't want to shout as loudly what it was or from where. She had never spoken to the actress directly before because she had had no reason to.

"Can you come back later?" Winnie knew she couldn't and had to be persistent. They couldn't have a valuable piece of jewelry floating around when the directions were to put it in the hands of the star herself. It had to be in her possession, on her body or in a safe, for insurance purposes, as the PA had explained. There was a safe in her trailer for the jewels she wore on the show.

"I'm sorry, no, I can't come back," Winnie said firmly, and she heard a male voice raised.

The door opened a moment later, and Elizabeth Cornette was wearing a white satin bathrobe, with her makeup smeared and running down her face. She had obviously been crying. Beyond her, Winnie could see Bill Anders, the equally important male star of the show. He looked angry at Elizabeth, and annoyed when he saw Winnie. She was obviously interrupting something unpleasant and it gave credence to the rumors that the two famous actors were having an affair. Both of them were married to other people, but according to gossip on the set, their romance had been going on for months, ever since he'd joined the show. He was a recent addition.

"It's from Cartier," Winnie said as she handed it to her.

"Why the hell are you bothering us?" Bill Anders shouted angrily at Winnie.

"It's a four-hundred-thousand-pound bracelet," Elizabeth said, turning to him. "She can't just slip it under the door. They're lending it to me for the shoot tomorrow, when we go to the queen's ball." She was trying to reason with him, with a tone of exasperation in her voice. He was usually difficult on the set too. He had been famous for many years and was used to people kowtowing to him, and he was known to have affairs on every show.

"Fuck the queen's ball, Elizabeth. My wife is threatening to divorce me. Do you have any idea what that will cost me? I think she's having me followed," he said, ignoring Winnie, as he paced in the small trailer, while Elizabeth looked at Winnie in despair. And Winnie didn't know whether to leave or not. It was an awkward moment, and Elizabeth told her to come in. She had something to return to Cartier too, the forty-carat emerald ring she'd worn the day before. "Why the hell did you let her in here?" Anders complained when he saw Winnie walk into the trailer and wait for Elizabeth to get the box with the ring out of the safe. It was twice as valuable as the bracelet, and Elizabeth wasn't supposed to keep them. Winnie hadn't been told about the emerald ring. And Bill Anders stood glaring at her. "Who've you been talking to?" he shouted to Elizabeth, as she nervously pulled the ring box out and was about to hand it to Winnie, but hadn't yet. "I told you to keep your mouth shut." He was wearing a satin bathrobe too. Winnie felt as though she had walked into their bedroom, and wished Elizabeth would just give her the box and let her go.

"I didn't tell anyone a damn thing!" Elizabeth shouted back at him, still clutching the box that Winnie was waiting for. "You're not exactly discreet yourself. I told you this would wind up all over the press." A scandal of that nature would be good for both their careers, and add spice to the show, but Anders obviously had a lot at stake, and his wife was going to make him pay. Winnie knew from reading about him that he'd had numerous affairs before, always with big stars.

"This is your fault if she nails me for it. I don't know about you, but I'm not willing to give up what we're making this season for the privilege of sleeping with you." His tone was disrespectful and his words were cruel. Elizabeth was crying again, and she opened the door wider and looked straight at him over her shoulder.

"You'd better go," she said clearly, and he looked like he was going to hit her. For a minute, Winnie was afraid for her.

"I'll go when I goddamn want to," he said angrily and strode to the door. He stopped where Elizabeth was standing. "Let's not forget that you seduced me, this was your idea," he added viciously. "We both know you're a whore, and now my wife knows it too." And with that, he pushed past both of them, hurried down the steps of the trailer in his dressing gown, and went back to his own. Elizabeth collapsed in a chair then, sobbing, still clutching both the package with the brace-let and the ring box, and Winnie gently closed the door, so no one could see what was going on. She went to get Elizabeth a drink of water and handed it to her without saying a word.

"Thank you." Elizabeth took a sip, set the glass down, and blew her nose on a tissue she had in her pocket. "I'm sorry you had to hear all that. Please don't tell anyone." She looked humiliated and deeply upset.

"Of course not," Winnie said, feeling desperately sorry for her. She had a reputation for sleeping with her leading men, but she didn't deserve to be berated and abused. He was just as guilty as she was, and Winnie hated the way he treated her. She couldn't stop herself from saying what she thought. She'd been through it herself with Rob. "He shouldn't talk to you like that. You can't let him. And if his wife is angry at him, it's his own fault." Elizabeth nodded and looked gratefully at Winnie. She handed her the ring box, and put the enve-lope with the bracelet in the small safe. "What he's doing to you is abuse," Winnie said in a small voice, sure that she'd be fired for say-ing anything at all. "I've been there myself."

"And did he stop eventually?" Elizabeth asked hopefully. "I'm in love with him. He's not always like this. He's just worried about what his wife is going to do and what it will cost him."

"That's no reason to talk to you that way. And no, he didn't stop," Winnie said honestly. "He cheated on me. I caught him, and I walked out."

"You're a brave woman. Men have cheated on me for years, and I've never walked out." She looked sad as she said it. It was as bad as if he'd beaten her with his fists. She was a spectacular-looking woman. She didn't have to put up with this. Nobody should, star or not. "Please don't tell anyone about what you heard just now." She looked imploringly at Winnie.

"I promise I never will. Just try to walk away from it the next time. You'll feel a lot better when you do." Elizabeth wiped the tears from her face again. And they were both thinking about Bill's harsh words and insults, which had hit the actress with full force. She looked badly shaken and depressed.

Winnie left her trailer a few minutes later, and tried not to think about it as she went to find the production assistant to return the emerald ring. She looked horrified when Winnie found her.

"Oh my God, I forgot to get that back from her last night. Thank you." And then in an undertone, "Please don't tell anyone, I'd get fired."

"Of course not," Winnie assured her. She was suddenly keeping everyone's secrets, but the scene in Elizabeth Cornette's trailer haunted her all afternoon.

It was still on her mind when she left work. Nigel had told her that he'd meet her at her place. She had barely had time to make the bed, and put her breakfast dishes in the dishwasher, when he rang her doorbell and she let him in. She just had time to say hello to him, when he gently pulled off her clothes and wanted to make love with her. She'd been looking forward to it all day too.

They almost didn't make it to the bedroom, and he carried her the last few steps, kissing her, and then he laid her on the bed, and she reached up to him, and he entered her as they both gasped. Their lovemaking went on for hours, until they finally fell away from each other, and she smiled at him as they lay on their sides facing each other. "That was very nice," she whispered to him.

"Yes, it was," he whispered back, "very, very nice indeed." And with a peaceful smile, he fell asleep.

Chapter Eight

Despite Elizabeth Cornette's insistence that she hadn't told anyone about her affair with Bill Anders, it was all over the papers two days later. They were both just too famous for anything about their love lives to stay quiet for long. Someone inevitably talked and usually got paid by the press to do so. Winnie saw Bill Anders slip into Elizabeth's trailer several times after that. Nothing about their affair had slowed down, no matter what he was risking with his wife. The paparazzi were pursuing both of them, on and off the set, and it was bothering all the other actors. The paparazzi crawled all over them like ants.

And to complicate matters further, one of the other principal actresses had a stalker. She was young and beautiful, and played an ingénue on the show. The stalker was an obsessed fan who claimed he was madly in love with her, and constantly left her letters on the set, or on the steps of her trailer. It became so extreme and intrusive, they had to get a security guard to accompany her everywhere she went. The fan seemed relatively harmless, but you never knew with someone like that if he could suddenly turn and become violent when he realized that his sentiments weren't returned.

A few days later, Elizabeth Cornette's assistant gave notice. She had worked for Elizabeth since the beginning of the show, but her boyfriend was moving to Paris and she wanted to go with him. After six years with Elizabeth, she gave her a week's notice, and Elizabeth was frantic to have them find her someone else *now*. People were away for the summer and on the day the girl left, the PA still hadn't found a replacement, Elizabeth was having a tantrum over it, and the PA turned to Winnie in desperation.

"You do it," she said, looking desperate.

"Me?" Winnie looked horrified. "I can't be her assistant. I don't know what the job is. She's the biggest star on the show. I'll screw it up and she'll kill me." Winnie was panicked.

"All you have to do is help her get dressed, put on her jewelry for her, answer her phone if she wants you to. Call hair and makeup when she's ready for them and keep the paparazzi out of her trailer. It's not very complicated. What you're doing now as an errand girl for the cast and crew is harder. And when she's on the set, you get to read a magazine. Working for one person is easier, and she's not crazy like a lot of actresses. She probably won't even want you around most of the time, so she can sneak around with Bill Anders. You've got to do it for me, Winnie." The production assistant was near tears. "I don't have anyone for her. I'm going to get fired over this. Just do it till I find someone. I'll owe you my life if you'll do it." Winnie hesitated and felt sorry for her. She was a nice girl, about ten years younger than Winnie, with a lot of pressure on her and constant demands. She was always jumping through hoops of fire for someone.

"Okay, but only until you find a real one. I guess I can fake it until then." She wasn't enthusiastic about it. She was doing it as a favor to save the PA's neck.

"You might get to like it. Assistant to the star of the show is a cushy job, and a lot of perks come with it. People will be giving you presents all the time to get to her."

"I like the job I have. I don't have to deal with any personal issues or divas. All I have to do is run around the set, and do everyone's errands. What you're describing sounds like being a lady-in-waiting in the court of Marie Antoinette. That's too complicated for me." It actually sounded like being a lady's maid on the show too, which didn't appeal to Winnie either. But she thought she could do it for a short time.

She showed up at the star's trailer half an hour later, knocked, and stepped in when Elizabeth answered. She looked surprised when she saw Winnie, and remembered her immediately from when she'd had the big fight with Bill about his wife. But things had calmed down since.

"Hello, reporting for duty, Miss Cornette. I'm your new assistant." Winnie felt awkward when she said it, because she could see that the star remembered her from an unpleasant moment.

"You're my new assistant? Aren't you the errand girl on set?"

"I am." Winnie didn't try to deny it. "It was the only job they had open when I applied here."

"Have you ever been a personal assistant before?" She looked skeptical.

"No, I haven't. I'll do my best until they find you a real one. I'll try not to screw up too badly," she said humbly, and Elizabeth Cornette smiled.

"Don't worry about it. I forget my lines every day. We'll manage till they find somebody." Winnie nodded, and hoped it would be soon. This was more of a job than she wanted, with a high-strung actress and an abusive boyfriend, it sounded stressful to her.

"What can I do for you?" Winnie said, feeling like the lady's maid she didn't want to be. She felt faintly obsolete, or anachronistic, and could almost see herself wearing a black maid's uniform and lace cap and apron.

"I'm going out to dinner with Bill tonight. Will you help me get dressed? Call Angelica in hair, and Ivan to do my makeup." She had already taken her stage makeup off. "If there's press out there, I don't want them to see me like this." Winnie didn't dare ask her how things were going with Bill's wife. "There's a white silk dress with a pleated skirt and beading around the neck in my closet. Why don't you grab that? You may need to press it. I'll wear the high-heeled silver sandals," she said and then started sending text messages, while Winnie went to look for the dress and shoes. She found them easily, and mercifully the dress didn't need ironing. She would have been terrified to do it and ruin what was obviously a very expensive dress. She called Angelica and Ivan in hair and makeup, and they showed up five minutes later. As they got started, Winnie asked Elizabeth if she wanted something to drink.

"I'll have a glass of water," she said easily, and chatted with her hairdresser, which left Winnie with nothing to do.

An hour later, Elizabeth was dressed and ready. She looked very glamorous, and thanked Winnie for her help. She left as soon as Bill showed up, looking equally dashing, and Winnie tidied up the trailer and left a few minutes later, feeling as though she had climbed Everest. It was stressful being there, tending to someone's every need. Nigel was waiting for her outside in the Jeep.

"Where were you? I haven't seen you all day." He had missed her.

"I'm not sure if I got a promotion or a demotion. They haven't been able to find an assistant for Elizabeth Cornette. Hers quit. So they asked me to fill in until they find one. I'm kind of a lady's maid, waiting to cater to her every whim. It scares the hell out of me. What if I screw up? I'll get fired and they'll send me away, after she kills me, but I guess by then it won't matter."

"She's usually pretty decent, or that's what I've heard. She's nice to the tech guys on the set. Was she tough on you?"

"No, she was fine. I was just scared to death. I hope they find someone for her soon."

"Listen," he said to her seriously, "that's a big deal. Assistant to the star is a plum job around here. And I'm sure you'll be fine at it. It's way more money and half the universe will be kissing your ass trying to get to her."

"That's what the PA told me today. I don't need to have my ass kissed. I just want to do my work."

"Maybe you need to be more of a diva yourself," Nigel said, glancing at her. "You're so easygoing and helpful, you never demand anything for yourself." It was how she had gotten through eleven years with Rob, expecting nothing, which was pretty much what she got. Nigel was right. "There's nothing wrong with your making some demands too. Everyone will respect you more if you do."

"My old boss at the printing company was always rude to me. He was rude to everyone, so I figured it wasn't personal. Except of course, he was charming the girl he was sleeping with, who got the promotion I was supposed to get. He acted like the rest of us were cockroaches, and I was no different."

"You know, Matthew Stevens is smart about these things. It shows in what he writes. The people he writes about demand respect, they have boundaries, most of the characters don't take crap from anyone. The ones who do always take it on the chin and have to learn the lesson. It's something to think about."

"I never thought about it that way, but I think it's why I love the show so much. The good guys are very clearly that, and you know who the bad guys are, and they usually get their just deserts. And the weak ones learn to be strong. It's the way we all want to be. Funnily enough, I think it's why I quit my job when I didn't get my promotion. It happened right after an episode where Annabelle finally put her foot down and stood up for herself. So I quit, and threw Rob out when I found him in bed with my best friend. I think the show gives me courage." He smiled at what she said. "I've been feeling guilty about it, but lately I've been thinking about when I dropped out of college to take care of my mother. I never insisted on going back. I loved her dearly, and I had some precious moments with her, but I sacrificed seven years of my life, and all my dreams. And after she died, it seemed too late, so I just gave up. But my sister never helped or offered to pitch in. She was having babies by then, and she just assumed I would do everything since I wasn't married and didn't have kids. She should have helped. It's water under the bridge now, but looking back, after that it didn't matter to me that I had a job I hated, and a boss who treated me like shit. The pay was good so I put up with it. And I didn't expect Rob to treat me any differently. I kept telling myself it was just temporary, but one day temporary becomes your whole life. You wake up, and you're not twenty or twenty-seven anymore, you're thirty-eight and you've given up all your dreams. I don't want to do that again. That's why I came here. From now on, I want things to be different, and this was the first step. I want to make decisions, not just float along letting life happen to me. I want more than that." He was touched, listening to her.

"I want that too," he said gently, "as long as it lasts."

"What does that mean?" she asked, frowning at him. It sounded like he expected them to fail. She was disappointed to hear it, now that she had decided to take a chance on him. He was an improvement over Rob, but he had his own issues, since he was still single at thirty-nine.

"We're in a business where everything is temporary, Winnie. It's all stage sets and illusions. Nothing is built to last. The show feels like it's forever, but it isn't. One day we'll get canceled, or Matthew will want to stop writing it, take what he made and go live in the South of France, or start another project, and then the coach turns into a pumpkin, and we all turn into white mice and scurry off in separate directions. It's hard to have a relationship living like that."

"Is that what you see happening to us?" She looked sad as she said it. She was hoping for better from him. He seemed to be so willing to be defeated. He was already preparing for it, which Winnie found discouraging.

"I've been on a lot of shows and that's how it happens," he said, convinced that he was right, and they would lose in the end. "No matter how much people like each other while they work together, when the show is over, they scatter. *Beauchamp Hall* looks solid, but nothing ever is. And it's damn hard for two people to get jobs on the same show. When the time comes, we'll have to figure something out if we're still together. I told you, it's a nomadic life. That's why a lot of people in this business are single. Or eventually, you give it up, and find a different way to use what you know. That's why I want my own sound business one day, maybe in London, working on commercial videos and films, either for industry or advertising. I've thought about it a lot. It's the only way I'll be able to settle down, get married, and have kids. It's in my plans," he said, smiling at her, as they got out of the car. She hadn't thought as far ahead as he had. She had just arrived and was new to the business, but she was impressed that he was making plans for the future. She suspected that a lot of the people in the business didn't. They just moved on, and created new relationships wherever they went. Nigel was smarter and more thoughtful than that, and at least he wanted a more stable life. It was why she was falling in love with him. Maybe she could help him start his business one day. For the first time, she was starting to think about her future. For Winnie, it was a big change. She had drifted from year to year till then. And woke up at thirty-eight.

They cooked dinner that night in her tiny kitchen, and went to bed right afterwards. They made love until after midnight and fell asleep in each other's arms.

Working as Elizabeth's assistant was less frightening than Winnie had feared it would be. It was even fun at times, and interesting. She was learning a lot. They did research together in books and magazines on her costumes and hair styles, which Winnie then transmitted to the costumer. And Elizabeth took Winnie's advice seriously. Winnie was intelligent and had good taste, and was supremely efficient. The rest of the time she was a combination social secretary, psychiatrist, and maid.

Elizabeth's affair with her male costar was turbulent. Winnie discovered that he drank a lot, and most of the time when he was abusive to Elizabeth it was because he'd been drinking, but he was also a fierce narcissist, and felt that the world should revolve around him. His wife was still threatening to divorce him, not just over Elizabeth, but because of the dozens of women before her, and every time his wife upped the ante and wanted a bigger settlement from him, he blamed Elizabeth. He even suggested that she should contribute to what his wife wanted. She asked Winnie what she thought about it, and Winnie told her it was outrageous. He had to take responsibility for his own behavior, and bear the weight of it himself. Winnie saying it gave Elizabeth the courage to stand up to Bill. He didn't like it, but he had new respect for her after she did. He didn't ask her to contribute again, which was a victory for Elizabeth that she attributed to Winnie. The two women were becoming friends. Elizabeth was two years younger, although she looked older than Winnie, who had more natural looks. The artifice of Elizabeth's makeup, hair, expensive clothes, and jewels subtly aged her, but it was part of her identity and essential to her career.

After two weeks, they hadn't found her a "real" assistant yet, and Winnie was surprised by how comfortable she was in the job, and startled when she got the wrong pay envelope. She opened it by mistake, and was mildly envious of the salary the other person made, whoever it was. She took it to the production assistant and ruefully handed it back.

"I got someone else's salary by mistake," she said, smiling. "I'd love to know what they do. I could use some of that." The PA looked inside the envelope, checked some notes in a stack on her desk, and glanced back at Winnie.

"That's not a mistake. It's your salary, as personal assistant to the star. We're still paying you in cash." She was still part of the budget for "miscellaneous expenses on set," since she didn't have her visa yet.

"That's what I make as an assistant?" She looked shocked and grinned. "But I'm just temporary."

"Yeah, but it's what you're doing right now. She's crazy about you, by the way. She says she's never had such an efficient assistant. I haven't found anyone for her yet. Are you sure you don't want the job?" The salary was five times what she'd been making as the errand girl on the set. Winnie hesitated for a moment, thinking about it. It was tempting and she was enjoying the work. She liked Elizabeth more than she'd expected to. The one she didn't like was Bill Anders, he was pompous, pretentious, and the most self-centered human on the planet in Winnie's opinion. And Elizabeth was madly in love with him. She and her husband had just separated officially, so she was free now, but Bill was hanging on to his marriage, and didn't want to give half of what he owned to his wife. "Let me know if you decide you want the job. HR tells me we can get the work permit to go with it," which they couldn't do for her as an errand girl so they paid her in cash.

The next morning, she had made her decision, she wanted the job. Elizabeth was thrilled and so was she. They celebrated with champagne at lunch.

"Now you're really my assistant," she said, looking pleased. Winnie had talked it over with Nigel the night before, and he agreed. She discussed all her decisions with him now, he wanted to be involved in every part of her life.

Everything was going smoothly until an actor came on the show who'd been signed on for three episodes, as a brief romance for one of the younger female members of the Beauchamp family. He was sexy, handsome, and thirty-two years old. He looked like a player, and two days after he arrived, he was trying to seduce every woman on the set, and had slept with one of the hairdressers on his first day. His name was Gillian Hemmings, he was one of the hot new young talents, and had just made a movie in the States. He was expected to become a big star, and it was a coup to get him on the series for three episodes. They were considering making him long-term, but he hadn't agreed so far. He was more interested in feature films in Hollywood than a British TV series.

He had Winnie go out and buy his new underwear, he said he'd run out. Then he needed T-shirts, a bathing suit, a prescription filled for a sore throat. He wanted a bottle of very expensive malt whiskey in his dressing room. And then asked Winnie to pick up a box of condoms for him, the largest box available, for an extra-large penis, he explained to her, with ribbed sides. He asked for it as though he was ordering a ham sandwich and she did it equally straight faced, although she reminded him it wasn't her job.

"I'm Elizabeth Cornette's assistant, Gill. I don't have time to do your errands." She had done it to be nice, but he was stretching her boundaries with the box of condoms, and his precise instructions supposedly to show off his size.

"They told me you were the errand girl on the set," he said, looking boyish and apologetic. "Besides"—he lowered his voice conspiratorially—"I thought maybe you'd like to try out the condoms with me, and let me know how you like them. I'm staying at the Hoste." He had come down from London, driving a new Rolls, and was starting to ruffle feathers on the set. Bill Anders particularly didn't like him, and said that he would object strenuously if they kept him around for more than three episodes. None of the men liked him, but most of the women adored him, and were flattered by his attentions, which were indiscriminate. He had already hit on most of the younger women, and considered Winnie a challenge since she paid no attention to him. She thought he was ridiculous and she was happy with Nigel, sexually and otherwise. Their relationship was growing like a flowering plant.

"I think you'd better get the condoms yourself. I don't have time," Winnie said brusquely. She didn't want to flirt with him, or give him the mistaken impression that she was interested. She wasn't.

"Sorry, darling, I'll pick them up myself. See you tonight at my hotel?"

"No, thanks, Gill. I'm busy. I've got a boyfriend."

"That's fine. A little variety never hurt anyone. I'm only in for three episodes."

"Try someone else," she said coldly and walked away. She checked in with Elizabeth to see if there was anything she needed, brought her an iced latte, and went to find Nigel just to say hello. She couldn't find him on the set. He sent her a text at the end of the day, to say that he had to go to a production meeting and couldn't drive her home. She didn't mind, since the weather was warm and she liked the walk. But she found it strange when he didn't call her or show up that night. It wasn't like him, and had never happened before.

She texted him in the morning. "What's up? I missed you last night."

"Sorry. Busy," he responded, and she walked to work wondering what was going on with him. She didn't see him until she went to the commissary truck to get some fruit for Elizabeth and saw Nigel eating lunch alone. She walked over to him with a smile, and he looked at her icily.

"Did you have a nice night?" he asked in a glacial tone.

"Very exciting. I did laundry." She could see that he was furious with her, but she had no idea why. "Would you like to tell me what's going on? I don't like mysteries. What are you pissed about?"

"I hear you've been testing condoms with the Boy Wonder," he said, glaring at her.

"Are you kidding? Do you think I'd sleep with that little jerk? He asked me, and I told him to find someone else, and that I have a boyfriend. Was I wrong? I thought I did. It doesn't sound like it right now."

"How do I know you didn't sleep with him?" He still glared at her suspiciously.

"Hopefully because you trust me. I wouldn't lie to you. He's ridiculous. Do you actually believe I'd sleep with someone like him, or that I'd cheat on you?"

"I don't know. Maybe you would." It was the first ugly side she'd seen of him. He was insanely jealous. Gillian Hemmings was undeniably handsome, but she thought he was a total horse's ass, and another narcissist. She was starting to discover that they were rampant in the business, men and women who made their living because of how beautiful they were, not how intelligent or talented. Although a few had both looks and brains, they were rare. Many of the pretty ones had slept their way to where they were. It had been said about Gillian, and that he was equally willing to sleep with women or men to get ahead.

"If that's what you think of me, Nigel, I have nothing else to say to you," Winnie said, looking as angry as he was, and she took the fruit for Elizabeth and left.

He came looking for her on the set an hour later, while they were watching Gillian do a scene with their ingénue. Elizabeth was due to enter the shot in a few minutes, and Winnie was putting her jewelry on, carefully checking the list of what she was supposed to be wearing for continuity from the day before.

"Can I talk to you for a minute?" Nigel asked, ignoring Elizabeth, and Winnie didn't look up at him.

"No, you can't. I'm busy." He looked embarrassed and skulked off a minute later, and Elizabeth smiled up at her.

"Pissed at him?" she whispered.

"Very," Winnie said emphatically, and the two women exchanged a smile.

Winnie didn't see Nigel again until she left work that night. He was waiting for her outside.

"I'm sorry. I shouldn't have said those things to you. I get jealous, and he's such a good-looking guy."

"He thinks so too," she said coolly. "I think he's a jerk. And you're much better-looking." He fell into step beside her as she walked home.

"I just thought . . . One of the guys I work with overheard what he said to you."

"Then he should have heard what I said back." She stopped walking and turned to look at him. "I'm not going to cheat on you, Nigel. If I wanted to be with someone else, I'd leave you. I don't play those games."

"I'm sorry . . . I've just been played so often, sometimes I assume all women do it."

"I'm not one of them," she said and started walking again.

"I'm a jealous guy," he confessed, looking sheepish. "I just didn't see how I could compete with someone like him."

"You have everything to offer, he doesn't, except his looks. And you're a good person. I'd have to be crazy to want him." They walked on in silence then, back to her cottage, but she had seen a side of him she didn't like. She didn't like that he had been so angry and assumed the worst from her. But at their age, they each had their scars from the people they had been with. And she had hers from Rob.

They had a quiet dinner that night, and went to bed afterwards, and when they made love, quietly and gently, she forgave him for what he had assumed so wrongly about her, but she didn't forget it. He had a strike against him now.

Chapter Nine

The following weekend Nigel surprised her. He'd been trying to make it up to her for his jealous fury over Gillian Hemmings. Gillian finished up his three episodes that Friday, and left the set. Winnie and Elizabeth amused themselves by trying to figure out how many women he had slept with while he was there. They guessed that in ten days, he had slept with thirteen members of the cast and staff, and Winnie suspected he had slept with one of the grips as well. He drove off in his Rolls and no one was sorry to see him leave. He was a walking sex machine but not much else.

But Nigel surprised her by asking her to spend the weekend at his home in Leighton Buzzard. He said it wouldn't be exciting, but he wanted to introduce her to his parents and one of his sisters who lived nearby. She was married and had three children. And Winnie was touched by the invitation.

They drove for three hours to get there in his battered Jeep, and Winnie was looking forward to it. She had just told Marje about him, and that she was going to meet his parents for the weekend, which made Marje nervous. She didn't want Winnie putting down roots in England, but Winnie said he was a great guy.

Marje talked to Erik about it afterwards, and he told her not to worry. Winnie had gone away for an extended vacation to get over a breakup and the loss of her job, she hadn't run away from home. Marje wasn't so sure, and she missed her. It made her even lonelier for Winnie when she saw her on Skype. But Winnie seemed happy, had a job she was having fun with and experiences she would never have had at home. Working on the set of a hit TV series was an incredible opportunity Winnie was grateful for every day. It was a dream come true for her.

They got to Leighton Buzzard before dinnertime, and his parents were having tea when they walked in. His mother looked thrilled to see him, and his father smiled to see his youngest son. Nigel hadn't been home in several months, and they were intrigued to meet the American woman he said he was bringing with him. She would be sharing his childhood bedroom with him.

His parents were retired, his father had been an electrician, which was what had gotten Nigel interested in sound equipment when he was young. He had a brother who was an accountant in London, a sister in New Zealand, and the sister who lived nearby was a nurse. His youngest brother worked at a resort hotel in Spain. His mother had worked for the post office. They were solid middle-class people and loved their son. The house was small, but tidy and well kept. His parents looked older than their age, and had worked hard all their lives to provide for their five children. And Nigel was grateful for all they'd done for him and was happy to see them.

They were very polite to Winnie, and asked her about her life in Michigan. She showed them pictures of Marje and Erik and her nephews. And after tea, they went to visit Nigel's sister Julia, who was just coming back from work. She was a surgical nurse in orthopedics and had three young children who were running wild in the house while they chatted. Her husband was a policeman, and had recently been promoted to detective.

She asked about the show, and she and Winnie discovered that they were both addicted to it. Winnie told her that was why she had come to England, and now, through a series of coincidences, she was working as a personal assistant to the lead actress.

"Well, aren't you the lucky one?" Julia said, ignoring the screams of glee from her children and the pandemonium around them. "It all sounds very glam to me. And very brave of you to come to England just to watch the show from close range. I'd love to do something like that." She looked envious as she said it. "Do you think you'll stay here?" she asked, curious.

"I haven't figured that out yet." Winnie smiled easily. "I'm just letting things unfold for now." She glanced at Nigel and he smiled at her. His sister could see that he was very taken with Winnie, although none of his relationships had lasted so far and were usually short-term, which she said to Winnie. Nigel looked annoyed, and gave his sister an angry look to stop her from saying more.

Nigel and Winnie stayed for dinner that night. Patrick, Julia's husband, was Irish, and the four of them had a good time at dinner, and the children entertained themselves while the adults finished the meal.

The following day, he took Winnie to see where he'd gone to

school, and they had dinner with his parents. His father was a history buff, and an expert on World War I. He had made a model of the *Lusitania,* which was displayed in their living room.

And on Sunday, they drove back to Burnham Market, with a tin of cookies his mother had made for them. It had been a relaxing, cozy weekend, which helped Winnie to get to know him better. She liked his family a lot, particularly his sister Julia. She was a smart, sensible woman, and very down to earth.

On Monday, they both went back to work, and Winnie was happy to see Elizabeth and hear about her weekend. She had flown to Nice, and met Bill in Saint Tropez, where the paparazzi had besieged them, which was to be expected there. He could hardly complain about being in the press after that, or blame Elizabeth for it, as Winnie pointed out. They were going to Spain together later that summer. He had rented a house in Ibiza, and a yacht to go with it. It was a far cry from Winnie's weekend in Leighton Buzzard, but they each had their own lives, and liked each other despite the differences between them.

Winnie made a decision after her weekend away with Nigel, and she called Marje on Monday, told her about the cottage she'd rented and that she wanted Marje to rent out the house in Beecher for her.

"Does this mean you're never coming back?" Marje asked in a choked voice, and Winnie felt sorry for her. She didn't want her to feel abandoned. But she wasn't willing to give up her dreams this time either.

"I haven't made that decision," she said honestly. "I want to stay here for a while. It's all working out so far. And it seems stupid to let the house just sit there. I might as well make some money on it. I'll split it with you," she offered, since they both owned the house. "Why don't you rent it for six months? You can put my clothes in boxes, so the renters can use the closets." It made Marje sad to think about it, but it sounded sensible to her too.

"Why don't you try to come home for Christmas?" Marje suggested, and Winnie nodded and said she didn't know yet. She'd been gone for three months, and Christmas was four months away.

"That would be nice, though," Winnie said, thinking about it. They both knew a lot could happen in the next four months, good and bad. Things might be really established with Nigel by then, or over, it could go either way, although things seemed to be getting more serious between them. They were talking about going away in September, during the hiatus before they started shooting the next season. But they hadn't figured out where to go yet. They had time to decide.

Marje promised to list Winnie's house with the realtor in town as a six-month furnished rental. She wouldn't get a lot for it, but it never hurt to make some money. Both sisters were sad when they hung up: Marje because she felt as though Winnie was slowly severing her ties with Beecher, and Winnie because she felt guilty for leaving her sister. But Marje had her own life, and now Winnie had to try and figure out what to do with hers.

"I wish she'd gotten something else in that damn white elephant game at her office last Christmas, instead of the DVDs of the show she's so crazy about. Another set of coasters maybe," she said with tears in her eyes, and Erik smiled at her.

"Don't worry, she'll be back," he said, sounding certain. "She's just spreading her wings a little. She'll be happy to come home eventually." He didn't doubt it for a minute, but as Marje cleared away the dinner dishes, she wasn't nearly as sure. She sounded much too happy in England, and she was leading a fantasy life, watching the series she loved being made, working for a big TV star, and now she had a boyfriend on the wrong side of the Atlantic. It was fun for Winnie, but it did not sound good to her.

Elizabeth was strangely quiet for the next week or so, and Winnie was worried she had said or done something to offend her. Their joking and friendly exchanges had suddenly stopped. She wondered if Elizabeth felt ill at first, but she claimed she was fine whenever Winnie asked her. And after a few days, Winnie didn't want to bother her. It was obvious she didn't want to talk. She spent a lot of time conferring with Bill Anders in private, and frequently asked Winnie to leave them alone, which she hadn't done till then either. Winnie didn't want to pry but she began to believe she was going to be fired, and talked to Nigel. She asked if he'd heard any gossip. The rumor mill was very active on the set. But he said he'd heard nothing about it.

"It probably has to do with his divorce. They can't go on having a flagrant affair like that forever. Everyone loves a love story, but sooner or later, the viewers will just think they're cheaters and the sponsors won't like it." Winnie hadn't thought of that.

"I guess so. But they clam up every time I walk into the trailer. Before, she wasn't afraid to say anything in front of me. Now she barely talks to me. I think I must have done something to offend her."

"Don't be so paranoid," Nigel teased her, but Winnie had a weird feeling in the pit of her stomach that wouldn't go away.

The following Monday, she and Elizabeth were picking which wig to wear in the next shot. Elizabeth had tried several and didn't like any of them, and they'd just asked the wigmaker on the set to bring over more, when Michael Waterman, the executive producer, burst into her trailer without knocking. His face was purple and he was waving several sheets of paper in his hand.

"When did you cook this up?" he shouted at Elizabeth, as she lowered her eyes and didn't look at him. He waved the papers in her face and tears sprang to her eyes. "You couldn't have the guts to talk to me about it? You had to send me a goddamn *letter*? We work together for six fucking years and you tell me four weeks before we go on hiatus? Do you know what this is going to do to us? You just torpedoed the ship. The *Titanic* is going down. Is that what you wanted? Well, I've got some news for you. I'm not going to let it sink. We've all worked too hard and love this show too much to let you destroy us. I thought you had a heart, Liz. We can sue you, you know."

"No, you can't," she said, speaking for the first time, as she raised her head to look at him. She was deathly pale, in contrast to his face, which was scarlet and looked like it was going to explode. "My agent checked the contract, and I have three escape clauses that apply. I can't help it. I have a right to take a better offer. That show is going to make my career. I can't turn it down." She looked deeply regretful, but he couldn't sway her. And Winnie suddenly realized that she had been so silent because she was making a major decision. It had nothing to do with her.

"Make your career, and destroy mine and everyone else's on this show. Does that seem right to you?" They both completely ignored Winnie, who shrank into the background in the small trailer, and when the wigmaker showed up, they sent her away.

"I can't turn down an opportunity like that. I love this show, but they're offering me three times the money, and an incredible opportunity. I can pick my own cast. They're giving me everything I ever wanted. And one of these days you're going to shut down *Beauchamp Hall,* or Matthew will get tired of writing it, and I'll have passed this up."

He ignored what she said, which wasn't entirely unreasonable, from what Nigel had explained to Winnie. "And who are you picking for your cast?" He took a step closer to her, and glared at her ominously.

"I'm only taking Bill with me," she said in barely more than a whisper.

"Oh my God, you bitch. He hasn't even told me yet." If it were possible, Michael's face went from red to purple.

"I asked him to let me tell you first."

"How could you do this to us? And why didn't you tell me sooner and give us a chance to negotiate with you?"

"Because you'd never give me that much money. And the deal just finally came together a week ago. I thought they were just bullshitting before that, but they're not."

"I don't know what to say to you. I like you, Liz. You've been great on the show. But you have no heart. You're just like everyone in this business. It's all about you, and you don't care whose lives you destroy to get ahead. Well, I'm sorry to disappoint you. We'll make it without you. *Beauchamp Hall* has a lot more going for it than you and Bill Anders."

"This is just business," she said limply, which was the phrase everyone used to stab someone in the back. Even Winnie already knew that, and she felt sorry for the producer.

She fully understood what had just happened. Elizabeth was leaving the show, and taking Bill Anders with her, to star on another show. They were the two biggest stars on *Beauchamp Hall*. They had lost Tom White when he was killed earlier in the season they were shooting. And Miranda Charles had left shortly after. Matthew had compensated for it admirably, with new storylines and several new actors. But Elizabeth and Bill leaving would be an even bigger blow, and would be much harder to make up for, to keep the show interesting to their loyal viewers who were emotionally attached to every one of the players, as Winnie had been when she got there. It had changed subtly for her now, because she was part of the behind-the-scenes making of it, which made it seem less real to her, though even more fascinating. And she knew what went into making it convincing. She saw the artifice now, not just the plot.

He stormed out of the trailer then, and there was dead silence after he left. Elizabeth stole a careful glance at her assistant, and Winnie looked at her.

"I'm sorry you had to hear all that."

"I thought you were mad at me for the last week."

"Of course not. I was just stressed out trying to make the decision, and I wanted Bill to come with me. He wasn't sure at first. He's made the decision now. I'm leaving when we finish shooting the season in four weeks."

"Matthew will have to work hard to make up for it. Do you think he can do it?" Winnie asked, looking worried. It hadn't even occurred to her she was about to lose her job too. She was the assistant to someone who was about to leave. But her job was minimal compared to everyone else's. And she cared deeply about the show.

"I hope Matthew can do it," Elizabeth said seriously. "I love this show. I don't want to hurt it. But I have to think of my career too. Shows like this rarely go past six or seven seasons. Viewers either get tired of them, the cast wants to do other things, or the writer runs out of gas, or wants to quit before it all falls apart. The handwriting was on the wall before I did this. Michael just doesn't want to see it, but he knows it too." Winnie nodded, trying to absorb it. "And I'm sorry, Winnie. You've been the best assistant I've ever had. Do you want to come with me? We'll be shooting in London, with location shoots in Monte Carlo, Dubai, Las Vegas, and Macao. It's about a professional female gambler, who's basically crooked, an embezzler and a thief, so we'll be on location in the gambling capitals of the world. The scripts are great. Bill is going to play the sexy, handsome James Bond–style detective who's always trying to catch me, but never does. But I sleep with him occasionally." She smiled.

"It sounds like a great show," Winnie said sincerely. But not a family show with strong values like *Beauchamp Hall.*

"I think it will be. Want to come on board?"

She thought about it for a minute and shook her head. "I didn't come here for a career in show business. I came here because I love this show, and everything it represents. It won't be the same without you, but I think I'll stick with the *Titanic,* if that's what happens. I'm not ready to get in the lifeboat yet." Elizabeth nodded and respected her for it. She admired Winnie's integrity.

"Loyal to the end. I think Matthew will be able to keep it going for another season or two, if he wants to. But I don't think he could have done it for longer than that anyway. Almost no show has ever made it to ten years. What'll you do?" she asked Winnie, worried about her for a minute.

"Go back to being an errand girl on the set," she said philosophically. "I had a lot of fun working for you. Thank you for giving me the chance to do it. As long as I don't have to buy super-sized condoms for Gillian Hemmings and test them with him, I'll be fine." They both laughed at that, and Winnie asked the wigmaker to come back. Elizabeth picked two she wanted to wear that day, and her performance was brilliant. Winnie knew she would be sorely missed. She was a pro and a terrific actress, one of the best, even if she wasn't loyal. She had her eye on her own career, which came first for her.

The news was out by the end of the week, and there was mass panic on the set. At first, everyone thought it was just a rumor and didn't believe it, but management confirmed it. A brief announcement was issued, with the assurance that they would be shooting another season after this one, as planned, but the more experienced players and technicians were dubious that the show would survive Elizabeth and Bill leaving, and that Matthew would want to write it without them. They all felt the sands shifting under their feet. The more optimistic members of the cast and crew wanted to believe it would go on. Others didn't. Fear was rampant and tangible on the set.

Nigel took the news badly, and said it wasn't handwriting on the wall, it was a neon sign that the show would be canceled.

"I was there when she told Michael. He said he's not going to let the ship go down." Winnie tried to reassure him.

"It's not up to him, it's up to the network, the viewers, and the sponsors. If the ratings blow, it'll be over in five minutes. Why didn't you tell me if you knew?" He looked angry about that too.

"I only heard it a few days ago. I wasn't supposed to be in the room, and I was told to keep it confidential."

"And that includes me?" he asked and she nodded. "I'm about to lose my job, and you couldn't warn me?" He wanted to blame her for what was happening.

"You're not about to lose your job. They say they're going to do another season."

"Don't count on it. You don't know this business. I do. I guarantee you we'll be out of work by the end of the year. I'm going to start putting out feelers," he said, with a grim look. He went to stay at his own place that night, and left for London for the weekend to see some producers he knew. He acted as though the show had already been canceled and he was in a black mood. They had all signed confidentiality agreements about Elizabeth and Bill leaving, so Winnie couldn't talk to Marje about it. She spent a quiet weekend watching reruns of *Beauchamp Hall,* which always calmed her, and reading her dog-eared copy of *Jane Eyre.* She wondered what Matthew was going to do to bring the show back to life without Elizabeth and Bill. It made her realize how difficult his job was. She used to fantasize about writing a show like this, and now she realized what it took to do it. She didn't envy him the task ahead.

Nigel was in no better spirits when he came back from London. He couldn't tell anyone he'd met with why he was looking. He'd just said he was getting restless and thinking about moving on, but no one had had any hopeful suggestions for him.

"What about starting the sound business you've been talking about if they cancel the show?" Winnie was trying to be helpful and he looked annoyed when they talked about it over dinner.

"I'm not ready to do that yet. I don't have the money. It'll cost a fortune in equipment. That's probably ten years away. If the show goes down, I need another job, Winnie. I can't do what you've done, and come over here and hang out for six months and play around."

"I didn't come over here with a fortune. I did it with my savings."

"Yeah, and if you run out of money, you can sell a house in Michigan."

"Half a house," she reminded him. "My sister owns the other half. You make me sound like an heiress. I saved most of what I have, and the money my mom left me eleven years ago, which wasn't much."

"Well, I haven't saved my money like you did, I don't own half a house, and my parents barely have enough to live on now that they're retired. I'll have to go to work on another show if *Beauchamp* dies, or when it does, since it's not an 'if' anymore, it's a 'when.' Sometime in the next year or two, if it takes that long, I'll be out of work."

"So will I," she said quietly.

"And then what? You'll go back to Michigan?"

"Let's figure that out when it happens."

"I told you, Win, everything in this business is temporary, that's why I never married and don't have kids. Because all you do when you work on shows like this is go from one to the next, if you're lucky and get another job." She had come to understand that. It wasn't like working for a bank or a business that would be there forever. It appeared, it had its moment of glory, and one day it disappeared. It made her sad to think about it. She didn't want *Beauchamp Hall* to end either. Coming here had been her dream. But for Nigel, it was a matter of earning his livelihood. This was his career.

A few days later, she got a note addressed to her that was dropped off at Elizabeth's trailer. Elizabeth was out when she found it, and she sat down to read it. It was from Edward Smith, one of the actors on the set, who asked her to give him a call. She had hardly ever spoken to him. He played the oldest son in the Beauchamp family. He was in his early forties and played a married man with four children, with a wife he had married out of duty and didn't love. He'd had an affair with his true love for years, and had a second family with her, living in secret in a home he'd built for her a few miles away. The actor who played the part was Australian, from a fancy family. He had gone to the best British boarding schools, and had no trace of an Australian accent, only an aristocratic British one. He was good-looking, and a wonderful actor, and Winnie had no idea why he wanted her to call him. She thought about it, and finally called him that night from home.

"It's good of you to call me," he said as soon as she said who it was. "I would have talked to you on the set, but it seemed awkward. There's so much angst these days with Liz and Bill leaving." Winnie couldn't figure out if he was asking her for a date or something else, but he came to the point quickly. "I've been envious of Liz ever since you went to work for her. I saw how efficient you were, even when you were the errand girl on the set. I don't know what your plans are now that she's leaving. But my assistant is having a baby and wants to stop working for good. Her husband has a good job and she can afford to. She wants to leave as soon as I replace her, so she can stay home and eat ice cream and relax. I wondered if you'd come to work for me. It's less glamorous than working for Liz, but I gather that we both have a need, possibly you for a job, and me for a new assistant. I thought I'd put it out there before someone else snaps you up." He made it sound straightforward and clean, and she was flattered by everything he'd said. "You'll have fewer wigs to deal with, and more hunting weekends to arrange," he said and they both laughed.

"Wow, that's amazing. It certainly solves the problem for me. They're going to shoot all Elizabeth's shots now, and Bill's, so they can leave before the hiatus. To be honest, the producers are pretty upset so I think they want her off the set. So I'll be available as soon as she leaves."

"That works perfectly for me, Rebecca would love that. They hadn't found anyone for me yet, and then I thought of you. It sounds like it could be a good thing for us both."

"Yes, it would. Thank you, Mr. Smith," she said respectfully.

"Edward, please. Well, I'm very glad I dropped you the note, and you called. I'll let them know that we're all set. It's a pretty simple switch."

She was pleased with the new arrangement, and relieved to know she'd still have a job when Elizabeth left. She told Nigel with a big smile as soon as he got home. He didn't say anything at first, and then came to discuss it with her while she was making dinner, and she could see from the look on his face that he was upset.

"So now you're going to be the assistant to a man? What's that all about? Why isn't he hiring a guy? Is he after you for sex?"

"Not everyone sees me as an opportunity for hot sex," she said smiling at him. "I'm thirty-eight, not nineteen. His assistant is leaving, and he needs a new one. And she's a woman too. So he wants me to work for him when Elizabeth leaves. It's pretty simple, and works for both of us."

"I'm not so sure it works for me," Nigel said, picking at his food at dinner. He was too disturbed to eat. It reminded her of when he'd had a fit over Gillian Hemmings. But Gillian had been a creep, and had propositioned her. Edward Smith was a stand-up guy, and a gentleman. Nothing about his offer had been lascivious, and she'd never heard of his having affairs on the set, which was unusual. From the rumor mill, she thought he had a girlfriend, who had a title and lived in London.

"I need a job, Nigel, and he seems like he'd be nice to work for. If he's not, and he puts the make on me, I'll quit and go back to being an errand girl. But if it's okay with you, I'd like to make a decent salary too. This is about your being jealous, not about who he is."

"I don't like him. He's too good-looking. And what happens when he struts around his trailer in his underwear, or bare-ass naked. Then what will you do?"

"If he's a decent guy, he won't. If he does, I'll quit. You have to trust me on this."

"I don't trust him."

"Well, I do."

They argued about it all evening, and Nigel went to bed mad. He was still angry when he woke up in the morning, and roared off to work in his Jeep without breakfast or saying goodbye to her, and she didn't see him all day. He didn't come for dinner that night.

They argued about it until she started work for Edward. She had decided to work for both him and Elizabeth for Elizabeth's last week on the set, so she could get used to him before the hiatus. And Nigel never relented for the entire time. He got angrier and angrier, convinced that Winnie would have an affair with her new boss.

"Nigel, you have to stop," she said finally. "I'm not going to give up a job just because you're jealous. He's done nothing inappropriate."

"He will." Nigel was convinced of it and didn't trust either of them.

"This is ridiculous!" She wasn't going to give in on principle. "I make five times the money as an assistant than I do as an errand girl, and I get a work permit with it. The salary pays my rent. Be reasonable, for God's sake."

"He's a TV star. How do you expect me to feel?"

"You're a handsome guy and I love you. You have nothing to worry about." Winnie finally gave up and stopped discussing it with him. She kept the job, Nigel would have to learn to live with it, and grow up, as far as she was concerned. His jealousy was one of the things she liked least about him, and she wasn't going to indulge him. But his jealousy and paranoia were beginning to erode the good times and the relationship they'd had. He was worried and angry now all the time.

She told Elizabeth about it before she left, and Elizabeth said she'd had a boyfriend like that once.

"How did you deal with it?" Winnie wanted all the advice she could get, and she was closer to Elizabeth than anyone else.

"I started cheating on him because he thought I was anyway.

153

Eventually he was right, so we broke up." Winnie laughed at her so-lution, which was typical of her. She had confessed to Winnie that she had never been faithful to any man. "But Edward Smith is so serious and straightlaced. I doubt he'll even make a pass at you. I tried with him once," she said with a laugh, "and he turned me down. I thought maybe he was gay, but he's definitely not. He's a one-woman man and I hear he's been with the same girl for years. I think you're perfectly safe with him."

"So do I. But I can't convince Nigel of that. He's been furious ever since I told him."

"I hate jealous men, they're such a bore," Elizabeth said with a sigh, and Winnie agreed. The first time she thought it was flattering, and a little childish. This time it was just upsetting. She had thought he was better than that, but he wasn't. It was his worst flaw, and a serious one if it was going to interfere with her job. And she couldn't only work for women to please him. This time a man had offered her a job, and a very good job she liked. He was an excellent, considerate employer.

Winnie was sad the day Elizabeth left the set. She gave Winnie a gold bracelet to thank her and told her to come and visit her new show, and Winnie promised to do so if she came to London. Winnie waved as she drove away, gathered up her things, and walked down the road to Edward's trailer, where he was waiting for her with a stack of work and calls to make. She liked working for him. He was more businesslike than Elizabeth and treated her more like a secretary, and he was unfailingly respectful and appropriate. She never even saw him in a dressing gown when he got his hair and makeup done. He was entirely proper. Nigel had been totally wrong. But he still spent a lot of their time together complaining about him, to the point of being bitter about it, and she was beginning to understand why none of his relationships had worked out. His jealousy and rages were hard to overcome. Her new boss was a perfect gentleman, which Nigel refused to believe. Day by day he got worse, and Winnie loved him less and less, until she could barely remember what it was she loved about him. His jealousy burned white hot and consumed everything she'd liked about him until there was nothing left.

Chapter Ten

Despite Nigel's constant unpleasant comments, Winnie enjoyed working for Edward Smith. He was professional, intelligent, had a good sense of humor. He studied his lines diligently so he was always prepared on the set, and followed direction easily. He was well liked by the cast, and Winnie couldn't imagine having such an easy boss. It turned her workdays into a pleasure.

And one day, while they were trying to guess how Matthew was going to rewrite the next season without Elizabeth and Bill, Winnie admitted that she had done some writing in college, and had dreamed of working in publishing in New York, and being an editor.

"I wanted to be a commercial fisherman, or a big-game hunter when I was growing up. That didn't happen either." They both laughed at the fallen dreams of their youth. "Do you ever do any writing now?" She shook her head. "You should. Who knows, maybe one day you'll write a screenplay, or a bible for a show like this. Stranger things have happened. I know plenty of actors who've given it up to become screenwriters and been very successful. And you're around the show enough to get an idea of how it works, and it sounds like you know all the episodes verbatim," he teased her. She had long since confessed her addiction to the show, and said that was why she had come here. "You should study the scripts." He gave her a stack of old ones to take home with her, and she started reading them at night, to see how they were constructed, and how they moved from one scene to the next. She found it fascinating. But her doing it annoyed Nigel intensely. He had started spending the night with her less and less often, and would show up without calling her, acting as though he expected to find her in bed with someone, presumably Edward. Instead, he would find her at the kitchen table, making notes on a script.

He annoyed her particularly one night, when she opened the door for him in her pajamas. Nigel looked like he'd been drinking, and he staggered slightly as he said, "No Edward?"

"I locked him in a closet when I heard you coming," she said tartly. She found his jealousy childish and a waste of energy and time and refused to take it seriously. He was basically a decent guy, but he was obsessed by his concern about her with other men.

"Why are you always fooling around with the scripts?" he asked her, as he sat down across the table from her.

"Edward thinks I should try and write a script one day," she said innocently, thinking Nigel would be intrigued by the idea, and pleased for her.

"Oh, Saint Edward, of course. Are you going to try and save the show?" he said bitterly.

"I wish I could. I think Matthew can do that without my help," she said quietly. "At least I hope so."

"We'll be lucky if we get another year out of it," Nigel said, "and then we'll all be out on our asses, and looking for jobs again." It was a possibility she couldn't deny, and Edward was worried about it too. They all were, but their attitudes were more positive than Nigel's. His fear of the future and jealousy over Winnie were slowly poisoning him, and making him toxic to be around. His mood was very dark.

"Well, let's enjoy it while it lasts," she said calmly.

"This is just a hobby for you, Winnie," he accused her, and there was truth to it. But she was learning a lot from reading the scripts, and her dream of writing was coming to life again. It had been dormant for nearly twenty years, but she could feel it stirring.

"This is a job for me, my livelihood. If they cancel the show, I'm liable to wind up on some show I hate. Like one of those sick reality shows, with a family of drug addicts who all go in and out of rehab." His comment made her think of Marje and her Las Vegas housewives.

"My sister loves those shows, but not about drug addicts. About housewives who look like hookers." She smiled as she said it and he relaxed a little. She could still see glimpses of the Nigel she knew and loved from time to time, but anxiety had him in its clutches and he was tense and different than he had been when she met him. His bitterness was toxic.

He spent the night with her that night, but the beer he'd been drinking caught up with him and he passed out the minute his head hit the pillow. It reminded her of Rob and the nights they spent together when they didn't even talk to each other. She didn't want to face it, but she could sense that what she had shared with Nigel was slipping away. She wasn't heartbroken over it, but disappointed. He wasn't a bad person, and he had a kind side to him, but he had become hard to live with. Impossible in fact.

Edward said something about it one morning. "I've seen you with one of the sound men a few times, away from the set. Is that your boyfriend?" She nodded.

"He has been, it's a bit on and off at the moment. We've only been dating for a few months, since I got here." She didn't tell him that Nigel was consumed with jealousy of him. He didn't need to know, and Nigel wasn't dangerous, just neurotic about it, which made him unattractive. She didn't find it charming, in fact less and less so.

"Relationships are like that," he said, thinking about it. "We all make compromises about something. It's never perfect. I've been dating the same woman for thirteen years. We get along brilliantly, although we're not together all the time, or maybe because of it. Her father is in the House of Lords, and he doesn't want her to marry an actor. I don't want to give up acting. I've put too much into it, and I don't know what else I'd do, and she doesn't want to defy her father. So we've never married. I'm forty-two, and she's thirty-seven. It's not a drama for me, but she's getting anxious about having children, so we'll have to figure it out one of these days. It's awful to say, but he's quite old, and I think she's been waiting for him to die before we get married. But he's made of sturdy stuff and quite a tyrant. I'm sure he'll outlive us both." He smiled as he said it. "And she's not the sort to have babies without being married. I wouldn't mind it. Things seem to change as you get older. The things one used to think were so important turn out not to be. And the things you thought didn't matter actually become very important one day. What matters to me about Grace is being with her. I don't care if we marry or have children. She's the only woman I've ever loved. That's worth hanging on to. And you never know what's going to happen."

"I think I'm getting there too. I spent eleven years with the wrong man before I came here. I realize now that I don't really care if I get married or have children. I want to be with the right person. Being with the wrong one is pretty miserable." She smiled and he nodded agreement.

"You don't know what surprises life has in store for you."

"Coming here was the best surprise I've ever given myself," she said happily. And she wasn't going to let Nigel spoil it for her.

"How are you doing with the scripts, by the way?" he asked her.

"I've been studying them every night. Writing a screenplay seems easier than writing a book. The construction is simpler and more economical."

"Precisely. And it's all visual. It's all in the actor's face, if he's any good." He gave her a list of calls to make for him then, to his banker, his lawyer, a dinner reservation. He was planning to go to London in the morning for his days off. He and Grace had separate apartments, but she stayed with him when he went to London. Listening to him talk about her made it even clearer how absurd it was that Nigel was jealous of him. He was madly in love with his girlfriend, and Winnie loved the way he talked about her. She would have liked to have a man say things like that about her.

She tried telling Nigel about it that night, and he didn't want to hear it. He left shortly after, to meet up with friends at one of the pubs he'd been frequenting recently. He was drinking more than he used to, she suspected out of anxiety about his job and his future. The atmosphere on the set was tense these days, and Bill and Elizabeth's departure had made everyone's anxiety that much more real.

The phone rang a few minutes after he left, and she assumed he was calling to apologize or ask if he could come back later, which wasn't as much fun as it used to be. He was fine if he was sober, but having him stagger in drunk and pass out in her bed next to her was a déjà vu of Rob for her, and she didn't enjoy it or want to relive it.

But it wasn't Nigel on the phone, it was her sister. Marje sounded hysterical and she was crying. Winnie couldn't understand her at first, but it was obvious that something terrible had happened. The first thing that came to Winnie's mind was Erik. He had just turned fifty and sometimes bad things happened to men his age with no previous history.

"Calm down . . . take a breath . . . try to tell me what happened . . ."

She managed to get out one word. "Jimmy." Her seventeen-year-old son. Winnie froze as she tried to guess what might be wrong.

"He was swimming in our neighbor's pool. They were having a pool party," which made no sense to Winnie either. The people they knew in Michigan didn't have pools, they hardly ever got to use them. But Marje's neighbor was a contractor and had built it himself for his kids. "The kids were horsing around, and he slipped and hit his head."

"Oh my God, is he okay?" Obviously not, with Marje sobbing, and Winnie was starting to panic too.

"He's in a coma. He fractured his skull and has a severe concussion. I've been with him since last night and my cellphone doesn't work at the hospital. Erik is with him now. I came home to see Adam. Win, they said if he doesn't regain consciousness soon, he'll be brain damaged."

"That's not going to happen," Winnie said automatically, rejecting the thought as soon as her sister said it.

"He's got swelling of the brain, and they want to see if it goes down. If it doesn't they'll have to operate. They might have to take out part of his brain." She collapsed in sobs and Winnie looked at her watch, wondering how fast she could get to London, and on a plane. It was nine o'clock at night. She had no idea what time the last train left, but if there was one around eleven o'clock or midnight, she could be on it, which would get her to London at one or two in the morning. With luck, she could catch a morning flight to Chicago, and from there to Detroit. The time difference was in her favor, and even with all the stops she had to make, she could be in Beecher by early afternoon.

"Marje, hang in. I'll get home as fast as I can. I'm going to get off now so I can get organized. I'll call you as soon as I know what time I'll be there."

"You can't, you're working. . . ."

"Never mind. I love you. It'll be okay." She had no idea if it would, but she didn't know what else to say. Her mind was racing as she hung up, and the first thing she had to do was call Edward, and tell him what she was doing. He was going to London for four days, and she didn't want him to think she'd disappeared. She glanced at her watch again, it was still early enough to call him at just after 9:00 P.M. He picked up, and was in good spirits. He was excited to be going to see Grace.

She told him what had happened to her nephew, and he sounded shocked.

"How awful, Winnie, I'm sorry."

"I hate to do this to you, but I've got to go home for a few days. I'll try not to be gone too long, depending on what happens."

"For Heaven's sake, don't be ridiculous. Stay as long as you have to. I can manage on my own. I won't even be back on set for five days. When are you flying out?" He sounded deeply concerned.

"I don't know yet. I called you first. I'm going to try to get on the first morning flight to Chicago, or New York if I have to. I need to get to Detroit after that. My hometown is two hours out of Detroit. I'll see if I can get on a train to London tonight."

"No, you're not. I'm all packed. Grace is having dinner with her father tonight, so I was going to drive up in the morning. Call the airline. I'll pick you up in an hour. I can get you to London in three hours, or less. You can stay with us until your flight if you need to."

"Are you sure?"

"Of course. Grace never lets me drive the way I want. I'll enjoy it," he said, trying to make it seem lighthearted. He was very sorry for her. He had a nephew the same age.

Winnie didn't waste time arguing with him. She called the airline, and they had a 7:00 A.M. flight to New York, which connected to a direct flight to Detroit. The flight to Detroit was due to land at 12:30 P.M. local time. With luck and no delays, she could rent a car at the airport, and be in Beecher at 3:00 P.M. She threw jeans and a stack of clean shirts into her small rolling bag, got the toiletries she needed, a nightgown, some sandals, and some papers she thought she might need. An hour later, she was ready when Edward arrived in his Aston Martin. She turned off the lights, locked her front door, ran out to the car, and hopped in.

"I can't thank you enough for doing this for me," she said gratefully, and as soon as they cleared the village, he put his foot on the gas, and never picked it up. They were on the freeway in no time, and they talked from time to time, but mostly he kept his mind and eyes on the road.

They reached the outskirts of London at 1:00 A.M., and they agreed that it made the most sense to take her directly to the airport, since she had to check in by 5:00 A.M. for the 7:00 A.M. flight.

He called Grace from the road and told her that he was coming in that night and why, and just listening to him talk to her made Winnie realize that what she wanted was a man who spoke to her like that. The tone of his voice told the woman at the other end how much he loved her, and couldn't wait to see her that night.

Edward dropped Winnie off at the international terminal at Heathrow at 1:30 A.M. and wished her luck. She had three and a half hours to spare before she had to check in, and could doze in a chair in the airport, and then get something to eat. She thanked Edward profusely again and he hugged her and told her to text him and let him know what was happening. He was worried about her and her nephew. She waved as he drove away, and walked into the terminal.

She couldn't call Marje because she was back at the hospital by then, so Winnie texted her to see how Jimmy was doing, and Marje texted back "No change," and Winnie responded with "Yet." She texted Nigel after that, and said that her nephew had had an accident, and she was flying home on a 7:00 A.M. flight, and would be back as soon as she could. She was sure he was sound asleep by then after a night at the pub, but at least he wouldn't worry when he didn't see her at work in the morning, or think something had happened to her.

She sat thinking about Marje and Jimmy until she boarded her flight. He'd been so sweet as a baby, and was so grown up now. This couldn't be happening to him. He had to wake up. She wanted to will him into opening his eyes and looking at his mother.

The flight took off on time, and she fell asleep almost as soon as it did, exhausted from being up all night, and before it took off, she texted Edward to thank him again. He had turned out to be even nicer than she'd expected, and she loved working for him. He was intelligent and down-to-earth, talented and disciplined, and modest, which was rare in his business. And thanks to the show, he was a rising star and his career had taken off. She was thinking about him when she fell asleep, and how lucky he and Grace were to have found each other thirteen years before. She hoped she met someone like him one day, minus the Aston Martin. She didn't need all the trappings of success and riches, just a good man to spend her life with.

The plane landed in New York at 9:00 A.M. local time, after a seven-hour flight. And she had an hour and a half before her flight to Detroit. She called Nigel then, and hoped he wasn't on the set. He couldn't answer if he was, and would have his phone on vibrate, but he was outside taking a break, and he picked up immediately, and sounded angry when he did.

"Where are you?"

"I'm in New York. On my way to Michigan. I'm between flights. My nephew had an accident. I sent you a text last night. Didn't you get it?"

"Yes, I got it. I went by your place last night. It was dark. Where are you, Winnie? Really. In London with Edward? I saw the call sheet. He's off for five days."

"He's with his girlfriend," Winnie said, shocked. "You think I'm lying to you? Do you want to call the hospital and check on my nephew? He's in a coma." Nigel sounded mollified for a minute, but uncertain as to whether to believe her or not.

"I'm sorry, if it's true."

"You know what, Nigel," she said, suddenly furious, "you're pathetic. Edward is madly in love with a woman he's been with for thirteen years. He treats me with respect, I don't think he even notices that I'm a woman, and you're so busy trying to catch me cheating on you that you can't even think straight and think I'm lying to you about my nephew being in a coma. This is sick."

"How did you get to London?" Nigel asked suspiciously.

"Edward drove me, so I could make a seven A.M. flight. Is that considered cheating too? We both had our clothes on, and he dropped me at the airport at one-thirty this morning and then he went home to his girlfriend. I'm sorry if that doesn't work for you, but with my nephew in a coma with a fractured skull, I was damn glad to get a lift."

"Why didn't you call me?"

"Because I'm sure you were drunk out of your mind by then, and you would have killed us both. Besides, you had to be at work this morning. He was going to London today anyway. It all made sense."

"How bad is your nephew?" he said, returning to the human race.

"It sounds bad. They might have to do brain surgery. I couldn't let my sister go through that without being there with her. I'll come back as soon as I can. But I don't want to hear about Edward anymore. It's gotten old, Nigel, it's just too much."

"I'm sorry. I just keep thinking that . . ."

"I know what you keep thinking, but you're wrong. I'll let you know when I'm coming back." She hung up then and texted Marje again. Marje wrote back that there was still no major change. Jimmy was still in a coma, but the swelling of his brain had decreased a little. At least that was a hopeful sign, but nothing else was encouraging. Her neighbor was taking care of Adam.

The flight to Detroit left only a few minutes late, and landed shortly before noon. She went straight to the rental car desk, picked up a car, and was on the road fifteen minutes later. She was going to go right to the hospital to meet her sister. She saw Erik crying in the parking lot when she got there and nearly had a heart attack. She parked the car at an angle in the nearest parking spot, jumped out of the car and ran over to him.

"What happened?"

"Nothing. I was just calling my office. Thank you for coming home, Win." He put his arms around her and hugged her and they both cried, and then went upstairs to the ICU together. Erik said they had picked Jimmy up by police rescue helicopter right from the neighbor's front lawn.

Marje saw her and came out and hugged her. She looked ravaged and pale and frightened, and Winnie wasn't prepared for the sight of her nephew, with tubes and monitors attached all over his body. His heart was beating steadily, and Marje said he had brain waves but he hadn't regained consciousness since the accident. But the swelling of his brain was coming down, so they had postponed surgery for now.

"I just want him to stay alive. I don't care if he's a vegetable," Marje said, sobbing, and Winnie turned to talk to Jimmy, and told him she had come to visit him all the way from England and she had a lot to tell him, so she expected him to wake up. She talked to him for about half an hour and then went out to the hall with Marje while Erik stayed with him.

They walked up and down the corridor for a while, and then went back, the trauma team was checking Jimmy, and left after a few minutes. And at six o'clock Erik went to take Adam to dinner, who was worried sick about his brother too. When Erik left, Winnie went down to the cafeteria and brought back sandwiches for her and her sister, and the nurses brought them each a cup of coffee. It was one in the morning in England by then, and the time difference and travel were starting to catch up with Winnie. She needed the coffee. They took another walk around the floor, after they ate the sandwiches while sitting in the hall outside ICU, and when they went back, Winnie saw that a whole team of doctors were with Jimmy. Winnie couldn't see past them, with their backs turned, and both women were terrified of what they'd see when they entered the cubicle, but when they got there, one of the doctors turned and smiled at them. Jimmy opened his eyes, and looked straight at his mother. They had taken the tube out of his mouth, and his voice was a hoarse croak when he spoke to her.

"Hi, Mom," he said, and then he looked at his aunt. "Why are you here?"

"I missed you," she said as tears filled her eyes and spilled over onto her cheeks. "Actually, I came to beat you up for scaring the hell out of your mother," she added, and he smiled.

"Sorry, Mom." Marje was smiling through her tears and hiccupping on sobs.

"I love you. Thank you for waking up," she said to her son and touched his leg.

"Yeah, you've been pretty boring. I drove to London in an Aston Martin. I wanted to tell you about that," Winnie said to him.

"Cool," he said, and closed his eyes, tired from the effort he'd made, and he drifted back to sleep for a few minutes as the chief neurologist ushered them out of the room, walked out to the hallway with them, and gave them the rundown on his condition.

"He's not out of the woods yet. He's still at risk for seizures and complications from the brain injury. But I'm guardedly optimistic. We're heading in the right direction. And it's a great sign that he's regained consciousness." Marje was still crying in relief, and Winnie's legs felt like Jell-O. She had been terrified that they had lost him when they walked back in from the hall. "We should see ongoing progress from now on," the doctor told them. "Pool accidents can be ugly. Boys his age usually get cervical injuries from them, and wind up quadriplegic."

"I'm cementing over the neighbor's pool myself when we get home," she whispered to Winnie after the doctors left, and they walked back into Jimmy's room in the ICU. Erik returned from dinner ten minutes later, and Marje had saved the surprise for him. Jimmy said, "Hi, Dad," when Erik walked in, and Erik burst into tears like Marje and Winnie. He kissed Jimmy's cheek and told him how worried they'd been about him. And then Jimmy turned to Winnie.

"Where'd you get the Aston Martin?" he asked her, and they all laughed.

"Now we know you're not brain damaged. It belongs to my boss. He drove me to the airport."

"I want one, one day," he said dreamily.

"You must have fallen on your head," Winnie joked with him. It was a very different scene than it had been when she'd arrived five hours earlier. "Tell you what, I'll buy you one someday, if you promise never to scare us like this again." They talked to him for a while, then the nurses wanted him to go to sleep and get some rest. Marje had been planning to spend the night with him, but they told her she didn't need to, and they'd call if there were any problems. The three of them left Jimmy a few minutes later, and walked out to the parking lot together. The two sisters hugged each other in relief, and then Marje kissed her husband, and said she wanted to pick up Adam on the way home. They wanted to tell him the good news too.

Winnie followed them back to the house in her rented car, and when they got there, Marje turned to her sister.

"Do you want to stay here tonight?" Winnie nodded. She didn't want to go back to her place just yet. She wanted to be with them. They'd all been through a lot worrying about Jimmy. Marje pulled out the convertible couch in the playroom for her, and they made the bed together, and then Winnie put on her nightgown while she talked to her sister. She had been terrified of a very different outcome when she caught the plane at Heathrow that morning. And from every-thing the doctor had said, Jimmy had been very lucky.

"You're happy over there, aren't you?" Marje asked her sadly.

"I like my job, and I love the show. I'm glad I went. I don't know how I got the guts to do it, but I'm glad I did."

"And Nigel?"

Winnie shrugged in answer. "It's kind of up and down. They've had some problems on the show, and he's worried about his job. That doesn't bring out the best in anyone. And he's insanely jealous of my boss, and afraid I'm going to sleep with him." She looked tired as she said it.

"And are you?" Marje looked interested and Winnie shook her head.

"No, he's a great guy, in love with a terrific woman. They've been together for thirteen years, and I actually think he's faithful to her. But Nigel doesn't believe it. I'm not sure we're going anywhere, or that we should. His jealousy has really turned me off." Marje was disappointed to hear it. There was no point going all the way to En-gland to wind up in another dead-end situation. And Winnie thought that herself, she just hadn't dealt with it yet.

"I ran into Rob and Barb the other day," Marje said cautiously, not sure if she should tell her.

"Separately or together?" Winnie asked her.

"Together. I gather from her mother that the dentist found out about Rob and canceled the wedding, so she and Rob have been dat-ing since you left."

"They deserve each other," Winnie said without regret and lay down on the bed. Marje bent down to kiss her and the two sisters smiled at each other. "I'm glad you got your boy back. I think telling him about the Aston Martin did it." They both laughed and Marje walked up the stairs from the playroom, feeling a hundred years old. They had been the worst days of her life, and she was grateful to Winnie for coming home. Erik was waiting for her in their bedroom, and Adam was already in bed.

Marje was so tired she could hardly brush her teeth and put her nightgown on, and Erik put an arm around her as she got into bed.

"Thank God he woke up," Erik said with deep emotion in his voice.

"I don't think I could have survived it if he didn't," she said, exhausted.

"We'd have had to for Adam. We don't have to think about that now."

"The doctor said he may have headaches for a while. And he's not going back to that pool again." Erik smiled at what she said.

"How long is your sister here for?"

"I didn't ask her. I'm just glad she came." He nodded and turned off the light. They lay in bed, holding each other, slowly returning from the terror they'd lived through. Winnie was already sound asleep in the playroom. It had been the longest, most terrifying day of her life.

Chapter Eleven

Winnie texted Edward and Nigel when she woke up the next morning to tell them that her nephew was out of the coma, though still under observation and in the ICU. Edward texted her back immediately to tell her he was relieved, and to stay as long as she needed to. Nigel sent a message a few minutes later, telling her he was happy for her and wanting to know when she was coming back. She answered him that she didn't know, but would let him know when she did.

They stopped at Winnie's house on the way to the hospital. Everything looked clean and in good order. It hadn't rented yet. Marje said the realtor had shown it to a doctor who had just come from Detroit to work at the hospital, and liked the idea of renting a furnished house until he got situated and found something to buy, but he hadn't made a decision yet.

"How long do you think you'll stay over there?" Marje asked when they were back in the car, on their way to see Jimmy.

"I just don't know. I have a job I love, and I have nothing to rush back for here except you and the kids. And I won't find a job here I like as much."

"Not working for a TV star," Marje said regretfully. And as they drove down the street, everything looked familiar to Winnie, but she suddenly realized she had no attachment to it. It didn't feel like home anymore. It felt like someone else's town, her mother's, her sister's, but no longer hers. Something inside her had come unhooked, but she didn't mention it to Marje. It would panic her sister if she thought Winnie wasn't coming back. Winnie didn't know if she would or not. But it was interesting being here, and being aware of how little she felt. It was good seeing Marje, Erik, and the kids, but not much else.

"Thanks for telling me about Rob and Barb last night. I'd have been pissed if I'd seen them walking down the street together and you hadn't told me."

"That's what I thought. Do you care?"

"Not a bit," Winnie said honestly. "They're both dead as far as I'm concerned." Marje nodded and didn't comment. She didn't think she could have recovered from it herself.

Jimmy was sitting up in bed when they got to the hospital. He said he had a headache, but the nurses weren't surprised. They got him out of bed and had him walk a few steps, but he got dizzy very quickly and had to sit down, which they said was to be expected. He wanted to hear about the Aston Martin again and how fast they'd gone. And when the doctor saw him, he said they wanted him in the hospital for a week for observation, to make sure he had no complications before he went home. Jimmy was upset about it, but all the adults thought it made perfect sense. Adam came to see him that afternoon and brought him a pizza, and they shared it for dinner. Jimmy's appetite hadn't come back yet. Adam was beaming and peaceful after he saw him. Winnie drove him home after the visit.

"I thought he was going to die, Aunt Win," Adam said in a small voice.

"I think that occurred to all of us, but he's going to be fine now. He's very lucky, and so are we." Adam nodded again and looked subdued when he got out of the car. Almost losing his brother had been terrifying for him, and for all of them.

When Marje came home from the hospital, the adults had dinner together, and Winnie told them about her work on the set and how interesting and rewarding it was, and how huge a crew it took to film the show. She told them about Alexander Nichols, their historical consultant, and the manners coach, who advised them about every aspect of appropriate behaviors and manners of the time, how the women should sit and stand, what they could and couldn't say, and he was just as rigorous about the men in the cast. He would stop them from filming the instant anyone made a faux pas about the customs of the period.

"I thought he was a pill at first," Winnie said to them, "but he's brilliant. He knows everything about the era. He goes around with a ruler measuring how far apart people should sit. He's what keeps the show historically accurate and so believable. It's fascinating to listen to him," she said, her eyes shining brightly in admiration of how the show was made. "And the castle they use is beautiful. I took a tour when I got there. The descendants of the original family that built it still live there. Having the show use their castle as the location helped them to keep from selling it. They were dead broke before the show.

There's a book about them I can send you if you want." She loved everything she had learned and what she was doing there and they could see it.

"I'd rather watch a reality show about them," Marje said and all three of them laughed.

The day after, Winnie made a reservation to leave the next day. There was nothing more for her to do, and Jimmy was out of danger. She had to get back to work. She wanted to get back and be on the set the same day that Edward returned, which seemed only fair. She'd come to Michigan for an emergency, not a vacation. Her stay had been action-packed and had a happy ending. And more than ever, she felt as though she didn't belong there, although she never said it to Marje. She had found greener pastures in a bigger world, not where she'd expected to find them, but in a place that suited her. She was eager to get back to her cottage and daily routine.

She said goodbye to Jimmy at the hospital that night, and to Adam and Erik the next morning at breakfast. She had another half hour of sisterly gossip with Marje and then she had to leave for the drive back to Detroit. She was following the same route that she'd come by.

"I get the feeling you don't feel like you belong here anymore," Marje said cautiously as they shared a last cup of coffee.

"In some ways I don't," Winnie said honestly, "in other ways I always will. I like living in England for now."

"Mom always said you don't belong here, and would end up somewhere more sophisticated." It was odd how different the two sisters were. Winnie couldn't imagine Marje anywhere else and neither could she.

She hugged Marje close before she left for the drive to Detroit, and realized how much she had missed her. "I'll call you when I get back," she promised. Nigel had been driving her crazy with texts every day, asking when she was coming back. But she was getting in too late to see him, and would meet up with him at work the next day. It seemed soon enough. She wasn't in the mood for his jealousy and accusations, and crazy assumptions about her boss.

She turned the car in, in Detroit, and caught the flight to New York. She texted Marje that she'd landed safely, and walked around the airport before the next flight. She felt as though she were going home. She watched two movies and had a meal on the flight to London, and slept for an hour before they landed. And although she'd only been at Heathrow twice before, it really did feel like home when she got there. She took a train back to King's Lynn, a taxi from there to the village, and smiled when she walked into her cottage. She didn't even want to call Nigel, or miss him. She was thrilled to be there in her bed alone.

In the morning, she got up, showered and dressed and made breakfast, and walked to work. She was happy to see all the familiar faces, and then she saw Nigel watching her. He walked over slowly and gave her a hug.

"You didn't call me last night when you got in," he said softly.

"I got in very late. I didn't want to wake you." He nodded and went back to work. She walked to Edward's trailer to report for work, and she saw Nigel watching her when she left the set.

"How did it go?" Edward asked as soon as he saw her. He looked fresh and happy and relaxed.

"He'll be fine. He came out of the coma the day I got there, and he's making steady progress. He has headaches, but it could have been a lot worse." It could have been a tragedy, and she was grateful it hadn't been. "How were your days off?"

"We went to Venice for the weekend, and I proposed," he said proudly. "We're going to get married next year. Grace is going to break the news to her father next week."

"Congratulations!" Winnie smiled at him. "Where are you going to get married?"

"Someplace gorgeous and romantic that we both love. The Caribbean, St. Bart's, Tahiti, the top of a mountain, or in our apartments. We haven't figured it out yet. Her father will probably want us to do it at his club. We want to avoid that at all cost. But wherever we do it, it's time. We've waited long enough." Thirteen years seemed like more than enough to Winnie. And she hoped Grace's father didn't give them a hard time. They didn't deserve it and Edward would be a wonderful husband.

He gave her some projects to do for him while he studied his lines and got ready for their shooting schedule that day. His costumes were lined up on a rack, and the hairdresser was coming to trim his hair. Winnie handed him his schedule a few minutes later and he smiled at her.

"It's nice to have you back." He loved how organized she was, and how efficiently she kept his life on track.

He was on the set on time for every shot, knew his lines flawlessly, as he always did. The day unrolled smoothly like a carpet, and they both left work on time at six o'clock. And when she left, Nigel was waiting for her outside.

"Want a ride home?"

"Sure." She smiled at him and got in the Jeep, and hoped he wouldn't mention Edward again. He didn't, and he came in while she made dinner for both of them, and they enjoyed a relaxed evening together and went up to bed. Their lovemaking was tender and sweet. When he was that way, she always hoped that things would work out between them. But when he played the jealous lover, all she wanted to do was get away from him. She was happy he hadn't done that tonight. It was a perfect homecoming, and just what she needed from him.

For the next week on the set everything went smoothly, and everyone seemed in a good mood, even Nigel. Winnie noticed Matthew sitting on the sidelines several times that week, and then conferring with Michael and nodding. She wondered if he had figured out a storyline yet to cover Bill and Elizabeth's absence the following season, and if they would be bringing in new actors. At the end of the day on Friday, before a weekend off, the production team called a general meeting, and when she got there, Winnie saw Matthew waiting to speak to all of them, and she got an odd feeling about it. He waited until everyone was there before he started.

Before saying anything else, he praised them for how exciting the season had been. They had a week left in their shooting schedule before the hiatus, and he said he thought it had been their best season. The most impressive and the most professional, and breathtaking in every way. He said what they'd been shooting would play in the coming months as their seventh season. They were due to return in October to shoot the following season, but he didn't mention it. Everyone knew it anyway. He said he'd been working frantically to come up with alternate plot lines to explain Elizabeth and Bill's absence from the series. And he had come to the conclusion that no matter how many new actors they added or plot turns he devised, they had already given the viewers their best work, and it would be a mistake to dilute it now or trivialize it in some way, and disappoint people. He said every show had its lifetime and he had realized that *Beauchamp Hall* had reached the end of its natural life, and trying to extend it artificially would be a grave mistake. So with gratitude to everyone involved and great regrets, they were canceling the show, and ending it when they finished shooting the remaining episodes. He had tears in his eyes when he said it, and added, "I will never be able to thank you enough for the life you have breathed into this series. We have pleased people all over the globe and given meaning to their lives, just as you have to mine. From the bottom of my heart, I thank you. I'll miss *Beauchamp* as much as you will, and much, much more," he said, and then walked quietly off the set with tears running down his cheeks. The entire cast and crew sat mesmerized, watching him go, as though they hadn't understood what he told them, and then burst into tears and hugged each other. It was over. They had pulled the plug. *Beauchamp Hall* would never have another season beyond the one they were shooting now. It would be over forever in a week, and all the joy it represented for the viewers and for those who made it. After almost seven years, it was finished.

There was chaos on the set for half an hour, and then people disbanded, to discuss it among themselves, digest it, mourn it, and celebrate it. Winnie made her way to where Edward was sitting and he looked like he was in shock.

"Are you okay?" she asked him and he nodded.

"I'm stunned. I didn't expect that, but maybe I should have when

Liz and Bill left. I thought he'd pull a rabbit out of the hat one more time. But no more rabbit, no more hat. I'll be okay," he reassured her, and also himself. "I'd better call my agent tomorrow."

"You'll get another series," she said with conviction. He was one of the best actors on the show, and the most reliable, even if he didn't have top billing, which was the problem. The actors who had left them flat were their strongest and most marketable, and Matthew didn't think they had a viable series without them, no matter how talented the rest of the cast was. He didn't want to weaken the show now with inadequate support, and new stars who couldn't carry it.

When Edward left the set to call his agent and fiancée, she went to look for Nigel and couldn't find him at first, and then she saw him in a knot of sound technicians who looked thunderstruck. They had feared that the end was coming, but no one was sure until now. Now it was certain. The worst had happened. The end had come for all of them. Matthew had always pulled it off before, but this time he refused to. He didn't want people comparing the show to what it had been and not liking it as much, or sponsors abandoning them. It was a reasonable concern, and had been a wise decision, and surely a hard one, that would affect a multitude of people, all of whom had just lost their jobs.

"Are you okay?" she asked Nigel when she walked over to him. He looked both angry and sad at the same time.

"Do I have a choice?" he said with an ironic look.

"There's always a choice," Winnie said gently. "Especially in how you look at it."

"Don't give me that philosophical Pollyanna bullshit. I just lost my job, and God knows where I'll be working two months from now.

Probably somewhere heinous on a shit show, or wherever the union sends me. There's something to look forward to. And they certainly didn't give us much notice. They never do when they cancel a show."

"So I've been told," she said, sympathetically. "I think they just made the decision. Bill and Elizabeth didn't give them much notice either. Do you want to come home with me?" she offered. This was a blow and a loss for her too.

"I'm going out with the guys," he said with a hard edge to his voice, as though their canceling the show was somehow her fault. She was sad about it, very sad, but it wasn't as devastating to her. She loved the show, but didn't need it to survive. He did. She had come here on a lark, taken a break from her life, and fallen in love with the people involved and the production. But she could still go back where she came from, in theory. Except she didn't want to, even now. She wanted it to go on forever, but destiny, and the writer, had decided otherwise. She had no idea what to do or where to go next.

She walked home alone, feeling sad about the show being canceled and almost like a symbol of closure, she saw Rupert with his food truck. She had seen him when she first arrived, and now here he was again. She hadn't noticed him in weeks.

She stopped to say hello, and he looked as devastated as the crew and cast when they left the set. "I just heard. That's terrible news for all of us. The town will never be the same without *Beauchamp Hall*. The show saved us. There won't be any jobs here again now. All the life will go out of the place."

"What about you, Rupert?" she asked him with concern. "Will you be okay?"

"I'll have to give up the truck. I'll sell it. No customers after you lot go. There may be a few tourists for a while, but not enough to live on. I feed the crew every day. They won't be here now. Another week and it's all over for me, and a lot of people around here. This is a hard blow for us. I guess I'll go back to what I was doing before. I'm a chimney sweep. I hate it, but there it is. My father was too. I sold the business when I bought the truck. I'd rather sell tea and orange juice than be crawling up everyone's chimneys with a black face for the rest of my life." His voice quavered as he said it, and her heart went out to him.

"I'm sorry," she said gently, listening to him for a few more minutes, and then they said goodbye and she went home. It was going to be a tough situation for the villagers, not just the cast and crew. Matthew Stevens had made a big decision that had hit them all hard, and as Winnie walked the rest of the way to the cottage, she was crying too.

Chapter Twelve

Winnie spent a quiet night watching old *Beauchamp* DVDs from previous seasons. There had been some incredibly wonderful episodes and twists and turns of events. Unforgettable moments, and spectacular performances from amazing actors who had brought their talents and well-honed skills to the show. Many who had grown from being on it. And a few who had gone, thinking they were forging ahead to greatness, and instead had disappeared, as often happened when actors left a successful series. Thinking about ending the show now made her sad. But losing two major players, shortly after losing two others, was a crippling blow Matthew Stevens didn't think the show could recover from, and possibly he was right. They couldn't afford to lose that much. The hole in the hull was too big now for the ship to sail on. And he was left to wrap up all the plots and subplots as elegantly as he could with the cast and material on hand. Winnie was sure it would be a challenging task.

When she got up in the morning, the day after the announcement, she realized that Nigel hadn't called her the night before. His concern about his future had given him a sharp edge recently, and that coupled with his unfounded jealousy of Edward had impacted their relationship considerably, and it wasn't likely to get better now. She hadn't come to any definite conclusions about it, but he wasn't seeking solace with her, instead he was at the bars with his coworkers. And she suspected he'd been too drunk to come over the previous night, so it was probably just as well that he hadn't.

She was thinking about him when she made a stop at the dry cleaner on her way to work. They had all gotten a text asking them to work through the weekend to shoot the final scenes until they wrapped. They had a lot of work to do with new scripts to conclude the show.

She dropped off her laundry too. She didn't have the convenience of Mrs. Flannagan's two big washing machines now that she had her own cottage. There was a tiny machine that didn't work very well.

She found herself standing behind a familiar blond figure ahead of her. When the woman turned around, Winnie could see that it was Lady Beatrice Haversham, and this time she didn't smile when she saw Winnie, although she recognized her.

"Bad news yesterday," Lady Beatrice said cryptically. She didn't know what Winnie's job was, but knew where she worked. "It'll be back to Poverty Flats for us, when the show goes. My brother and I will be selling scones and pencils on the street one of these days." Winnie hoped she didn't mean it, but clearly the castle was expensive to maintain, and the show had provided a big cushion for them, and been their primary source of income for the last seven years. "And not much notice on top of it. It'll be all over in a week. It's quite a shock." There was a sad look in her eyes.

"People will want to come and visit here for a long time," Winnie said, trying to sound encouraging, but the young noblewoman shook her head.

"Not for long. They'll forget. They'll fall in love with some other show, and we'll fade back into the mist like all the other great houses with owners who've run out of money. Faded curtains run out of charm rather quickly, when there's nothing else going on there. The show was a great blessing for us for a long time. I'm grateful for it, but the situation is going to be dire for all of us who depended on *Beauchamp Hall*. My brother is going to have to sell his horses, like it or not."

"Just so you don't sell the house," Winnie said, deeply moved by her admissions.

"It could come to that. That's where we were when they decided to set up the show here. We had just come to the conclusion that we'd have to sell. We've had a nearly seven-year reprieve. But half the businesses in town will be closed this time next year, and us along with them." It was in fact the situation the British aristocracy had been in for the last hundred years, their lifestyle dramatically changed, their homes in jeopardy, trying to squeeze out enough to live on however they could. There was a long list of houses in England, castles, manor homes, and great halls that the public could tour.

"Don't give up yet. You'll figure something out. The show must have come as a surprise when it happened. As they say, 'They're not the only show in town.'"

"They are in this town," Lady Beatrice said realistically. "No one will set up a show here again. It's been done. We'll have to get creative, but I haven't figured out how yet. My brother is more inclined to wait for a miracle to fall from the sky." Winnie remembered that it was Lady Beatrice who had written the book, and whom she saw from time to time on the set, conferring with the producers and consulting on the show. She knew everything there was to know about the history of the house, who had visited there and stayed there, and colorful anecdotes that turned up in the plot. Her brother never seemed to be around, although he lived at Haversham too. He looked more aloof the few times Winnie had glimpsed him. Lady Beatrice seemed more down-to-earth, and engaged with people around her, as she was with Winnie now. "I suppose I'll see you around for a while longer," she said almost wistfully and Winnie smiled.

"We'll all be sad to leave and I've only been here since May."

"We'll be equally sad to see you go." She smiled warmly and then left, and Winnie paid for the sheets they had laundered and the skirt she'd had cleaned. She thought about Lady Beatrice as she walked up to the castle, and what a blow this was for them. Winnie felt very sorry for her. Others weren't as interested in the family, and thought they were just a bunch of silly old snobs who were no longer relevant, but Winnie had been intrigued by them since the first time she'd seen the show. The history of the castle and the family gave credibility to the whole series, and the issues they had dealt with at the time. And what they were dealing with now wasn't much different. They were fighting to keep their heads above water and were the last survivors of a lost world.

Winnie went to look for Nigel as soon as she got to the set, and forgot about the Havershams. She was worried about him.

"How was last night?" She tried to sound light about it, but he looked rough.

"About the way you'd expect. Sorry I didn't make it over. At least I had the good sense not to knock on your door. You should be glad I didn't. I called the union yesterday. There are half a dozen new shows starting. The new ones are pretty well staffed by now, but something will turn up." He tried to sound optimistic, but didn't look it, and she knew pride had kicked in. He didn't want to look pathetic to her. She kissed his cheek lightly and headed for Edward's trailer. He was reading the London *Financial Times* when she walked in, and seemed surprisingly calm, when he looked up and smiled at her.

"Wow, everyone's in an uproar all over town. The food truck, the Havershams, the sound guys," she said to him.

"It's going to make a hell of a difference to the locals. The rest of us should be used to it. It's the nature of the business. I called my agent last night. He's not worried. We've turned down some good parts in new series recently. If they haven't filled the parts, I liked a couple of them very much. One in particular, and I hated to turn it down." He was the consummate professional, and Winnie was impressed by how calm and philosophical he was. "The ones who will probably take a hard hit are the small businesses who depend on us and have done well because of us for all these years. And the Havershams were probably hanging by a shoelace when we got here. Running a place like this costs a fortune. They won't be able to afford to without the show."

"I saw Lady Beatrice at the laundry this morning, and that's pretty much what she said. And I get the feeling they may not have been saving a lot of it, between upkeep and expenses." She had looked seriously worried.

"Her brother has some very fancy horses and cars. He gave me a tour of all of it one day."

"She said he'll have to sell his horses."

"I'm not surprised. That's the trouble with the aristos, they always put their money on the wrong stuff. They have no sense of commerce or investment, they're not equipped for the modern world. You'd think they'd have learned that much by now."

"She seems pretty practical," Winnie defended her.

"I'll wager you her brother isn't, not with a stable like that. And he has some fabulous antique cars in the barn. He has three or four Bugattis, he let me drive one of them. I'd have bought it from him, but I couldn't afford it, and he wouldn't sell it. Great car to own, just for the thrill of it." Edward loved cars, and had several of his own, including a Ferrari, a Lamborghini, and the Aston Martin he'd used to drive Winnie to the airport.

Other than Edward, who seemed remarkably stable, the whole cast seemed distracted, anxious, and off-kilter that day. Actors who normally learned their lines perfectly were stumbling and blowing them, with new scripts they had to learn rapidly. One of the producers had distributed new scripts to the entire cast. Matthew had reworked the storylines and outcomes leading up to the end, to conclude the show. It was a challenge to make it all go smoothly and tie up all the loose ends, so people who had studied the scripts and knew their lines had to learn an entirely new script for each remaining day. It would be that way now for the next week until the end. And they all expected to work overtime to finish it.

It was a long stressful day, and even Edward looked tired by the end of it, and Winnie felt drained. She was so worried about everyone that she was distracted too. She hadn't called Marje to tell her the news about the show being canceled. She didn't want to mislead her and give her the impression that she was coming home. Going back to Beecher after Jimmy's accident had convinced Winnie that she didn't belong there, at least not yet. She hadn't played out her hand in England, and Edward had said that day that he wanted to take her with him if he got a part on a new show. It was an appealing idea and she was flattered. But he didn't have a new show yet and they still had *Beauchamp Hall* to deal with, before she thought of anything else. For now, and for some time, Michigan was not in her plans.

Marje called her a few days later, and had heard a rumor that the show had been canceled. They'd said it on *Entertainment Tonight*.

"Is that true?" She sounded shocked.

"Unfortunately, yes. They announced it to the cast and crew a few days ago. They're not going to shoot a new season. After this one, we're done. They're wrapping up the conclusion now. Everyone is very upset about it, even the local townspeople." Marje could hear that she was sad as she said it.

"Does that mean you're coming home, Win?" She sounded hopeful, which was exactly what Winnie had wanted to avoid. "Should I take your house off the market to rent?"

"I don't think I'll come home for a while. I still want to rent it."

"What would you do there without the show?" Winnie could tell she was disappointed.

"I'm trying to figure it out, we all are. My boss offered me a job as

193

his assistant, if he gets another series, and he probably will. He's hot right now. *Beauchamp* really put him on the map. I could do that. I like working for him. He's very businesslike and matter-of-fact and polite, not like a lot of other actors." She hadn't been favorably impressed by many she'd seen, except him. She liked working for him even more than she had for Elizabeth, who had been very flighty, although she was sweet and good to Winnie. But Elizabeth's personal life was a mess, with the affair with Bill Anders. They were still all over the press, even after she left the show. Edward kept his private life much more discreet. "I'll let you know what I'm doing, when I know." She asked about Jimmy then, and Marje said he was doing well, and the headaches had gotten better.

Nigel came over that night and hadn't been there in three days, a long time for him. But he just hadn't been in the mood. He was quiet that night too. She didn't ask if the union had called about upcoming jobs. She didn't want to upset him more than he was.

"I may stay with my parents for a while after we wrap," he said quietly. "Or go to stay with my cousin in Ireland. Would you want to come, Winnie?"

"I might," she said vaguely. "I haven't figured out my plans yet either." And then she decided to tell him. "Edward offered me a job on his next show, when he gets one. I might do that. He's good to work for. Simple and direct, and no nonsense. He's a pro." Nigel looked depressed by what she said.

"Are you in love with him?"

"Not at all. He just got engaged, and he's crazy about her. They're getting married fairly soon. He's not a cheater. And neither am I."

Nigel had heard it all before and didn't believe her, but this time he looked as though he might. He was so down and lethargic he was even less jealous.

"I don't know if that's true about him. But I think it is about you," he said fairly, for the first time. "What do I have to offer you anyway? You'd have a much better life with him. I'm just a broke sound guy, about to be out of a job."

"You'll have another job soon. And he's not offering me a 'better life,' he's offering that to his fiancée, some lord's daughter in London. I'm no fancier than you are. He's offering me a job, not marriage."

"You won't go home to Michigan?" He seemed surprised.

"I don't know yet. I haven't decided. It seemed pretty dreary when I went back. I've gotten spoiled here. I love it."

"Well, you can't stay here when the series ends. It'll be a ghost town, half the shops will be closed, and people will have to go to other towns for jobs. That's what England is like these days."

"Beecher isn't exactly a hot job market either. That's why I left. I didn't want to work at a motel, or the hardware store."

"You'd look cute in a set of overalls," he teased her. "Small towns are like that."

"I should have gone to New York fifteen years ago, but I didn't. I missed my chance. I can't start out there at my age. And I really love it here. I'll be sad to move on."

"Won't we all," he said wistfully.

They made love that night, but he didn't spend the night. Their relationship seemed more tenuous now, like a summer romance as the leaves begin to fall. They could both sense a reckoning time coming and needed to face if the relationship was viable or not. She wasn't looking forward to that either. And she didn't think their brief romance would survive.

She picked up the book about the Havershams from her night table after Nigel left, to help her sleep. She liked reading in bed. She fell asleep with the light on and the book in her hands. She slept fitfully, woke, dozed, and woke again, with strange people she didn't know in and out of her dreams. She was in a grand house surrounded by people and there was a woman in a wedding gown, and a director shouting at all of them that someone had been murdered and everybody laughed. It felt like a nightmare, but it wasn't, and she sat up in bed with a jolt at four in the morning, shaking, and everything about the dream came clear. She thought it was important, and wanted to remember all of it. She grabbed a yellow pad she kept on her night table for lists of things she had to do, found a pen beside it, and began writing down the dream frantically, before any of it could slip away.

The people the director had been shouting at were actors, but at the same time she knew they were guests. They were all in elaborate period costumes like the ones on the show, she even recognized one or two of them as gowns Elizabeth had worn. The bride in the midst of it was real, and the murder a hoax, which was why everyone laughed. And then they had all taken a tour of the castle, where scenes from the series were being played out in different rooms by the actors, but Winnie could see now that they were being played out on giant video screens. They all left the castle via some kind of museum where Rupert was selling souvenirs, cups and mugs and plates, beautiful hats and tiaras, and they were all being interviewed by reporters. She realized that the bride she had seen was Edward's fiancée, Grace, and he was with her. She'd only seen Grace in photographs so far, but she was sure it was her. Grace looked ecstatically happy, and everyone including the reporters threw rose petals at them as they drove away in Rupert's food truck with JUST MARRIED written on the back. The dream was crazy, but parts of it made sense to her. She read what she'd written over and over again, and added to it, and then divided it into sections. Some sounded more lucid than others. She tried telling herself that the whole thing was ridiculous, and turned off the light at five-thirty and tried to get another hour or two of sleep, but she was too excited to drift off, and kept thinking of more things she remembered to add to her notes. By eight o'clock, she was certain that the dream had been an inspiration, and she knew who she wanted to share it with.

She dug through some production notes and papers, and found the general number for the castle, in case of some major problem on the set, if there was an emergency like a flood or a leak, or a major power outage. She wasn't sure if a butler or a janitor or a property manager would answer, and instead she recognized the voice of Lady Beatrice Haversham. She was having breakfast and sounded surprised by the call.

Winnie explained who she was, and reminded her of where they'd met.

"Yes, yes, I know," Lady Beatrice said, sounding worried. "Do we have a leak from the upstairs master bath into the library again?"

"No, everything's fine. I know this sounds a little odd, but could I meet with you at lunchtime or after work today? I had an idea I'd like to share with you."

"If it incorporates murdering an irresponsible brother, I'd be most willing," she said crisply. "He drove my car into a pond yesterday. Odd, he never does that kind of thing with his own, or his Bugattis." Winnie laughed, but Lady Beatrice did not sound amused. "Might I ask what this is about, by the way?"

"It's too complicated to explain on the phone."

"Ah, very well. After I dispose of my brother's body and fish my car, or what's left of it, out of the pond, I'll be free at noon. Come in through the door to the family living quarters. I'll meet you in the main parlor. It's a bit dusty, I'm afraid, I haven't had time to hoover in there for three weeks, but meeting you in our boot room seems a bit rude." Winnie had seen all of it on the tour except the private quarters, but it suddenly seemed more personal going there to see Lady Beatrice. It sounded exciting, and so was her dream.

Edward noticed her high spirits when she got to work, but she didn't explain it to him. He guessed it was due to a romance, but didn't ask her. She warned him before he walked onto the set to play a scene that she would be leaving a few minutes before noon for an appointment. He had no problem with it. Alexander Nichols, their historical consultant, was on the set, correcting them just as intensely right to the end. He wanted everything to be perfect and was relentless to ensure it.

She left the set and walked around to the back of the castle, and wandered in through the back door the Havershams used now as their private entrance. There were two small sitting rooms for visitors to wait in, but most of the furniture and paintings had been removed to use as props on the set, and she walked past them into an enormous parlor filled with sunlight, overscale antiques and magnificent paintings, some as high as six and seven feet tall, and the ceilings were high too. It was a splendid room. They had filmed there a few times in the first two seasons, then decided there were other rooms they preferred, and the Havershams had been happy to reclaim it for their own use. It had been called the "day parlor" in the heyday of the house.

Winnie wandered around looking up at the paintings, and stood gazing intently at one of a woman riding sidesaddle on a white horse, and she jumped when she heard a voice behind her.

"That's my great-great-aunt Charlotte. She was quite mad apparently, but lovely to look at, and very amusing." Winnie turned to see Lady Beatrice in a crisp white men's shirt, tailored to fit her, jodhpurs that were obviously custom-made, and perfectly polished tall black riding boots, with her blond hair cascading down her back. She was every bit as beautiful as the woman in the painting.

"Thank you for seeing me," Winnie said, somewhat cowed by the surroundings, and feeling shy now that she was face-to-face with the lady of the house, who would surely think she was "quite mad" too, once she explained her dream, and her interpretation of it.

"Don't be silly, of course. Won't you sit down?" Winnie did, at the edge of a large antique chair covered in deep red velvet that was frayed but still impressive. "Would you like some tea?"

"No, I'm fine, thank you."

"Sorry I look like this. I got the damn car out of the pond. I'm not sure we can get it running again. My brother is an incredible nuisance." She looked as exasperated as she had sounded that morning on the phone. "No one should have to live with their siblings past the age of eight. We shipped him off to Eton and Cambridge, but he always came back. And now we're stuck with each other, trying to run this place. And there's always some little actress to chase, with the show here, although that will be all over now. He'll be bored to sobs once they leave. But so will I. And broke as well, so dreary." She sank into a velvet couch facing Winnie, with an enormous painting over it, of another of her ancestors, but didn't explain who it was. "So what did you have in mind?" She talked a lot, but was lighthearted, articulate, and funny, and very British. The series was full of people with accents just like hers, which they imitated to perfection, with the help of diction coaches to make them sound upper crust, whatever their origins. Lady Beatrice always found it amusing.

"I had a dream last night," Winnie started cautiously.

"Oh dear, not a bad one, I hope. I hope you haven't come to warn me of some dreadful premonition. I'm frightfully superstitious and shan't sleep for weeks."

"No, a good one. At least I think so. And I know it sounds terribly presumptuous, but you mentioned the other day how concerned you are about the fate of Haversham, and even the village, once the show moves on. And it worries me too. I love it here, I fell in love with the show months ago, but now I've fallen in love with the people here, the village, and the castle, and what it means to everyone. It's been troubling me, and I think that's how the dream happened. It was all an insane jumble, but I pulled it apart when I woke up, and made some notes. I think you have some amazing possibilities here to make Haversham Castle even more important, and even more lucrative than it was as Beauchamp Hall."

"How do you imagine that?" Beatrice Haversham looked skeptical. "I've rattled my brain too and all I can come up with is selling lemonade and biscuits at the door after our beastly tour, which will be even more boring now."

"It doesn't have to be. You have some opportunities you may not have explored yet. First of all, weddings. What more fabulous place to have a wedding? Holkham Hall does them near here, and I'm told they do very well with them. There have been several weddings in the series, and they've been spectacular. People will want to get married here because they've seen the weddings on the show, which makes this a highly desirable location. You can do less expensive weddings in the house, all carefully organized in a package. They could be period weddings in costume, if you like. You might be able to buy some of the costumes when the show leaves. You could do more elaborate weddings with tents outside. All you need is a good caterer and florist, and this would be an ideal venue in the future. If you can organize some of the rooms, the wedding party could stay here." Beatrice nodded, thinking about it.

"Getting the costumes would be a great idea. They had five hundred extras for one of the weddings they did here," she mused pensively.

"Second, mystery weekends. Again in period costumes. People love them. They do them in the States. A group of people rent the castle for the weekend, it doesn't have to be many. Fifteen or twenty, which is manageable. They wear costumes. You have a script, and they enact a mystery, usually a murder. And they have to solve it by the end of the weekend. Wonderful for a birthday or a house party, or some sort of small corporate event. You could charge a lot of money for it. Someone would have to write the scripts they can all follow. A bit like the game of Clue, but in a real castle in real life. You could use the same script for each group, except for repeat guests.

"Third. A *Beauchamp* museum for crazies like me who love the show. You could set aside a few of the rooms that were used regularly on the show, have screens in the room with scenes playing in the rooms where they were shot. You could add that as a piece of modern history, as part of the life of the castle. And I know it's embarrassing, but a gift shop somewhere with souvenirs of the castle and the show, mugs, plates, tea services, all the things that the fans love and buy on the Internet. You can have some local girl selling them after the tour, with your book of course.

"And, lastly, you may hate it, but it's a possibility. A reality show on television of the life of the castle today, with you and your brother. They could film weddings that happen here, and mystery weekends. Your brother with his cars and horses. They'd even enjoy your car falling into the pond. It's a vulgar idea, but could be done tastefully. People love royalty and aristocracy, and a peek into life at the castle might excite them as much as the series now. And the truth is you could make a fortune on it, if you can stand doing it. And seeing what's happening here on a reality show would make them flock here in droves. They'd be throwing money at you to get in." Winnie fell silent when she was finished as Beatrice Haversham stared at her.

"Good Lord! That wasn't a dream, it was a nightmare! You dreamt all that?" Winnie nodded. "But what an amazing lot of ideas. I have to think about it, but some part of it actually might work. Why on earth did you trouble yourself about how to solve our problems?" As

she spoke, her brother walked into the room frowning, with a puzzled expression.

"Have you seen my riding crop, Bea? I can't find it. I'm going out
on Comet in a few minutes. Oh, sorry, I didn't know you had a guest,"
he said when he saw Winnie.

"I did see it. I broke it in half and threw it in the rubbish. Thank
you for drowning my car."

"Don't be silly, it'll be fine. And you should have thrown it in the
rubbish years ago. What are you doing throwing my crop away?" He
glanced from his sister to Winnie as he said it. He was an incredibly
good-looking man, with all the marks of good breeding, and was
wearing jodhpurs and boots like his sister.

Lady Beatrice turned to her brother with a disgusted expression.
"My brother, the Marquess of Haversham," she said for Winnie's benefit to introduce them. Winnie wasn't sure if she was supposed to
curtsy or bow, and looked flustered.

"How do you do?" she said shyly as he shook her hand.

"Very well, thank you, other than my sister's bad temper. And
Freddie will do. I hate titles, don't you?"

"I don't know, I've never had one," Winnie said meekly.

"How fortunate for you." His smile was dazzling and full of mischief.

"I have to buy groceries," Beatrice interrupted him. "Which of
your Bugattis would you like to give me to replace my car? And by
the way, this is Winona Farmington." Winnie had used her full name
when she made the appointment, in order to sound more credible
and formal. "She has a wealth of extraordinary ideas to help us stay

on our feet when *Beauchamp* leaves." Beatrice stood up then, and Freddie disappeared again to find another riding crop in the boot room. "I have to think about what you said. I don't know if I'd have the courage to do any of it. But it's certainly worth a thought. I'll call you when I've had time to digest it." Winnie nodded and stood up, and thanked her for allowing her to come and share the ideas. "What part would you play in it?"

"None," Winnie said simply. "I wasn't in the dream. I just thought some of it might be helpful."

"How kind of you," Beatrice said, smiling at her. They were about the same age, and Winnie had a feeling she'd like Bea if she got to know her. And her brother was handsome and funny. They were like people in a book or a play, not real life, or not Winnie's real life at any rate. "I don't know where we'd get the manpower to pull it off," Beatrice said thoughtfully as she walked Winnie to the door.

"There will be lots of people out of work here shortly. They'd be grateful for the jobs," Winnie reminded her. Beatrice nodded agreement and Winnie left a minute later. After she left, in the distance, Winnie saw Freddie cantering toward the hills on a white horse. He looked like a good omen. She thought about it as she headed back to Edward's trailer. There were parts of her life now, in fact all of it, that felt like someone else's life, surely not hers. Titled aristocrats and movie stars, castles and hit TV shows. It still took her breath away at times. But Beatrice Haversham seemed almost normal to her, down-to-earth, and practical. She had listened intently to Winnie.

In the family side of the castle, Beatrice was pouring herself a cup of tea and shaking her head, wondering if fate had just saved them again, or was it all too absurd?

Chapter Thirteen

N ew scripts appeared daily on the set now to try to wind down the series to a satisfying conclusion. Viewers had to be pleased, mysteries solved, Matthew didn't want to leave anyone hanging, but to wrap everything up neatly. It took new scripts and storylines to do it, and learning all the new lines was challenging for the actors and confusing for everyone, even the crew. Nothing was going according to previous plans. Scenes were being shot in different places, costumes were changed. The costumers were going crazy trying to keep up and remaking old dresses from previous seasons. The producers wanted to maintain the same high standards to the bitter end.

Winnie was studying one of Edward's new scripts in the trailer, when her cellphone rang, it was Beatrice Haversham. She was surprised to hear from her for a minute. It was two days after their meeting, and Winnie was beginning to assume that they had decided she was crazy and had no interest in any of her ideas. It was entirely possible and she wouldn't blame them.

"Is this a bad time?" Beatrice asked her.

"No, it's fine."

"I'm sorry I didn't call you yesterday. Would you have time to come by and talk to us sometime today? My brother's going to London tomorrow, and I never know when he'll get back."

"I could come by after work," Winnie said softly, she didn't want to disturb Edward, who was trying to learn new lines, only a few feet away.

"Perfect. We'll have tea together. Six o'clock?" which Winnie knew meant a light dinner at that hour.

"See you then," she said and hung up.

She was hurrying out of the trailer at five to six when she saw Nigel coming toward her. He caught up with her a minute later.

"Do you want to go to dinner with me now?"

"I can't," she said, looking apologetic. "I've got an appointment. I don't know what time I'll be finished. I can call you."

"Never mind," he said, annoyed. "Who's the appointment with?"

"The Havershams," she said simply.

"The bloke with the Bugattis?"

"And his sister."

"What for?" He was suspicious.

"I had an idea they want to talk to me about."

"See you tomorrow," he said, turned on his heel, and left, and she didn't chase after him. She didn't want to be late for Beatrice and Freddie. She rang the bell at the door three minutes later, after she walked around the castle to their private entrance. The bell system was the same one that had existed there for over a hundred years and they used on the show. It still functioned, with occasional repairs. Beatrice opened the door a few minutes later. She was wearing jeans and a sweater and short riding boots. She and her brother both spent a lot of time on horses.

She walked Winnie into a small sitting room after following a circuitous route down a back hallway. It was the room Beatrice used as an office, and was a combination library and sitting room, with a fireplace and two comfortable couches, and several big leather chairs. The room was cozy, and her desk was piled high with papers. She handled all of their accounts with the production company, and kept track of all the schedules for the shoot, and which rooms they'd be using when, so there was never a conflict.

"Sit down," she said warmly to Winnie. "I'll be back in a flash." She reappeared a moment later with an enormous, ornate, antique silver tea tray, piled high with plates of scones and clotted cream, impeccable tea sandwiches of chicken, egg salad, cucumber, watercress, a silver tea pot, three cups, china, and silver. It looked like a scene from *Beauchamp Hall,* and worthy of the fanciest home, hotel, or restaurant. It smelled delicious, and as soon as Beatrice set it down, her brother appeared in jeans and a T-shirt.

"Are we meeting in here?" he asked his sister. "Who made the tea?" He looked impressed too.

"I did. Sit down. We have a lot to talk about." She passed Winnie the plate of sandwiches and Winnie took one of each. Freddie helped himself to several, while his sister poured tea and handed Winnie a delicate cup with a linen napkin and silver spoon. The light meal, the silver and china were a civilized relic of a bygone era.

Once they were all served, Beatrice addressed Winnie. "We've been talking about your ideas, and some of them are quite mad and positively frightening, but *very* interesting. We're wondering how much of it would really be possible, and how much manpower and expertise it would take. We don't have a big staff here. This isn't *Beauchamp Hall.*" She smiled.

"I don't think it would take a lot of people, and you could hire the ones you'd need. What part of the dream appealed to you?"

"The mystery weekends," Freddie said, smiling, helping himself to more sandwiches and his sister gave him a quelling look.

"The weddings first," Beatrice intervened. "I never thought of it before, but I think weddings could be quite marvelous here. We'd have to limit the number of guests, of course, but God knows we've got all the china and crystal and silver we'd need. And I suppose we'd have to know who the people are, so we know they're not the sort to steal the silverware."

"The bridal family could make a security deposit, as part of the price. You could design packages money-wise, depending on size and how elaborate they want it, and additional fees if they stay here or not. You could even provide a hairdresser and makeup artist, manicurist, everything they'd need. It could be very lucrative. You could hire someone just to do weddings," Winnie suggested.

"I could do it myself," Beatrice said thoughtfully. "We've all seen how they do it on the set. I think I could pull off a creditable wedding. I've never had one myself, but I've been to enough."

"I could masquerade as a priest," Freddie interjected. "Then the wedding wouldn't be legal, and they wouldn't have to bother getting divorced if it doesn't work out later."

"You are *not* being helpful." His sister glared at him. "And I loved your idea about buying wedding gowns and costumes from the production company when they leave. It could be very glamorous, and I think we have a few in the attic also."

"They might give them to you for free," Winnie said thoughtfully. "And you should probably have an assistant to help you with the weddings, a young local girl. Do you know a good caterer?"

"Actually, I do," Beatrice said. "And they're not very dear. I think our doing weddings here is a fantastic idea. We could advertise in bridal magazines, or some newspapers. Maybe British *Vogue*. I think we should keep it high-end, so it's something people are begging to do. Their dream wedding."

"I completely agree," Winnie said, pleased that her idea had spawned something useful for them. She liked Beatrice and she thought her brother was funny. "You'll need a florist and a photographer, and a calligrapher. And catering staff of course."

"What about the mystery weekends? Do you think we could actually pull that off? I've never been to one." Beatrice was intrigued.

"I have." Freddie leapt in. "It was amazing. I loved it. I was the murderer twice, and no one guessed me." He described what it had been like, and it sounded less complicated than the weddings.

"Someone will have to write the script. I can barely write a letter." Winnie nodded in response to what Beatrice said.

"And we like the idea for the Beauchamp museum. The rooms with the video screens showing scenes from the series is brilliant. They'll eat it up, and it will keep the spirit of the show alive for tourists who come here. And the gift shop is incredibly vulgar, but they'll probably like that too. We'll likely need the show's permission to sell the merchandise, but we can split the profits with the studio if we have to. And we'd need someone in the gift shop, again some nice young girl from the village. What kind of staff do you think we'd need to do all this?"

Winnie thought about it for a minute. "Would you both be working on it?" She glanced cautiously at Freddie.

"Yes," Beatrice said immediately. "I'd do the weddings. Freddie can do the mysteries. And I can manage the museum. Freddie is good with technical issues, like the video. It would be full-time work for both of us." She glanced meaningfully at her brother, who nodded.

"You could get one girl to help with the weddings, and another one to handle the gift shop. You need a technical person to set up the videos in the rooms on the tour, but you can hire an outside firm for that. You can do a lot with independent contractors, like the caterer. I think two willing young local girls would do it at first. You can always add another person later, if you need it. If you're both willing to do the work, you don't need much staff. And someone would have to keep the costumes straight, but you could do that," she spoke to Beatrice again.

"I know a nice seamstress in the village who could do fittings for us, and her husband is a tailor," Beatrice volunteered, and then she frowned again. "I had another thought. People have been watching the show for years. There's a very convincing butler on it, and houses like this are expected to have one. I was thinking that we should hire a butler, not a real one, but someone to act as one. He could even help with the tours."

"I can play the butler," Freddie said happily. He was enjoying the fantasy immensely, and smiled several times at Winnie.

"You *cannot* play the butler," his sister said firmly. "You're the marquess, you can't be the butler. We need someone who looks the part."

Winnie nodded, thinking. She agreed with Beatrice if they were going to re-enact something close to *Beauchamp Hall* and put on a real show for visitors or wedding guests, and then she had an idea.

"Do you know Rupert with the food truck in the square?" Freddie smiled when she said it.

"I went to school with him in the village for a year before I went to Eton. He's a good chap. He gives me free bangers whenever I see him. Actually, he'd be perfect."

"Brilliant," Beatrice approved. "Do you think he'd do it?"

"He was telling me last week that he's going to have to sell his food truck when the show closes, and go back to being a chimney sweep, which he hates," Winnie explained.

"I'd forgotten about that," Freddie said sympathetically. "I'm sure he'd rather be a butler than go around with soot on his face." It didn't sound like a fun job to Winnie either.

"I can ask him," Winnie said politely. She had made notes of several of the things Beatrice had mentioned. She had to hire two young girls to help her. And they needed to inquire about buying wedding dresses and costumes for weddings and mystery weekends. Haversham was a perfect venue for them. "We can also buy period gowns at auctions if we have to." Beatrice nodded agreement. They were thinking of every detail.

"And now for the horrible part," Beatrice said, looking at Winnie. "I can't even bear the thought of turning our home into a reality show, and my parents and grandparents would roll over in their graves, but I have a feeling there could be some real money in it. I hear that those shows can make a fortune. Do you suppose there's some way we could do it, without having them film us in the bathtub, or cooking breakfast in our underwear, or fighting with each other to keep them happy? We don't either of us have any 'love children' to produce to shock them. But maybe if they filmed a wedding or a mystery weekend and the preparations for it, it would satisfy them. Some of the brides might love it." She looked pained as she said it.

"From what I hear, there's some real money in it," Winnie said. "I understand your hesitation, but commercially speaking, it would feed the wedding business and mystery weekends. People would be begging to come here, better yet if they could be on the show." Beatrice groaned at what she said, and leaned back against the couch, as her brother looked at her.

"Don't be such a snob, Bea," her brother accused her. "If we want to stay here and keep the place going, we have to be smart about it. And they can film me in the bathtub, if they insist, or driving a Bugatti naked. It's all for God and Country." He said it nobly, and all three of them laughed.

"Do you know anyone who produces those reality shows?" she asked Winnie.

"No, but I can find out. I'm sure someone on the crew knows who they are."

"I have another important question," Beatrice said, jotting something down on her list. "How soon do you think we have to start putting all this together?"

"Yesterday," Winnie said without hesitation. "I think you should try to open by Christmas. That gives you almost four months to get everything in order and ready to roll. I think you can do it by then, if you start now. There actually isn't much preparation, because you have everything right here already, and you don't need a lot of staff. And the rooms they've been using for the show are camera ready now." Both Havershams were in agreement. It sounded feasible to them too.

"And one more thing," Beatrice added, looking shyly at Winnie. "We can't do this on our own, and it was your idea. We'd like you to be our creative director."

"Me?" Winnie looked shocked. She hadn't expected to include herself in the deal when she suggested it to them. She just did it to help, because she felt bad about their being left high and dry by the show being canceled, and she liked Beatrice when she'd met her. "I've never done anything like this."

"Neither have we, and you've worked on the show. You've seen how these things work."

"So have you," Winnie said modestly. "You don't really need me. You can run with the idea without me."

"Now, hear, hear," Freddie said to Winnie in a firm voice. "You can't just hallucinate this kind of thing, dump it in our laps, and then just leave us to it. We'll muck it all up. Or I will, certainly."

"*You* might," his sister said to him. "I'm not going to muck up a damn thing." And then she turned to Winnie. "But we do need you. I think your ideas are fantastic, and we're grateful to you. Would you consider being partners with us? We could split the profits three ways." Winnie was stunned and didn't know what to say, but it sounded exciting and fun and like a whole other chapter after her months hanging around the show. It was another dream coming true.

"I did some writing in college, I could try writing the scripts for the mystery weekends," she said hesitantly, "and see if you like them."

"The whole thing is your idea. If you hadn't suggested it, we'd never have thought of it, and we'd be broke again in six months."

"We might be anyway, if it doesn't work," Freddie said realistically, but it had the potential to become a real moneymaker and they could all sense it. She looked at them both for a moment. She had nothing to lose. And all three of them were excited to try it.

"I'll do it," she said, smiling at both of them. "I'd love to! Thank you for asking me."

"And if it doesn't work, we'll sell the house and all go live in the Caribbean together," Freddie suggested.

"Let's hope that doesn't happen," Beatrice said with feeling. "So what do we do now?" Beatrice looked at her list, as Winnie glanced at her own.

"You start looking for two girls in the village," Winnie said. "Freddie, will you talk to Rupert and ask him about being the butler? And I think Beatrice and I should talk to Michael Waterman about the costumes as soon as possible. I think we should do it together. He's very impressed by you and your title." She looked at Beatrice. "Should I be calling you Lady Beatrice all the time?" She wasn't sure, and Freddie answered the question.

"Yes, and you have to curtsy to her whenever you see her."

"Oh, shut up," his sister said to him. "Of course not. Beatrice or Bea is fine. But Freddie should always be 'His Lordship' when others are around, so visitors are impressed that they're in the presence of a marquess. We can charge more for that." She grinned.

"Maybe we should tell them I'm a duke and charge them even

more. 'Marquess Masquerades as Duke in Wake of *Beauchamp Hall* Scandal. . . .'"

"You don't need the producers' permission to run the museum, since the show is part of Haversham's history now, and the life of the castle. We can ask them for film clips, though."

"I think we've made some amazing progress," Beatrice said, looking pleased. It was nine o'clock at night, and they had covered a lot of ground in three hours. They had a partnership, and a plan, and a fledgling business.

"I hope it's a huge success," Winnie said sincerely, as Freddie disappeared, then returned a minute later with a bottle of champagne and popped the cork. He poured it into three glasses he'd brought with it, and they each raised a glass.

"To Haversham Castle and the three musketeers!" Freddie toasted them and they took the first sip of the champagne.

"I can't wait to get started," Winnie admitted. She wasn't even out of one job yet, and she already had another, and it was a way of holding on to the last memories of *Beauchamp Hall*. Her DVDs in the white elephant game the year before had changed her whole life. And the next chapter had just begun.

Chapter Fourteen

"W hat's up with you?" Edward asked her with a grin the next morning at work. "You look like the cat that swallowed the canary. New guy?"

"Better than that. New project. I met with the Havershams last night. I'm trying to help them compensate when the show wraps." It was only days away. They had just been notified that the shooting schedule for the final episodes had been extended to get all the new scenes in. All days off had already been canceled and they were doing night shoots too. They were working as fast as they could.

"And can you help them?" Edward was impressed by how resourceful she was. It was why she was such a good assistant too. She was full of energy and ideas.

"I think so. We have some promising avenues to pursue. They're fun to work with, and really nice people." And as she said it, she had another idea. "I just thought of something. They're going to start hosting weddings at the castle by the end of the year. What would you think about you and Grace getting married here? They're going to do period weddings, with costumes for those who want them, but obviously, you could wear whatever you want. Do you think Grace would consider it as a wedding location?" He looked pensive for a moment and then at Winnie with a slow smile.

"I love it. This show has meant so much to me. And the castle is exquisite. I think Grace would love it too, and so would her father. He knew the Havershams' father and grandfather. He's mentioned it to me several times. Let me ask her, and I'll let you know."

He called her that afternoon and after he did, he smiled at Winnie. "Grace loved the idea. She wants to get married at Haversham Castle. In costume!"

"Do you have your date yet?" She was so excited she could hardly stand it.

"The Saturday before Christmas, if that works for you."

"You're our first wedding customer, and we're going to keep it that way. I love that you'll be our first wedding, and you've been on the show." And it would be fantastic publicity for them for future weddings.

Winnie was so excited that she waited until she had a break in the late afternoon, and ran to the family entrance to the castle and rang the doorbell. Freddie opened it, he had just gotten back from a drive in his favorite Bugatti.

"Is Beatrice here?" Winnie asked shyly, as she walked into the hallway and was surprised to see Freddie. She wasn't as comfortable with him yet as she was with his sister. He was a little more daunting and flamboyant, and she didn't know him as well. Beatrice appeared a minute later. "Edward Smith is going to get married here the Saturday before Christmas," Winnie told both of them. "He'll be our first wedding and every magazine will want to cover it." She was ecstatic as she told them.

"Fantastic!" Beatrice was beaming. "How many guests?"

"I forgot to ask him. Do we have a limit?" The three of them looked at each other and decided they didn't in his case. "I'll ask him. And they want to do it in costume. I think he should probably keep his own, and I told him he'd be our first wedding." The three of them laughed and talked as they walked into the kitchen, and Beatrice said she'd call the caterer and wedding baker she'd already contacted to announce their new business, and they were excited about it. Beatrice had the list of everyone she had to contact. And when Winnie asked Edward, he said they wanted between two hundred and three hundred guests. She promised him a "family rate" for being their first client, and a celebrity on top of it. He said Grace's father would be delighted with the discount since he was as tight as a tick, and he had said repeatedly that he'd had some very good times at the castle in his youth. This would be one more, and great publicity for them.

Beatrice and Winnie had decided to approach Michael Waterman that evening after they finished shooting to discuss the costumes with him, now that they had their first wedding booked. He looked startled to see them both waiting outside the room he used as an office. He was always impressed by Lady Beatrice, particularly since she had a title, and thought her a lovely-looking woman. He would have loved to ask her out but had never dared.

"To what do I owe the honor, Lady Beatrice?" he asked her.

"We have something we want to ask you," Winnie said nervously. They outlined the project to him, and Beatrice added that they would be willing to pay for the costumes.

"How many do you have in mind?" Beatrice glanced at Winnie before she answered, and decided to shoot for the moon.

"As many bridal gowns as you'd be willing to sell or give us. And for the wedding guests, perhaps two hundred and fifty evening gowns and two hundred and fifty sets of tails." They both knew that they had at least that many for extras and possibly more, since some of the weddings on the show had been huge.

"Let me see what I can do," he said. He had a lot on his plate now that the show was going to close.

"We'd be grateful to buy as many as you can spare," Beatrice said politely.

"I can't give them to you until we end the show," he reminded her. But that wasn't far off now.

"That's fine." She and Winnie had already picked a room to outfit with racks for women's costumes, and a second one for men's. They had plenty of storage on the old servants' floor.

"Do you think he'll do it?" Beatrice asked Winnie as they hurried away after the meeting, giggling like young girls. She had just learned a few days before that Beatrice was only a year older than she was at thirty-nine, and Freddie was forty-one. "But he acts twelve," Beatrice said about her brother.

True to his word, Freddie approached Rupert the next day. He said he hadn't had time until then, and one of his horses had gone lame a few months before and he wanted to see the vet himself to discuss the horse's progress. But with Edward Smith's wedding date set, their project suddenly seemed very real. And he agreed with Beatrice, they needed a butler to add credibility and the right look and dignity to the house.

Rupert laughed at him when he asked him. "Are you serious? You expect me to act all la-di-da and be a butler?"

"Winnie Farmington, our new partner, said you're worried about what will happen after the show ends, and you'll have to sell the food truck," Freddie reminded him.

"True," Rupert said pensively.

"We're going to do murder weekends, and weddings, and better tours than we've been doing till now. Bea thinks we need a butler to impress the guests."

"She's probably right. My grandfather was in service at the castle. He was a footman. My father thought it was a step up to own his own business and be a chimney sweep. I never thought I'd be in service."

"You wouldn't be. We're talking about a Hollywood-style butler to impress people, open the door, and parade around in white tie and tails, not a real one to polish the silver." Rupert laughed at what he said. They had always liked each other as boys and gotten into mischief together, despite the social gap between them, which hadn't mattered to either of them, although it had to their parents.

"I'll be lucky to get a job once the show is gone," Rupert said ruefully. "You're on, mate. A Hollywood butler it is. When do I start?"

"As soon as you can sell the truck, or whenever you want to. The show will be leaving very soon. They're shooting the final episodes now at full speed. And it'll take them a couple of weeks to move out all the equipment."

"It sounds like fun. Give me until they've all left, so I can catch the last of the wave and feed the crew, and then I'll sell the truck. I should be free by the end of September."

"You've got it." They shook hands on their agreement, enjoying the same complicity they'd had as children.

Freddie texted Winnie and his sister on the way back to the castle. "Ladies, we will have a butler before September ends." His name was Rupert Tilton, and they were going to call him "Tilton," in proper form, when guests were present.

Winnie had been so busy working for Edward, meeting with Beatrice, coming up with new ideas, and making lists that she had hardly had time to see Nigel. And he was working day and night on the final episodes. He showed up late one night after a night shoot and looked exhausted. She could already feel the distance between them.

Things had been hectic on the set, and everyone was worried about their futures, calling agents and producers they knew, and unions for the crew.

"How's it going for you?" he asked her as he lay down on her couch. It was almost midnight and he had just finished work.

"It's been crazy," she said, smiling at him. "I'm starting a wedding business with the Havershams." It was the simplest way to explain it.

"What do they need you for? They've already got the castle." He looked surprised.

"It was my idea. Sometimes it takes an outsider to see the obvious." She mentioned her idea of having video screens in some of the rooms on the tour, with film clips of the show, as a kind of museum tour. She asked him who he thought she should speak to on the set for technical advice of what to buy. He told her who to see on the video team, and then he told her that he'd been busy too. They hadn't spent a night together all week. And at least he hadn't asked her about Freddie again, or Edward.

"I've had an offer to work on a show that shoots in Ireland, and another that spends a lot of time on location in Italy. The food would be better in Italy, but Ireland would be easier. I speak the language, and I lived there for a year. I'll probably do it, Winnie. I'll have to live in Dublin. Any chance you'd come with me?" He knew the answer before he asked her. It was obvious since she was starting the wedding business and all the rest. And they'd been drifting apart inexorably, and neither of them was trying to stop it. They knew they couldn't.

"I can't leave them stranded. We're just getting started," Winnie said quietly. But they both knew she wouldn't have gone with him anyway, their relationship had gone flat in the last month or two. His jealous fits had cooled her feelings for him, and she'd have nothing to do in Dublin if she went with him.

"I figured you wouldn't," he said sadly. "We're kind of done, aren't we?" She hesitated and then nodded. "I told you it was like that. It's like a family while the show lasts, and when it's over, everyone goes their separate ways. I'll be lucky if you remember my name a year from now." He looked sad as he said it and she touched his hand. His obsessive jealousy had ruined it for her, not the end of the show. But she didn't say it to him.

"Don't be silly. I've loved being with you, but I can't see how it would work for the long run. Sooner or later I'll go back to Michigan. Your life is here. I can't see myself in Dublin now. And I want to stick around Haversham for a while." He nodded again. He understood, or thought he did. He didn't ask to stay with her that night. They both knew it was over. Like a summer romance, autumn had come, sooner than expected. He kissed her one last time before he left. She watched him as he walked to his Jeep and he turned to look at her, as though to engrave her in his memory. She stood in the doorway and watched him as he drove away. They both knew their time had come and gone, and it was better that way.

Michael gave them an answer about the costumes the next day. Decisions had to be made quickly now. He called Lady Beatrice to tell her, and she was stunned when he told her that she could have the five hundred extra costumes she'd requested as a gift. They were going to sell her the wedding gowns for the equivalent of five hundred dollars each. There were five of them that had been prominently featured in the show. She was welcome to choose any of the other costumes for considerably less. He was doing it as a gesture to thank her for how gracious she and her brother had been for the past six years. He told her to make an appointment with the costumer, and they could collect them as soon as they wrapped the show. She was breathless when she called Winnie to tell her.

"We'll have five wedding gowns to offer brides!" Gowns well-known actresses had worn, which gave them even more cachet. Winnie told Edward about it that afternoon, in case Grace wanted to wear one of them, and he thought she might, since she loved the show too. But he had another gown in mind for her.

Beatrice and Winnie spent an evening setting up racks for the costumes in two of the old maids' rooms in the attic, and a separate room just for wedding gowns, and the accessories that the producers were giving them too.

"Should we set up a fitting room?" Winnie asked her.

"I think we should recarpet my mother's old dressing room. It's very elegant and has mirrors everywhere, and would make a perfect fitting room for our brides." The two women smiled at each other. Everything was falling into place, and had since the beginning. The fates had been smiling on them since Winnie's dream. "I don't know how to thank you. You turned a disaster into a miracle for us." Just as *Beauchamp Hall* had six years before by coming at just the right time.

"I'm loving it too," Winnie said. "I've never enjoyed anything so much in my life." It was the best job she'd ever had. And it had all happened because she'd had the courage to leave Michigan, come to see the making of the show she loved, and follow her dream. In spite of what had happened with Rob and Barb and her job, it had turned out to be the best year of her life, even though the show was ending. They had found a way to keep it alive, for the people who had been so devoted to it, and for themselves.

"I found a source for the *Beauchamp Hall* souvenir china, by the way," Beatrice told her. "The show has a licensing agreement on it, but we can buy it from them at a discounted rate."

"Is it very expensive?" Winnie looked concerned. She was going to commit some of her savings to their project. At least they would be saving a lot on costumes. She was prepared to put in some of what her mother had left her. And Marje had just rented her house in Beecher, which was additional income too. Every penny mattered, although it was not a very costly business to start. They had so much of what they needed on hand.

"It's not too bad," Beatrice said about the china, "and I think it will sell like crazy." Winnie agreed with her, which was why she had suggested it in their initial plan. Beatrice had hired a nice woman for the gift shop, Bridget Donahue, who was thrilled with the job, and a bright young girl, Lucy, as their assistant. She had done a year at university, was working as a maid at Mrs. Flannagan's B and B, wanted to better herself, and was willing to do whatever they needed. Lucy was starting in two weeks. They weren't opening the gift shop until December when they were fully up and running, so Bridget could start a week before to organize their inventory.

"The guy who handles the video equipment on the show is coming over tomorrow, by the way, to give us advice and tell us what we need," Winnie said, and Beatrice nodded as Freddie walked in. They had just come down from the attic and setting up the racks, and he'd been in the stables with his horses, which he was keeping now, hoping their business would be a success. He could always sell them later if he had to. He hoped not.

"What are you two tittering about?" he asked them. It was easy to see how well the two women got along. Beatrice was the closest friend Winnie had made in a long time. It was nice having a woman to talk to again. She had missed Barb.

"We were agreeing on how ridiculous you are," his sister teased him.

"We need another man around here," he complained. "Thank God Rupert will be here soon. I don't know what I was thinking, starting a business with two women. You're always ganging up on me."

"Sorry, Your Lordship." Beatrice grinned at him.

"You may call me Your Majesty," he said haughtily to his sister. "Where are we on the reality show?" he asked Winnie seriously.

"Edward is talking to someone he knows in London. He says they're all pretty rough, but it's a sure moneymaker. People like the scandalous stuff better, so we may have to come up with some sexy angle for them. Or maybe your titles will be enough," she said hopefully.

"Maybe we'll have to include your flock of girlfriends," Beatrice said seriously.

"Or your illegitimate children," he tossed back at her.

"I don't have any, just for your information," she told Winnie again.

"She's a virgin," he added, and Beatrice took a swat at him with the notepad that never left her hand.

"Seriously, though," Beatrice said pensively, "maybe they do expect us to have lovers on the show or a boyfriend or girlfriend. We're not a very interesting lot." Even Freddie hadn't had a girlfriend in months. There was no one local he was interested in.

"I don't have one at the moment," Freddie said practically, "but I can start auditioning if you want. All for the good of the cause, of course."

"What happened to the last one? The girl from Brazil?" Beatrice asked, surprised.

"She ran off with a race car driver and is living with him in Monte Carlo. We could tell the producers we're a ménage à trois. That might be interesting."

"Maybe they won't care about our sex lives," Beatrice said hopefully. "I haven't had a serious man in my life in years."

"It's your own damn fault," her brother reproached her. "The village has been teeming with actors and movie stars for six years, you could have made some effort to pick one up, or a few of them."

"They're all spoken for, or gay, or cheaters," Winnie corrected him. "To be honest, most of them would rather have you," she said, looking at Freddie. "The one I work for is terrific, but he's been with the same woman for thirteen years and he's faithful to her."

"How depressing for him. Fidelity is so overrated," Freddie said and both women laughed. "But thank God he's marrying her, since they're our first wedding. What about you?" he asked Winnie. "No boyfriend?" They were all three getting to know each other and curious about their lives.

"No, I dated a sound technician for a while when I got here, but it fizzled out, and now I don't have time. I've got two jobs and a business to start."

"You two should have been nuns," he scolded them both. "But I'm not much better these days. At forty-one, you've seen it all. I'm beginning to like my horses better."

"I might as well have been a nun," Beatrice complained, "locked up with you all my life. And don't tell me you're reformed. I don't believe you."

"You should go to London more often," he said seriously. "You'll never find a man hanging around here. Unless you want Rupert. He's perfectly nice."

"Our butler?" she said, putting on airs. "Don't be ridiculous!" But Rupert had never appealed to her, and wouldn't. She was sophisticated despite her country life.

The three of them got along well and were becoming friends. Building something together was a strong bond. Beatrice said privately to Winnie that her brother hadn't been this busy in years, or as happy. He didn't do well when he was idle and always got into mischief that didn't serve him well. "Women, mostly," she explained to Winnie, while they waited for a carpet layer to measure the dressing room one night after work. They had decided to do the carpet in pale pink and have the room repainted so it looked fresh. The room hadn't been used in years, since Beatrice still slept in her childhood bedroom, which was huge. Freddie had his own, with a library and sitting room attached, and a dressing room that had been their father's, paneled in mahogany, at the opposite end of the castle. Winnie loved discovering more and more about the house, and seeing things she hadn't been able to see on the tour, since their living quarters weren't on it.

It struck her as odd that neither of them had ever married. Beatrice told her in confidence one day, when they were going through the guest room to see what, if anything, they needed for mystery weekenders or bridal party guests, that her brother had been very much in love with a French girl ten years before. She had run off with someone else and broken his heart, and he had become a determined womanizer after that, and seemed intent on staying that way.

"I don't think he'll ever marry at this point, he enjoys variety too much, and they all bore him after a while. And I suppose by now I've missed that boat too. When I go to parties in London, all the sweet young things are twenty-two, and thirty-nine looks quite elderly in comparison. One can't really compete with that." She was matter-of-fact about it and didn't seem to care. "The only unfortunate thing is that the bloodline, the name, and the title will die with us. We don't have any cousins. And if Freddie doesn't have children, then it's all over. My father would have been disappointed by that. So we're the last Havershams." That mattered to her more than any regret about not having married or having children herself, but it was important to them. "Maybe Freddie will marry when he's eighty and produce an heir," she said with a grin.

"Who produced an heir?" Freddie asked, as he walked through the room.

"No one. I was saying to Winnie that you should one day."

"I'd rather wait till I'm ninety, I don't want to miss all the fun before that. Are the brides fair game while their husbands are getting blind drunk on their wedding night?"

"I forbid you to touch any of the brides, you'll put us out of business. You can have all the bridesmaids you want, you have my permission for that," his sister told him.

"Excellent. Don't accept any brides with ugly bridesmaids. I'll vet them for you, with full approval rights." He smiled at Winnie as he said it.

"And why aren't you married? Beatrice is much too outspoken for any man to put up with her, and I can't seem to stay with any woman for more than three months, six at best. But you seem quite normal and easy to get along with. I would have thought someone would have snatched you up years ago." It was a backhanded compliment for Winnie and she smiled, and he seemed to expect an answer.

"I had a bad boyfriend for eleven years. He slept with my best friend, so that was that."

"How rude," he said disdainfully, "and not very imaginative of him. So tiresome. You're well rid of him."

"I think so." She smiled back at him. She could guess the kind of women he went out with, very young and very beautiful, debutantes or maybe models. "I came here when I left him, so it worked out very well for me."

"And for us. You've turned out to be our fairy godmother," he said, and went off to do something in the wine cellar. They were going to have to stock more wine for the weddings, especially Edward's, who wanted Cristal. Freddie was in charge of that.

They had another good surprise when the video technician from the set came to look at the rooms where they wanted to set up the screens with film clips from the show. They wanted to install three large screens, with scenes shot in the rooms they were placed in. He measured the spaces Winnie and Beatrice indicated, and made note, and then called them back two hours later to tell them that the production company had five screens they would be getting rid of when they left. He'd been told he could give them away, and offered them to the Havershams for free and said he would set them up for them in his spare time before they left. The show was like a retreating army, giving out bounty to the village, but it was going to save them money to have the screens. He set them up just exactly the way they wanted them, and Winnie knew just which episodes she wanted to play in each room while people took the tour. She had watched the DVDs dozens of times. The producers said they had no problem with it.

Rupert came to check out what they'd been doing right after the screens were installed, and he was impressed. It was beginning to look very professional and Beatrice and Winnie had freshened things up and moved some things around, but not too much. Freddie had selected a set of tails for Rupert, and had them dry cleaned, and Rupert looked the part of a butler once he was dressed. He put on a stern face and they all laughed. He was perfect in the role, and very convincing.

"I should have had this for the food truck. I could have doubled the prices," he said and they all teased him and played around with him.

The four of them had a light dinner one night in the kitchen, when Winnie finished work, and on her way home, she stopped in to see Mrs. Flannagan in her cottage. She told her what they were doing at the castle.

"I'm so pleased you're staying here with us." She'd been happy to hear it. "It's such a shame they've decided not to go on with the show," she said sadly. "I'll miss it." But their weddings and mystery weekends were going to generate business for her too.

"So will I," Winnie agreed with her. "I'll be watching the DVDs for years." She still watched it at night now that she was alone. Nigel had stopped coming over after they broke up. She had glimpsed him on the set, but they hadn't spoken. She knew he would be moving on shortly, and going to Ireland. And her DVDs of the show populated her nights alone. She didn't really miss him.

She promised Mrs. Flannagan she'd come to dinner soon when she wasn't so busy. And despite everything they had to do at the castle, she was trying to focus on the final moments of the show and be helpful to Edward. They were all feeling emotional about the end of *Beauchamp Hall,* and there were frequent tears on the set. It seemed to heighten everyone's performances, and they wanted to make the last episodes as memorable as they could.

"How's it going at the castle?" Edward asked her one afternoon as he waited for the production assistant to call him for his shot. He was about to get engaged to the woman he had loved all his life on the show. His cold, nasty wife had died and he was going to marry his true love, the mother of his other, clandestine children. His mistress could come out of the shadows now. Matthew had done a masterful job with several very emotional scenes to wrap up Edward's story on the show. And there wasn't a dry eye on the set during Edward's performance with the girl who played his mistress and future wife.

Matthew had outdone himself in his rewritten scripts for the end of the show. Many of them were very poignant, and even brought tears to the crew's eyes as they watched. And the actors were giving it their all.

"We're getting ready for your wedding," Winnie told Edward with a smile. "Your real one."

"We're both excited to be doing it at Haversham. I think what you're planning to do up there sounds wonderful. I guess your days as an assistant are over."

"For now. You never know what will happen. They won't need me around forever. I think the whole operation will run itself eventually, they won't need a creative director. Just in the beginning."

"Maybe you'll marry the marquess," Edward said, and she laughed at the suggestion. She knew Freddie better than that now, and had heard the stories from his sister, about all the mischief he got into, and the women in his life.

"Not likely. He has a whole lineup of women."

"You're a very special woman," Edward said. "I hope you know that, Winnie. You're a powerful positive force to have around. I've been lucky to have you. Now they are the lucky ones." She was touched by what he said, and cried when she watched him propose to his true love on the show. It was a perfect ending for their characters. And they were going to show his wedding in the last episode, which was a secret, but he had told her. He had an eye on the wedding dress for Grace. It was spectacular, an antique the costumer had bought for a fortune at a Sotheby's auction and well worth it, with a thirty-foot-long antique lace veil and train. It had been made for a princess.

Winnie was making room for more racks in one of the old maids' rooms on a Sunday, when Freddie came to find her upstairs.

"Beatrice says she's busy and won't come riding with me. Do you want to take a break and come with me? Do you ride, by the way?" She was startled by the invitation, but he looked restless and bored.

"I haven't in years. I used to ride on a friend's farm when I was a kid. I love horses."

"I'll give you an easy horse, if you want to join me." She'd never thought of it before, she'd been too busy working, but it seemed like a good excuse to get some air. The weather had been unusually hot and muggy. And she was caught up on her work, for Edward and for them.

"Okay." She was wearing jeans and lace-up shoes with low heels that she could ride in.

"Do you ride English saddle?" She nodded, and didn't tell him she liked to ride bareback too. A few minutes later, she followed him out to the stables, and he had the stable boy saddle up a mare for her, who looked as tame as he had promised. She heard him ask the stable boy about a horse called Black Magic. And then he mounted the white stallion she'd seen him ride before, an elegant Thoroughbred with a lot of spirit. She stepped up on the block and got into the saddle, and followed him on the mare at a slow trot. It was a beautiful early fall day, and they headed toward the nearby hills, on a path on their land. It was a wonderful change of pace from the show and their work in the house.

"I come out here to get sane again." He looked calmer than she'd ever seen him, and at peace once he was riding. "I get cabin fever in the house."

She laughed at what he said. "You would hate my cottage, it's about the size of your boot room."

"I know, we're spoiled," he said, faintly embarrassed. "What really brought you out here, Winnie?" He was curious about her. She had a strong creative streak, and a practical side. It was an interesting combination. There was no pretense or artifice about her, which he found pleasant to be around and refreshing. He knew so many arrogant, ambitious women who always wanted something or had an angle and thought they were clever, but were never as clever as they believed.

"An old dream," she answered him honestly. "I always wanted to get out of my hometown. It was just as small, but not as charming as this. In fact, it's not charming at all. Most people there settle for jobs they hate, men they don't really love, or not enough, and a life I never wanted. I was hoping for a job in publishing in New York, as an editor. My mother got sick, I dropped out of college to take care of her, and it never happened. I did what everyone else did, got stuck in a job I hated with a bad boss, and a boyfriend I didn't want to marry, who turned out to be a bigger jerk than I'd thought. Then one day, it all fell apart. The job, the man, my best friend. I felt sorry for myself for a while, and then on the spur of the moment, I came here to watch them film the show. I learned a lot from it, about good people and bad people, and having the courage to go after what you want. That's what they do on that show." Matthew wrote the plot and characters so well, which was why people loved it.

"You're lucky you knew what you wanted. I never did. We're supposed to protect our land, our history, and our homes, and follow a lot of traditions that are meaningless now. The old ways don't work anymore, but I never found new ones that work any better. I hate fakery and dishonesty and there's a lot of it in the way we live. Beatrice isn't good at it either, which is why she seems to be winding up alone. We're both allergic to all the nonsense that goes with who we are. She's too honest, and I just run away all the time. Except when I'm here. I come out riding, and it all makes sense again. I love it here. This land and our home mean everything to me. Thank you for helping us to keep it. It probably seems foolish to you, to hang on to an old house like this, but all of our history, our values, the traditions that matter to us are here."

"I can feel it when I'm in the house. It's what I love about the show. Matthew captured that in the scripts. I fell in love with *Beauchamp Hall* and everything it stood for."

"Matthew isn't a particularly warm person," Freddie commented. "But he's a wonderful writer, with an amazing instinct for people," he added, with surprising insight. And she realized as she listened to him that there was more to Freddie than she'd thought. He hid behind the jokes and the banter, but he was just as thoughtful, deep, and kind as his sister, and observant. He just didn't like to show it, although he just had to her.

They rode on in silence, and got to the top of the hill where they could look out over the land, most of which was still his. "If we have to sell something one day, I'll sell some of the land. I would hate to give up the house."

"I hope you never have to," she said sincerely. "What we're planning to do now should shore things up for you, hopefully for a long time. You could make some real money from it." Some very big money in fact, and the whole franchise was theirs, other than what they'd offered Winnie. But no one would be telling them what to do.

"It's a bit of prostitution," he admitted ruefully, "especially the reality show, but if it works, so be it. It's worth it." They rode back down the hill then, and took another path toward the stables, past the stream, and under the cover of ancient trees in fields of wildflowers. She could see why he loved it. "Will you go back to Michigan eventually?" He was curious about it. She seemed so at home here in England, and reluctant to go back where she came from.

"Probably. I don't really want to. I'm loving it here, especially now that I'm involved in our project, it's like a continuation of the love I have for the show, only in real life. But I have a sister and two nephews in Michigan. They're my only family and I suppose one day I should go back." He nodded, and she added, "I have no valid reason not to."

"Maybe what we're all doing together will be that reason. It's ample justification to stay here. We need you," he said simply. "You made it all happen, and saved us, just like the show did. But your concept may last longer."

They rode past a small elegant house on the property then, with gardens around it, where his grandmother had lived, and Freddie pointed it out to her. "That belongs to my sister, and the land around it. I gave it to her when I inherited the rest. She owns some of the tenant farms as well. It seemed only fair. She'd rather live in the castle now with me. But she'll have the dower house, whenever she wants it. No one can take that away from her." Winnie nodded. It touched him that the castle meant so much to Winnie, the land, and the village and all it stood for. It was as though she had been drawn to exactly where she was meant to be, and she felt it too.

"It's funny how you find your right place accidentally," Winnie commented as they rode. "I thought New York would be it for me. But it turns out to be here." He smiled at her.

"It's damn lucky you found us. Lucky for us, that is."

He helped her dismount when they got back to the stables, and she thanked him for the unexpected treat of riding with him. She liked getting a deeper look into who he was. She was getting to know Beatrice and felt a bond with her, but Freddie was more elusive and harder to get to know. He joked and played all the time, and stayed hidden.

She was thinking about it as the stable boy led a spectacular-looking black stallion out of the stables and took him toward the ring where Freddie said he and his sister had been taught to ride as children. The horse looked skittish and took off at a gallop around the ring once he was in it, and then switched directions as Freddie watched him intently.

"He got spooked a few months ago," he told her. "He slipped when I had him out riding and he fell near the river. His leg has healed but no one's been able to ride him since. It was my fault. The bank was too steep, and slippery from heavy rains. It lamed him for a bit, nothing serious and he's fine now, but he still won't let anyone ride him. He's a fabulous horse but he's not himself now." They were standing at the railing watching him, as he stopped running and pawed the ground. Without hesitating Winnie hopped the fence as Freddie tried to grab her, but she was already in.

"What are you doing, you mad girl? Come out immediately." He didn't want her to get hurt, and Black Magic was watching her from the center of the ring, with a look of panic. Winnie had already made eye contact with him as she ignored Freddie and walked slowly and confidently toward the black stallion. "Winnie, come back here!" Freddie said and headed toward the gate, but he didn't want to frighten the horse any more than it already was.

Winnie looked totally at ease as she walked toward him, speaking softly, as Black Magic continued to watch her and Freddie was mesmerized by what he was seeing. She walked right up to the horse, patted his neck, and then gently touched his muzzle, still talking to him. You could see the tension go out of him, as he leaned toward her and nuzzled her, and then rested his head on her shoulder. They walked around the ring together for a few minutes, the horse totally relaxed as he followed her. Freddie watched with fascination.

She stayed with Black Magic for ten minutes, still talking to him, and then she patted him again and left the ring. Freddie was in awe of what she'd just done.

"Do you realize I've spent hours with him since we fell and couldn't get near him? Who are you, Winnie from Michigan? You have an incredible gift with horses." Freddie was floored by her gentleness and her courage.

"I just like horses, and they know it."

"You're some sort of magician." They walked back to the castle then in silence. Freddie was too stunned to say more about it, until he saw his sister, waiting with tea for them, and he described the scene to her, as Winnie looked casual about it.

"He was just scared, that's all," she said gently.

"He's been half mad for two months, no one's been able to ride him or get near him until you today."

"We had a nice time riding before that and saw your house," Winnie told her as Beatrice handed her a cup of tea. She had prepared one of her wonderful tea trays, with elegant little sandwiches and scones with clotted cream and jam.

"I'm saving the dower house for my old age, or for when Freddie marries some intolerable girl who hates me, and has ten children with her. Until then, I'm happy here," Beatrice said, smiling.

Freddie still wanted to talk about Winnie's extraordinary handling of the black stallion. "You're a woman of hidden talents," he said with open admiration as Winnie smiled at him. She knew she had won him as a friend that afternoon, for her innate ability with horses. He couldn't wait to go riding with her again.

Winnie and Beatrice started talking about the wedding dresses they were acquiring, and the evening gowns Winnie still wanted to buy. Freddie left them then, in awe of Winnie's performance with Black Magic. One thing was for sure, she was indeed a woman who loved horses. He was beginning to think there was nothing she couldn't do. And he was suddenly absolutely certain that their joint venture was going to be a stunning success. She was a totally amazing woman.

Chapter Fifteen

When the reality show producers Edward had recommended came to talk to the Havershams and Winnie, their suggestions for the format of the show made all three of them shudder at first. But Beatrice was very direct with them, and told them it wouldn't fly. She told them what their boundaries were, what they were willing to show and what they weren't, and what their goals were in doing the show, as publicity for the castle. It was the first show of its kind. No titled aristocrats had opened their homes to reality TV. The weddings and mystery weekends had the potential to make it a fun show for the viewers. Both sides had something to gain, and Beatrice handled the meeting well and took control of it while Winnie and Freddie watched. She had been equally good with contacting magazines and getting them PR. She was fearless about getting what she wanted, and a great spokesperson for their project.

The reality producers agreed to modify their plan and send them an outline more in keeping with what Beatrice said. Their main producer, Paul Evans, was deeply impressed by her. And true to their word, they sent an outline for the show that respected most of Beatrice's parameters, though not all. They showed it to an attorney, and after two more attempts at negotiation and compromise, all three of them were somewhat anxious but satisfied with the results. Beatrice had done a good job defending their interests. They were all discovering their hidden talents and covering new ground.

The producer of the show came to Haversham for a final meeting and called Beatrice "Your Ladyship" every time he addressed her, and she didn't tell him not to. Freddie teased her about it after they left, after their final meeting.

"You are such a bitch, Bea, you had the poor guy terrified. He acted like he thought you'd send him to the Tower of London."

"Good. It will keep him in line." They had agreed to an introductory show, with a tour of the castle, with all three of them present. They liked that Winnie was American, to balance the Havershams' titles. And the second show would take place at Edward's wedding. Winnie had asked his permission and he thought it was fine. It would add spice to the wedding, and it was good publicity for him too. It was a factor he had to consider as an actor, to be kept visible at all times, and Grace understood it, although her father undoubtedly wouldn't.

There was a big article in the *Mirror,* in the 3 A.M. column, about Edward's engagement, and a photograph of Haversham Castle, where the wedding would be held. Beatrice got them to say that the castle could be rented for weddings by select guests. And each bridal couple was carefully chosen, to make it seem even more exclusive.

They had five inquiries for weddings the day after the article appeared.

"Yes!" Beatrice shouted when she hung up after the fifth one. "We just got our second booking, and we might get two more. This is so wonderful! It's working!" She hugged Winnie, and Freddie looked delighted too.

He and Winnie had taken to riding together whenever she could spare an hour, although she didn't have much free time now. He had let her ride Black Magic, who was now back to his old self.

They were working double time on the set, with night shoots that went very late and all weekends. The show was drawing toward its dramatic close. The final episode would be two hours. Everyone was working hard.

Winnie was on the set most of the time now and could only come to Haversham at night. They had three weddings booked by then, including Edward's, two of them in January, Edward's right before Christmas. A mystery night for a party of twenty was booked on New Year's Eve. It would be their first. The reality show was filming all four events, and the introductory show that would be more about the Havershams and Winnie than the guests. After that, the guests would be heavily featured.

Marje was fully aware of what they were doing now, and kept telling Winnie how proud of her she was. She was the creative director of Haversham Castle, and the co-producer of a reality show.

"We want to come over and visit," Marje had said.

"Wait till we're up and running and have all the kinks ironed out, then I'd love it." Winnie knew they were going to be insanely busy from the time the show wrapped for *Beauchamp Hall,* and for three months after, through January. They were nervous about it, but exhilarated too. This was a new world for all of them. Rupert had taken to strutting around the house in his white tie and tails, practicing his role, and got quite good at it. He was a very convincing butler and very proud.

The final days on the set were unbearably stressful, bittersweet, and agonizingly nostalgic, as people who had appeared in earlier seasons and episodes came back for final appearances. And each character and plot twist on the show was brought to its final denouement to tie it all together in the final two hours.

Predictably, the last day was the hardest. Beatrice and Freddie had come to watch discreetly from the sidelines, but with less sadness now that they had something to look forward to. Winnie did too, but it was painful for her, watching the last scenes and knowing that there would be no more after this. *Beauchamp Hall* would be syndicated and shown for years, but there would be no new episodes. It made Winnie's heart ache to think about it.

She and Nigel had a few minutes to talk on the set, and he said he was leaving for Ireland in a few days.

The final scenes were achingly beautiful. Matthew had outdone himself with the script and so had the costumer. The costumes in every scene were remarkable. And Edward's wedding to his true love was the last segment they shot, with a wedding gown that took everyone's breath away, and was now earmarked for Grace to wear at their wedding. Michael had given it to them as a gift.

The very last shot was of Edward and his bride, and there were tears in their eyes as they were declared man and wife and kissed, as everyone on the set was crying openly, and so was Matthew. Winnie wondered if he regretted now having the show end here, but if so, it was too late. The die had been cast.

When the director shouted "Cut! That's a wrap!" for the last time, there were sobs all over the set. People were hugging and crying, congratulating each other, and wishing each other luck. A family was being disbanded, and friends would never meet again, except by chance one day on another soundstage.

Edward hugged Winnie after he kissed his costar, and thanked her for the time she'd spent with him, and how helpful she'd been. But they knew they would meet again in December at his wedding. He had already signed to be the star of a new show and was excited about it. He had two weeks off and then he was starting again. He was to have top billing and be the main character on his new show. *Beauchamp Hall* had helped him get there.

Freddie and Beatrice came over to hug Winnie as the chaos started to die down. And almost as soon as people stopped hugging and kissing, the crew started tearing down the sets and packing up the equipment. It would be days before it would all be dismantled and removed.

There were already moving vans outside and in the square to take costumes and props and equipment to studios and storage to London. A whole world was being dismantled, one that would never come again. *Beauchamp Hall* would only be a memory now in the hearts and minds of the millions of fans who had loved it, Winnie among them. It had changed her life forever and that of so many others. Its subliminal message had revived her dreams. She owed a lot to Matthew, whether he knew it or not.

When the cameras stopped rolling, the stars packed and left quickly. By that night, only the crew remained, and Winnie had dinner with Freddie and Beatrice in the castle kitchen reserved for their use. The main kitchen had been part of the show, and would be on the tour now, with one of the screens they'd been gifted with set up there, with clips of the lovable cook and kitchen staff from the show. The actress who played the cook had decided to retire. In an interview, she said that nothing could match *Beauchamp* for her.

"I feel like I left home forever today," Winnie said sadly, as Freddie poured them each a glass of wine. "It's so sad knowing it's over."

"But it isn't over," he reminded her. "Now you're part of the real story, and the family, and its future, not the fake one. You're part of Haversham now." Not *Beauchamp Hall,* which had faded into the mists that night. By morning the sets would be gone, the costumes and hats and wigs would have vanished, the familiar faces would disappear as if they had never existed. She was woven into the future of Haversham now, but the past was a tender memory for her, and had brought her here in the first place. *Beauchamp Hall* was an important piece of the Havershams' history too now, a turning point for them, and had led them to the next chapter with Winnie. It was all intertwined, like the roots of a tree that had been planted, and had grown to maturity on the show.

"You can't get maudlin now," Freddie told her. "We have too much to do." They had to focus fully on Edward's wedding, and their first night of the reality show before that. Beatrice was trying to decide if she wanted to wear one of the costumes they'd been given, or a dress of her own, and said she had nothing decent and hadn't shopped in ages, nor had Winnie. And Freddie couldn't decide whether to wear a suit or jeans.

They sat and talked late into the night, and drank a lot of wine. Freddie walked Winnie back to her cottage afterwards. He would have driven her, but knew he'd had too much wine. They saw the crews working straight through the night breaking down equipment and packing up.

When they got to her cottage, he looked surprised. "It looks like a dollhouse, but it suits you. I didn't realize it would be so small." He smiled at her. He'd never seen her cottage before. He had talked to Beatrice about offering Winnie the dower house to live in since it was empty, but she thought Winnie might not want to live on the property so close to them. She suggested that Winnie might want to have some distance and independence, but Freddie didn't see why. And he hadn't gotten around to asking her about it yet. He thought it would be convenient to have her even closer than she was now. They would have so much work to do together. "I think you need a bigger house," he said cryptically.

"No, I don't. This is fine. Do you want to come in for a nightcap?" she asked. It had been a special day. One chapter was ending, and another one starting.

"If I do, you'll either have to let me sleep on your couch, or call a cab to get me home and there are none at this hour." It was two in the morning.

The reality show technicians were coming the next day to decide on the path the house tour would take on the first show. They wanted the contrast between the private quarters and the more public ones.

Freddie and Beatrice had agreed to show certain rooms, but not all. It was still in negotiation.

Freddie decided that he wanted to see the inside of Winnie's house and would have a glass of water. He walked in and she handed it to him, as he looked around. It was comfortable and cozy. He peeked around the ground floor and didn't ask to see her bedroom upstairs, although he was curious about it, and sat down on the couch with her.

"I like it," he admitted, "it's like a pair of comfortable old slippers that are nice to come home to." She nodded, it was how she felt about it too.

"My sister and I have been talking about selling my mother's house, where I live in Michigan. If I do, I might buy something here, maybe this cottage or something a little bigger."

"I have an idea about that. We can talk about it tomorrow. I like the idea of your being closer to us. You belong at Haversham now." She was startled by his saying it, and she didn't see why.

"I'm only a short walk away."

"I'd feel better if you were under our wing. If you ever need anything, we'd be right there." He felt suddenly protective of her, and she felt as though she had acquired a brother. He had his own wing at the castle, at the opposite end from his sister, so they both had privacy, though neither of them took advantage of it. Whatever dalliances he had, he had in London when he went there, and stayed in his pied-à-terre. When Beatrice went to London, she stayed with friends, and preferred it that way.

He swayed slightly when he stood up, but other than that, he seemed sober. He hugged her when he said good night, and told her he'd see her in the morning.

After he left, he had a mad impulse to turn around and go back to the tiny cottage and spend the night with her. He just wanted to be close to her, but he was sure they'd both regret it in the morning, so he didn't, and walked back to the castle alone.

The trucks were still there in the morning when Winnie walked past, and let herself into the castle kitchen. It was her first day of not going to the set and it felt strange. Beatrice was drinking a cup of coffee and looked up at Winnie with a rueful smile.

"Was I drunk last night or do I have a brain tumor?"

"I think we drank a lot." Freddie had brought out some very good red wine to mark a special night and the end of the show.

He came down half an hour later and looked fresh and rested and in good spirits. He had slept off the wine more successfully than his sister.

Two hours later the reality show crew showed up with Paul Evans, the producer, who looked respectable and serious, and was still nervous around Beatrice. Edward had told Winnie that he was the most successful reality show producer in the business, and everything he touched turned to gold. She hoped it would be true in this case.

He walked the suggested route with Beatrice, and they debated which rooms to use, and agreed on all of it. Not knowing what else to do, she invited him to stay for lunch, and he sent his crew to a restaurant in the village. During lunch, Winnie was surprised to learn that he had gone to Oxford and to Eton, like Freddie, but he was four or five years older. Freddie said he actually remembered him, although he looked different then, and now he had a beard.

"How did you get into doing reality shows?" Freddie asked him.

"Money," he said simply and they all laughed. "I started doing reality with rock stars, which was pretty grim, and moved on to movie stars, which was a little more civilized, but just a little. And then real people, which is actually very interesting. The others are so predictable, and you know what it's going to be about, sex, drugs, and rock and roll, which gets old very quickly. The real people always surprise you, and the viewers like them better. They can identify with them. You're going to be an intriguing case, because you're real and you're not real, like the royals. People love them and want to reach out and touch them, but they know they're different. Your titles and this house make you special. And Winnie is a commoner and American, which they'll love, because she's like them, but she's with you, which makes them feel they could be too. Then you'll have movie stars and the rich and famous in for weddings, and mystery weekends. This show has every ingredient it needs to be a smash hit. Aristocrats, real people, stars, a castle, a young American woman. It's pure gold." He smiled as he said it.

"Thank you for the 'young,'" Winnie said, laughing.

"You look even younger than you are," Paul said kindly, then turned to Freddie. "It's too bad there's no marchioness in the mix, but that also makes you an eligible bachelor. Every woman in England is going to want to show up here and meet you, and be your fairy princess."

"Now there's a frightening thought," Freddie said, looking worried.

Paul left shortly after lunch to join his crew and drive back to London, and the three of them went to pick up the costumes waiting for them on racks at the set. They rolled them around to the back of the castle, and spent the rest of the afternoon carrying the clothes upstairs. It was exhausting, since many of them were heavy. Freddie called Rupert to come and help them. He came over quickly, and carried armloads of them to the rooms Beatrice and Winnie indicated and had set up for them. There were day clothes, evening gowns, morning coats for the men, and all the suits of tails they needed for Edward's wedding. They had a separate room set aside, with sheets on the floor for the five wedding gowns they'd purchased for very little money. There were veils and headpieces to go with them, and every dress had a long train, which would look magnificent going down the stairs.

Beatrice had developed a checklist for Edward's wedding, and they already had several items ticked off. And they had three months to complete the rest.

After they put all the costumes on racks upstairs, Winnie was about to leave at six o'clock when Freddie stopped her and asked her to take a walk with him so he could show her something. She had no idea what he had in mind but assumed it was for the tour for the reality show. He led her down a path she hadn't noticed before. There was a narrow gate and a garden, and then she saw the small elegant stone house with dark-green painted shutters. He had told her when they were riding that it had been his grandmother's. She hadn't paid much attention to it, other than that she knew it belonged to Beatrice now.

He took a key out of his pocket and walked to the front door. "Traditionally, when the marquess died, and his son inherited the title and took over the castle, his widowed mother would move to a smaller house on the property, and live out her days there. The tradition is a bit sad and very British. In France, they live the rest of their lives in their chateaux, but here we put the widow in a small house, and her daughter-in-law takes over the castle. But some dower houses are very pretty. I rather like ours," he said as he led her inside to gracious rooms of livable proportions that managed to be both elegant and not too daunting. "It's a bigger version of your cottage, by quite a bit." He smiled at her.

"It's a lot bigger." She looked around, not sure why he had shown it to her except for its historical value. She wasn't sure it would be interesting for the tour.

"No one lives here now. I thought you might like to try it, Winnie. It would be nice to have you close by."

"Have me move here?" She looked shocked for a moment. "Wouldn't Beatrice mind?"

"I asked her, she likes the idea too. You're part of our family now. You've protected our home, so now we want to protect you."

"But I'm safe where I am." She liked her cottage, although the dower house was truly lovely and very elegant.

"I'm sure you are, but you'd be more comfortable here. And you could come and go as you want at the castle. We have my grandmother's furniture in storage in one of the barns. Will you let me set this up the way you want it?" He looked gentle as he said it, and he put an arm around her, as she sank against him. It was a comfortable place to be, like the house, under his wing.

"Are you sure?" She felt like an intruder or an impostor, but she didn't want to hurt his feelings and refuse. She could see that it meant a lot to him, and was a gesture of his thanks for everything she was doing, and had done for them.

"Yes, I'm sure," he said, smiling at her. "I'll have it up and running for you in a few days. I had it cleaned up for you last week. And I want to get a few things painted." She had never known him to be so organized and serious since she'd met him. It wasn't like him. "I think my grandmother would like knowing you're here. You've become the family savior."

"With a reality show? I doubt she'd be happy about that."

"True," he said with a laugh, "but these are modern times. We all have to adjust." And he liked the producer a great deal more since he'd learned he'd gone to Eton. He knew it was small-minded of him, but he found it comforting nonetheless. Surely he wouldn't betray or embarrass one of his own. He hoped he was right about Paul Evans.

"So do we have an agreement, and you have a new home?" She nodded, overwhelmed. He looked happy as they left the house together.

"I don't know how to thank you," she said softly.

"Oh, we'll figure out something. Tithing maybe, or you can give me your firstborn when you have a child," he teased her, "or call me 'Your Grace,' so people think I'm a duke. Or 'Your Majesty.'"

They were laughing as they walked back to her cottage, and she saw that there were only a few trucks left. The last of *Beauchamp Hall* had almost disappeared. But they still had the best part, with the castle.

He walked into her cottage again as he had the night before and it looked familiar to him now. "Well, it won't take you long to pack up. I'll tell Beatrice you've agreed, she'll be pleased." He seemed very satisfied with the arrangement.

At the end of the week, she moved into the dower house and found an enormous bouquet of white roses from the garden in a vase in the living room, with a note: *Welcome home. Love, Freddie and Beatrice.* She texted photographs of the house inside and out to Marje, who sat in her kitchen looking at them, frowning, and handed her phone to Erik. "She'll never come home now," she said unhappily, and he nodded.

"No, maybe not," he agreed when he saw her new home. It was impossible to compete with that.

Chapter Sixteen

The first episode of the reality show was a two-hour special, and took a week to film. They did it in the first week of December. Freddie showed off the stables, with a great many explanations about the horses. Then he showed his car collection, which included the Bugattis. There was no mention of what they were worth, which was one of Beatrice's conditions and they stuck to it. So far, Paul had kept all his agreements with them.

They began the tour of the house then, with Beatrice in the lead. They walked the path of the rooms that had been most used by *Beauchamp Hall,* and then explored the family rooms, and some of the most stately rooms of the castle, including the ballroom. Freddie and Winnie joined her eventually, and they talked about the history of the house, who had stayed there and when, all the way back to Queen Victoria, who they explained had been a frequent visitor and a cousin of the Havershams, which Winnie hadn't known.

They showed some film clips of *Beauchamp Hall,* and the important actors who'd been in it, Winnie handled that part of the inter-view. It saddened her for a moment that it was only history now and no longer the present. Then she told them of their plans for Haver-sham Castle, and Edward Smith's wedding, although they didn't give the date to protect his privacy, and so they wouldn't be besieged by paparazzi. They described the mystery weekends they were planning, and how they would work, showed off the costumes, and described what a weekend would include. They also interviewed Winnie about her life in Michigan.

Paul stayed with them for the week. They set him up in a guest room and he ate dinner with them every night. He was good com-pany and had a great sense of humor, and seemed fascinated by Beatrice, and continued to call her "Your Ladyship" for the entire week, even after she'd asked him not to.

Rupert played his role perfectly, looming throughout as the digni-fied butler. He thoroughly enjoyed it.

Paul invited them all out to dinner at a pub the night before he left. He walked ahead with Beatrice on the way back, and Winnie tucked her arm into Freddie's and pulled him back and whispered to him.

"I think he likes her."

"So do I." It amused him.

"Do you think she likes him?"

"You can never tell with my sister. She can be a terrible snob, or she can like people, and men, who have absolutely nothing in com-mon with her."

"Like me," Winnie added.

"I wasn't thinking of you. You two get along like two peas in a pod.

I was thinking of men. I can never figure out who's going to strike her fancy. But he's smart, has a good job, and seems to be crazy about her, although if he calls her 'Your Ladyship' one more time she may slap him." They both laughed at that, and then Freddie walked her to the dower house so she didn't trip in the dark. He usually took her home at night to make sure she got in safely. She had given up her cottage by then.

When the show aired, it was a mind-boggling success, with fantastic ratings, and they had over a hundred inquiries about weddings and mystery weekends, and sixteen firm bookings, with deposits in the mail. And their rates weren't cheap.

"We did it! We did it!" Beatrice said when they got the first check, and she waved it in their faces at breakfast. "Take a look at *that*!" she said to her brother and Winnie. "And that's all thanks to Winnie's dream!"

"Thank God you listened to her," he said seriously.

"I thought she was mad for a minute," Beatrice confessed, and they laughed.

Edward's wedding was two weeks away by then, and Beatrice wanted every detail to be perfect. She went over it again and again with Winnie to double-check everything and make sure they hadn't missed a single detail.

The bridal party showed up on schedule on Friday morning. British *Vogue* and assorted members of the press were staying at nearby B and Bs and the village's best hotel. Grace had a maid of honor and two bridesmaids. At his insistence, Beatrice gave Grace's father the room he had occupied at the castle sixty years before, and Rupert helped him up and down the stairs so he didn't fall. Winnie had given up the dower house to Edward so he would be comfortable, and wouldn't see Grace on the morning of the wedding. His family was in Australia, and couldn't come, so the wedding party wasn't large. A parade of masseuses, manicurists, and a yoga instructor came to minister to Grace and her attendants, and the morning of the wedding, the press appeared in earnest, and makeup artists and three hairdressers got to work, while Winnie and Beatrice orchestrated all of it, with Lucy, the young girl they'd hired from the village who came in as needed. She remained mostly in the background but came running when they called her. And Bridget came to pitch in.

The caterer had been serving delicious meals for two days.

Edward had his own exquisitely tailored set of tails, Freddie had the ones that he'd worn since he was twenty, and Grace's father had his. The guests began arriving on schedule. The music Grace had chosen was being played by the orchestra Beatrice had hired from London. There were flowers throughout the house, fabulous white orchids and fragrant lilies of the valley. The minister was there on schedule, and Freddie went to get Edward from the dower house at the appointed time. His best man was staying at Mrs. Flannagan's along with the photographer from *Vogue*. Every single detail came off without a hitch. The bride came down the grand staircase just as Miranda Charles and Elizabeth Cornette had on *Beauchamp Hall,* and the wedding gown from the last episode of the show was a masterpiece and perfection on Grace. Her father had tears running down his cheeks when he walked her down the aisle, and Edward's eyes were damp when he saw her.

The valets had dispensed with the cars for all three hundred guests, and Winnie and Beatrice agreed it was the most beautiful wedding they'd ever seen. They had both worn black dresses so as to be unobtrusive. The reality show filmed every moment of it, and interviewed the guests afterwards, particularly the famous ones. Edward had invited a number of fellow actors that he had worked with, all of whom were major stars. It was an extraordinary wedding.

Halfway through the evening while the guests were dancing and before the bride and groom cut the cake, Beatrice and Winnie slipped into Beatrice's office for a break, and found Freddie sitting on the couch with his shoes off, drinking champagne.

"What are you two doing here?" he asked, pleased to see them.

"Same thing you are," his sister said. "My shoes are killing me." She took them off and Winnie sat down in a chair, relieved not to be on duty for five minutes. She had been watching every detail, as had Beatrice and Freddie. Their future depended on the success of the first event, which could make or break them.

"I'd say it's a great success, wouldn't you?" he asked them, and they all agreed that it was fantastic. And Edward and Grace were a particularly lovely couple. They looked like a fairytale prince and princess.

Winnie, Beatrice, and Freddie went back out among the guests ten minutes later, and after Edward and Grace cut the wedding cake, Freddie asked Winnie to dance, and Paul stepped forward and invited Beatrice to dance with him. He said the filming was over, and he had stayed to enjoy the rest of the evening. He had been seated with them at their small table for dinner.

The wedding went on until 4:00 A.M., with a buffet breakfast of eggs and oysters, lobster, and caviar before everyone left and the wedding party went to bed. The bride and groom had reluctantly left at 2:00 A.M., after tossing the bouquet, and departed in a shower of rose petals to be driven to London in a Bentley, and catch the plane Edward had chartered to take them to Tahiti. Every single moment of it had been gorgeous and exactly what Edward and Grace hoped it would be. Edward had left them a huge additional check to thank them. Paul had gotten his crew going again to film the bridal get-away, and the *Vogue* photographer had stayed until the bitter end too. And in the morning, they were going to put Grace's father in a Rolls and send him home, and the bridesmaids in another, after they shared a hearty breakfast of eggs and crèpes.

When the last guest and bridal attendant had left, Freddie, Beatrice, and Winnie danced around the front hall and hugged each other. There wasn't a single detail that had backfired or been overlooked.

"It was *unbelievable*! You did such a great job," Freddie complimented his sister and Winnie.

"We all did," they both said generously. Their suppliers had proven to be reliable and skilled and had done their jobs well.

"I've never been so tired in my life, but it was worth it," Beatrice said, collapsing on a couch in the main living room. "I'm not sure how often I can do that."

"A lot more," Winnie said to her. "We have eleven more weddings booked, and six mystery nights. And twenty-six calls I haven't returned yet." And when Edward's wedding turned up in *Vogue,* and the reality show of the wedding aired, their phone would be ringing off the hook.

"Oh God," Beatrice groaned at the thought. "I'm going to wear orthopedic shoes to the next one."

"We're going to become the primo location for weddings after Las Vegas," Winnie said happily.

Their cleaning woman from the village had come in early and cleaned up the dower house by then, and Freddie walked Winnie back to reclaim it. He walked in with her and she smiled at him.

"Do you want a drink or a cup of tea?" she offered.

"A transfusion . . . actually, tea." She made him a cup of Earl Grey and handed it to him. "How did you ever come up with this idea, and why didn't we think of it before? It was so obvious," he said to Winnie, "to have weddings here."

"It was all in that crazy dream I had." He was smiling at her as he set his cup down. He had changed in the last few months, Beatrice had noticed it too and mentioned it to Winnie. He was more serious and reliable. He was just as funny, but they could count on him to do what they needed and he promised. He was very much a functioning member of the team, and took care of both women. "Did you see your sister with Paul last night, by the way? I thought he was going to kiss her on the dance floor." Freddie looked amused at what she said.

"I think he might have. Or she might have kissed him. She won't admit it because she's such a prude around me, but I think she likes him, quite a lot in fact. I like him too."

"So do I," Winnie agreed. "I can't believe we've got the mystery night coming up in ten days. And a wedding two weeks later. This is positively athletic!"

"We can do it," he said confidently. And then he looked at her in an odd way, and she had the feeling he was going to ask her some-thing, and then his mood changed and he didn't. "Do you want to go for a walk later?" he asked her.

"Yes, if you carry me."

"We can take turns."

In the end, he stayed for an hour while they talked about the wed-ding and the upcoming mystery night. Then he went back to the main house, and she promised to come over for dinner. She had the option to eat by herself or with them, but most of the time she went over to join them. It was always warm and friendly being with them.

When they met up for dinner in the kitchen, they were all wearing jeans and old sweaters and running shoes, and helped themselves to whatever they wanted from the neatly organized leftovers arranged by the caterers. Edward had sent them a text saying it was the most beautiful wedding he'd ever been to, and they were thrilled.

"Did you see the check Edward left us last night as a bonus? I nearly fainted," Winnie commented.

"Me too," Beatrice agreed, munching on a perfectly trimmed lamb chop left over from the wedding. The food had been superb.

"So tell us about Paul," her brother teased her and she gave him an evil look.

"Mind your own business. And yes, I like him. But he's divorced and has two children I haven't met yet, who will probably hate me. Both teenage girls."

"At our age, most people have been married and are divorced with kids," Winnie said practically. "And if they haven't been married, they're weird." Freddie looked insulted the moment she said it.

"I've never been married and I'm not weird," he defended himself.

"You're just crazy, that's different," Beatrice said easily.

"I'm not crazy or weird, I just haven't found the right woman."

"Well, you've certainly auditioned enough of them," his sister reminded him.

"I've reformed," he said weakly. "I don't think I'd want a big wedding like that if I got married," he said, thinking about it.

"Neither would I," Beatrice agreed. "I think I'd elope to Las Vegas, or somewhere else vulgar and fun. I don't want all that formal stuff, hundreds of guests and a white dress trailing down the stairs. I'd probably trip and fall flat on my face. But it was certainly pretty. They're stars, so people expect all that, and after thirteen years, she earned it."

"Her father looked happy," Winnie commented, enjoying rehashing the wedding with them. It was like having roommates, which they were in a way.

"If you drank as much as he does, you'd look happy too," Freddie added. "And he had a flask in his pocket."

They sat in the library afterwards, and Freddie poured them each a glass of port as Winnie groaned.

"I think I'm becoming an alcoholic. Are we drinking too much?"

"I don't think so," Freddie reassured her. "I wonder what the footage for the reality show looks like."

"Gorgeous, I hope," Beatrice said, and stood up when she finished her drink. "I'm going to bed before I pass out. I'm sleeping till noon tomorrow."

Winnie and Freddie sat talking for another hour after that. He made her laugh, telling her stories about Eton, and the pranks he used to play on his teachers and friends.

"Were you and Beatrice always close?" she asked him.

"We hated each other growing up, and then I turned around one day and we were best friends. Especially after our parents died. We were both very young, and she needed a big brother to protect her. And once she grew up, I could go back to being an adolescent," he said, and she laughed. "But lately, I'm growing up or getting old. This business of ours has forced me to be responsible. I think I rather like it." He seemed surprised.

"I've noticed. It suits you. I like you as a grown-up," she commented.

"I think I do too." He looked at her for a moment, and held her hand. "You're a brave woman, Winnie. I admire that about you. It took guts for you to come here all alone."

"Brave or foolish, I'm not sure which. But it's worked out well. I've been very lucky." She smiled at him.

"So have we," he said gratefully.

He walked her back to her house then, kissed her on the cheek, and looked serious when he left. After that she got into bed and watched an old episode of *Beauchamp Hall* before she fell asleep. It was almost Christmas, but with the success of their first wedding, she felt as though she'd already had the best Christmas gift of all.

Chapter Seventeen

C hristmas was a quiet affair, and anticlimactic after the excitement of the wedding. They shared a simple dinner in the
kitchen, reminiscing about their childhoods, when their parents were
alive, and they relaxed on Christmas Day and Boxing Day. Winnie
called Marje and Erik and spoke to the kids, and the day after Boxing
Day, they got to work, to get everything ready for the first mystery
weekend.

The preparations were almost as complicated as those for the
wedding had been. They were doing it on New Year's Eve, so everyone's expectations were heightened.

Winnie had written the script for the mystery with Freddie's help.
Beatrice and Winnie organized the costumes. There were maps and
clues to hand out. The food had to be flawless, the rooms perfectly
prepared. They had put appropriate accessories with each outfit. The
evening was going to be black tie, evening gowns for the women.
The murder was to occur the night they arrived, and be solved by the

time they all left late the next day. The weapon, cleverly concealed somewhere in the house, was used as part of the guessing game and would have to be found and identified.

The whole process was intricate, and the three partners worked hard on it before the guests arrived. Not all of them spoke fluent English. There were twenty people in the group, among them a couple of Italians, a very exotic-looking French woman, a Turkish man, and the rest were English. The reality show crew was on hand to film it. Paul had come with them, and Beatrice looked pleased to see him, especially since it was New Year's Eve.

Everything went off smoothly during dinner, while Winnie and the Havershams supervised and Paul hovered near the guests, offering to help. After dinner, the guests were sent off to various locations in the castle to do errands they'd been assigned as part of the mystery, which was confusing for the film crew, who weren't sure which group to follow. Paul instructed them to stay with each group for a short time.

And then a scream rang out, according to the script, when a body was found in the main salon. It was the French woman, who was supposed to be dead, but was actually lying in an enticing position, smoking a cigarette.

"You're supposed to be dead," Beatrice reminded her. She spoke no English, so Beatrice repeated it in French.

"I am dead," she assured her. "I am smoking in the afterlife." The others circled around her, trying to guess how she had died.

"From smoking," someone suggested, and Freddie and Winnie tried not to laugh. They were a group of friends who had all chipped in for the evening, as a fun way to spend New Year's Eve. And the price they were paying was appropriately steep.

The guests were offered after-dinner drinks from a large silver tray that was a Haversham heirloom, and the smoking corpse ordered a cognac.

It was finally decided, per the script, that she had been strangled with her pearls, and there were lengthy interrogations about where they had last seen her alive and when.

Beatrice put music on then, and the murdered French woman got up and wanted to dance.

"Is it a language problem?" Freddie whispered to Winnie. "Or is she just difficult?"

"Both, I think," Winnie whispered back, as Beatrice gave them pleading looks to rescue her. Freddie took over as the police detective, and narrowed it down to nine possible murderers, which was several too many. The guests were all dancing by then, and put the murder on hold.

"They're not following the script," Beatrice complained with immense irritation. "Who has the script? Do you have it?" she asked Winnie.

"I gave it to Freddie," she explained.

"I don't have it." He looked blank.

"Sorry," Paul said, pulling it out of his pocket. "I forgot to give it back to you."

"I'm not sure they care who killed her," Freddie commented.

"I don't blame them," Beatrice said. "I'd like to kill her myself." And Paul laughed.

"It's going to make a great show, so don't worry about it," he told them. "Murder goes awry at Haversham Castle. Do you want to dance?" He had finally stopped calling Beatrice "Your Ladyship," which was a relief. They all began dancing to the music Freddie had set up on the sound system. The guests were dancing too. A few minutes later, Freddie and Winnie joined them. It was almost midnight. As the hour approached, Freddie began a loud countdown to warn them, and at the stroke of midnight, he blew a horn and put "Auld Lang Syne" on the sound system, and all the guests kissed each other, far more ardently than he had expected. They were still kissing when the song ended, several with their tongues halfway down each other's throats and their bodies pressed together.

"Now what do we do?" Freddie asked his support group. "They're still kissing."

"At least they haven't taken their clothes off yet," Paul said and kissed Beatrice with equal ardor. And they didn't come up for air for a long time either.

"Oh, sod it," Freddie said, took Winnie in his arms, and kissed her.

"What are you doing?" Winnie said, shocked for an instant. She hadn't expected it, and thought he was kidding.

"Don't worry, it's in the script," he insisted.

"No it's not, I wrote the script."

"Yes, it is, I added it," he said, and kissed her with all the pent-up passion he'd felt for her since he'd met her, and she melted into his arms and kissed him back. They were still kissing when Beatrice and Paul stopped and looked at the scene around them, which the film crew was recording diligently. The mystery guests were starting to grope each other. Winnie and Freddie had come apart by then, as Beatrice stared at her brother.

"Do you realize you just kissed Winnie? Are you drunk?"

"Not yet, but I'm considering it. And yes, I do know I kissed her. It was intentional, not an accident."

"That's like kissing your sister!" she said, looking outraged. "She's family!"

"Not exactly. Although I hope you kiss like that, for Paul's sake." As Freddie and Beatrice were discussing it, the guests hurried up the stairs in pairs to disappear into their rooms, the murdered woman among them, her arm linked through the arm of one of the Italians, whom she hadn't arrived with. His wife was with the Turk.

"Wonderful evening," they all murmured as they rushed past their hosts. "Great party! . . . So much fun . . ." And with that, the last of them disappeared, their doors closed, and Freddie, Winnie, Beatrice, and Paul were left alone in the grand salon and started laughing. It was obvious what the guests had gone upstairs to do, to celebrate the New Year, hopefully in pairs, not in groups.

"Maybe they're a sex club of some kind," Freddie suggested.

"Aren't they a little old for that?" Beatrice responded, as Paul's film crew came over and asked if they should continue filming.

"I don't think so, they all went to bed. You can stop now," Paul told them.

"Should we film you?" they persisted.

"No, that's fine." Freddie suggested the crew each have a glass of champagne, which they did, conferring quietly with each other, as Freddie looked at Winnie intently, dropped quietly to one knee in front of her, and gazed at her lovingly as she stared at him, and Beatrice looked at him in astonishment.

"Freddie, *what* are you doing, for God's sake?"

"I'm proposing to Winnie," he said, never taking his eyes off her face, and she started to smile and look shy.

"Now?" Beatrice scolded him. "Are you mad? You've never been married before."

"No, I haven't, so I'm free, which is a good thing. If I weren't, this would be awkward. It's already hard enough." Realizing that he was serious and something major was happening, Paul signaled frantically to his camera crew to get the cameras rolling again.

"Winona Farmington," Freddie said in a louder voice, as he reached for Winnie's hand and held it, "I'm totally mad about you, and have been from the first time I laid eyes on you, and I can't wait a moment longer to share my life with you. Will you marry me?"

"Freddie, for Heaven's sake," Beatrice complained. "Can't you do something like that in private?" She saw the cameras rolling then and shrieked. "Oh my God, you just proposed on a reality show. What's wrong with you?"

"Nothing," he assured his sister. "Winnie, will you?" he asked the woman he wanted to marry in a gentler voice, oblivious to the cameras rolling, and Paul was beaming. It was the best show they'd filmed in years.

"Yes," Winnie said in a hushed voice. "Yes, I will." Freddie stood up and kissed her then, as Paul's crew got the kiss and their smiles afterwards, and Beatrice rolled her eyes.

"I can't believe you just did that. How can you be so undignified? You proposed on a reality show, Freddie." Her feathers, and her

nerves, were seriously ruffled by the entire evening. "Congratulations of course, and best wishes to the bride." She kissed Winnie on
the cheek and glared at her brother. "You're incorrigible, and I
thought you'd finally grown up."

"I think I have," he said, undaunted by his sister.

"Now we can be sisters," Beatrice said, smiling at Winnie. "And
you will be the Marchioness of Haversham." The thought of it suddenly hit Winnie like a lightning bolt.

"Oh my God. How do you do that?"

"It's easy," Freddie said, still holding her hand. He looked over at
his sister then. "I tried to get Grandmama's ring out of the safe to
give her when I proposed, and I couldn't get into it. Did you change
the code?"

"No, it sticks," she informed him, as Paul told the cameraman they
could stop rolling film. They had everything they needed. The newly
engaged couple then retired to a quiet corner and he kissed her
again, more discreetly, as Paul walked Beatrice to one of the other
couches.

"I need a drink. This has been a ridiculous evening. We have to
work on these murder evenings a little more," Beatrice said, looking
exhausted.

"They were a tough group," Paul said comfortingly, and then
kissed her, and both couples sat lost in their own worlds for a while
until Beatrice said good night to Paul, announcing that she was going
to bed. He left without bothering Winnie and Freddie, and a little
while later, they got up, Freddie found her wrap, and walked her to
the dower house. The cameraman had disappeared with Paul.

"Do you really mean it?" she asked as he walked her home. The proposal had been so crazy and theatrical, she wasn't sure if it was a joke. It didn't feel real yet.

"Of course I mean it. I wanted to propose to you on New Year's Eve. I decided weeks ago. Tonight just got a little out of hand. The delivery was not as smooth as I would have liked. When do you want to get married? Let's do it soon. And where?"

"Here," she said without hesitating. "Just us and our sisters. I want to get married in this house. That's my dream." They had reached the dower house by then and it was cold outside. They were both shivering. "Do you want to come in?" She looked at him lovingly. He nodded in answer to her question, she opened the door, and he followed her in, to finish what he had started.

Their first murder group appeared at noon on New Year's Day and ravenously ate breakfast. They left as soon as they had finished, although they weren't supposed to leave till that afternoon. But they all seemed very happy. They thanked their hosts profusely, and said it had been perfect, just what they'd hoped for. They added generous tips to the bill, and looked delighted when they left. The mystery remained unsolved and the designated murder victim looked hale and hearty, with a cigarette pressed to her red lips when she left.

"I think we need to work on that script some more. She was the most uncooperative murder victim I've ever seen," Freddie said.

And with that, Beatrice came up to her brother and put something in his hand discreetly. "I think that's what you were looking for." He glanced at it, and recognized the beautiful rose-cut oval solitaire diamond that had been their grandmother's. He nodded and smiled at his sister and slipped it on Winnie's left hand. She looked down at it in amazement.

"I love you," he whispered to her and kissed her, as Beatrice walked away quietly, smiling.

They called Marje a little while later and told her the news, and she laughed and cried, and couldn't believe what had happened.

"And you're going to be a marchioness. I can't even pronounce it."

"Neither can I," Winnie said happily.

"I'll teach you," Freddie whispered, and they smiled at each other, as Winnie thought how incredible it was.

It had started with two DVDs in the white elephant game at Christmas in Michigan a year before. They had turned out to be the best gifts she had ever received and the key to her future. The dream had become a reality once she had the courage to pursue it. Who could have known? Who could have dreamed it or imagined it? *Beauchamp Hall* had changed her life. And in turn, she had come to Haversham and changed the lives of those who lived there. Reality had turned out to be so much better than her dreams.

About the Author

DANIELLE STEEL has been hailed as one of the world's most popular authors, with over 650 million copies of her novels sold. Her many international bestsellers include *In His Father's Footsteps, The Good Fight, The Cast, Accidental Heroes, Fall from Grace, Past Perfect, Fairytale,* and other highly acclaimed novels. She is also the author of *His Bright Light,* the story of her son Nick Traina's life and death; *A Gift of Hope,* a memoir of her work with the homeless; *Pure Joy,* about the dogs she and her family have loved; and the children's books *Pretty Minnie in Paris* and *Pretty Minnie in Hollywood.*

Daniellesteel.com
Facebook.com/DanielleSteelOfficial
Twitter: @daniellesteel

About the Type

This book was set in Charter, a typeface designed in 1987 by Matthew Carter (b. 1937) for Bitstream, Inc., a digital type-foundry that he cofounded in 1981. One of the most influential typographers of our time, Carter designed this versatile font to feature a compact width, squared serifs, and open letterforms. These features give the typeface a fresh, highly legible, and unencumbered appearance.

The Introduction of
Group Technology

By the same author

Principles of Production Control
Standard Batch Control
Group Technology (Ed.)
Production Planning

The Introduction of Group Technology

JOHN L. BURBIDGE

C.Eng., F.I.Mech.E., F.I.Prod.E., M.B.I.M.

Professor of Production Management
International Centre for Advanced Technical
and Vocational Training, Turin

133 417895

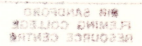

HEINEMANN : LONDON

William Heinemann Ltd

15 Queen St, Mayfair, London W1X 8BE

LONDON   MELBOURNE   TORONTO

JOHANNESBURG   AUCKLAND

Printed in Great Britain by Butler & Tanner Ltd
Frome and London

Preface

This book describes the new approach to the batch and jobbing production of components, which is called Group Technology, and shows how it can be introduced in a factory. It is my hope that it will provide a helpful do-it-yourself manual for companies who are planning to introduce Group Technology, and that it will also provide a useful text on the subject, for students of management in business schools, universities, and technical colleges.

I start with the premise that Group Technology is already a proven and desirable innovation which can, if it is well introduced, result in both major economic gains and improved job satisfaction for the workers in industry.

The economic advantages have been convincingly demonstrated by the few companies which have already made the total change to Group Technology. Of these one of the earliest and best documented is Gordon Ranson's application at Serck-Audco. This is still a good example of a complete change, involving not only production but the whole of management.

The sociological advantages are more difficult to prove. There is a lot of indirect evidence in the research by behavioural scientists into the effects of group production on job satisfaction. Most of this research has been concerned with assembly and office work, and very little has been done in component processing groups. It is a fact, however, that Group Technology makes it possible to delegate the making of many decisions to groups, which could not be delegated efficiently with our present forms of organization. I believe that Group Technology holds out the promise of a big improvement in the quality of working life and that in the long run this will be its major contribution.

In some ways the book breaks new ground. The early exponents of Group Technology saw this new approach as essentially a technological development. I see it as a new strategy of management, which extends the economic benefits obtainable with mass production into the fields of batch production and jobbing. Many authorities again—including those who take a broader total management view—have linked Group Technology with a need for prior rationalization of the product range; value analysis and simplification of design; classification and coding for variety reduction; extensive tooling development, and some investment in new plant. Although I admit the importance of these types of development, I do not believe that any of them are necessary prerequisites for the introduction of Group Technology. I believe, in fact, that there are advantages if these

A*

types of development are left until certain other changes, essential to Group Technology, have been introduced.

In my opinion, the changes which typify Group Technology and are essential for its successful introduction, are: the change from functional layout to group layout; the change in production control from multi-cycle stock control to single-cycle flow control; a big reduction in ordering cycle times, and the introduction of a planned loading sequence. Changes in the design, marketing, purchasing, personnel management, accounting and wages systems, will also be desirable, but these are secondary changes.

One other innovation in this book is that it advocates the use of 'Production Flow Analysis' for finding the groups and families for group layout. This technique finds the best division into families and groups by analysing the information contained in the component route cards for the parts produced in a factory.

Most of the early applications of Group Technology were based on component classification and coding, using the information contained in component drawings. Most of the existing literature describes this approach as though it were the only one possible. There is today, however, a considerable amount of experimental evidence that analysis based on the information contained in route cards finds a better division and finds it quicker and at less cost.

My own work in this field is described in the book. Other experimental evidence comes from the work of Mr. Graham Edwards and his post-graduate students at U.M.I.S.T., Manchester University, with whom I had the pleasure of collaborating for a number of years. Early work by Fatheldin, Crook, and Fitzpatrick was concerned with evaluating the techniques of classification and coding and Production Flow Analysis. Later work, by El Essawy in particular, has been concerned with practical applications of Group Technology in industry. There are now two factories with fairly complete installations and many groups already installed in other factories, all planned on the basis of analysis of the information contained in route cards.

Some companies have been frightened away from Group Technology, because it appeared to be indissolubly linked with a high initial investment in classification and coding, in rationalization, in tooling development, in the purchase of new plant, and in the installation of a computer. In my opinion none of these are necessary prior commitments. There is evidence that Group Technology can be largely self-financing, finding the money for its introduction from the induced reduction in the stock investment. With the methods described here, I believe that Group Technology can be introduced without the need to make a major prior investment increase and without the need to wait for years before achieving any savings. For the same reasons, I believe that Group Technology can be introduced in small companies, as well as larger ones, and that in some ways the smaller company will find introduction simpler.

As I write this preface, Britain and many other countries are facing a major industrial crisis. Due to inflation, rising material costs, rising wages, price controls, and heavy taxation, many manufacturing companies are facing serious liquidity problems. Experience with Group Technology shows that companies can double their rate of stock turnover and be much more efficient after the change than before. Group Technology offers many struggling companies the only real hope for survival.

There is no doubt in my mind that Group Technology is a major breakthrough in production. I hope this book will encourage many companies to take the plunge and introduce this important new innovation.

JOHN L. BURBIDGE

Acknowledgments

Acknowledgments are gratefully made to the following:

1. Mr. J. R. Morgan of the Institute for Operational Research, for introducing me to the technique of AIDA.
2. Ferranti Ltd., and Mr. J. Durrie, for permission to reproduce the illustration in Figure 2.2.
3. Mr. J. Szadbovski and the *International Journal of Production Research*, for permission to reproduce Figures 8.2 and 8.3.
4. Messrs. Olivetti, for permission to publish the results illustrated in Figures 9.6, 9.7, 9.8, 9.9, 9.10, and 9.15.
5. Mr. J. Gombinski—an old friend and early pioneer of Group Technology in Britain—for permission to use Figures 2.1, 12.1, and 12.2.
6. The publishers of *The Production Engineer* for permission to reproduce Figure 1.3.
7. Mr. Fatheldin of Manchester University for permission to reproduce Figure 1.5.
8. Mr. J. Livingston of the Turin International Centre, for his help and advice on the paragraphs dealing with computer applications in Chapter 6 and Chapter 9.
9. Mr. G. Ranson of Serck-Audco, who introduced the first successful application of Group Technology in Britain, for allowing me to quote from his book *Production Planning and Control* in Chapter 3.
10. Mr. C. Manton, who carried the manuscript to London twice and helped with the last paragraph.

J.L.B.

Contents

1 An Outline of Group Technology

1.1 INTRODUCTION

Group Technology is a new approach to Production Management, which seeks first to obtain similar economic savings in batch and jobbing production, to those already achieved using line flow in the simpler process industries, and in mass production, and second to provide a better type of social system for industry, in which improved labour relations are easier to achieve.

The key features required for a successful Group Technology application are Group layout, short cycle Flow Control, and a planned machine loading sequence. As most batch and jobbing production factories at present use Functional layout and Stock Control, the introduction of Group Technology means changes for most companies in both plant layout and production control. These key changes can produce major economies on their own, but they also make it possible and profitable to make other changes in management systems and in technology which will further increase the possible savings.

This chapter gives a brief outline of Group Technology. It introduces Group layout, Flow Control, and Sequence Planning, and it also describes some of the other desirable innovations which these changes make possible.

1.2 FROM LINE PRODUCTION TO GROUP LAYOUT

Early in the present century, when Henry Ford and others started to mass-produce automobiles, they are reputed to have reduced car production costs and the normal level of investment in stocks, both by a factor of four. The principle they adopted was the principle of line flow which prior to that time was only used in the simpler process industries. They laid out the machines and other work centres close together in lines, in the sequence in which they were used. They then balanced the output rates from all the work centres in each line, so that materials could flow down the lines in a continuous stream.

The early mass production lines were designed to produce one particular component, or assembly. For this reason they could only be used for standard products with a very high and continuous demand. Line flow production has been confined therefore to the production of only a small proportion of the world's product needs. The rest are made using material flow methods, which have changed very little during history.

In recent years it has been discovered that lines can be used efficiently, not only in simple process industries and for single components in mass production quantities, but also for 'families' of similar components. Lines are now in use which make hundreds of different parts. The tooling on the machines in the line is so designed, that it can be reset in seconds for each different item in turn. In effect the large quantities required to make lines economical, are obtained by adding together many small batches of similar components, which all use the same machines in the same sequence. This principle can be seen applied in both batch and jobbing production. In a mechanized jobbing foundry for example, all castings will follow the same route from moulding to pouring, to knockout, to fettling. There can be a continuous flow of materials with a large measure of automatic control, even though the moulding machines will be re-set at frequent intervals to make many different castings.

These multi-component lines are similar to mass production lines and have again only limited applications. It has been discovered however, that even if machines are used in different sequences by different parts, and even if all the parts don't use all the machines, many of the advantages of line flow can still be obtained, merely by laying out machines close together in *groups*, each capable of completing all the operations on a particular list, or *family* of parts.

It is this last discovery, that big savings are possible even without line flow, which is the essence of Group Technology. This family-group approach can be applied to nearly all batch production and jobbing industries. The big economies which it provides coupled with the very wide possibilities for its application, make it one of the most important discoveries of the century.

1.3 GROUP LAYOUT

The first of the key features of Group Technology is Group layout. In most factories it is possible to divide all the made components into Families and all the machines into Groups, in such a way that all the parts in each family can be completely processed in one group only. When the plant is laid out in this manner, with each group of machines and its team of workers established together in one special area, the factory is said to have Group layout.

The three main types of plant layout, known as Line, Group and Functional layout, are illustrated in Figure 1.1. Line layout is used at present in simple process industries, in continuous assembly, and for the mass production of components required in very large quantities. Functional layout is by far the most common form of layout and Group layout is only now beginning to be used, at present mainly in the engineering industry.

With Functional layout all machines of the same type—all lathes, or all milling machines in a machine shop for example—are laid out together in the same section under the same foreman. Each foreman and his team of workers specialize in one process. The workers in each team work independently. Co-operation between them in the execution of their tasks is only rarely needed, because the different workers in the section seldom do

(a) Line layout (Machines grouped by component family)
[Component specialization]

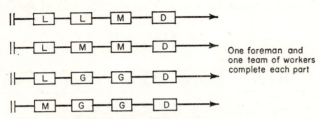

One foreman and
one team of workers
complete each part

Machines in each line always used in the same sequence.

(b) Group layout (Machines grouped by component family)
[Component specialization]

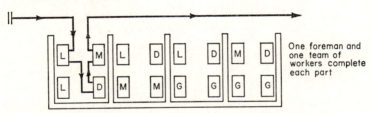

One foreman and
one team of
workers complete
each part

Machines in each group need not be used in the same sequence.

(c) Functional layout (Machines grouped by M/C type)
[Process specialization]

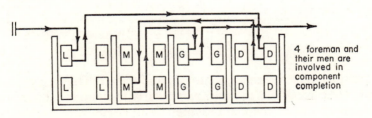

4 foreman and
their men are
involved in
component
completion

Key L = lathe M = miller G = grinder D = driller

Figure 1.1. Types of plant layout

work on the same items. This type of layout is based on process specialization.

In Group layout on the other hand, each foreman and group of workers specialize in the production of one list of parts and co-operate in the completion of a common task. This type of layout is based on component specialization. Because the products produced in component processing departments are components or parts of products, a change from functional layout to group layout can also be seen as a change from process specialization to product specialization.

Perhaps the main reason why mass production is economically successful, is that it greatly simplifies the material flow system. This simplification of the system of routes along which materials flow through the factory, simplifies management and makes it possible to reduce throughput

Total flow charts

(i) Complicated

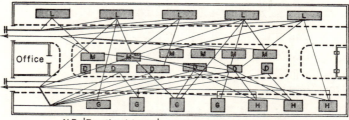

N.B. 'Functional layout'–machines grouped by process type

(ii) Simplified
(By laying out in family machine 'groups')

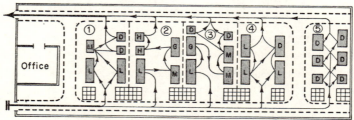

N.B. 'Group layout' – machines grouped for component 'Families'

Figure 1.2. Simplification of material flow system

times, reduce the investment in stocks, and reduce handling costs. It also induces other important savings, particularly in indirect labour costs.

With group layout the main savings again come from simplification of the material flow system. This simplification is illustrated diagrammatically in Figure 1.2. It is very much simpler to plan and control material flow through a workshop with group layout, than it is through a workshop with functional layout. Although a few savings arise directly from a change to group layout, the main savings require other changes as well, particularly in production control. Group layout is in effect a key which opens the way to savings which are unobtainable or very difficult to obtain with functional layout.

1.4 A TYPICAL GROUP

Before considering the more theoretical aspects of Group Technology, it will be useful to consider the composition of a typical Group, in a factory using Group Technology. This group has fourteen machines, employs a work force of twelve, and produces a family of 300 parts. The parts are all ordered to the same two-week cycle.

The labour force of twelve consists of ten machine operators; one 'skilled' man who does pre-setting, major machine set-ups, marking-off when required, and first-off inspections; and one 'unskilled' man who does sweeping, cleaning, and swarf removal, and helps with handling, deburring, and other similar work. One of the operators is the 'working chargehand' of the group, and six of the operators are capable of operating more than one of the machine types in the group.

The fourteen machines are of five different types, consisting of five lathes, two horizontal milling machines, one vertical milling machine, five drilling machines, and one key seater. Two of the lathes used for first operations are normally fully loaded, the remaining machines have lower loads down to only 30% for the key seater. Three of these machine types are special to the group. Among the drilling machines however, there is one of a type which is also used in two other groups, and the two horizontal milling machines are of a type found in one other group.

In addition to the machine tools, equipment has been provided for pre-setting, together with inspection fixtures, a marking-off table, and other equipment special to the parts in the family. Tool racks and cupboards have also been provided. With ordering to a two-week cycle, the use of a central tool store would require at least fifty tool handling moves per tool per year, and Group storage is considered preferable.

The items produced in the group are relatively light in weight and the only handling equipment consists of roller track and bins. The materials arrive either as forgings or as blanks, and finished parts are despatched in the same types of bin as those used for handling inside the group.

At the beginning of each two-week cycle the group receive a 'list order' showing all the parts to be produced by the common due-date for the cycle. The task of the group is to schedule this work so that it is all completed to the required quality standards by the common due-date for the cycle.

It will be seen that an independent group of employees works together as a team, to complete specified quantities, of a specified list or family of finished parts, by a specified due-date and that they are provided with all or most of the facilities, needed to achieve their target.

1.5 FAMILIES

The word '*Family*' is used as a name for any list of similar parts. The families used with group layout are lists of parts which are similar because they are all made on the same group of machines. This type of family is called a 'Production Family' when it is necessary to differentiate it from other types.

Some parts appear in a production family, which are similar in shape, like those for example in Figure 1.3. Because they are similar in shape and size, these particular parts can be made on the same machines. However,

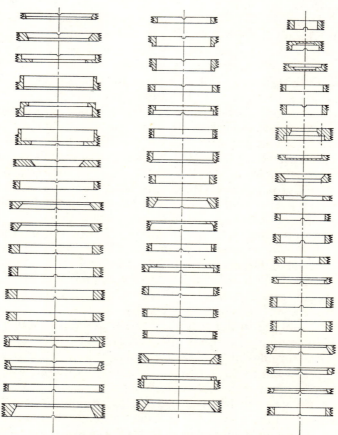

Figure 1.3. Parts which are similar in shape

not all parts which are similar in shape will appear in the same family. For example, Figure 1.4 shows four components which are almost identical in shape. Because there are major differences in manufacturing tolerances, requirement quantities, materials, and special features, which will require the use of different machines, it is unlikely that these parts would all be in the same family.

Many parts appear in a production family which are dissimilar in shape. Figure 1.5 shows a number of parts which are very different in shape. Any production engineer looking at these parts however, will see that they are all approximately the same size and can all be produced on a lathe, a drilling machine, and a miller. They would almost certainly all appear in the same production family.

Some components come together in the same production family because they all have a particular feature, requiring the use of a special machine. Examples from engineering are splines, gear teeth, broached holes, and special heat treatment operations. If there is only one broaching machine and all components requiring a broached hole are in the same family, it

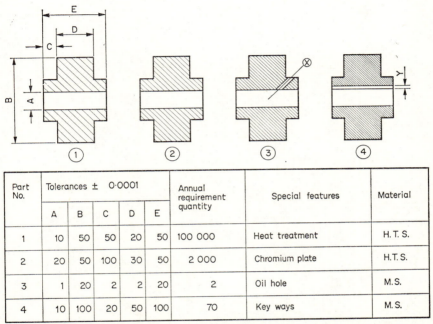

Part No.	Tolerances ± 0·0001					Annual requirement quantity	Special features	Material
	A	B	C	D	E			
1	10	50	50	20	50	100 000	Heat treatment	H. T. S.
2	20	50	100	30	50	2 000	Chromium plate	H. T. S.
3	1	20	2	2	20	2	Oil hole	M. S.
4	10	100	20	50	100	70	Key ways	M. S.

Four parts of identical shape and size which require different production processes, due to different requirement quantities, tolerances, and special features.

Figure 1.4.   Parts similar in shape, but in different families

may be that some of these components are similar in shape to parts made in other groups, and that apart from the hole they could be produced more economically in one of these other groups. To obtain the advantages and savings of Group Technology in this case, one must either accept the additional costs of other-processing in the broach group, or buy new plant to reduce these costs in the broach group, or buy one or more new broaching machines for the other group. The transfer of partly finished work between groups is normally unacceptable, because it will make it impossible to obtain the much larger general savings due to Group Technology.

Some simple parts might be made in more than one group. They may be

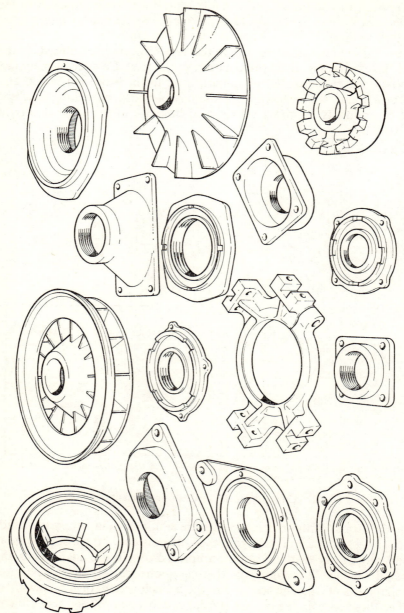

Figure 1.5. Parts different in shape, but in the same family

placed in one family rather than another because there is no spare capacity on the machines in another group which might have been more suitable or because the choice gives a better balance of load between machines.

There is a large number of factors which affects the choice of family for a component. There is no reliable method of finding families which looks only at components. Components only come together in production families because they use the same machines. The significant information when looking for families, is that which tells on which machines each part is made.

1.6 GROUPS

A *Group* is a list of machines, selected for layout together in one place, because it contains all the necessary facilities to complete the processing of a given family of parts. It will be seen that the definitions for family and group form a circle. A family of parts can only be defined by relating it to a particular group of machines, and a group by relating it to a family.

Groups vary greatly in type and size. They vary widely in the number of machines—from one to twenty-five or more. They may also vary widely in the number of different machine types, again from one type only—say, drilling machines only—to all different. If a family of parts can be completely machined on a number of machines of the same type, they still form a legitimate group, even though they are all of the same type.

There will normally be the possibility of choice between using large or small groups. Large groups can be formed with most plant types existing in one group only. As group size is reduced more types of machine will be needed in more than one group and there is an increased risk that some new machines must be purchased. Economic factors tend therefore to influence the choice towards large groups.

Another important factor in choosing the size of group is the number of people who will be employed in them. Sociological research seems to indicate that teams of two, or of six to twelve inclusive [1] are likely to be the most effective and cohesive. In the long run it is probable that sociological factors are the most important in deciding the optimum size of group.

In any factory there is always imbalance between the work loads on the machines. There are always some machines which are heavily loaded and others which are necessary, but are only very lightly loaded. The balance of load is dictated by the product design, production methods, choice of machines, and sales programme. Only minor temporary adjustments are possible by drawing on work for the future, or by replanning work from one machine to another. For this reason there will always be some groups where there are more machines than there are men. In some types of industry the machine:worker ratio is 2:1 or more. Group Technology will not change the ratio significantly.

In one sense each group is a small factory, specializing in a particular range of components, and able if necessary to make any other components, which can be made with the same machines. Inside any industry—say, the sewing machine industry, or the tractor industry—the percentage of components made by the same combinations of machines tends to be approximately the same from product to product. Once the groups have been found therefore, they tend to be semi-permanent, only requiring changing when product designs change, new processes are introduced, or there is a significant change in production volume.

There is a large number of factors which affect the choice of group for a particular machine. There is no possible method of finding groups, which looks only at machines. Machines only come together into groups, because they are all used to make the components existing in a particular family. The significant information when looking for groups, is that which tells what components are made on each machine.

1.7   FINDING THE FAMILIES AND GROUPS

It is not difficult to form one or two families and groups in any factory. A walk round the stores, or better still a look through the drawing files of a classification and coding system, will quickly find two or three hundred parts, which are similar in shape, or function and can all be made on, say, a capstan lathe, a vertical drill, and a horizontal milling machine. Taking one or more of each of these machine types out of general use, a '*trial group*' can be set up quickly and another enterprising company has apparently made its first step towards Group Technology.

Each new family and group provided successively by this method, will be a little more difficult to form. First of all, it must be created from a reduced population of parts and machines. Secondly, this population has been corrupted by the addition of parts, which used to have some operations on machines allocated to the early groups, but were found unsuitable for the associated families. They will therefore have been re-routed on other machines. Thirdly, it will contain some parts, which ought to be in early groups—because they are made on the machines provided in these groups—but are not in these groups, because there was no simple method of discovering this similarity, by looking solely at components, or at information about component designs.

Eventually there will be a large remnant of parts and machines which appear to offer no possibilities for further grouping. Some companies which have used this approach now say, 'We have $x\%$ of our parts being made in groups. The rest are unsuitable for Group Technology'. It isn't true. They've just used a method which doesn't find the families and groups.

One cannot find the natural total division into families and groups by making a series of arbitrary abstractions from the list of parts, followed by an independent and equally arbitrary series of allocations from the plant list. One cannot find the natural division into families by looking only at components. The groups and their associated families already exist in all factories. The problem is not to create some completely new relationship, but to find the relationship which already exists. Finding the groups and families can be seen as an analytical process, which progressively divides, sub-divides and sub-sub-divides the plant list and the list of made components, into very large, large, and required size groups and families.

The first major division into very large groups and families finds little, or no duplication of plant. In an engineering factory for example, this first division into very large families and groups of departmental size, might find a forge, a sheet metal shop, a machine shop, and an assembly shop, with only one or two simple machine types being required in more than one of these major groups. Although apparently based on process differences, these departments are still true major groups if they carry out all the operations needed to make completed parts, or completed material items.

Further sub-division in say the machine shop might find three main groups. One might contain the plano-millers, horizontal boring machines, and heavy radial drills used to make gear cases and other box-like parts. Another containing bar lathes, sensitive drills, a horizontal milling machine, and a keyseater, would make studs, bushes and other similar parts, machined directly from bar. The third group would contain the rest of the plant and would make the rest of the parts. Once again with a major division of this type, very few of the machine types used in the department are likely to appear in more than one of the three major groups.

In a small machine shop with, say, thirty-five machines and twenty-five operators, this division into three groups might be all that was necessary. In a large machine shop, further sub-division would be needed. Some new groups can probably be formed with no further duplication of plant types between the groups, but each further sub-division will increase the need for duplication.

It is probable that in the majority of factories, group layout can be introduced without purchasing additional plant, providing that the groups and families are found analytically and are not too small. The technique for finding groups and families, described later in this book, is called Production Flow Analysis. It finds progressively: first, the best division of plant and parts between major groups; second, the best division into families and groups inside each of these major groups; third, the best arrangement for the layout of the machines in the groups; and fourth, the division into 'tooling families'. The only information required for this technique is an accurate set of route cards, showing the operations and machines used to make every component.

1.8 PRODUCTION CONTROL

The second of the essential features of Group Technology is short cycle Flow Control. One of the main reasons why mass production reduces costs and requires a much smaller investment in stocks per unit of output than is needed for batch production, is that it uses a type of production control system which is different from that normally used in batch production.

Most mass production factories use flow control systems for ordering materials and parts. They forecast product sales and produce production programmes, at short intervals to a regular ordering cycle. By 'explosion' from these programmes, they find the component and material requirement for each cycle. Because with lines, throughout times are short, they can use very short production control ordering cycles. They are thus able to follow changes in market demand very quickly and to work with a minimum of stock.

Most, but not all batch production factories use stock control systems. A so-called Economic Batch Quantity is fixed for each component. Each is given a re-order level and when the stock drops to this level, a new order is issued for a further supply. Because the system only works with heavy stocks, it requires a very big investment in stock. Because the system cannot produce parts in balanced product sets, it induces heavy losses due to material obsolescence. Because the system produces orders at random, it generates a very uneven load of work on the machines.

The stock control system of ordering is an anachronism even with functional layout. Flow control is the best system for ordering made parts for standard products, with any type of layout. With a flow control ordering system, the amount of stock depends on the ordering cycle. As the cycle time is reduced the stock level falls. The type of layout however, affects the throughput time as shown in Figure 1.6. The cycle time cannot be less than the longest component throughput time. Because with functional layout the different machines used to make each component, are far apart, cycle times cannot be much reduced below the sum of the operation times plus queuing time for the critical parts, without a large increase in handling costs. Functional layout therefore imposes the use of long cycle times. Because group layout brings the machines used to make each part, close together and under the same supervision it reduces throughput times, and makes it possible to work with shorter cycles than is possible with functional layout. It also makes it possible therefore to work with a much smaller investment in stocks.

Flow control is essential for efficient Group Technology. There are factories with good group layouts which have achieved only minor savings, because they are still trying to operate with stock control. Group layout is also highly desirable for efficient flow control. Flow control achieves its major savings when it uses very short cycles. With functional layout in a factory making assembled mechanical products, it is difficult to use flow control with a cycle of less than four weeks. With group layout in the same factory, a cycle time of one week is possible.

The change to flow control is not only a change in production control. It

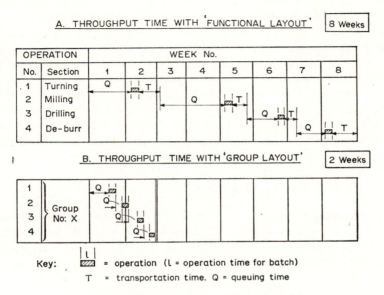

Figure 1.6. Effect of layout on throughput time

Note: With *functional layout* each operation is done in a different section, under a different foreman. There are delays for transport and then queueing delays while preceding work is completed on the required machines. With *group layout* all operations are done in the same group, under one foreman. Transport delays are eliminated. With unified control, it is possible to schedule the work with a big reduction in average queueing time and to eliminate queueing time for critical parts.

also requires important changes in sales forecasting methods and in purchasing. Flow control systems are much simpler to operate than stock control systems. The changes required are not generally difficult ones, but they do require careful planning and co-ordination for efficient introduction.

1.9 SHORT CYCLES AND A PLANNED LOADING SEQUENCE

The change from long cycle stock control to short cycle flow control, is highly desirable. It both reduces the stock investment and also increases 'flexibility', or the ability of Production to follow changes in sales demand quickly. The reduction in stocks is partly in work in progress due to run quantity reductions, and partly in finished products because with short cycles one need only make products which can be sold.

If cycles are reduced with stock control and functional layout, the stock control system becomes very inefficient. Handling costs, setting costs and administration costs are inflated. The increase in setting time reduces capacity, and the reduction in output which this induces, further increases costs.

Group layout saves some of these losses. Because the machines used to make each part are close together in one group for example, reducing the cycle now has a negligible effect on handling costs.

The remaining losses can be eliminated by using a flow control ordering system with a planned loading sequence for loading work on the machines. This brings parts together for loading, which can use the same or similar tooling set-ups. In this way setting times per part are reduced and capacity is increased.

1.10   GROUP TECHNOLOGY AND AIDA

It has been stated that the essential features of any Group Technology application are group layout, short cycle flow control, and a planned sequence for loading machines. The O.R. technique called AIDA can be used to support this thesis.

(a) AIDA

AIDA, or 'Analysis of Interconnected Decision Areas', is a technique used to find optimum solutions for design problems involving many different decision areas and interrelated options. It has been used to assist in the design of products as diverse as shoemaking machines and bridges. In a study undertaken at the Turin International Centre, the technique was applied to the design of an optimum production system.

AIDA first recognizes the different decision areas involved in any problem, and the different options open in each area. Next it studies the relationship between options and finds out which are incompatible. Combinations of options which contain incompatible pairs are eliminated and carefully specified criteria are then applied to the remaining combinations, or in other words, the remaining possible solutions.

(b) Decision networks

Figure 1.7 shows part of the AIDA decision network for a production system. The circles represent decision areas; the spots inside the circles are decision options, and the straight lines between spots join incompatible options which cannot be used together.

The design of any production system is mainly concerned with the design of the material flow system, or system of routes between work places, and the design of the production control system, to be used to regulate the flow of materials. Four main decision areas can be recognized, with two main options in each.

Decision Area	Option
1. Production Control	(a) Stock control
	(b) Flow control
2. Plant layout	(c) Functional layout
	(d) Group layout
3. Order cycle	(e) Short ($\leqslant$ 2 weeks)
	(f) Long ($\geqslant$ 10 weeks)
4. Job loading sequence	(g) Planned sequence
	(h) Random sequence

Many other decision areas were considered, but they are either not linked, or only weakly linked with each other, or with the above four. These four can therefore be treated as the primary decision areas in the network.

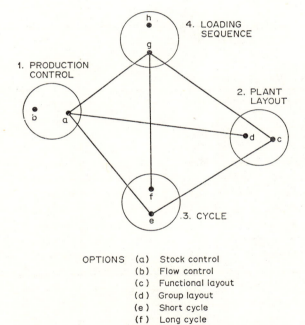

OPTIONS (a) Stock control
          (b) Flow control
          (c) Functional layout
          (d) Group layout
          (e) Short cycle
          (f) Long cycle
          (g) Planned loading sequence
          (h) Random loading sequence

Figure 1.7. AIDA decision network

(c) Incompatibility links

The links joining incompatible options in Figure 1.7 can be explained as follows:

1. *Link ag.* A planned loading sequence and stock control ordering

cannot be used together, because the stock control ordering system releases orders at random, and not together in tooling families.

2. *Link ae.* A short cycle cannot be used with stock control ordering, because this ordering method requires large order quantities sufficient to cover about 50% more time than the replacement lead time, if it is to work efficiently.

3. *Link ad.* Stock control cannot be used efficiently with group layout.

(a) *Elimination of combinations precluded by links*

Y	N	1	2	3	4	5	6	7	8	9	10	11	12	13	14	15	16
a	(b)	Y	Y	Y	Y	Y	Y	Y	Y	N	N	N	N	N	N	N	N
c	(d)	Y	Y	Y	Y	N	N	N	N	Y	Y	Y	Y	N	N	N	N
e	(f)	Y	Y	N	N	Y	Y	N	N	Y	Y	N	N	Y	Y	N	N
g	(h)	Y	N	Y	N	Y	N	Y	N	Y	N	Y	N	Y	N	Y	N

(b) *Five remaining possible solutions*

No.	Options	Prod. control	Layout	Cycle	Loading	Notes
4	acfh	S.C.	Funct.	Long	Random	TRADITION
12	bcfh	PBC	Funct.	Long	Random	
13	bdeg	PBC	G.L.	Short	Planned	G.T.
14	bdeh	PBC	G.L.	Short	Random	
16	bdfh	PBC	G.L.	Long	Random	

Figure 1.8. Possible solutions

The stock control system releases orders at random. This produces substantial and unpredictable variations in machine loads which are exaggerated by the division into smaller groups.

4. *Link ce.* A short cycle cannot be used efficiently with functional layout. Because the machines for successive operations are far apart throughput times tend to be longer than the cycle time and therefore unacceptable. Reducing the cycle also inflates handling and control costs.

5. *Link cg.* A planned loading sequence cannot be used efficiently with

functional layout. Too much co-ordination between different foremen is involved to make efficiency possible.

6. *Link gf.* A planned loading sequence cannot be used efficiently with a long cycle. It is naive to expect that detailed loading plans covering ten or more weeks ahead can be implemented without changes.

There are four decision areas in Figure 1.7, each with two options. There are therefore 2^4 or 16 possible combinations. Excluding combina-

	1		2		3		4		TOTAL COST	TOTAL INVESTMENT
Decision area										
Options	a	b	c	d	e	f	g	h		
Effect on cost	x	o	x	o	o	o	o	x		
Effect on investment	z	o	z	o	o	z	o	z		
SOLUTIONS 1 (13)		1		1	1		1		o	o
2 (14)	1			1	1		1		x	z
3 (16)	1			1		1	1		x	2 z
4 (12)	1		1			1	1		2 x	3 z
5 (4)	1		1			1		1	3 x	4 z

Figure 1.9. Solutions in order of preference

tions precluded by links, leaves the five possible solutions shown in Figure 1.8.

Considering the two criteria of cost and investment, it is apparent that in each decision area one option will always cost more, and require a greater investment than the other, with one possible exception in the case of cycle time and cost. Figure 1.9 shows the five possible solutions. In each case where the more costly option has been chosen a symbol x has been added to indicate increased cost. In each case where the option requiring the larger investment has been chosen, a symbol z has been added to indicate an increase in investment.

The best solution is the Group Technology solution of group layout, flow control, short cycle and planned loading sequence. The worst solution is the traditional combination of functional layout, stock control, long cycle and random loading sequence.

B

1.11 WAGES AND ACCOUNTING SYSTEMS

One other change which is desirable with Group Technology, needs special mention. This is in the wages and accounting systems.

(a) The wages system

First of all, it is desirable to substitute a fixed wage, or group bonus, for individual incentives. With group layout the emphasis must be on team spirit and group co-operation. Individual incentive schemes tend to destroy this type of co-operation, due to jealousies about such things as who should get the best-paying jobs.

Individual incentive schemes are concerned mainly with the minimization of operation times. We now realize that throughput time is equally important to profitability. The traditional individual incentive schemes provide a disincentive to the achievement of this second aim, because they make it more difficult to split batches, to move men from one machine to another, and to arrange continuous flow between machines for critical components.

With functional layout and stock control, machine operators have the opportunity to increase their output and earnings by doing extra work for the future. With group layout and flow control on the other hand, they have no such opportunity. The amount of work assigned to the group is fixed when the programme is adopted. Because there are no large banks of material in the group, the speed of the operator even if he is 'tied' to one machine, is controlled by the speed of other operators who feed him with part-finished work. Under these circumstances an individual incentive scheme has very little to offer, and only provides a costly and bureaucratic source of irritation.

(b) The accounting system

Traditional costing systems are normally based on operation costing. They seek to control the cost of components by controlling the costs of operations. Because all parts are normally made in many departments and sections, there is no cost centre smaller than the factory as a whole, which could be used to obtain a comprehensive control of component costs.

With group layout the obvious cost centre is the group itself. It is in effect a single machine which makes finished parts and there is very little point in making a costly running analysis of its internal operations, Control of expenditure can be effected, to mention only one possibility, by measuring the work content and standard cost of all components; calculating the total standard cost value of the output each cycle and comparing this with the sum of the actual expenditures in the group. In effect the group becomes a profit centre and as long as it improves its performance, it is unprofitable to record the details of what is happening inside it. If things go wrong it is simpler and cheaper to make a special investigation in the group.

One company which adopted this approach found that reduced accounting cost was a substantial item in Group Technology savings.

1.12 THE STRATEGY OF INTRODUCTION

So far this chapter has covered the minimum Group Technology 'package with a pay-off'. It is possible to make substantial savings in both the stock investment and in costs, by a change to group layout, coupled with the introduction of a flow control ordering system and a planned loading sequence, plus some modifications to the wages and costing systems. It is the recommendation of this book that the best strategy is to make these changes and take these savings early, before continuing with further longer term, more capital intensive developments. Planned in this way, the introduction of Group Technology can be self-financing, capital requirements for later development coming from the reduction in the investment in stocks, induced by group layout and flow control.

There are other reasons why it is better to plan for an early change to group layout and flow control. To examine these, it is necessary first to consider what are the other developments which might possibly be introduced earlier. These come under two headings: first, rationalization; and second, technological development.

(a) Rationalization

Rationalization covers such subjects as variety reduction, simplification and standardization of the raw materials, parts, assemblies, and finished products made and also of all the tools and equipment required to make them. Among the principal techniques used to attain these ends, are classification and coding, and value analysis. When stock control ordering is used in a factory, rationalization will generally induce heavy initial losses due to material obsolescence particularly in the case of direct materials and parts. Because material and parts are never in balanced product sets with stock control ordering, a change in design tends to scrap large numbers of parts. There are then some advantages in leaving major rationalization until operation with flow control has brought the stock into balanced product sets. If there are any possibilities for rationalization, which will not cause obsolescence and will not delay group layout, they are of course desirable, at any time.

(b) Technological development

Technological development is concerned with the development of machines and tooling for group production. It deals with such subjects as the design of tooling for tooling families of similar components; the design of tooling for quick change of set-up; the development of automatic transfer lines and machining centres for batch production to replace the present generation of machine tools; and finally it looks toward the complete automation of batch production. It is impossible to plan technological development effectively until one knows what parts are in the families and also has some experience of group working. The traditional approach of designing new machines on a hunch, and then looking for parts to make with them, is putting the cart before the horse. A more effective approach is to analyse component processing needs and then design machines to suit them. Ideally technological development should also follow rationalization of products and parts, to avoid making tools which are not needed after rationalization. Again technological development is capital consuming and it is wiser management to recover the capital needed for investment, before spending it, by first introducing Group Technology with existing methods.

This book concentrates mainly on the practical problems of introducing group layout and flow control. These problems are general in nature and can be described in a manner suitable for any industry. The problems of rationalization and technological development tend to be special to different types of industry. They are however covered again briefly, in the next chapter, and in Chapter 12.

1.13 LIMITS TO THE APPLICATION OF GROUP TECHNOLOGY

Before leaving this chapter, consider what are the limits to the application of Group Technology. The first limitation is that Group Technology should not normally be used where simple line flow is possible. Group Technology achieves many of the savings of line lay-out, but not all of them. Line flow is usually better, where it is possible to use it, providing that work tasks are not reduced excessively to a series of trivial, repetitive, short cycle motions. Simple flow process industries making products like bricks, cement, steel, castings, many chemicals, beer, and bread, will continue to use line flow. Most continuous assembly operations will still be laid out for line flow in the future. Complex components made in very large quantities will also still use line flow.

After these limitations, it is difficult to find any other general limitation to the application of Group Technology. What is left is all either the batch production of standard products, or jobbing production. Group Technology has already been applied in both these types of production. Even though in jobbing, the products may be new with every order and there are no fixed families, it is normally still possible to use group layout. Most jobbing companies tend to specialize in a restricted range of processes and product types. It is possible in this case to find a division into groups, which will accept any component for which the company would normally accept an order.

Group Technology has been applied to date mainly in the engineering and electronics industries, where it has been used in factories making a wide range of very different products, including airborne radar sets, machine tools, oil valves, brake linings, cars, and television sets. Partial applications have also been reported from the chemical, and furniture manufacturing industries. Applications following Group Technology principles have also been reported in the textile and clothing industries. The type of product appears to provide no general limitation to application.

Most of the present applications of Group Technology have dealt with the mechanical engineering processes. In particular it has been used with the metal cutting, sheet metal forming, forging, and metal founding processes. Once again however, there seems to be no reason why it should not be applied to any process.

Group layout can be used for assembly as well as for component processes. As one example, a recent study by the author, in a shipyard making supertankers by the block welding method, showed that group layout could also have advantages for the welded assembly of ships. A ship may consist of 300 or more blocks, or welded assemblies. These fall into families requiring similar welding skills and equipment, similar quality checks, and similar scaffolding. As the blocks in each family are mostly required progressively during the erection of the ship, there are advantages to be gained from group layout, with teams of men specializing in particular families of blocks.

A recent development has been the use of group assembly instead of line assembly for mass production products. Companies such as Saab and Volvo (cars), Phillips (television sets), and IBM (typewriters), which have pioneered this development, claim increases in productivity due to increased job satisfaction and a reduction in scrap, absenteeism, and rates of labour turnover.

Finally the quantity of each item to be produced appears to offer no bar to the application of Group Technology. It has been applied successfully with the very small quantities found in jobbing production, and there is also one application in the car industry, where the batch quantities are very large.

1.14 SUMMARY

The main features which typify Group Technology are the use of group layout, short cycle flow control, and a planned loading sequence. Used alone, none of these features will give significant savings. Used together however, they provide a powerful new production strategy, of great economic and sociological importance.

The introduction of these features will make it desirable to change traditional working methods in management functions other than production. Those most likely to be affected are Personnel, Marketing, Purchasing, and Accounting.

Rationalization and technological development are easier to achieve and more rewarding after the introduction of Group Technology than before it. There are advantages in leaving the major effort in these fields, until after the introduction of group layout, short cycle flow control, and a planned loading sequence.

Group Technology is applicable to all types of batch and jobbing production. It does not generally take the place of line production, but is normally used where line flow is impossible. In many factories group layout for some components and line layout for others will exist side by side.

With Group Technology most men will work together in teams, or independent groups with common aims, rather than as isolated individuals. There is some evidence that this change can lead to better human relations in industry.

2 Production Technology and Group Technology

2.1 INTRODUCTION

It is usual with all new innovations for a name to be chosen which is a good description of the initial concept. With time however, the concept grows and changes. The name eventually becomes a poor description, but is still the best possible name, because all those who are involved with the subject know what it means. To change the name would only cause confusion.

The name 'Group Technology' has had very much this type of history. It came into the English language in translations from Russian works dealing with the technological aspects of machining families of parts. Group Technology is now more important as a managerial break-through than as a technological revolution. The term is now a poor description of the subject, but it is still a reasonable name, because it has a common widely-understood meaning, and because there is no universally acceptable substitute.

Group Technology is also a reasonable name, because it was the technological break-through which made the managerial break-through possible. Previous generations of managers saw setting-up time as a fixed and unalterable factor. Starting with this premise, it was easy to accept as normal and inevitable: the multi-cycle stock control system of ordering; the theory of the economic batch quantity; a high investment in stock; long delivery periods; big obsolescence losses; and all the other deficiencies of traditional production methods. It was only when Mitrovanov in the U.S.S.R. and Patrignani in Italy, showed that setting times of one hour could be reduced to a few seconds, that it became possible to conceive of batch production following similar principles to those followed in mass production.

This chapter starts by examining the problem of machine setting and then goes on to consider possible trends for machine development in the future.

2.2 MACHINE SETTING

In mass production one can find some machines which have been specially designed to make one component. In batch and jobbing production on the other hand, and also widely in mass production industries as well, parts are made on standard machines which are adapted to the special needs of particular components, by the addition of jigs, fixtures, and special tools.

The task of changing this tooling, when changing from one component to another, is known as machine setting, or *setting-up*. The time required is known as the *setting time*. The early technological phase of Group Technology was important because it showed that setting time is not an inflexible constant factor, but is a variable which can easily be reduced. The following are the principal methods by which setting times can be reduced:

1. Planned sequence of loading
2. Tooling families and composite parts
3. Training of the setters
4. Pre-setting
5. Co-ordinate setting and digital read-out
6. Improved measuring devices
7. Improved tooling design

Each of these methods will now be considered in turn.

(a) Planned sequence of loading

The time required to set-up a new job on a machine tool depends very much on what was the previous job. If two very similar components follow each other on a capstan lathe, for example, which have a similar shape, but involve a change in say two diameters, necessitating the repositioning of only two already-fitted tools, the setting time may be five minutes. If two very different components follow each other however, requiring machine cleaning and a complete change of all the tooling, the setting time may be more than an hour.

By choosing the sequence in which components are scheduled on the capstan lathe, so that similar parts are machined one after the other, with the same or similar set-ups, substantial reductions can be obtained in total setting time and setting cost. Because savings in setting time can be used for useful work, they represent an equivalent gain in capacity. Similar savings can be obtained by this means, with most types of processing plant, but the amount of the savings varies greatly for different types of machine.

Note that these savings can be obtained with the existing plant, tooling, and methods. The savings can be obtained, in other words, without any new investment in machinery or tooling. Further savings can of course be obtained later by improvements in tooling design and in machine design. There are however sufficient savings, merely from the change in scheduling sequence, to make Group Technology possible and profitable in most factories, with the existing machines and tooling.

The simplest method for finding a reasonable scheduling sequence is to delegate the job to the group foreman. If the company uses a single cycle ordering system with a two-week cycle, he can be given at the beginning of each fortnight, the materials for two weeks work. By looking at the materials, the drawings, and the routes, he can find a reasonable sequence without great difficulty. If the products are standard products he will receive the same list of parts every two weeks and can gradually improve the sequence by trial and error. If the products are special, as in jobbing production, he must live with his first choice each cycle, but with practice again, he will improve.

If the company already have a classification and coding system, it can be used with advantage to simplify the choice of scheduling sequence. The coded information can in this case be analysed, to find the sub-families of parts made from the same materials, or having similar shape, or similar features, necessitating similar set-ups.

Another even more efficient method analyses the actual tools used to make different parts and divides them into sub-families using the same tools. This method is known as Tooling analysis and is described in a later chapter.

(b) Tooling families and composite parts

It has been shown that even if the processing methods for each component are planned individually, there are inevitably enough similarities in approach, to make significant savings in setting time possible. If the routing methods are now modified to take advantage of and encourage these possibilities, even greater savings are possible.

The parts in any production family will tend to divide for each machine used, into a number of tooling families, the parts in which can all be produced at the same set-up. By establishing these families and planning new jobs so that they can be produced by the existing tooling, it is possible to reduce both setting costs and the investment in tooling.

Some of these tooling families exist because the parts are similar in shape. This idea was stated by S. P. Mitrovanov in his principle of the composite component. Figure 2.1 shows a number of similar but different parts and one part—the composite component—which combines in its design all the features of all the others. One can set up a capstan lathe to make the composite part, in such a way that it can also make all the real components.

Other tooling families exist because they all have one common feature, such as a particular size of gear tooth, or tapped hole. For example there may be a turret drilling machine in a group which holds eight different sizes of drill and has a vice on the drill table which with replaceable jaws, can hold a wide variety of shapes. This combination can accommodate a tooling family for which the only criteria are that all parts must require holes of the sizes of the drills in the turret, and all parts must be such that they can be held in the vice.

If these tooling families and their set-ups are established and recorded, it is possible either to add new parts to the original family as they arise, or to extend the family by increasing the range of tooling provided.

Once again this approach to setting time reduction is more a question of good planning and organization than of new investment. Most engineering

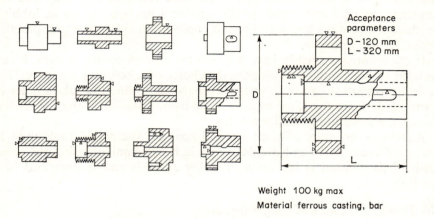

Acceptance parameters
D – 120 mm
L – 320 mm

Weight 100 kg max
Material ferrous casting, bar

Figure 2.1. The composite component

companies, could apply the idea of the tooling family to a large proportion of the components they make, using mainly existing tooling. It is possible in some cases to find the division of a 'family' into tooling families by eye. For more complex cases there are special techniques described later in the book. This task of finding tooling families is again one which can be facilitated by using a classification and coding system.

(c) *Training of the setters*

Setting times can also be reduced by improving the skill of the setters. Because each set-up tends to be different, it is difficult to provide training economically, for specific set-ups. However nearly all setting-up jobs in the same process shop require the same types of skill. It is possible to analyse the setting up process for different types of machine and to specify the specific physical and mental skills required to complete different parts of the process. Exercises can then be used, to improve these skills. This approach to training is known as 'Operator Training' in Britain, or alternatively as 'Skills Analysis Training'.

'Operator Training' is of course just as successful with functional layout, as with group layout. It cannot claim any special advantages for Group Technology. It is mentioned here only to reinforce the point, that the reduction in setting time needed to make Group Technology possible, does not necessarily involve any investment in new machines and tooling.

(d) Pre-setting

Further savings in setting time can now be obtained by improvements in tooling design involving some additional investment. The key to this type of reduction is pre-setting. With pre-setting the positions of the tools are accurately set in their tool holders, away from the machine. The tool holders are designed so that they can be quickly and accurately mounted on the machines. In this way the setting time on the machine itself is

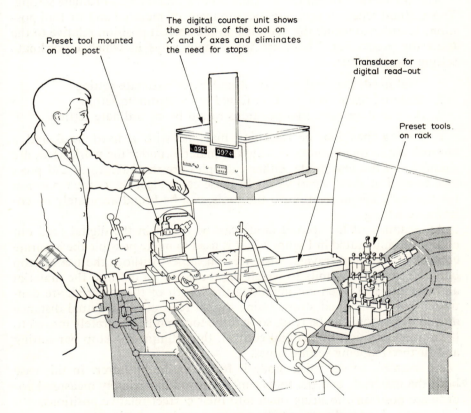

Figure 2.2. Quick change tool holders for lathes

reduced, even though the total setting time reduction, including pre-setting, may be small. The main gains are in machine capacity, reduced material throughput times, and reduced stocks.

As an example Figure 2.2 shows a lathe equipped for quick tool change. With this equipment the change from one tooling family set-up to another can be effected in a matter of seconds.

Pre-setting has been successfully applied to several different processes. The die-set for sheet metal press work is an example. The punches and dies for different jobs can be mounted in these die-sets away from the power press. The die-sets hold the punches and dies in correct relation and reduce the time required to set-up the tooling on the press. Another very successful example can be found in the printing industry. Using special pre-setting fixtures, the setting time on stop-cylinder printing presses can be greatly reduced, giving a significant increase in their capacity.

(e) Co-ordinate setting

Another method of reducing setting times is based on co-ordinate setting. This method relies on accurate measurement of material and or tool position, in order to locate the materials in the correct position relative to the tools for processing. There are three main ways in which co-ordinate setting can be used:

1. Tool fixed, material position found by co-ordinate setting
2. Material fixed, tool position found by co-ordinate setting
3. Both tool and material positions found by co-ordinate setting

A drilling machine, or punching machine with a fixed head and a co-ordinate setting fixture to locate the material under the work head, are examples of the first mode. Other examples are the guillotines and press brakes used in sheet metal work. In these cases also, the correct position for the materials in relation to the tools, can be found accurately by co-ordinate setting.

An example of the second mode can be found in the digital read out equipment illustrated in Figure 2.2. It is used to make possible the accurate control of feed and traverse distances on lathes, without the use of stop bars. Normally the limits to which the tools can be fed into the material and can traverse when cutting along the length of the material, are controlled by setting fixed stops. Using digital read out, the actual distance moved by the tool can be read, so that the tool can be accurately moved to the correct position by manual control, thus eliminating stop bar setting and further reducing setting times.

An example of the third mode is found in the jig borer. In this case both the materials and the tools can be moved to precisely measured co-ordinate positions, to bring them into their correct relative positions.

In general co-ordinate setting tends to reduce setting times, but to increase operation times. At the same time it also reduces the investment in tooling. It is possible therefore, for the introduction of co-ordinate setting to increase profitability in comparison with the provision of special tooling, even if the sum of the setting time plus operation time is increased by the change.

(f) Improved measuring devices

Savings in setting time are also possible by the use of measuring devices which measure the size of the work during processing. Special measuring equipment can be used, for example, to measure the diameters of shafts while they are being ground. The grinding wheel can be fed in manually to the correct depth without the need to set stops on the machine. It will be seen that as far as setting time reduction is concerned, this is a similar method to the digital read-out method described earlier, but is based directly on actual component size rather than on the tool position required to obtain this size.

(g) Improved tooling design

In most companies setting time can also be reduced by the redesign of tooling and by the redesign of machines. In many instances setting times are long because they were never even considered by the machine or tool

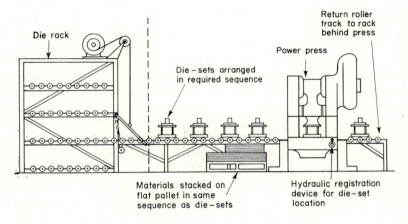

Set-up time : 15 seconds

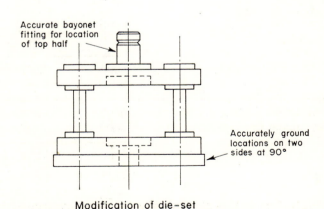

Modification of die-set

Figure 2.3. Power press arrangement for quick setting

designer, or because he showed little inventiveness, or initiative. An important point is that accurate locations should be provided on both the tools and the machine, so that the tools can be rapidly located in their correct positions during setting. A large part of setting time with present tooling is consumed in finding the correct location in which to clamp the tools and materials on the machine.

As an example of what can be achieved by good design, Figure 2.3 shows an arrangement of power press and die-set storage rack designed by the late Signor L. Patrignani. With this equipment he reduced setting times on a 90-ton power press from 40 minutes to 15 seconds.

2.3   THE CHOICE OF MACHINE

Consider now the factors which should regulate the choice of machines. When considering a new machine it is comparatively simple to estimate the investment required to obtain it and the expenditure necessary to run it for the purpose for which it is required. Such estimates have little value on their own however, because it is impossible in all but the simplest industries, to estimate the revenues which one individual machine will earn. It is always necessary to compare two alternative estimates. Even two estimates cannot be compared safely by eye however, to find which of two alternative machines is the best investment. It is necessary to consider the machine with the higher total investment and find the rate of return earned by the marginal investment in this machine, in the form of savings. In practice it is necessary to use some such techniques as the Discounted Cash Flow method to find this rate of return. The simple tabulation below however, is sufficiently valid to demonstrate the principles involved.

Item	M/C 'A' £ p.a.	M/C 'B' £ p.a.	Savings £ p.a.
1. Materials	1000	1000	
2. Labour (*i*) Setting	1100	100	
3. Labour (*ii*) Operation	900	1300	
4. Overheads	3000	3000	
5. TOTAL COST (p.a.)	6000	5400	600 (p.a.)
6. Investment (*i*) The machine	4000	7000	
7. Investment (*ii*) Tooling	3000	500	
8. TOTAL INVESTMENT	7000	7500	500 Marginal Investment

It will be seen in this case that the marginal investment of £500, required to buy Machine *B* instead of machine *A*, earns £600 per annum, or a rate of return of 120%. This is in spite of the fact that the other machine—machine A—costs £3000 less, and £400 per year less to operate.

The important point about this case is that as far as profitability is concerned, it is the total cost and total investment which matter. It is possible to pay more for a machine and to increase operation times, but at the same time to make substantial reductions in both total annual cost and the total investment. It is also possible to change profitability from methods which have short operation times and long set-up times, to methods which have longer operation times and compensating shorter setting times.

This point is important, because speed of setting is a required quality for efficient Group Technology, and because a reduction in setting times may in some cases induce some increase in operation time. The short cycle flow control systems used with Group Technology use only small run quantities and require a reduction in setting times to make them usable. Without this reduction they would induce a severe loss in capacity due to the increased number of set-ups.

2.4 MACHINES FOR QUICK SETTING

Earlier in the chapter seven different ways were described by which setting times can be reduced. Other factors such as accuracy being equal, the best machines for group technology are those which are best adapted to take advantage of these possible methods. The setting time reduction methods can be reclassified into three main types:

1. Tooling family method
2. Quick tool change method
3. Co-ordinate setting method

Looking only at the present generation of machines, consider some of the ways in which differences in machine design will affect setting time by each of these methods.

(a) Tooling family method

The principle here is that the machine is set-up so that many components can be machined at the same set-up. Setting time per piece is reduced by sharing the set-up time. In general the greater the number of tools which can be accommodated on the machine, the greater will be the sizes of the tooling families which can be found to use each set-up, and the greater, therefore, the reduction in setting time per piece. Machines with many usable tool positions tend therefore to be ideal for Group Technology.

Turret lathes, capstan lathes, and the automatics derived from them, are ideal for the tooling family method, particularly in the case of parts of similar shape where the composite part approach can be used. These same machines can, however, also be set-up to handle families of dissimilar parts. Other machines with particular advantages for Group Technology for the same reason, are turret drilling machines, turret presses, and machines with automatic tool change features and tool banks.

(b) Quick tool change method

Setting time is reduced in this second case by designing the tooling so that it can be pre-set in special tool holders, which can then be changed on the machine in seconds.

To use this method, machines must be adapted to take the quick change tool holders. Some modern makes of machine are already sold fitted for quick change tooling. Many older types of machine can be modified for the purpose. In the case of capstan lathes, for example, the tool posts will have to be changed and the capstan will need modifying so that capstan tooling can be pre-set and complete capstans can be interchanged.

Drilling machines are another type of machine for which quick change tooling methods are well established, and the power press arrangement already illustrated in Figure 2.3 gives another example. Outside these few instances however, little has been done to develop the idea. One does not have to look long at a milling machine, or a rod mill, for example, to realize that with some development of machine design, very similar savings could also be achieved.

(c) Co-ordinate setting

Co-ordinate setting reduces setting time, first because it generally uses fewer tools, and second because in some cases it also eliminates stop setting.

To use co-ordinate setting, machines must either be produced with the equipment for accurate measurement along two or three axes, or must be modified to take it. The principles of co-ordinate setting have already been described. The methods of measurement include simple scales—suitable for sheet metal working machinery—optical methods such as those commonly used on jig borers, and electronic methods such as that used on the digital read-out equipment illustrated in Figure 2.2.

For simple two dimensional work, the reference surfaces, or points and the values for x and y co-ordinates will be shown on the drawings. The same method can also be used for three dimensional work, processed on jig borers for example. Copy machining from a model, is also an example of co-ordinate setting. In this case the co-ordinates of the tool position are found by sensing the position of the equivalent point on the model. This information is transfered directly to the tool. Numerical control is also a further example of co-ordinate setting. In this case the co-ordinates for each cutting path are stored on tape, and this information is used to control the machining cycle. Setting-up in this case also involves changing the tapes.

2.5   FUTURE MACHINE TOOL DEVELOPMENTS

The machines for quick setting described above, were all present generation machines. They were nearly all designed for functional layout. Each carries out one very narrow range of processes. When a number of different machines of this generation are placed together in a group, they become in effect a single machine, capable of carrying out a range of processses on a family of parts.

The parts in most families will use the machines in their groups in many different combinations and in different usage sequences. At the other extreme, the parts in a few other families may all use all the machines in the group and all use them in the same sequence. In the second case, where there is the same usage sequence for all parts, it is comparatively simple to build lines with conventional present day machines, and even to achieve some measure of automatic material transfer between machines. In the first case where the sequence of usage is highly varied, automation is extremely difficult, or impossible with conventional machines. Starting from this basis, it seems likely that machine development for Group Technology will follow two main lines. First there will be some demand for automatic transfer lines and second there will be a demand for tape controlled machining centres.

(a) Automatic transfer lines

The late Sig. L. Patrignani—an Italian engineer—designed and built an automatic transfer line, for producing families of different parts. A standard machine unit could be fitted with equipment for a wide range of metal cutting processes. These machine units were arranged in line, with an intermittent conveyor type transfer mechanism which moved the work up one station every cycle. The tooling was designed for pre-setting and at any station the tools could be reset for a new component, inside one cycle.

Due to the type of transfer mechanism on the Patrignani machine, the cycle time was the same for all components. It is also possible to design automatic transfer lines based on total balancing. Using hopper storage between the machines with automatic positioning and feeding equipment, lines can be established which will accommodate some ebb and flow of stock between machines.

An interesting fact about automatic transfer lines is that they already exist in large variety in the form of multi-spindle vertical and horizontal automatics. With a little ingenuity it is possible to tool these machines to handle families of many different, but similar parts.

(b) Machining centres

Automatic transfer lines become very complicated if one starts to vary the combination of machines used from one part to the next, and also to vary the sequence of usage. In this case another idea, the so-called Machining Centre, becomes more attractive.

Machining centres are single machines fitted with machining heads capable of carrying out many different processes. They are generally arranged so that the material is held in one place and the different heads are fed into the work automatically to a fixed cycle for each part. This cycle can be controlled mechanically, with or without the assistance of electronic, hydraulic, pneumatic, and/or fluidic controls.

A recent development is the numerically controlled machining centre. Although not yet fully developed, it is hoped eventually that such machines can be programmed to select the correct head cycle and the correct tools from a tool bank, for a family of parts, which have widely different processing sequences. Numerical control has not on the whole lived up to its early economic promise, when used as a substitute for conventional tooling on the present generation of machine tools. It should come into its own now, however, with the development of numerically controlled machining centres for Group Technology.

2.6 DEVELOPMENT POLICY

The difficult question to answer is how much technological development must be completed, before the introduction of Group Technology. Some authorities appear to suggest that all tooling methods must be revised and a lot of new plant must be bought, before Group Technology can be successfully applied. Others, including the author of this book, take the view that Group Technology can be successfully applied with very little prior technological development. They say that the setting time reduction required, can be obtained by a better sequence of loading, and by the use of tooling families.

There is some evidence that the second view is correct. There is one highly profitable installation of Group Technology, which made no major contribution on the technological side prior to introducing group layout and flow control. There are two companies which have made extremely sophisticated contributions to technological development, with trial groups. Neither has earned a worth-while return on a very considerable investment.

Wise management does not embark on projects which involve a leap into the dark. No Board of Directors in its right mind is going to abandon most of its present tooling and most of its present tried and proven processing methods, in the hope that by so doing it will later be in a position to use Group Technology. Group Technology wouldn't be worth-while, if it involved this kind of gambling.

The best technological policy is to change to group layout and flow control first. When the production families and their component tooling families are well established, then is the time to start advanced tooling development and the introduction of more sophisticated machines. With this policy, the reduction in the stock investment will release the capital required for good technological development, and make it self-financing.

2.7 SUMMARY

Large reductions in setting time and increases in capacity are possible even with the present generation production machines, by such methods as the use of a planned loading sequence and tooling families.

These setting time reductions can be further reduced by intelligent tooling design, using in particular pre-setting and quick change tooling techniques.

A group of machines is in effect one complex machine. In a few groups where parts use the machines in the same sequence, it is possible to join the machines by automated transfer and feeding mechanisms. In the future automatic transfer machines will probably be specially designed to meet this type of need.

In most groups different parts use the machines in the group in different combinations and different sequences. In this instance, the solution for the future is probably the numerically controlled machining centre.

3 Advantages of Group Technology

3.1 INTRODUCTION

The key features of Group Technology are group layout, short cycle flow control, and a planned sequence of loading. No one of these features will give major savings on its own. Used together, however, they do generate significant savings and they also create a new environment, in which other important savings can be obtained, which are impossible to achieve with functional layout and stock control.

Only a small part of the potential savings arise automatically from the changes in layout and production control system. The remainder are only achieved if action is taken to gain them. For this reason it is essential that anyone who attempts the introduction of Group Technology should have a deep understanding of what savings are possible.

This chapter describes the advantages which can be obtained with Group Technology and also seeks to explain why they occur.

3.2 SETTING TIME

As mentioned in the previous chapter, the discovery which made Group Technology possible, was the discovery that long setting-up times are unnecessary. Once it was realized that the same tooling and set-up could be used to make many different parts, and that tools could be accurately pre-set and changed in seconds, if provisions were made to do so, the door was opened to a complete rethink of existing production practices and prejudices.

The beauty of this setting time discovery is that it is not new, or difficult to accept. Anyone who has ever set-up machines knows that the savings are possible. Anyone who has ever set-up machines for a living has probably taken advantage of some of the methods by which setting times can be reduced, either to reduce his work, or to increase his bonus.

Although set-up time reduction is vital to Group Technology, it does not itself depend on the introduction of Group Technology. Set-up savings can be obtained in part, with functional layout and stock control. Consider four main cases.

(a) Standard products, functional layout, and stock control

Consider first the case of standard products. With functional layout and stock control the savings will be small, because the stock control system throws up orders at random and the whole of any tooling family is never likely to be an order at the same time. Before a complete tooling family has been processed, the same tooling will have been set-up many times.

Some increase in the number of parts per set-up may be possible, by waiting for orders for parts in the same tooling family to accumulate, but this will increase the investment in stock and delay completion. Some increase in the number of parts per set-up may also be possible if, when the tooling is set-up for one part from a tooling family, a special review is made of all the remaining items in the tooling family and new orders are released for components whose stocks are approaching re-order level. This method will again increase stocks and at the same time will also increase production control costs.

(b) Standard products, functional layout and flow control

In companies making standard products to their own designs, the change from stock control to flow control will still further reduce setting time. Because most parts will be re-ordered every cycle, most of the parts in any tooling family can generally be machined at the same set-up, at least in the case of simple components with few operations.

With complex components and functional layout, this bringing together of the parts in the same tooling family, is more difficult. Tooling families are related specifically to particular machines and not to particular parts. Each of the machines used to make a component, will accommodate a number of entirely different tooling families. The tooling family lists containing the part will tend to be different on each of the machines it visits. In a particular tooling family there may be fifty parts. When they come together, different parts may have reached, say, Operation No. 2, No. 3, and No. 4. They may already have visited anything from one to three other functional processing sections. It will be realized that with functional layout, it is not a simple task to plan and control the schedules, so that the parts in each tooling family all arrive at the correct machine at the same time. With complicated parts complete success is probably impossible.

(c) Standard products, group layout and flow control

Considering again the same case of standard products made to company designs, it will be found that the change from functional to group layout, still further increases the savings obtainable in setting time. Because all the machines used are under the control of one foreman, he is in a much better position, first to find the optimum schedule, and second to control output to follow the schedule.

(d) Jobbing production

With jobbing production the savings in set-up time are less than those obtainable with standard products. Components suitable for combining in tooling families are only found when customers' orders are received. Some method of production planning must be introduced which finds the tooling families among new component orders, and finds the correct tooling from stock for the processing of the family.

It is probable that tooling can be designed which will continually accommodate new parts as they are ordered. The similarities between the components made in one industry, are in many ways more significant than their differences. For the same reasons as with standard products, the reduction in setting time will tend to be greater with group layout, than with functional layout.

3.3 ADVANTAGES OF SETTING TIME REDUCTION

It has been shown that savings in setting time are not entirely dependent on the introduction of Group Technology, but that they are much larger with Group Technology than is possible with traditional methods of production. The development of methods for setting time reduction was important to Group Technology, mainly because it made short cycle flow control economically attractive for batch production.

If the set-up times for components are high, there are apparent economic advantages to be obtained by making some parts in large batches for stock. If the set-up times for components are low, increasing the size of batch ceases to give any significant economic advantage.

In these circumstances there are obvious advantages to be gained by:

1. Ordering parts in product sets to avoid material obsolescence and facilitate family machining (single cycle ordering)
2. Making parts in small batches, or in other words to a short cycle, to reduce stocks and improve flexibility

In addition to this major advantage of setting time reduction, that it makes Group Technology possible, the same change also induces a number of other savings. Of these the most important are:

1. An increase in machine capacity
2. A reduction in the tooling investment
3. A reduction in setting costs
4. A reduction in operation costs

(a) An increase in capacity

A recent survey conducted by Professor N. A. Dudley of Birmingham University* in engineering machine shops in Britain, showed that on average the machines were cutting metal only 41% of the time available.

---

* DUDLEY, N. A., *Comparative Productivity Analysis*, Dept. of Engineering Production, University of Birmingham.

The remaining 59% was non-productive machine idle time and ancillary time, including 45% for setting.

Assume that in a particular factory, setting time is 45% of available time, and productive time is 40%. Reducing setting time to one third of its present total would increase factory output capacity by 75%. An increase in output of 75% would be possible with no further investment in buildings or machinery. Reductions in setting time of even greater magnitude have been obtained in practice on some types of machine allowing the number of set-ups to be increased three or four times due to the introduction of short cycle flow control. Most companies which have introduced Group Technology have also reported an increase in capacity.

(b) A reduction in the tooling investment

An essential method for setting time reduction is the development of tooling families. The use of tooling families also reduces the tooling investment. If each set of tooling handles an average of ten parts, the tooling investment will be much less using tooling families than with individual tooling for each part, even if the family-tooling costs twice as much as one set of special component tooling. The traditional method of making special tooling for each operation for each component is extremely wasteful of capital.

(c) Reduced setting cost

Setting cost is almost directly proportional to setting time. Reducing setting times, therefore, induces an equivalent reduction in setting costs.

(d) Reduced operation costs

The reduction in setting time, finally, indicates a very important way in which operation costs can be reduced. At present the choice of machine and tooling for an operation depends on the requirement quantity. If a part requires a turning operation, a centre lathe would normally be chosen for up to say ten per month, a capstan lathe for more than ten a month, and an automatic lathe for five hundred a month, or more. Each choice requires progressively a larger investment in tooling and a longer set-up time. Each progressively gives a lower operation time and lower operation cost per piece.

A production planner would not normally choose the higher output rate automatic machines for a requirement of only thirty per month, because the high tooling investment and cost of setting would make it economically unattractive. Where it is possible, however, to share existing tooling on the automatic lathe, and to reduce the setting time between components to nothing or to a matter of seconds by using set-ups already in use for long-run jobs, the high output method can be used for the low requirement components, with a big reduction in costs.

3.4 ADVANTAGES OF GROUP LAYOUT

A number of the benefits obtainable with Group Technology, spring directly from the use of group layout. A list of the principal benefits of this type is given below. It includes only those advantages which can be obtained with group layout and cannot be obtained with functional layout to anything like the same degree.

1. Reduced throughput time
2. Improved ability to follow market changes
3. Reduced stocks
4. Centralization of responsibility
5. Reduced handling and setting costs
6. Simplification of paper work
7. Reduced indirect labour
8. Improved human relations
9. Reduced investment per unit output

(*a*) *Reduced throughput time*

With functional layout throughput times are inevitably long. Any batch of parts will normally be completed in each processing section it visits before it is sent on to the next one. When it gets to the next section it must

Cycle 6		Week 9		Week 10					Week 11				
Machine		Thur	Fri	Mon	Tue	Wed	Thur	Fri	Mon	Tue	Wed	Thur	Fri
1539	C/Cap	2067 Op 1											
1552	C/Cap						2067		Op 4				
736	H/Mill		2067		Op 2								
859	H/Mill				2067		Op 3						
702	Drill											2067	Op 5

Note   Part No. 2067 is critical. The sum of its operation times is 13 days which is longer than the cycle time. Because the machines are close together with group layout, close planning can be used for this part without inflating handling costs

Figure 3.1. Throughput time with group layout

wait in the queue for its turn to be processed. As a consequence, the average throughput time for a component in a typical engineering machine shop with functional layout will be ten or more times the sum of its operation times.

With group layout, some component throughput times can be less than the sum of their operation times. Because the machines in a group are close together, continuous transfer is possible, at least for the critical components as illustrated in Figure 3.1.

The reduction in throughput time has some direct advantages. It makes it possible to quote shorter delivery promises to customers, for example. The two major advantages of reduced throughput time however, are indirect advantages. The first of these is that it allows a reduction in the ordering cycle, which improves the ability of production to follow changes in market demand quickly. The second is a reduction in stocks.

(b) Improved ability to follow market changes

One major advantage of the reduction in throughput time is that it makes it possible to use a flow control ordering system with a very short ordering cycle. The limiting factor which controls the reduction in cycle time is the component processing throughput time. Ideally all the parts required for assembly in one cycle, should themselves be processed in one cycle. With functional layout it would be very difficult, in one engineering factory, to use flow control with a cycle time of less than four weeks. With group layout a cycle time of one week would be possible in the same case.

Each reduction in cycle time reduces the time ahead for which a firm forecast of future sales must be made. It also therefore improves the accuracy of the sales forecasts. At the same time the reduction in cycle time increases the frequency with which new programmes are issued and increases therefore the frequency of occasions when errors in previous forecasts can be corrected. With flow control and a short cycle, production can rapidly follow changes in market demand, with a minimum of finished product stock. If long delivery times are acceptable in the market and a very short cycle is used, production may even be able to make to customers' orders. In this case production will be based on certainties rather than on predictions.

In the past we have expected our Sales Managers to guess what they should sell many months ahead. Today we realize that this is both impossible and unnecessary. It is possible to plan production so that the need for guessing is eliminated.

(c) Stock reduction

A reduction in throughput times reduces both work in progress and finished product stocks. The reason why work in progress stocks are reduced by a reduction in throughput times, is illustrated in Figure 3.2. The reason why finished product stocks are reduced has already been seen in the previous paragraph. Reduced throughput time allows the use of short cycle flow control, which in turn makes it possible for production to follow market demand changes, without a big accumulation of unsold finished products due to inevitable forecasting errors.

The reduction in run quantity induced by the reduction in cycle time, also contributes to stock reduction, as shown in Figure 3.3.

It has been claimed recently that a computer programme for machine loading can reduce throughput times and stocks so much, even with functional layout, that a change to group layout is not necessary. The computer

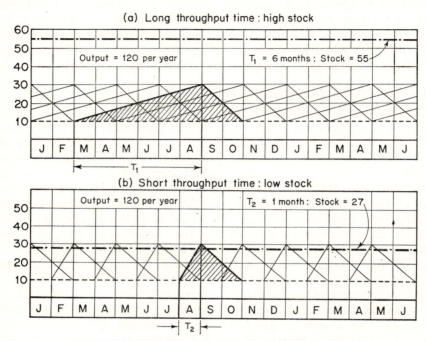

Figure 3.2. Effect of throughput time on work in progress

certainly shows significant gains over manual loading with functional layout. In practice, however, it cannot compete even with manual methods of loading and group layout. It cannot compete because it cannot overcome the physical limitation that with functional layout the machines are far apart. Continuous transfer requiring the immediate transport of some parts to the next machine as soon as each one is finished, is therefore economically impossible, due to the increase in handling costs which it would cause.

(d) Centralization of responsibility

Another big advantage of group layout is that it centralizes the responsibility for producing each component in one group, under one foreman. With functional layout, it is often difficult to decide which of the several foremen who have handled a component, is responsible for a quality defect, or a failure to complete processing by due-date. With group layout there is never any doubt. The foreman of each group can be made completely responsible for both quality and completion by due-date.

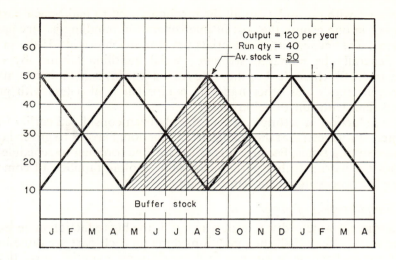

(a) High 'run quantity' – high stock level

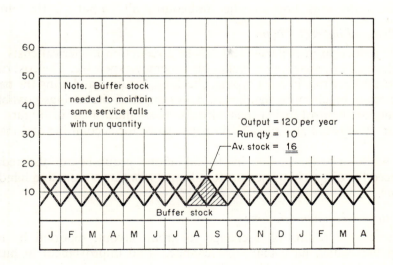

(b) Low 'run quantity' – low stock level

Figure 3.3. Effect of run quantity on stock

(e) Reduced handling and setting costs

Because with group layout all the machines used to make each part are together in one group, the cost of inter-operation handling is very greatly reduced. The movement of materials between machines inside the group, can generally be managed without special handling labour, by using roller track, for example. For the same reasons the investment in containers, industrial trucks and other handling equipment is also less with group layout than with functional layout.

The reduction in setting cost has already been considered earlier in the chapter. It was seen that the change from functional layout to group layout reduces setting times, because it is easier for one foreman to schedule and control the work, so that parts in the same tooling families all come together for processing at the same set-up.

(f) Simplification of paper work

Another advantage due to group layout, is the big reduction in necessary paper work. Because all the operations done on each part are done in the same group, documents such as tool requisitions, material move tickets, job cards, and progress records are not needed. With, say, ten operations per part, thirty-five pieces of paper may be necessary to control the production of only one part, in a machine shop with functional layout. With group layout, as shown in Figure 3.4, one list order per cycle, is all that is needed in the workshop, to order and control all the parts in the family.

(g) Reduced indirect labour

The reduction in paper work leads to a reduction in clerical costs. It is not the cost of paper which makes bureaucracy expensive. The cost of the indirect labour required for typing, checking, reading, and filing the paper, is generally much more significant. An example of the savings possible in production control paper has already been illustrated in Figure 3.4. Major savings are also possible in paper work for accounting and inspection.

In addition to the savings in clerical labour, group layout also reduces the need for dispatching clerks, store-keepers, progress men, and handling labour.

(h) Improved human relations

One of the results of a change to group layout, reported by most companies which have made the change, is an improvement in human relations. It appears that Group Technology has a contribution to make to industrial peace. Two possible explanations can be provided. The first is that group layout provides independent groups of people, working together towards common aims, with a significant and easily recognized task completion stage. The group is not only a collection of machines; it is also a group of people working together as a team. There is a growing body of

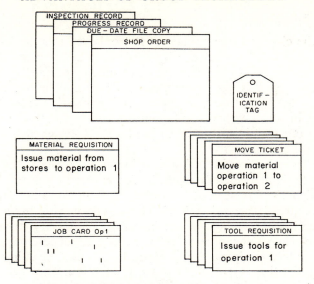

(a) Functional layout — paper required for EACH part

(b) Group layout — one list order per period for ALL parts

Figure 3.4. Simplification of paper work

research which indicates that this independence is important to both the workers' job satisfaction and the efficiency of the group.

The second explanation is that group layout reduces the need for co-ordination. With group layout most of the co-ordination needed in production takes place inside the groups. The foremen no longer have to co-operate closely with other foremen to do their job. This greatly reduces the amount of stress* in the organization.

* See CHAPPLE and SAYLES, *The Measure of Management* (New York: Macmillan).

(*i*) *Reduced investment*

Finally the change to group layout not only reduces the investment in stocks, but also reduces other forms of investment. It reduces, for example, the investment in buildings necessary per unit of output, partly because group layout requires less space than a functional layout of the same machines and partly because the capacity of the existing plant is increased. The savings in space with group layout are partly due to the reduction in work in progress and partly due to the fact that fewer machines require direct gangway access.

Because the reduction in setting time increases capacity, the investment in machine tools per unit of output, is also reduced by group layout. The way in which the investment in tooling and in handling equipment is reduced has already been described. The reduction in indirect labour will itself induce further savings in the investment necessary to support production, covering items such as office furniture, office equipment, office machines, canteen equipment, and so on. It will often be difficult to realize cash savings for these types of investment reduction. They generally represent only an increase in the capacity for expansion, and therefore a saving in future investment.

3.5   ADVANTAGES OF FLOW CONTROL

A number of the advantages obtainable with Group Technology spring directly from the use of flow control ordering. Others are greatly magnified by this change. The main advantages of changing from stock control to flow control are:

1. Reduced materials obsolescence
2. Reduced direct material cost
3. A contribution to the following savings already described under group layout:

> (*i*) Reduced throughput time
> (*ii*) Improved ability to follow market changes
> (*iii*) Reduced stocks
> (*iv*) Simplification of paper work
> (*v*) Reduced indirect labour

4. The elimination of inter-departmental stores

(*a*) *Reduced materials obsolescence*

In all cases where assembled products are produced, or where components are made which are used in sets, a change from stock control to flow control will reduce the costs of material obsolescence. With stock control each component is ordered independently to a different cycle. The parts are therefore never in product sets. Any modification to design, or the elimination of any product from the range, invariably leaves a remnant of stocks, which only has scrap value (*see* Figure 3.5). With some types of product a few of the parts, left after a product is taken out of production, may have a future sale as spare parts. Generally however, only a very small proportion have this possibility.

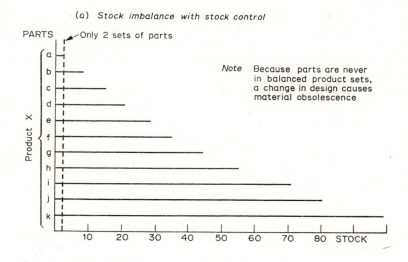

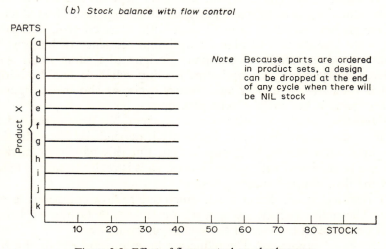

Figure 3.5. Effect of flow control on obsolescence

With flow control the ordering of parts is based on a sales forecast for products. Parts are ordered and made therefore in product sets and apart from minor variances due to scrap, they only exist in product sets. It is possible therefore to introduce design modifications and to take products out of production, with no materials obsolescence losses whatsoever.

(b) Reduced direct material cost

In the same instance of assembled products, or of components used in sets, flow control will also allow a reduction in the cost of general materials —such as sheet metal, plate, steel bar, and metal sections—which are used in products.

With flow control and standard products all components are ordered every cycle. Components made from the same materials can therefore be grouped for their first operations. In this manner it is possible to plan the cutting of material to give minimum wastage and maximum material utilization.

With stock control such planned material cutting is impossible, because the parts made from the same material are seldom on order together. Some savings may be made by the efficient use of off-cuts, but any financial advantage possible, is usually more than discounted by the need to store the off-cuts until the stock control system produces another suitable order. In any case the use of off-cuts for individual items does not give the savings possible with planned cutting.

(c) Contribution to group layout savings

A number of the savings attributed to group layout, depend also on the use of flow control.

(i) Reduced throughput time, for example, depends mainly on the fact that the machines used to make parts are close together. The reduction is however greater with flow control than with stock control, because it is easier with flow control to plan an optimum sequence of loading. With standard products made to company designs, the same items will be reordered every cycle. An optimum loading schedule can be adopted, which is used over and over again every cycle, as shown in Figure 3.6. This approach is known as Cyclic planning.

(ii) Improved ability to follow market changes, has been described as an advantage due to group layout. Indirectly it depends on the reduction in throughput time caused by group layout, but this particular advantage could not be achieved with stock control, so it is really equally due to the use of the flow control ordering system.

(iii) Reduced stocks again are as much due to flow control as to group layout. The major reductions in stock possible with Group Technology, cannot be made with either of these changes on its own.

(iv) Reduced setting cost. The reduction in setting cost obtainable by the use of tooling families, is very largely dependent on flow control. If stock control is used with group layout these savings are not obtained because the different parts in each tooling family are ordered at random and are not available for processing at the same time.

(v) Simplification of paper work, is still another case where the benefits come from the use of both group layout and flow control together at the

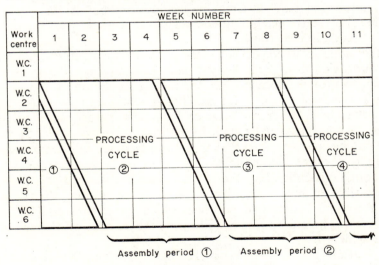

(a) A standard loading sequence is designed

N.B. The numbers above each bar on the chart, are 'part numbers'

Figure 3.6. Cyclic planning

same time. The savings in production control paper work illustrated in Figure 3.4, could not be obtained with either change on its own.

(*vi*) *Reduced indirect labour*, finally, is again partly due to flow control. Flow control systems are basically simpler than stock control systems, and they can normally be operated by fewer people even with functional

C

layout. With group layout it should be possible to run a flow control system with fewer people than stock control and with a much shorter cycle.

(d) The elimination of inter-departmental stores

One other major saving possible with flow control and group layout, is the elimination of inter-departmental stores. With stock control and functional layout, it is generally necessary to establish stores between each major process. Examples are casting stores between foundries and machine shops, forging stores between forges and machine shops, and finished parts stores between machining and assembly departments.

In the case of the first two examples, it should always be possible to eliminate the store. Because most castings and forgings go only to the machine shop, it should always be possible with group layout and flow control, to schedule production so that castings and forgings are delivered directly to the groups where they are machined. The amount of storage space required at the group, will depend on the standard ordering cycle, and on the sequence of loading. At one extreme, if the foundry finishes all the castings for a programme cycle before the machine shop starts work, space will be needed for all the castings used during one cycle, At the other extreme, if both foundry and machine shop use the same loading sequence, the foundry need only start making castings one or two days before the machine shop starts machining and very little storage space for materials will be needed in the groups.

In the case of finished part stores the problem is more difficult, due to the need to provide storage for bought parts and also, in some types of production, to provide storage space for the accumulation of assembly sets. Stores are usually essential for purchased items, because it is generally necessary to hold buffer stocks, as an insurance against random delays in delivery. A good case can be made for putting such stores under the control of the purchasing department, so that it can be made fully accountable for the supply of all purchased items.

Although it is difficult to eliminate all stores for finished parts, however, it is possible to make considerable savings by routing all made parts direct from the processing department which makes them to the assembly department. Three examples will illustrate the ways in which such savings can be achieved.

(i) *Standard products made on fixed assembly lines.* Where a company makes a small number of standard products, on a number of fixed assembly lines, made finished parts can be delivered direct to the assembly line. There will be a special storage place on the line for every item, with sufficient space to hold enough parts for one ordering cycle. If the same sequence of loading is used every cycle in the processing departments, the stocks of each part provided by the previous cycle will be running low, when the new batch of that item is delivered.

Class 'C' low value purchased parts, such as nuts and bolts, can be issued to replenish line stocks as necessary, on a free stores basis. Other purchased parts can be issued to the line from the bought part stores once a cycle, in the quantities required to meet the programme for the cycle.

If some of the made parts are required for sale as spare parts, they can be provided by adding a spares allowance to the production batches. These allowances plus any unused scrap allowance can then be removed at a quantity control check point between the processing departments and assembly for storage in a spare parts store. The only other problem likely to arise, is if some items are needed in more than one place on a line, or on more than one line. Arrangements must be made for the division of such batches, and their distribution between the different places where they are held and used.

(*ii*) *Many assembled products on impermanent assembly lines.* Examples of this type of problem can be found in the agricultural machinery industry, where different types of product are made at different seasons of the year, and new assembly lines are set up for each product in turn. In this case it is necessary to have a *transit store* where sets of parts are accumulated. As soon as the run on the previous product is completed, the new line is set-up, and the sets of parts are issued from the transit store. If a product is in production for two or more ordering cycles, the subsequent batches can be delivered direct to the line as in the first example.

Because with flow control the parts are always made in balanced product sets, it is unnecessary to route made parts into a controlled store, and incur the heavy costs which this involves. The parts need only be counted once, at a quantity control point between the processing departments and assembly, and can then be accumulated into assembly sets, in the containers which will later be used for storage on the line.

(*iii*) *Parts for welded assemblies.* It is possible to route parts for welded assemblies direct to the places where they are used. In one factory making mines equipment including conveyors, many different types of welded assembly are produced. The welding department is divided into groups, each handling a specified family of welded assemblies. The groups are so formed that each specializes in a family of welded assemblies requiring similar welding skills, similar positioning and welding equipment, and similar lifting and handling equipment. Each group has its own special storage racks on which sets of parts are accumulated for the different assemblies they produce.

The facilities for producing parts for welded assemblies are also organized in groups, including two flame cutting groups and one with saws for cutting pieces from steel bar and sections. Two of the groups have machine tools for those parts which require machining prior to welding. As soon as a batch of an item is completed, it is moved directly to the welding group which will use it.

(e) Savings from the elimination of inter-departmental stores.

The main savings achieved by the elimination of interdepartmental stores are:

(*i*) A reduction in handling costs
(*ii*) A reduction in storage costs
(*iii*) A reduction in throughput time
(*iv*) A reduction in work-in-progress
(*v*) The release of space for expansion

With functional layout and stock control, the use of inter-departmental stores may reduce the lead time for new assembly programmes. However they also increase the total lead time including the time required for ordering materials and for component processing. Even with functional layout and stock control, it is doubtful if inter-departmental stores give any significant increase in flexibility.

With group layout and short cycle flow control, inter-departmental stores serve no useful purpose. They only add unnecessary cost and increase throughput times and stocks. Under these conditions it should normally be possible to control the flow of materials right through the factory without inter-process stores.

3.6   PRACTICAL EVIDENCE OF SAVINGS

With one exception the companies which have introduced Group Technology, have published very little about the economic improvements they have made. The exception is a British valve-making company; Serck-Audco Ltd. The following results are taken from a booklet published for the National Economic Development Council, by Her Majesty's Stationery Office in London.*

Sales	: Increased 32%
Stocks	: Reduced 44%
Stock/sales ratio	: Reduced from 52% to 25%
Throughput time	: Reduced from 12 to 4 weeks
Overdue orders	: Reduced from 6 to less than 1 week
Despatches per employee	: Increased about 50%
Capital investment	: Cost of introduction recovered 4 times by stock alone

Other savings which were quoted in papers given at an International Seminar held at the Turin International Centre in September 1969, included the following:

(a) S. P. Mitrofanov, U.S.S.R.

The following savings were given in his paper 'The Scientific Bases of Group Technology':

* National Economic Development Office, *Production Planning and Control* (London: H.M.S.O.).

(*i*) The efficiency of group production is convincingly borne out, by manufacturing data from factories in Russia and elsewhere. The conversion of universal machines for group production increases work productivity by 40% to 50%.

(*ii*) The cost of standardized and specialized machinery can be reduced by 40 to 50%.

(*iii*) Process planning time can be reduced by 25–30%.

(*iv*) The time required to plan group equipment (tooling), can be diminished by as much as 50–60%.

(*b*) *Jacques Schaffran, France.*

The following saving is quoted in his paper 'The Application of Group Technology in the Société Stephanoise de Constructions Mécaniques': '. . . a reduction over 5 years (in the number of inventory items) of more than half . . .'

(*c*) *Professor V. B. Solaja of Jugoslavia.*

In his paper 'Optimisation of Group Technology lines . . .' he quoted a saving in working hours of 54% (455·231 hours reduced to 246·182 hours) in a metal working firm.

(*d*) *Ing. Frantisek Mändl of Czechoslovakia.*

In his paper 'Problems and Results of the Introduction of Group Technology', he quotes the following savings in tooling and equipment:

(*i*) It reduces the work expenditure in the designing of equipment (tooling) by 30–70%.

(*ii*) It reduces the cost of manufacture of equipment (tooling) by 40–80%.

(*iii*) It reduces the consumption of material (for tooling) by 50–90%.

(*iv*) Setting times cut by 60%.

(*v*) Unit times (including setting) cut by 23%.

(*e*) *A. Zvonitzky, U.S.S.R.*

In his paper 'Part Classification and Organisation of Group Production', he says: 'Within the last decade, (only) in the Russian Federation, the group machining method and its supreme form the organisation of group production, were introduced in more than 800 plants. . . . The annual saving was 7–8 million roubles'.

(*f*) *F. R. E. Durie, United Kingdom.*

In his paper 'Group Technology as Applied in an Electronic Firm', he quotes a reduction of 66% in setting time with one group.

Individual savings of these types may not be as convincing as the more comprehensive Serck-Audco figures, but they do at least indicate that

Group Technology is a development with wide possibilities and not just something special which has worked well for one company only.

3.7 ECONOMICS OF GROUP TECHNOLOGY

It is interesting to speculate why this new approach of Group Technology is so much more effective economically than the many other management techniques and new methods, which have been tried in recent years.

The main effect of Group Technology is a significant improvement in profitability. Profitability can be defined as the productivity of capital and is generally measured by the ratio known as the *rate of return on investment*, (R), in which:

$$R = \frac{Profit}{Investment} \times 100\% \tag{1}$$

or

$$R = \frac{(Output \times S.P.) - Cost}{Fixed\ assets + Stocks + Liquid\ capital} \times 100\% \tag{2}$$

Where *S.P.* = selling price

Group Technology is of major significance because it is a strategy of production management which gives important savings both above and below the line. By adopting a small number of changes from traditional policy—of which the most important are group layout, short cycle flow control, and a planned loading sequence—Group Technology at the same time increases capacity and output, reduces costs, reduces the investment in fixed assets per unit of product output, and reduces the investment in stocks.

Because it has this double effect—both above and below the line—it is a much more potent way to increase profitability than any policy which attempts solely to reduce costs, or solely to improve some other single variable. Consider some of the important savings made possible by Group Technology, and the way in which they affect profitability.

(a) Output

The reduction in setting times increases production capacity. The reduction in throughput time, shorter delivery times, better achievement in meeting delivery dates, and greater flexiblity to follow market requirements, all tend to increase sales output. None of these changes would be particularly significant on its own, but in combination they provide a powerful impetus towards increased output.

(b) Costs

The reduction in materials costs, in handling costs, in storage costs, in production control cost, in accounting costs, in setting costs, in materials obsolescence, in production planning costs, in tool design costs, and in the costs of paper and printing, may each be relatively insignificant on its own. When one set of changes makes it possible to achieve all these savings together however, the total saving can be extremely significant.

(c) Investment in fixed assets and tooling

The reduction in tooling investment, and the elimination of the need for building and services for inter-process stores, both reduce the investment required to sustain a given level of output. In effect, too, the increase in plant capacity also represents a reduction in the investment in plant and buildings, in relation to the level of output which it can sustain. Even if it were necessary to increase the investment in fixed assets initially, this would be unimportant if it resulted in a much greater reduction in the investment in stocks. As far as profitability is concerned, it is the reduction in total investment that matters.

(d) The investment in stocks

Finally the introduction of Group Technology has a major effect in reducing the investment in stocks. It reduces the stock of finished products and of work in progress at all stages of conversion, by an amount which has already in some firms, more than doubled their rate of stock turnover.

3.8 SUMMARY

Only a small part of the savings from Group Technology arrive automatically. To achieve the remainder, one must know what savings are possible, and take the appropriate action to get them.

Each of the key features of Group Technology makes some savings possible. These savings are however greatly magnified, if all four features are introduced together. Apart from these direct savings Group Technology also makes it possible to achieve other savings in other management functions outside production management.

The real test of Group Technology is that companies which have introduced it, have achieved savings which could not have been achieved by any other known approach. The main gain is in profitability. Group Technology is apparently a strategy of production management, where the same changes induce an increase in output, a reduction in costs and a reduction in the investment in stocks and fixed assets. The net result is a major gain in profitability, or profit per unit of capital invested.

4 Production Control and Group Technology

4.1 INTRODUCTION

One of the key changes for a successful application of Group Technology. is the change in production control from stock control to flow control, This chapter examines the nature of these two different approaches to the regulation of material flow in industry, and explains why the change is both desirable in its own right and necessary for the successful introduction of Group Technology.

Further information about the change in production control is given in the next three chapters. The first describes the most commonly used flow control system known as Period Batch Control. The second considers the problem of planning a new production control system—the third examines the special problems of Dispatching with Group Technology.

4.2 PRODUCTION CONTROL

Production control is the function of management which plans, directs, and controls the material supply and processing activities of an enterprise. A short description of the subject will serve to define the main terms used in the argument.

The work of production control is carried out at three successive levels of planning, known as:

1. Programming
2. Ordering
3. Dispatching

The work done at each of these levels is illustrated in Figure 4.1, which also shows the form of plan produced at each level.

(a) Programming

All production control is concerned with scheduling, or with planning the times at which different work tasks are to be started and/or finished. Programming first is concerned with scheduling the completion of finished products by the enterprise. The schedules produced at this level are known as 'Production programmes'.

The basic information required for Programming is contained in a

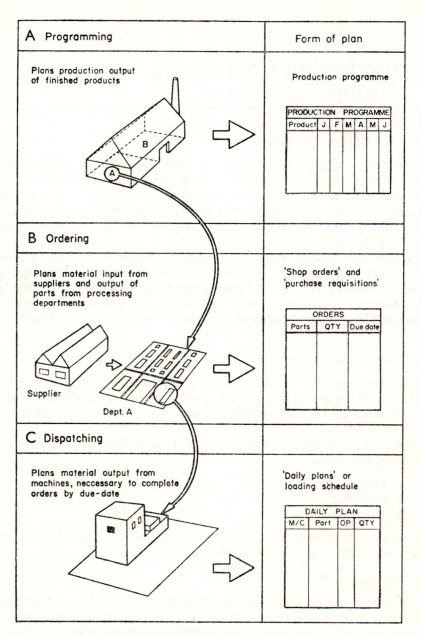

Figure 4.1. Levels of production control

'Sales programme', or 'Sales forecast'. This shows the number of products which can be sold and/or be delivered to customers in particular time periods. There is no sense in making products if they cannot be sold and this information is basic to all efficient production control. The sales programmes are generally produced by the Marketing department. Production control then translates these programmes into efficient production programmes.

Most enterprises make several programmes covering different times ahead, or to use another expression: with different 'terms'. For example they may have:

1. *A long-term programme*, covering six or more years ahead, reviewed and up-dated every six months, and used as the basis for long-term financial planning, plant development, product development, and training.

2. *Annual sales and production programmes*, covering one year ahead, reviewed and up-dated every two months, and used as the basis for the annual budget, for controlling purchase deliveries, and for sales control.

3. *A series of short-term sales and production programmes*, planned, say, every two weeks, and used as the basis for the control of processing inside the enterprise, and to control the delivery of some purchased items.

(b) Ordering

The next level of production control is known as Ordering. It is concerned with scheduling the output of processed components from processing departments and the input of materials and purchased parts from suppliers. The plans made and issued as 'orders' are commonly known as 'shop orders' if delivered to processing shops, and 'Purchase Requisitions', if delivered to a Buying department.

There are two main systems used to control the issue of orders, known as the 'Flow Control' and 'Stock Control' ordering systems. With a flow control system the quantities to be ordered and the delivery dates are calculated directly from a series of production programmes, a process widely called 'explosion'. A typical flow control system called 'Period Batch Control' is illustrated diagrammatically in Figure 4.2 and is described in detail in the next chapter.

With the period batch control system the time interval between the issue of orders is fixed and the order quantities are varied to regulate material flow. With the stock control ordering system the order quantity is generally fixed separately for each component and the interval between orders is varied to regulate material flow. A simple stock control system is illustrated in Figure 4.3. It will be seen that for each item there is a fixed order quantity and a fixed re-order level. When the stock drops to the re-order level, a new order is issued for the chosen fixed order quantity.

It will be noted that while flow control systems attempt to gear material flow inside the factory, directly to the sales and distribution flow, stock control systems use stock to isolate one part of the flow system from the

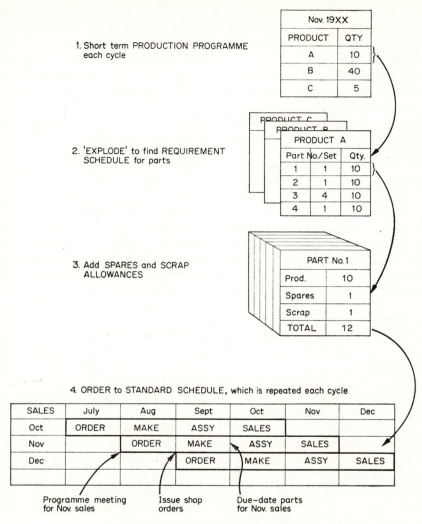

1. Short term PRODUCTION PROGRAMME each cycle

Nov. 19XX	
PRODUCT	QTY
A	10
B	40
C	5

2. 'EXPLODE' to find REQUIREMENT SCHEDULE for parts

PRODUCT C
PRODUCT B

PRODUCT A		
Part No./Set		Qty.
1	1	10
2	1	10
3	4	10
4	1	10

3. Add SPARES and SCRAP ALLOWANCES

PART No.1	
Prod.	10
Spares	1
Scrap	1
TOTAL	12

4. ORDER to STANDARD SCHEDULE, which is repeated each cycle

SALES	July	Aug	Sept	Oct	Nov	Dec
Oct	ORDER	MAKE	ASSY	SALES		
Nov		ORDER	MAKE	ASSY	SALES	
Dec			ORDER	MAKE	ASSY	SALES

Programme meeting for Nov. sales   Issue shop orders   Due-date parts for Nov. sales

Figure 4.2. A flow control ordering system

next. The production programme in this second case is used mainly to control assembly, but it also provides the data needed to fix batch quantities for component orders.

(c) Ordering Cycle and Phase

Ordering systems vary in cycle. The ordering cycle is the time between orders. A part which is said to be ordered to a monthly cycle then, is one for which a new order is issued every month. Ordering systems can be either multi-cycle systems, or single cycle systems. A multi-cycle system is one in which every part in use is ordered independently to a different

(a) The plan (different for each part)

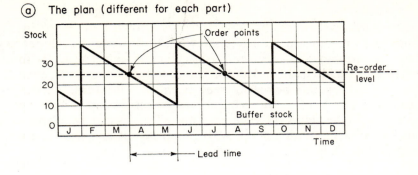

(b) The method

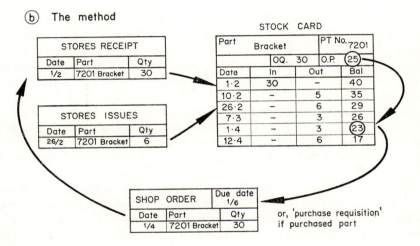

1. All finished items held in controlled store

2. All transactions recorded on receipt or issue notes

3. Notes used to maintain balance of stock record

4. When stock drops to order point issue new order

Figure 4.3. A simple stock control system

cycle. A single cycle system is one in which all parts are ordered to the same cycle.

Ordering phase is concerned with the time relationship between the cycles for different parts. With a single phase system all items are ordered on the same series of order days for completion by a related series of due dates. With a multi-phase system the order dates and due dates are different for each part. Most stock control systems are multi-cycle systems. They are always multi-phase systems. Most flow control systems are both single cycle and single phase systems.

(d) Dispatching

The third level of production control is known as Dispatching. It is concerned with the scheduling of the work to be done in each processing shop. In a machine shop in an engineering factory for example, the foreman will receive hundreds of orders for batches of different parts, each made by a series of operations on different machines. Dispatching is the job of scheduling or planning the sequence in which the operations on these parts should be done on each machine. The special problems of dispatching in a processing shop, with group layout and flow control, are examined in Chapter 7.

(e) Progressing and Inventory control

An essential process in all management is the process of Control. Control can be defined as the process of management by which events are constrained to follow plans. All management controls involve the comparison of actual output with planned output; the detection of significant variances, and the 'feed-back' of information about these variances to those in the organization with the necessary authority to take corrective action.

The two major controls used in production control are called 'Progressing' and 'Inventory Control'. Progressing is concerned with controlling the output plans made in programming, ordering, and dispatching. Inventory control watches the level of stocks, and gives warnings when the actual levels approach the planned safe levels for the enterprise.

With the stock control system of ordering, the ordering system itself fulfills some of the functions of detailed inventory control. The terms 'Stock Control' and 'Inventory Control' are therefore very often confused. In this book the term 'Stock Control' is only used to describe the type of ordering system in which the issue of new orders is based on a stock re-order level. The term 'Inventory Control' is reserved for all systems designed to control the level of stock in the enterprise.

4.3 DEFICIENCIES OF THE STOCK CONTROL SYSTEM

The stock control ordering systems are inefficient and unstable, particularly when used to regulate the issue of orders for parts used in sets. The most important deficiencies of these systems are:

1. They can only operate successfully with a high investment in stock

2. They are the major cause of losses from material obsolescence

3. They generate a widely fluctuating and unpredictable variation in the stock level

4. They generate an unbalanced and unpredictable variation in the load of work on the factory

5. If used to control a succession of processes, they magnify the demand and stock variation at each following level

6. They make it impossible to take advantage of the savings attainable with family processing

Each of these deficiencies is briefly considered below.

(a) High stock investment

With a stock control ordering system, the consumption time for a batch must be longer than the lead time for a replacement supply. This provision is illustrated in Figure 4.4. Attempts to reduce stocks by reducing

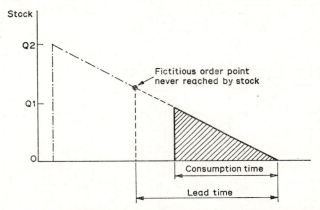

Figure 4.4. Consumption time and lead time

batch quantities will eventually fail, because lead times do not fall in proportion when batch quantities are reduced.

In practice it is difficult to make a stock control system operate reliably, if the lead time for a batch is more than two thirds of its consumption time.

(b) Materials obsolescence

Because with a stock control system each item has a different order quantity and a different cycle, the stock is never in balance in product sets. As illustrated in Figure 3.5, a change in design in any assembled product will tend to generate losses, due to remnants of unusable materials and parts.

(c) Fluctuating stock level

Because the stock cycles for the parts ordered by a stock control ordering systems are out of phase, the total stock varies widely and in an unpredictable manner.

Figure 4.5 shows the variation found by simulation for total stock in a hypothetical company. This type of variation is widely experienced in industry, but all too often is attributed to production control inefficiency.

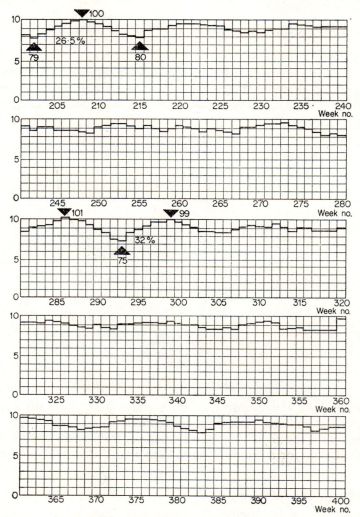

Figure 4.5. Stock level fluctuation with stock contro

In reality it is a natural characteristic of the stock control system. It is interesting to note that the total stock curve, eventually tends to assume approximately the same shape as the saw tooth stock cycles for individual components.

(d) Unbalanced load of work

For the same reasons as those which cause the fluctuations in stock level, the random issue of orders from a stock control ordering system generates a widely fluctuating and unpredictable variation in the load of work on the factory. Figure 4.6 shows the variation of outstanding load in

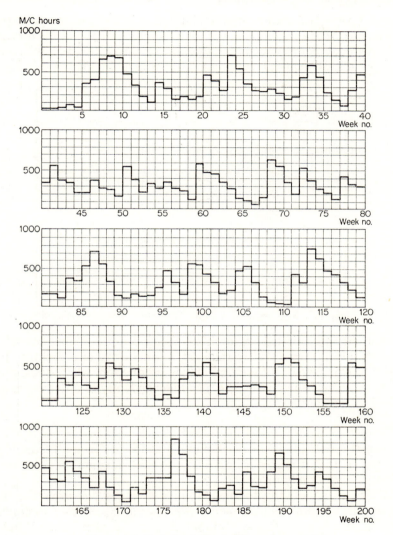

Figure 4.6. Variation in load with stock control

machine hours on a particular machine, which was found by simulation. The number of orders released by the stock control system will vary each month, and there will also be a big variation in the type of order. It is possible for example, that in one month most of the orders issued on a machine shop will be for bar lathe work, with very little work for other types of machine. In other periods there may be no work for the bar lathes and too much for the other machines.

(e) Magnification of demand cycle

Jay W. Forrester demonstrated by simulation in the research programme which he calls 'Industrial Dynamics', that stock control systems inevitably pass on a greater demand variation than they receive. This magnification of the amplitude of demand variation is illustrated in Figure 4.7. Jay W.

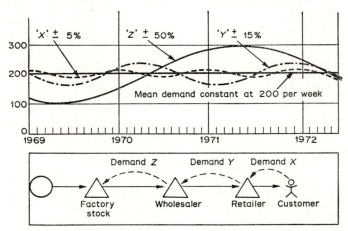

Figure 4.7. Magnification of demand variation with stock control

Forrester did his original research on distribution systems, considering chains of inventories held by retailers, wholesalers, and factory stores. Exactly the same effect is found in factory production, when stock control is used to order finished parts, and also independently to order the castings required to make them.

(f) Preclude the use of family processing

A special disadvantage of stock control as far as Group Technology is concerned, is that it makes it impossible to take advantage of the savings obtainable with family processing.

The idea of processing tooling families of parts one after the other, using the same tooling and the same set-up is central to Group Technology. To use this approach it is essential that the parts in each family should all be on order at the same time. Stock control releases orders at random and does not bring parts in the same tooling family together for processing one after the other.

4.4 THE PERFECT FLOW PROJECT

The deficiencies of stock control ordering described above, are widely known from experience. They can also be convincingly demonstrated by simulation.

The results shown in Figures 4.5 and 4.6 for example, were taken from a simple simulation project run by the author at the Turin International Centre and named the 'Perfect flow project'. The computer in this case was programmed to simulate perfect flow in which product output was at a perfectly even rate, there was no processing scrap and there were no delivery delays.

It was postulated that if even under these ideal conditions the stock control system was unreliable and unpredictable, the imperfections of reality could not make it stable. The imbalance of the stock; the wide, unpredictable variations in stock level; the unbalanced and unpredictable load on the plant; and the failure to bring families of parts together for family processing; were all demonstrated by the project.

4.5   ADVANTAGES OF FLOW CONTROL

The advantages of flow control ordering were described in the previous chapter. Here it is only necessary to show that flow control ordering systems overcome nearly all the deficiencies of the stock control ordering system, which are described above.

(a) The stock investment

The stock investment with any ordering system depends on the cycle. The shorter the cycle the lower the stock. The stock investment is lower with flow control than stock control because flow control systems can be operated efficiently with shorter cycles. This relationship is well known in relation to materials, work in progress, finished parts, and total component stocks. It may be less clear that reducing the cycle time with a flow control system also reduces the finished product stocks. This is so because reducing the programming and ordering cycle, both increases the accuracy of the sales forecasts—because they cover a shorter period ahead—and also gives more frequent opportunities for the correction of errors in previous sales forecasts. Shortening the cycle makes it easier for production to follow changes in market demand with a minimum investment in finished product stocks.

(b) Materials obsolescence

Because a flow control ordering system always orders materials and parts in balanced product sets, it is comparatively simple to plan product changes so that there are no losses due to materials obsolescence. If a product is taken out of production at the end of a cycle, there will be no stocks of obsolete parts, other than a small number of parts provided as scrap allowances and not used.

(c) Fluctuations in stock level

Figure 4.8 shows the changes in total stock level with time, for a flow control ordering system under conditions of perfect flow. These changes

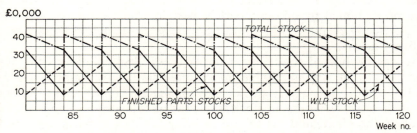

Note: This figure shows the stock variation for the whole 229 parts taken as one sample.

Figure 4.8. Variation in stock with flow control

are regular and predictable. The amplitude of the variation will depend on the chosen cycle, and will fall as the cycle is reduced.

(d) Balance of load of work

The balance of load on the different processing facilities in the factory, is much more even with flow control than with stock control. There may be minor changes in the proportions of the load on different machines, due to differences in the product mix in different period programmes, but these variations will always be much less significant than those generated by stock control and illustrated in Figure 4.6.

With a flow control system one starts by attempting to match the processing capacity level, with the mean load level imposed by sales. Thereafter one attempts to fill the selected capacity level in each successive period, in order to use the available facilities to the best advantage. This gives a much more efficient use of available processing facilities, than is ever possible with the random supply of orders provided by stock control.

(e) Magnification of demand cycle

The magnification of the demand cycle when stock control is used on a series of inventories, which is demonstrated in 'industrial dynamics', can be avoided if all orders on all successive processes or inventories are based on the actual or planned output of finished products. This principle is followed by the flow control ordering systems.

(f) Family processing

With standard products, or products made to company designs, the flow control system generally orders the same components every cycle. All the components in any tooling family are always therefore ordered together at the same time, and full advantage can be taken of the possibilities of family processing.

4.6 OPERATION TIME AND CYCLE TIME

Most of the advantages of short cycle flow control are obvious and desirable. The one great stumbling block to the general acceptance that this is a desirable change, hinges on doubts about the effect of such a change on operation costs.

It is widely reasoned that reducing the cycle times, reduces batch quantities and must therefore increase operation times and reduce production capacity. Experience with Group Technology has demonstrated the fact that this theory is wrong. The most successful applications of Group Technology have in fact achieved substantial component cost reductions and significant increases in product output capacity, in spite of a reduction in nominal batch quantities. The following are some of the probable reasons why these savings are achieved.

(a) Operation time and setting time

Traditional methods of costing tend to over-estimate the importance of operation time and to under-estimate the importance of setting time. In many factories operation times are closely controlled against standard times, while setting times and costs are recovered in costing by means of a fixed overhead rate.

The research carried out under Professor Dudley of Birmingham University has already been mentioned. It demonstrated that the machines in a sample of Birmingham factories were used on average as follows:

1. Actual processing: 41%
2. Setting up: 45%
3. Idle time: 14%

It is readily apparent that savings in setting cost can be just as effective in reducing costs, as savings in operation costs. In practice any losses due to increased operation times with small batches can be more than compensated by the savings in setting costs with flow control and family processing.

(b) Learning time

One basis for the belief that operation times per piece must increase with reductions in batch quantity, is founded on the theory of learning time. This theory says that any operator requires a certain 'learning time', every time he starts a job, before he achieves his optimum output rate. It is reasoned therefore that the average output rate will be higher with large batches because the learning time losses will be spread over a greater number of parts.

Against this simple theory it can be argued, that:

1. The learning time tends to be less with an oft repeated job (short cycle) than with a job seen only rarely at long intervals (long cycle).

2. The learning time for a tooling family of similar parts processed together at the same set-up, will be less than the sum of the individual learning times when each part is processed separately.

3. In practice there are compensating losses with large batches, due to fatigue and boredom which reduce the potential savings.

4. The significance of learning time is mainly restricted to manual operations. It does not apply to automatic machines.

Some of these effects are illustrated in Figure 4.9. There appear to be few logical reasons why operation times should increase significantly when batch quantities are reduced, with the same output rate. In the long run too, the reduction of setting time with family machining makes it possible to use high output methods economically for short runs, and makes it possible to achieve operation time and cost reductions which it would be impossible to achieve with traditional methods.

(c) Nominal and actual batch quantities

The significance of the reduction in batch quantities is easily over-estimated. A manager hearing that his present average batch quantity is eight weeks supply and that with flow control it will be reduced to two weeks, might imagine that all his batches were being reduced to a quarter of their original size. Allowing however for split batches due to scheduling difficulties and material shortages, and for stoppages due to shift changes; other routine stops; and maintenance, the true change would be much less significant.

He would also probably find that his present average batch quantity was inflated by very high batch quantities for a small proportion of the parts. The main impact of the change is only likely to affect a limited number of parts and processes.

(d) Summary—operation time and cycle time.

The real proof that short cycle flow control does not increase component costs, or reduce production capacity, can be found in the results achieved by companies which have made the change.

The actual change in batch quantities is less than the change in nominal batch quantities would appear to suggest. The larger the nominal batch quantity, the more frequently will it be necessary to split batches, to achieve a viable loading schedule. Because short cycle flow control with family processing, tends to reduce learning time per batch, and to reduce the boredom generated by very long runs, the actual output rates do not fall when batch quantities are reduced, as much as traditional learning theory suggests.

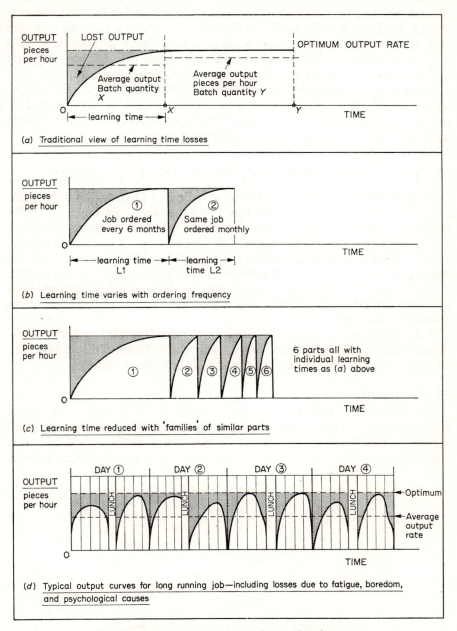

Figure 4.9. Learning time and operation time

Finally setting-up time represents a much higher proportion of total component time on the machine than has been realized in the past. Because short cycle flow control coupled with group layout and a planned sequence of loading, make it possible to reduce setting times substantially, it is possible to reduce batch quantities and at the same time increase capacity and reduce component costs, even if operation times increase.

While it is certain that large increases in annual output rate do tend to reduce component costs, it is doubtful if significant savings in cost or capacity can be made by increasing batch quantities and reducing batch frequencies for the same annual requirement rate.

4.7 ECONOMIC [*SIC*] BATCH QUANTITY   (EBQ)

One of the major obstacles to the introduction of Group Technology has been a widely held belief in the theory of the economic batch quantity. Originating in the United States at the beginning of the century—where it is better known as the Economic Lot Size theory—it has been repeated and is still being repeated in nearly every book on Production. Until the introduction of computers, the theorem was seldom applied in practice. Today however, most computer companies have standard library programmes for calculating EBQs, and a growing number of firms are introducing the method.

It is important that those who attempt to introduce Group Technology, should understand why, particularly as far as the ordering of direct materials for production is concerned, this theorem is completely false.

(a) The theorem

The theorem of the economic batch quantity is illustrated in Figure 4.10. It is assumed that costs can be divided into two types. First, preparation costs, which cover such items as ordering and setting-up. These costs are supposed to have a fixed value per batch. It is assumed that the pre-

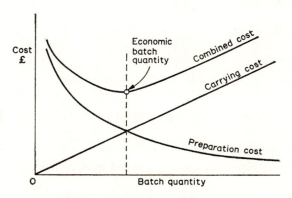

Figure 4.10. The Economic Batch Quantity

paration cost per piece falls rapidly at first, but at a gradually reducing rate as batch quantities are increased and the fixed preparation cost is spread over more and more parts. The second type of cost postulated by this theorem is Carrying cost. This type of cost covers all storage expenses and also an opportunity cost, or charge on tied-up capital. Carrying cost is supposed to vary directly with batch quantity. When plotted together, there is a point where the combined cost is at a minimum. The batch quantity at this point is known as the economic batch quantity.

In practice the EBQ is normally calculated using a mathematical formula such as Camp's formula, which is reproduced below:

$$Q = \sqrt{\frac{2PR}{CI}}$$

Where:

Q = Economic Batch quantity
P = Preparation cost per batch (£)
R = Annual requirement
C = Unit cost (£)
I = Inventory carrying cost (%)

It will be noted that it is very difficult to estimate values for some of the variables used in the equation. It will be realized that if there are 30,000 parts made in a factory, the preparation of the estimates needed for calculation, will itself be a major work. As many of the values will change with time, the estimates will also require revision from time to time. Strangely enough, some exponents of the method say that accurate estimating is not necessary. They say that rough estimates are good enough, because there is a wide range of values for batch quantity on either side of the EBQ, for which there is a negligible change in cost per piece.

It is supposed that if the EBQ is calculated for every part, and if these batch quantities are used in production, then the total cost of production will be minimized.

(b) *Changes of cost with changes in batch quantity*

If one takes a list of the main expenditures in a factory, and analyses them on a cash flow basis to find the probable changes in expenditure with changes in batch quantity, one finds that the curve produced is quite unlike that shown in Figure 4.10. Most of the expenditures will be found to be fixed expenses in relation to changes in batch quantity and batch frequency. Only a small proportion of the total expenditure varies with batch quantity. Figure 4.11 illustrates the type of curve found by economic analysis of this kind.

It will be seen that the experts who say that there is a wide range of usable batch quantities on either side of the EBQ are quite right. Looking at this curve, which is typical of those generally found in practice, it will be obvious that even with functional layout one could choose one common batch quantity for all parts, with a negligible increase in cost per piece, over that achievable by using the exact EBQ for each part.

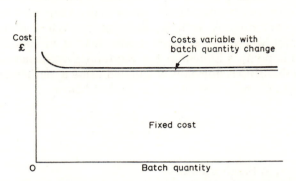

Figure 4.11. Cost change with batch quantity for one part

(c) Ordering cycle and phase

In practice a number of companies have achieved a substantial reduction in costs, by changing to one single order frequency, or cycle for all parts, and by ordering all parts together at regular intervals. This is the principle of the single-cycle single-phase flow control ordering system—known as Period Batch Control—which was described earlier in the chapter.

The substantial reductions in cost and investment which are possible with this system of ordering, are very much greater than any minor reductions which may be achieved by varying the order quantity separately for each part. Savings are obtainable even with functional layout, but these are greatly increased if, as in Group Technology, the change from a multi-cycle to a single-cycle system is coupled with a change from functional to group layout. Because the use of economic batch quantities imposes multi-cycle multi-phase ordering, it is impossible to achieve these major savings with the EBQ.

(d) Types of batch quantity (Made parts)

Another error in the economic batch quantity theorem, is that it suggests that there is only one batch quantity. In actual fact there are many kinds of batch quantity. Most of them can be varied independently, within certain limits. Because they generally have different economic effects, there are big advantages to be gained by fixing different values for the different types of batch quantity.

In the case of made parts there are four main types of batch quantity.

1. *The order quantity*, or quantity of a particular part, which is shown on the shop order.

2. *The run quantity*, or quantity of a particular part which is run off on a

machine consecutively. If the order is split, this can be less than the order quantity.

3. *The set-up quantity*, or quantity of parts—not necessarily all the same —which are produced with the same machine set-up. With *tooling families* this will be much greater than the run quantity for any one part.

4. *The transfer quantity*, or quantity of a particular part which is transported together as a handling batch between work centres. With line flow the transfer quantity will be 'one'. With other types of layout the transfer quantity may still be smaller than the run quantity.

Reducing either the run quantity or the transfer quantity, tends to reduce stocks. With functional layout and stock control, these changes will also increase some types of cost. With group layout and flow control however, most of these cost increases can be avoided. For example reducing the transfer quantity with functional layout increases handling costs, but has little or not effect on these costs if group layout is used because the machines are close together. Increasing the set-up quantity by using tooling families both reduces costs and increases capacity with no increase in stocks. Even though it cannot always be achieved in practice, the optimum production policy tends to be one which creates conditions, where it is possible and economical to reduce order and run quantities to fit a common cycle for all parts; to reduce transfer quantities to a value of as near one as possible; and to increase setting quantities to the maximum possible level.

Nearly all the published work on the economic batch quantity is based on the conditions imposed by stock control and functional layout. The authors assume that the values for all four of these batch quantity types must be the same, and they generally include the economic effects of all four at once, in the models used to find the EBQ. They also assume that there is a fixed preparation cost per batch, when in fact preparation costs vary greatly with ordering method and loading sequence.

(e) *Types of batch quantity* (Purchases)

A modified form of EBQ formula is again widely advocated for controlling the size of purchase batch quantities. Once again however, there is not just one type of batch quantity. The two most important types in this instance are:

1. The purchase order quantity, or total quantity covered by the purchase contract
2. The delivery batch quantity (transfer quantity) or quantity included in a delivery

In this case, increasing the purchase order quantity will tend to reduce purchase prices. On the other hand, reducing delivery batch quantities will tend to reduce the investment in stock.

In most cases the optimum purchasing policy will be one which selects reliable suppliers, increases purchase order quantities to the limit imposed by the risks of obsolescence and price reductions, and reduces delivery batch quantities to the point where a marginal increase in the costs of transportation will represent an uneconomic rate of interest on the equivalent marginal reduction in the stock investment.

In some text books transportation costs per piece are shown as rising sharply as purchase delivery batch quantities are reduced. This is not necessarily the case. For example, if one uses *input analysis* to analyse the geographical location of suppliers, it is possible to simplify the supply system, by reducing the number of suppliers and by giving preference to suppliers from particular areas. At constant output, the weight to be transported per week is approximately the same, whatever the delivery batch quantity. One lorry collecting ten different items once a week from the same supplier will cost little more than if the lorry collects 10 weeks supply of one particular item every week.

One particular danger of using the EBQ approach for purchased parts, is that it greatly increases the risk of obsolescence. When a product design has to be changed, there will be widely different quantities of different parts and special materials outstanding on order. A much safer approach is to use the Sanction method, widely applied in mass production, with which outstanding orders are maintained as far as possible in balanced product sets, covering a specified, 'sanctioned' time ahead for each product.

(f) Other points against the economic batch quantity theorem

Three further points may help to reinforce this case against the economic batch quantity.

There is a principle that the sum of a number of sub-optimum solutions does not achieve a total optimum. The EBQ theorem is the supreme example of sub-optimization. In a company making and buying 40,000 parts, it says that one must consider each part on its own—ignoring all others—and find in turn the optimum batch quantity for each of them. It then goes on to say that if you use these 40,000 sub-optimum solutions, you will achieve the total optimum of minimum production cost.

This assumption is false because the inevitable differences in order quantity imposed by the use of the EBQ, themselves impose the use of an extremely inefficient production system. The theory is based on an obsolete idea that the production system is a fixed immutable system like the systems studied in the natural sciences. In fact production systems are created by human beings. There is generally more to be gained by changing the system, than by optimizing the methods of regulation in the existing traditional systems.

Finally if the EBQ is the correct scientific approach for batch production, why isn't is used in mass production? Is it possible to believe that the applied science of production is so strange, that as one reduces production quantities, a point is reached where the economic laws of production are completely changed?

4.8 SUMMARY

Production control is the function of management which plans, directs. and controls the material supply and processing activities of an enterprise, It takes place at three main levels known as Programming, Ordering, and Dispatching.

Most existing production control systems are based on stock control. This system generates unpredictable and unstable stock levels and work loads. It requires a large investment in stocks to make it work, and causes high costs which can be avoided by other methods.

The acceptance of stock control is generally coupled with acceptance of the pseudo-scientific theory of the economic batch quantity which is mistakenly supposed to find the most economic order quantities for use with stock control.

Flow control systems for the ordering of direct materials are much more efficient than stock control and are essential to the success of Group Technology.

5 Period Batch Control

5.1 INTRODUCTION

Period Batch Control is a production control ordering system of the flow control, single-cycle, single-phase type, which is used mainly to control the ordering of materials and parts for assembled products to standard designs, in continuous or intermittent production.

The basis of the system is that ordering is to a fixed cycle. The quantities of components and materials to be ordered each cycle, are calculated directly from the numbers of products shown in a series of short-term production programmes, a process commonly known as 'explosion'.

In many ways this is the most important of the production control ordering systems. Systems of this type are used almost universally in mass production. Although not yet widely used in batch production, when it is used it is always much more efficient than the traditional stock control systems. It is fundamental to the successful introduction of Group Technology. In an adapted form it has also been used with success in jobbing production of single component products.

A pioneer in Period Batch Control, and the man who gave it its name, was an English management consultant, the late Mr. R. J. Gigli. He designed the system described in this chapter, and as a Director of A.I.C.— the British Management Consulting firm—he installed it in many different companies. Similar systems had been used previously in mass production. His contribution was to adapt the system for batch production.

This chapter is mainly concerned with the use of Period Batch Control in companies making a range of assembled mechanical products to standard designs. Ways are described later in the chapter, however, by which the system can be adapted for jobbing production and for the production of single component products.

5.2 OUTLINE OF PERIOD BATCH CONTROL

The basic steps taken in Period Batch Control have already been illustrated diagrammatically in Figure 4.2. The year is divided into equal cycles and a short-term sales programme is produced for each cycle in turn. The level of capacity is then fixed, and a short-term production programme is planned for the same cycle, which meets the sales programme requirement and also fills the capacity available.

The production programme is next 'exploded' to find the numbers of components and the quantities of materials which must be ordered for the cycle. These quantities are then ordered to a 'standard schedule', which allows time for raw material production or delivery, component processing or delivery, and assembly. This standard schedule is repeated every cycle.

The standard schedule in turn, sets the lead time required between the start of each sales period and the date of the programme meeting at which the two short-term programmes are discussed, amended, and accepted. The shorter the cycle and standard schedule, the shorter will be the time ahead for which marketing must forecast future sales. Short cycles and schedules therefore, give benefits in more accurate forecasts, more frequent occasions for the correction of past errors, and a system which is flexible and can quickly follow changes in market demand, with a minimum investment in stock.

Errors in the estimation of allowances for scrap and spares sales, and either under- or over-production against orders, will lead to component stock accumulation or shortages. All period batch control systems require some provision to correct these possible errors. Practical methods are described later in the chapter.

In any enterprise there are likely to be some components, which are better handled by some other ordering system, outside the period batch control system. Possible exceptions and complementary ordering systems are also described later.

5.3 THE CYCLE

For period batch control, the year must be divided into a number of approximately equal time periods, or cycles. Assuming that the production capacity is approximately in balance with the market demand, the choice of a cycle of say two weeks, implies that it is possible to assemble two weeks average sales requirement in two weeks; it is possible to make the parts for two weeks assembly in two weeks, and it is possible to make the raw materials for two weeks processing in two weeks.

The shorter the cycle, the more flexible will be the system to follow changes in market demand, with a minimum of stock. Reduction of the cycle is however, subject to two main limitations:

1. It cannot be less than the throughput time for any of the components.

2. It must not increase the proportion of setting time, so that capacity is reduced below the level required to meet the demand.

(a) Throughput time

With traditional methods of batch production, functional layout is used and the machines for successive operations on components are generally far apart in different sections. Under these conditions the component throughput time cannot easily be reduced below the sum of the operation times for all operations, plus handling and queuing time. Throughput time in this case is a major limitation to the reduction of the cycle.

With group layout, on the other hand, some measure of continuous transfer is possible, at least for the critical components. Following operations can be started before preceding operations are finished without increasing handling costs, thus reducing throughput times and permitting the use of much shorter cycles. An engineering factory, which with functional layout and period batch control can operate successfully with a cycle of four weeks, can probably use a cycle of one week if it changes to group layout.

(b) Setting time

Setting time is a much less serious limitation, because period batch control itself makes it easy to reduce setting times. Because all components are ordered together, it is possible to choose a sequence of machine loading, which brings together parts with similar set-ups and thus greatly reduces setting time. These savings are greatest when group layout is used.

With traditional methods of batch production using stock control ordering, orders are released at random. Parts which might be machined at the same set-up, or have similar set-ups are seldom on order at the same time. Setting time losses are always much greater with stock control than with period batch control.

(c) The cycle time scale

Period batch control has been used with a cycle of calendar months. This, however, produces certain complications. If, for example, the factory shuts down for two weeks holiday in August, it will be faced with the problem of making enough parts for the four weeks assembly in September, during only two weeks in August.

A better method is to divide the year into 50 working weeks, and use a cycle measured in working weeks. The minor differences caused by occasional national holidays, can generally be accommodated and this is the most widely used time scale. Some companies however, wishing to have an even more regular time scale, divide the year into 'working days' excluding all holidays, and use a time scale based on fixed numbers of these working days.

A difficulty with these 'working week' and 'working day' calendars, is that they complicate sales forecasting. Due to the wide use of monthly credit for sales, it is easier to forecast sales on a calendar month basis. This generally means that sales must first make their forecasts on a calendar month basis, and then re-allocate these sales to the special calendar periods needed for efficient production.

5.4 THE STANDARD ORDERING SCHEDULE

The form of the standard ordering schedule, will depend on the types of work to be controlled by the short-term programmes.

(a) Assembly only

The simplest case is where assembly is the only process. Figure 5.1 shows a possible standard ordering schedule of six weeks for this case, with a cycle time of two working weeks. Programme meetings will be held on Friday every two weeks. At each meeting the Sales Department will produce a forecast showing what they expect to deliver in the two weeks starting four weeks

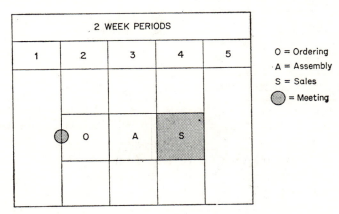

Figure 5.1. Standard ordering schedule—assembly only

ahead. During the first two weeks of these intermediate weeks, the production programme will be published and shortages will be made good, during the second two weeks the products will be assembled. This method is easy to introduce and can be recommended as a good first step in the introduction of period batch control. Before the time comes to extend the system to the control of component ordering, the programming system will be well established and working smoothly.

(b) Assembly plus component processing

The standard schedule for assembly only, can be extended to cover component processing, by adding one more cycle period between ordering and assembly, as shown in Figure 5.2(a). There is however a complication in this case. Imagine that the machines in the processing shop are listed progressively, with those used on first operations at the top and those used for last operations at the bottom. When one now prepares a schedule for one cycle's work, it will be found that it has more the shape of a parallelogram than a rectangle, as shown in Figure 5.2(b).

D

All parts must be finished, to provide complete product sets, before assembly can start. If one starts processing at the beginning of the cycle, there will be spare time between the processing cycles, as is also shown in Figure 5.2(*b*). Two solutions are possible. The first is to accept this gap as

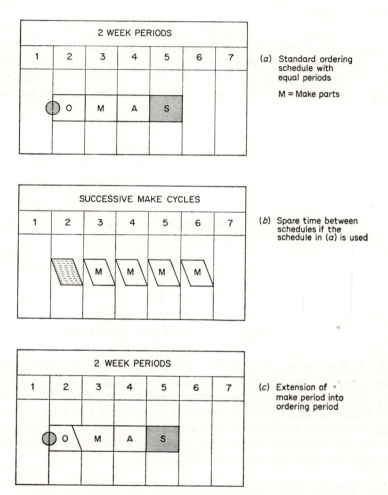

Figure 5.2. Standard ordering schedule, including component processing

an allowance for late work and to provide capacity for rush orders and other additional work. The second is to start processing during the ordering period as shown in Figure 5.2(*c*). To make this possible, either ordering must be speeded up, or the orders can be divided into two parts, the first issued early to cover the overlap and the second later, to complete the ordering up to the end of the cycle.

(c) *Assembly, plus component and raw material processing*

For safety, some companies prefer to add an additional cycle for raw material processing, as illustrated in Figure 5.3(*a*). In practice, however

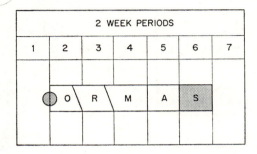

(a) Additional period for Make Raw materials

R = Make Raw materials

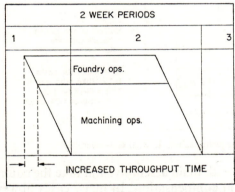

(b) Elimination of additional period by using same loading sequence in successive departments

Figure 5.3. Standard ordering schedule with raw material processing

this increase can be avoided if desired, as shown in Figure 5.3(*b*). Provided that the raw materials, say castings, are made and forwarded for processing in the same sequence as they are machined, they can be added to the schedule with very little increase in throughput time.

(d) *Sub-assembly*

The most difficult process to accommodate is sub-assembly. If there are two sub-assembly stages, it is very difficult to avoid adding two more full cycles to the standard schedule. Because full sets of sub-sub-assemblies are needed before sub-assembly can start, two full cycles must be added (*see* Figure 5.4(*a*)).

A possible method with one sub-assembly stage is illustrated in Figure 5.4(*b*). The parts for sub-assemblies are made in the first half of each processing cycle. Sub-assemblies are made in two batches per cycle. This method is, however, complicated to control, and it prevents the use of an optimum sequence of loading for processing.

Where possible, the best method is to treat major sub-assemblies as separate products and make them to their own programme, and then

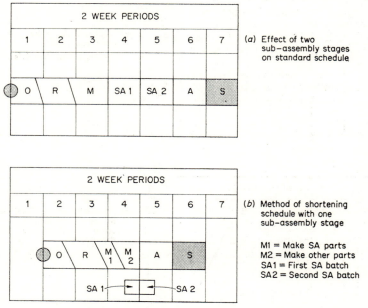

Figure 5.4. Standard ordering schedule with sub-assembly

consolidate minor sub-assembly with main assembly, and take the counter-advantages of job enlargement in compensation. In many cases however, where, for example, welded sub-assemblies are produced, the addition of an extra cycle cannot be avoided.

(e) Purchase delivery lead time

Note that the standard schedule fixes the purchase delivery lead time. If purchasing is based on long-term supply contracts, with 'call-off' at cyclic intervals, the 'call-off notes' can be sent to the suppliers at the end of the order period in the standard schedule. They will call for delivery by the start of the assembly period. In Figure 5.3(a) for example, the lead time is four weeks, and in 5.4(a) it is four weeks for parts used on sub-assemblies and eight weeks for parts used on main assembly.

It is often difficult to persuade suppliers to accept short lead times. When lead times are unacceptably short, the only solutions possible are to extend the standard schedule, which reduces flexibility, or to exclude certain classes of purchases from the period batch control system, and use some other ordering system to maintain supplies.

5.5 WHICH COMPONENTS TO INCLUDE

It will generally be necessary to exclude some components and material items from the period batch control system, for control by other systems. The usual reasons for such exclusions, will be that inclusion would increase either the cycle time or the standard schedule excessively, or would increase control costs.

(a) Made Parts

It should be possible to include the great majority of made components inside the period batch control system. The only likely exceptions are components with very complex routes, and some types of assembly.

(i) *Complex routes*. In all companies there are generally a few components which have very complex routes, involving, for example, operations in many departments or at outside sub-contractors. If the ordering system is designed to include these items, it will be so complicated and long-winded, that it will be uneconomic in its handling of the, say, 98% of components with simpler routes.

The commonest solution of this problem, is to abstract the items with

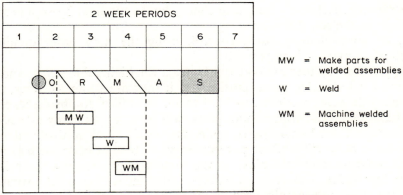

Figure 5.5. Standard ordering schedule with welding

complex routes, for special scheduling. Another possibility is to use the technique of 'Production Flow Analysis' to find the complex routes, and then eliminate them, by re-routing, re-design, change of method, or buying instead of making.

(ii) *Welded and sheet metal sub-assemblies*. Products which include made welded and, or sheet-metal sub-assemblies, pose a special problem, because they tend to increase the standard ordering schedule. Because welded assemblies generally require the three stages of component production, welded assembly, and machining, before main assembly, they generally require that there must be at least two cycles between ordering and main assembly, as shown in Figure 5.5. Normally this solution will be accepted, rather than control the manufacture of welded assemblies by some other method.

Note that, as with all assemblies, complete assembly sets of parts must be available before welding can start. Note also that one might plan the sequence of component processing to produce sets of parts for welding progressively. In this latter case however, one would lose the advantage of better material utilization, which might otherwise be achieved by cutting all the parts made from each type of material, one after the other. In spite of these limitations, a small amount of time overlap is generally possible in the standard schedule for welding, to make it fit into two cycles.

(b) Bought parts

As far as bought parts are concerned, the problem is more difficult. In most countries it is difficult to persuade suppliers to deliver small quantities to call-off notes against long-term supply contracts. Most bought parts must therefore:

1. Be scheduled for, say, monthly delivery, against schedules based on a long-term programme. Buffer stock can be used to compensate for variations between the long-term programme, and the series of short-term programmes. Relatively long lead times may be required by suppliers for changes in the schedules, or

2. Be controlled by stock control, using the high order quantities required to make this system work.

In general, the first method will be used for high value items, and the second for low value parts, particularly if they are common items, used on many different products, and not therefore subject to obsolescence.

The primary aim with bought parts, will be to get as many as possible of the high value bought parts, under the period batch control system. It may never be worth-while to put the low value bought parts, such as nuts, bolts, washers, and split pins, on the same system. Because these items have low value, excess stock makes little impact on total inventory. Because they are generally used on more than one product, consolidation to find the total requirement for ordering, would be expensive. For the same reason, obsolescence losses will tend to be lower than for special parts. Under these conditions stock control ordering is acceptable.

(c) Bought materials

In the case of bought materials, the aim should be to get as many as possible of the 'special material' items, such as castings and forgings, on call-off. Where this is impossible, they should be ordered to a schedule of deliveries based on a longer term programme, with buffer stock to compensate for differences between this schedule and the series of short-term programmes. Due to the high risk of obsolescence with these materials, stock control ordering should be avoided.

With 'general materials', such as bar, sheet, and plate, delivery against call-off notes based on the short-term programmes, is only possible if one takes supplies from a stockist. Theoretically this ought to be the most profitable method of buying for both the stockist and the supplier. In practice however, few stockists are organized to provide this type of service.

Alternatives are to order to a delivery schedule based on the explosion of a longer term programme; or in the case of widely used materials: to order to a delivery schedule based on a statistical projection of past usage; or in the case of low consumption, low cost items, to use 'stock control'.

5.6 THE SHORT-TERM SALES PROGRAMME

Each new cycle requires one further short-term sales programme. This short-term programme is merely a forecast of product sales for which despatches can be made to customers during the cycle. In the case of Figure 5.6, for example, the sales programme issued at the programme meeting for each cycle, covers the two week period starting six weeks ahead.

No corrections are made for overdue deliveries against previous sales

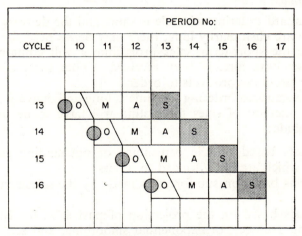

Figure 5.6. Successive cycles

programmes, or for errors in past forecasts. All errors of this type are corrected together, when the short-term production programme is prepared. A common error when designing production control systems, is to make the same corrections twice. To avoid this, it is better to make the short-term sales programme stand on its own each cycle, and to do all corrections together at the later stage.

(a) Sales orders and despatches

If all sales orders received, can be despatched as soon as the products are produced, the sales programme will be both a programme of probable despatches, and a forecast of probable sales orders received. Providing there is sufficient capacity to meet demand, delivery promises for new orders will be based, in this instance, on the time allowed for manufacture by the standard schedule.

If, on the other hand, it is customary to receive some orders for forward delivery, these will not be included in the short-term sales programme, until their delivery period is reached. A separate memorandum should be provided with the sales programme, showing all outstanding orders for future delivery, under their allocated delivery periods.

Finally, if demand has overtaken capacity and it has been necessary to extend the lead time for delivery promises, the sales programme will only show those orders which are due for delivery in the new period. Once again however, a memorandum should be provided showing all other outstanding orders.

An advantage of this method of only including products in the sales programme if they can be despatched, is that it simplifies the fixing of accurate delivery promises.

(b) Forecasting

If the standard ordering schedule is short and the delivery promises in the industry are customarily long, there may be no need for forecasting. In this case the short-term sales programmes will contain customer's orders, which have already been received. Under these conditions the factory only produces products to order.

Where the standard ordering schedule is long and delivery promises are short, some method of sales forecasting will have to be used. Typical methods include:

1. Forecasts based on the percentage of outstanding enquiries and quotations, which are likely to lead to orders
2. Forecasts based on sub-forecasts made by the salesmen in different areas
3. Forecasts based on the projection of past sales for each product, using moving averages, or exponential smoothing, and seasonal corrections
4. A combination of all these methods

5.7 THE SHORT-TERM PRODUCTION PROGRAMME

The next operation in period batch control is to plan a short-term production programme which will:

1. Provide the products, shown as required for despatch in the short-term sales programme
2. Use the full capacity provided for production

3. Provide for any accumulation of product stocks needed to cover future seasonal demand peaks, holidays, or large orders

This programme will be similar in form to the short-term sales programme. The products to be made will generally be the same as those to be sold. In some cases, however, where a wide range of products is made from a limited number of major assembled units, there may be advantages in using these units as the product units for the production programme. In this case an additional assembly programme will be needed to show how they are to be combined for sale.

A simple routine for planning the production programme has three main steps:

1. Estimate finished product stocks at the beginning of the sales period for the cycle

2. Calculate the 'Minimum make quantity' needed to meet the sales programme.

3. Plan the 'Fill quantity'—if any—to use the full capacity available.

(a) Estimate finished product stocks

Considering Figure 5.6 again, assume that when framing the production programme for Cycle No. 16 at the beginning of Period No. 13, it is necessary to estimate the free stock of finished products at the beginning of Period No. 15, which is the assembly period for the cycle.

A finished product stock check will have been made at the end of Period No. 12, and the present stock of all finished products will be known. A separate estimate will be made for each product in turn. The details of the calculation are given for one product below.

> (A) PROVISION:
>
> | | |
> |---|---:|
> | Stock end Period 12: | 15 |
> | plus Programmed Cycle 14: | 20 |
> | plus Programmed Cycle 15: | 21 |
> | plus Outstanding Production: | 2 |
> | *Total provision;* | 58 |
>
> (B) REQUIREMENT:
>
> | | |
> |---|---:|
> | Sales Programme, Cycle 13: | 12 |
> | Sales Programme, Cycle 14: | 15 |
> | Sales Programme, Cycle 15: | 25 |
> | Outstanding Sales orders: | 1 |
> | *Total requirement;* | 53 |
>
> (C) OPENING FREE STOCK:
>
> | | |
> |---|---:|
> | Period 15: | 5 |

(b) Calculate 'Minimum make quantity'

The minimum number of products which must be assembled to meet the sales programme is now found very simply, by subtracting the stock forecast from the sales requirement.

PRODUCT A   Sales Programme, Cycle 16   20
          less: Opening Stock, Period 15   5
                   Minimum make quantity, Period 15   15

If it is desired to hold a buffer stock of each product, the minimum make quantity may be redefined as the quantity required to meet expected sales and also maintain the buffer stock. If for example, the required buffer stock for product 'A' is 5, the calculation would change to:

PRODUCT A   Sales Programme, Cycle 16   20
             Buffer Stock   5
             Total   25

          less: Opening Stock   5
                   Minimum make quantity   20

Another method of maintaining a buffer stock, which is preferable when the demand is seasonal, is based on the use of a stock programme, and is also described later in the chapter.

(c) Plan the 'Fill quantity'

The next step is to find out how much capacity will be required to provide the minimum make quantity; how much spare capacity will be available, and what additional products should be made to 'fill' this spare capacity.

If the capacity level has been set accurately to match the mean demand rate, and if sufficient buffer stocks are held to cover random variations, it should normally be possible to meet the sales demand. If the sales demand

Product	MIN MAKE QUANTITY					FILL QUANTITY		MAKE QTY.	Code
	O/stock	Sales	Min. make	Man hrs each	Man hrs total	Quantity	Man hours		
A	5	20	15	100	1500	5	500	20	–
B	11	40	29	200	5800	10	2000	39	–
C	2	10	8	50	400	–	–	8	–
	–	–	–	–	x=7700	–	y = 2500	–	–

NB: x + y = Available capacity (10, 200 man hrs)

Figure 5.7. Calculating 'fill' and 'make' quantities

is above the mean rate during one period, the buffer stock will be used to complete the requirement. If the sales demand is below the mean rate in the next period, the spare capacity will be used to replenish the buffer stocks.

Occasionally special increases in demand may occur which overload production capacity, and the sales department must then be warned that there will be longer delivery times for some products. On other occasions it may be necessary to make for stock above the buffer stock level.

A simple tabulation which might be used to calculate the 'fill quantity', and the final 'make quantity' for the programme, is shown in Figure 5.7.

(d) Seasonal variations and the stock programme

With most companies there will be seasonal changes in market demand and stocks must be accumulated in some periods, to cover higher sales in later periods. To cover this situation, a finished product stock programme is prepared to show the required level of stock at different periods. This programme is used as a guide to show which products should be included in the 'fill quantity', during the periods when production is at a higher rate than sales.

The stock programme should be revised at regular monthly, or bimonthly intervals, as the year proceeds. Figure 5.8 shows the stock pro-

		PERIOD NO.								
		10	11	12	13	14	15	16	17	18	19
1	Opening stock	10	15	20	25	30	33	36	34	14	10
2	Production	15	15	15	15	18	18	18	–	16	15
3	Total	25	30	35	40	48	51	54	34	30	25
4	Sales	10	10	10	10	15	15	20	20	20	20
5	Closing stock	15	20	25	30	33	36	34	14	10	5
6	Actual stock	9	21	25	29	33	36	34	18	8	5
7	Variance (+):	–	1	–	–						
8	Variance (–):	6	–	–	1						

NB: The annual 2 week holiday is in Period 17.

Figure 5.8. Stock programme for product *A*

gramme for a particular product, together with a record of actual stock for control purposes. If a stock programme is used, it is unnecessary to consider buffer stock when calculating the minimum make quantity. Any buffer stock needed to smooth random variations in sales orders, will be included in the stock programme, and this programme will indicate which products should be included in the fill quantity.

(e) Production Programme period

Consider again the case illustrated in Figure 5.6. Although the production programme for Cycle No. 16 covers the requirement for sale in the sales programme for Period 16, it actually provides the assembly programme for Period 15, and the basis for calculating the machining programme for Period 14.

5.8 CAPACITY

One of the advantages of period batch control is that it provides a measured amount of work each cycle, which fills a carefully selected capacity level. The full use of all the available capacity could only be obtained if production capacity exactly matched market demand and if all the different production facilities had exactly the same output capacity in terms of product output. These conditions never apply in practice. Inside these limitations however, period batch control achieves a near optimum use of facilities.

An important part of any period batch control system, is the regular checking and regulation of capacity levels.

(a) Balance of capacities

The capacity of a material flow system is limited by the capacity of its weakest link. In most factories product output capacity is limited by only a small number of bottleneck machines, or by the number of skilled men available for one particular occupation.

A main aim in the regulation of capacity is to bring the capacities of all production departments into as near a state of balance as possible. Under this condition, if there is sufficient capacity in the assembly department to assemble a given programme, there will be sufficient capacity in the processing departments to make the parts. Under this condition again, it will be sufficient to balance each programme assembly load with the assembly department capacity in man hours, to ensure that it will also be possible to provide the parts. In some cases however, some differential adjustment of capacities may be needed. This point will be re-examined later.

(b) Adjustment of capacity

The level of product output capacity can be adjusted by a number of different methods. These are listed progressively below:

(A) Flexible methods

1. Work overtime
2. Work Saturdays

(B) Less Flexible methods

1. Take on more men (up to limit of machine capacity)
2. Start a second shift (for bottleneck processes)
3. Sub-contract some operations
4. Buy some parts instead of making

(C) Inflexible method

1. Buy additional plant
2. Engage new labour to run it

All changes of these types should be made in such a way that they improve the balance of capacities. Note that in human terms it is much easier to increase capacity than it is to reduce it.

(c) Regulating the assembly capacity

An annual capacity plan will be prepared for assembly, when the annual programmes for sales, production, and stocks are prepared. An annual assembly capacity plan for a company making three products is illustrated in Figure 5.9.

The sales, production, and stock programmes will be revised at regular intervals and where necessary the assembly capacity plan will also be changed. When changes are made in assembly capacity, any necessary

		PERIOD No.					
		1	2	3	4	5	6
1	'A' Qty	20	20	25	25	25	30
2	Man hrs	2 000	2 000	2 500	2 500	2 500	3 000
3	'B' Qty	30	30	35	35	30	30
4	Man hrs	1 500	1 500	1 750	1 750	1 500	1 500
5	'C' Qty	12	12	15	15	15	15
6	Man hrs	1 800	1 800	2 250	2 250	2 250	2 250
7	Total man hrs	5 300	5 300	6 500	6 500	6 250	6 750
8	No. men	67	67	74	74	74	74
9	Overtime	–	–	8 hrs	8 hrs	5 hrs	8 hrs
10	Saturdays	–	–	–	–	–	4 hrs
11	2nd shift	–	–	–	–	–	–
12	New plant	–	–	–	–	–	–

Figure 5.9. Long-term capacity plan for assembly

changes must also be made in processing department capacity to bring them into balance.

Careful records of demand trend will be maintained and capacity levels will normally be changed only when there is a positive change in trend. The frequent changing of capacity levels to match random variations in period demand, is seldom economical.

In some companies there may be limits to the numbers of some products which can be processed and assembled. For example, floor area may limit the numbers of certain products, if fixed assembly stations are used. Testing facilities may limit the output of other products. Such limitations may limit the choice of distribution between product types, even though sufficient assembly man-hours are apparently available for other distributions. The production controller must know these limitations and take them into account when framing his production programme.

(d) Load checking

As each programme is produced, the load which it imposes on the plant should be calculated. Figure 5.10 shows a 'load summary', for the machines in a machine shop, showing the load imposed by the production programme for a particular cycle.

Note that standard setting times are not used in the calculation. Component setting times vary so much with period batch control according to the sequence of loading, that it is cheaper and more accurate to use

LOAD SUMMARY							DEPT: M/C shop	PERIOD No. *14*	
Products	'A' = 20		'B' = 30		'C' = 12		M/C hours		
M/C number	M/C hours		M/C hours		M/C hours		Required	Available	CR
	ea	Total	ea	Total	ea	Total			
2067	4	80	1	30	3	36	146	150	x
2058	2	40	0·5	15	2	30	85	100	
2176	0·7	14	1·5	45	1	12	71	150	
210	1·5	30	0·5	15	–	–	45	70	
7169	–	–	1½	45	2	24	69	95	
8211	0·6	12	1·2	36	0·6	8	56	59	x
8171	3	60	4	120	5	60	240	300	
8096	–	–	0·7	21	–	–	21	·40	

Figure 5.10. A Load Summary

random observation studies to find the setting time losses, and use them to adjust the capacity.

If all the products produced are of the same general types, changes in product mix from programme to programme, will have a negligible effect on processing capacity requirements. If there are major differences between products, it may be necessary to make special capacity level adjustments in some departments, and for some machines. Whether this is necessary will be revealed by the load summary. Overtime and Saturday work will normally be sufficient to accommodate the variations. In severe cases it may be necessary to make temporary transfers of men between groups.

(e) Major increases in capacity

Major increases in capacity can be achieved by increasing the capacity of bottleneck departments and processes. The production controller should know which are the bottlenecks, and should encourage the early preparation of plans for their elimination, so that capacity can be increased quickly if necessary. Large increases in capacity, involving major increases in investment, are best tackled as a part of corporate planning.

5.9 'EXPLOSION' AND ORDERING

The next step is to calculate from the production programme, the numbers of each part to be produced, or in the case of purchased parts, to be delivered. A separate 'list order' must be produced for every department, or in the case of group layout for every group, and also for the buyer.

Figure 5.11 shows a type of 'list order' form which can also be used for explosion in a factory using group layout and making three products. The family of parts for the group in question, is broken up into 'tooling families' and these are listed in their optimum sequence of loading. Manual methods can still be used in more complex cases, but the work can be greatly simplified by using punched card machinery or a computer. Methods are described in the next chapter.

The stock adjustment column in Figure 5.11 is used to correct component stock accumulation, or depletion, due to errors in previous scrap and spares forecasts. The method will be described in the next section.

The two columns at the right hand side of the list order, are used by the group foreman to record actual achievement. Towards the end of each cycle he can see at a glance which parts need special attention, if they are to be completed by due-date.

The due-dates on each list order will be based on the standard schedule. Returning to Figure 5.6 for example, the due-date on all list orders for component processing in Cycle 16, will be the last day of Period 14. The same due-date will also be used on the purchase delivery lists for finished parts sent to the buyer. The list orders for bought special materials however, would have to have an earlier due-date during Period 13. In this case there is insufficient time in the standard schedule to base deliveries of bought special materials on the short-term production programme, and some other system of ordering will have to be used.

5.10 STOCK ADJUSTMENT

All period batch control systems require some method for correcting stock accumulation, or for replacing shortages, due to over- or under-production, or to errors in the scrap and spares forecasts. With period batch control it is generally unnecessary to have inter-process stores. Parts are only made in the quantities required for assembly, so they can be sent directly on completion to the point in the assembly department where they are used.

Item no.	Tool fam.	Part no.	Description	A=20 ea	A=20 Total	B=30 ea	B=30 Total	C=15 ea	C=15 Total	Total prod.	Spares	Total nett	Scrap %	Scrap Qty	Stock adj +	Stock adj −	Total gross	Record
1	207	20763	Plug	1	20	−	−	−	−	20	1	21	5	2	−	−	23	25 ✓
2		19989	Cover	−	−	1	30	−	−	30	3	33	5	2	−	10	25	21 ✓
3		45678	Ferrule	4	80	4	120	2	30	230	3	233	3	7	−	−	240	239 ✓
4		45901	Sleeve	−	−	−	−	2	30	30	1	31	5	2	20	−	53	50 ✓
5		31110	Cover	−	−	1	30	−	−	30	−	30	5	2	−	−	32	36 ✓
6																		
7	219	19965	Bush	1	20	−	−	−	−	20	2	22	5	1	−	−	23	21 ✓
8		19000	Bearing	2	40	−	−	−	−	40	2	42	6	3	−	−	45	42 ✓
9		17602	Brg. housing	−	−	1	30	−	−	30	1	31	4	2	−	12	21	−
10		23191	Sleeve	1	20	−	−	−	−	20	−	20	4	1	−	−	21	22 ✓
11		50011	Loc. bearing	−	−	−	−	1	15	15	5	20	4	1	6	−	27	25 ✓
12		61127	Thrust bearing	−	−	−	−	1	15	15	2	17	5	1	−	−	18	20 ✓
13																		
14																		

Figure 5.11. List order

(a) *Quantity control point—Made parts*

In the absence of a store, it is necessary to establish a quantity control point. All parts are routed to this point on their way to the assembly department. The quantities are counted and these quantities are checked against the quantities ordered. For this purpose the man at the control point will have a copy of all processing group list orders.

A simple routine for disposing of the parts and reporting failures would be as follows:

(A) *Disposing of the parts*

    (i) If the quantity received is more than the production requirement:

        1. Send production requirement to assembly
        2. Send remainder to spares store

    (ii) If the quantity received is less than the production requirement: Send all to assembly

Part No.	Description	Group	Gross rec'd	Variance +	Variance −	Variance x
	PRODUCTION VARIANCE LIST PERIOD: 14 DATE: 17_ 7_19XX					
20763	Plug	M 5	25	2	−	−
19989	Cover	M 5	21	−	4	✓
31110	Cover	M 5	32	4	−	✓
19965	Bush	M 5	21	−	2	−
23191	Sleeve	M 5	21	1	−	−
61127	Through bearing	M 5	20	2	−	−

N.B. The Production Controller may ignore minor variances. Ticks in last column show variances he decides to correct.

Figure 5.12. Production Variance list

(B) *Reporting failures*

    (i) If the quantity received is less than the production and spares requirements:

        Note shortage on production variance list (*see* Figure 5.12)

    (ii) If the quantity received is more than the total quantity ordered:
        Note excess on production variance list (*see* Figure 5.12)

The 'Production Variance list' will be sent to Production Control daily. They will have a set of list orders already prepared for the next cycle. All significant excesses and minor shortages will be transferred from the production variance lists, to the stock adjustment columns on these list orders (*see* Figure 5.11), so that production in the next cycle can be adjusted.

In the case of major shortages, if there is sufficient stock in the spares store to overcome the shortage and meet spares demand for one cycle, parts will be borrowed from the spares store, and the shortage quantity will be added to the quantity to be produced in the next cycle, on the appropriate list order. If there are insufficient parts in the spares store, a special 'RUSH order' will be raised.

(b) Control of spares stocks

When spare parts for sale are made with the production batches, and are provided by either special spare parts orders or by adding a spares allowance based on estimated usage rates, it is necessary to provide some method for the control of spares stocks.

A suitable system for the spare parts store might work as follows:

1. A stock card is maintained for all items showing receipts, issues and balance.

2. A maximum stock level is fixed for each part.

3. A minimum stock level is fixed for each part.

4. If the stock exceeds the maximum, or falls below the minimum, the fact is noted on a 'Spares stock variance list'.

5. This list is sent daily to the Production Controller.

6. If the stock exceeds the maximum, the Production Controller has three options:

> (*i*) He can raise the maximum stock level if he finds it is too low to cover random variations.
> (*ii*) He can transfer some of the stock to assembly, and reduce production of the part by the same amount in the next cycle.
> (*iii*) He can reduce the spares allowance on future list orders.

7. If the stock falls below the minimum stock level he has four options:

> (*i*) He can lower the minimum stock level.
> (*ii*) He can raise the scrap and/or spares allowance.
> (*iii*) He can increase the quantity produced in the next cycle to provide a special increase.
> (*iv*) He can raise a special RUSH order.

5.11 ADAPTION TO OTHER TYPES OF PRODUCTION

The system described so far, has been concerned with the manufacture of assembled mechanical products, made to standard designs. A few examples will show how the same period batch control can be adapted to other types of production.

(a) Single component products

Companies which make single component products like nails, rivets, nuts, spanners, and many others, generally make a number of different product types, with a large number of variants of each.

The short-term production programme in these industries will show main types. Stock Ratio Optimization (STROP), or some similar method is then used to determine how the total should be divided among the variants of each type.

Explosion and the stock adjustment step are unnecessary, and period batch control in these industries is very simple. Short cycles and very short standard schedules, of, say, three periods maximum, can be used.

(b) Shoes and hosiery

A similar solution can be used in the hosiery and shoe industries. These industries generally make a number of product types in a very large variety of different sizes, colours and patterns.

Once again the short-term programmes will show forecast sales and planned production in pairs for each type. STROP again can take the place of Explosion, to find the breakdown into quantities of each variant. Orders for these quantities will then be placed on the appropriate departments.

Another possibility in this case is to add an additional period to the standard schedule for the accumulation of orders, and then order the exact quantity of each variant. In this case the standard schedule will include:

1. *First period:* Accumulate orders for delivery in third period and issue orders
2. *Second period:* Manufacture
3. *Third period:* Distribution

With a weekly cycle, this allows delivery quotations of three weeks. If this is too long, stock must be carried, and the first method using STROP is preferable.

(c) Wallpaper and decorative laminates

The problem of ordering in these industries is similar to that described above for shoes and hosiery, and the solution is the same.

(d) Jobbing Foundries and Forges

The products of these industries generally fall into major groups, all of which use the same processes in the same sequence. They are normally suitable for line layout. Generally there will be one process, or machine which limits output.

Period batch control can be used to control ordering very effectively. Short-term sales programmes are maintained for as many periods ahead as the forward order book. As orders are received they are entered on the short-term sales programme for their delivery period. If the orders are for scheduled delivery, the appropriate quantities are shown on the appropriate sales programmes.

A three period standard production schedule is used covering:

1. Accumulation of sales orders and ordering
2. Manufacture
3. Distribution

During the first period the short-term programme is prepared listing actual items to be produced. Preference is given to overdue orders and orders for the delivery period under review. The loads imposed by each order on the critical machine are estimated and progressively totalled. When the full capacity is reached, the programme is 'sealed'. If there is a shortage of load for any programme, work for future delivery may be brought forward.

Copies of the short-term programmes are issued to the factory as orders.

5.12 COMPLEMENTARY ORDERING SYSTEMS

When introducing period batch control, equal care must be given to the design of the complementary ordering systems for excluded items, as is given to the design of the period batch control system. Two main types of complementary system will be needed in most cases.

(a) Stock control ordering

Stock control ordering has the deficiencies that it requires large stocks to make it work; it causes obsolescence; and it is unsatisfactory for ordering made parts, due to the large variations in the load of work, which it releases per period. It can be used however for low value purchased items, particularly if they are used on several different products and are not therefore liable to become obsolete.

All items controlled by this method should be stored in a controlled store. Stock records must be maintained for all items, and a special re-order level is set for each one. Purchase requisitions are sent to the buyer when the re-order level is reached.

To make the system work efficiently, the order quantities set for each item, should be at least 50% greater than the quantity required to cover the lead time. Reasonable buffer stocks should be carried to cover random variations in lead time and consumption.

If a good storekeeper is available, the cheapest method of running this system, is to let the storekeeper send requisitions direct to the buyer. There is little point in maintaining duplicate records in Production Control. Costs can also be reduced by using 'permanent purchase requisitions', which are used over and over each time an order must be placed.

(b) Maxmim control

With this ordering method, long-term supply contracts are issued and arrangements are negotiated for delivery against schedules. The frequency of delivery and the lead time required for changes in schedule, are a matter for negotiation with the suppliers.

This system will be mainly used for medium and high value purchased parts and materials. The quantities covered by purchase contracts can be controlled by 'sanctions' issued to the buyer at regular intervals, showing the number of future product sets for each product, which he is authorized to cover by purchase orders. Contracts should be drawn up to permit modifications to designs, when necessary.

The schedules for delivery can be found by a number of different methods, of which the following are the most important:

1. Explosion from a long-term programme
2. Projection of the trend of past usage

The first will normally be used for special parts and raw materials, and the second is possible for widely used general materials, such as pig iron, and widely used grades of steel plate and sheet metal. Arrangements must be included to carry some buffer stocks to accommodate random variations in delivery and usage, and to allow sufficient flexibility for the requirements dictated by the series of short-term programmes to vary from the requirement forecast based on the long-term programme. The long-term programme and the schedule should be revised at, say, monthly or bi-monthly intervals.

Control is maintained by setting maximum and minimum stock levels. If stocks stay within these limits, the schedule is meeting the requirements of production. If either limit is broken, the Production Controller will check deliveries and issues, and amend the schedule when necessary.

5.13 INTRODUCING PERIOD BATCH CONTROL

The safest way to introduce period batch control, is to break the job into a number of separate projects and introduce them one after the other. In this way the impact of the change is limited to a smaller number of people at any one time, and each project can be introduced and consolidated before the next is started.

A list of the projects necessary in a typical introduction is given below:

1. Introduce short-term programming for assembly only.
2. Use Pareto Analysis to classify all parts into A, B, and C value categories.

3. Plan and install system for the regular revision of the annual sales, production, and stock programmes and for capacity planning.

4. Introduce a stock control system for low value common parts (Class *C*).

5. Introduce 'Maxmin Control' for Class *B* purchased parts.

6. Introduce 'Maxmin Control' for ordering general materials.

7. Negotiate with suppliers for the delivery of special materials against call-off notes.

8. Negotiate with suppliers for the delivery of Class *A* purchased parts against call-off notes.

9. Use 'Production Flow Analysis' to simplify the material flow system and eliminate as many parts with complex routes, as possible.

10. Introduce a special scheduling system, for any parts with complex routes which cannot be eliminated.

11. Introduce ordering of made parts and delivery call-off of Class *A* purchases, based on 'explosion' from the short-term production programme.

A simple critical path analysis network can be used to find the best schedule for introduction.

A manual should be prepared for each project describing the method. Affected personnel should be trained before introduction. Frequent checks should be made, particularly in the early stages, to see that the planned method is being followed.

The early introduction of Project 4 above, introducing a simplified system for Class *C* common parts, has the advantage that it reduces the load on the Production Control department, and releases personnel for the planning of the other new systems.

5.14 THE PROGRAMME MEETING

Generally it is advisable to have a short programme meeting at the beginning of every period, to co-ordinate planning and approve the programmes for the new period. The Managing Director, Production Manager, Sales Manager, Purchasing Manager, Accountant, and Production Controller will generally attend the meeting. The agenda for this meeting will typically include:

1. *Trends.* A report on the trend of sales and on variations between the annual programmes used to frame the annual budget, and actual sales to date.

2. *Short-term sales programme.* The Sales Manager presents his short-term sales programme for the period and explains any major variance between his sales programmes and actual sales for previous cycles.

3. *Capacity.* The capacity level for the cycle is proposed by the Production Manager. Alternatives are considered, and where necessary action to change capacity levels is co-ordinated.

4. *Short-term production programme.* The Production Manager will

already have received a copy of the sales programme and presents his suggestions for a short-term production programme. Alternatives are discussed and a programme is approved.

5. *Delivery lead times.* The deliveries for each product, which may be offered by salesmen, are considered and fixed.

6. *Purchasing problems.* The Buyer reports on purchasing lead times, and on likely problems with future material supplies.

The planning of the programmes for a company, is much too fundamental to the success, or failure of the enterprise, to be delegated to any one functional specialist. The programme meeting ensures that all factors are considered, and provides an opportunity for the co-ordination of all the activities involved.

5.15 SUMMARY

A change from stock control ordering to period batch control produces major savings, particularly in the case of assembled products to standard designs.

As a general rule a cycle should be chosen which is long enough to accommodate the throughput time for any made part, through any major stage of processing. A standard ordering schedule is then adopted which allows one cycle per stage.

It is sometimes possible to shorten the standard ordering schedule, by using the same loading sequence in two successive processing stages. It is also possible to accommodate items with very long throughput times for certain stages, by allowing two cycles instead of one, in the standard ordering schedule for that item.

The system is simple to operate and is not difficult to introduce if the work is tackled progressively as a series of independent projects.

Period batch control is an essential pre-requisite for the successful application of Group Technology.

6 Planning the Production Control System

6.1 INTRODUCTION

Although flow control is one of the key requirements for Group Technology, it cannot generally be used for ordering all the parts and materials required for production. Normally the ordering of some of these items must be controlled by other methods.

This chapter considers the data processing problems involved in planning a production control system for Group Technology. It starts by examining the product parts lists, which provide information about the items to be ordered. It then considers the choice of ordering system for each item, the preparation of list orders, the method used to calculate load, and the advantages of computerization.

The chapter deals mainly with the most complex case of many standard assembled products, which is common in the engineering, electrical, electronics, furniture, and other assembly industries. The special problems in jobbing industries are considered at the end of the chapter.

6.2 THE PARTS LISTS

The parts lists for each product provide the information needed to list all the different parts and items of material which must be ordered. Normally these parts lists will be broken up into separate sections and sub-sections for main assemblies and sub-assemblies. This is the most convenient method for the designer, and is also the best for the assembly department. However, this method of listing has two main deficiencies from the point of view of production control.

1. It gives no indication of the source of each item.
2. Common parts may occur in several different assemblies in the same parts list.

The production control system has to be planned to overcome these problems among others.

When there is a standard product, with several different variants, it helps production control if all the parts common to all variants are on one parts list, and the special parts for each variant are on separate lists. Other arrangements which involve adding some parts and subtracting others to find the variant requirement, should be avoided where possible.

6.3 COMPONENT INFORMATION ON PARTS LISTS

Most parts lists already give the part numbers and names of all items included in each product, plus the numbers used per set. For the purposes of production control, four other items of information are needed and should be added to the lists, if not already included. They are:

1. The source: bought or made, and if made, where
2. The material used
3. A value code
4. Whether the part or its material is special or common

Why this information is needed is briefly described in the following paragraphs.

(a) Source and material form

These two types of information are needed for the same reason, to indicate to Production Control the number of different items which must be ordered to maintain supplies of all necessary parts, and the sources from which they are obtained.

Each 'bought finished part' is ordered from a single source—the buying department—and can be treated by Production Control as a single item. Each 'made part' on the other hand, must be treated as at least two separate items for ordering; first the part and second the material from which it is made. Some parts may involve Production Control in the ordering of three, or more different items. In a company which makes its own forgings for example, they will have to issue orders:

1. To the buyer (B) for bar
2. To the forge (F) for forgings
3. To the machine shop (M) for finished parts

In many companies this information is included on the parts list in the form of a simple material type code, e.g. *Fd* equals drop forging, plus a source code, such as: *M* = made; *BOF* = Bought Out Finished; and *BOR* = Bought Out Raw. The entry: '*Fd. BOR*' after a part, then, indicates that it is made from a bought drop forging.

This type of code is sufficient for finding the departments to which orders must be addressed in a company with functional layout. With Group Technology however, the Production Controller also needs to know the 'group' used in each department. The material form code is still required. The source information is given by ruling a column on the parts list for each department and entering the group numbers under each department for each part. In a factory with a buying department, a forge, and a machine shop for example, the following entries might be found for different parts:

Part No.	Material	B	F	M
1	P	1	—	—
2	Fd	2	3	5
3	BS	2	—	6

The first entry indicates a bought finished plastic part. The second indicates a part machined in Group 5 in the machine shop from a forging made in Group 3 in the forge, from bar purchased by Group 2 in the Buying office, which buys general materials such as bar, tube, and plate. The third entry indicates a part machined in Group 6 from steel bar.

(b) Value code

Another important item of information needed by the Production Controller is a code indicating the annual consumption value of the different parts on the parts list. It is important that the stocks of very high value items should be kept at a minimum, even if this involves high control costs, for the small number of items of this type. At the other extreme, it important that control costs should be minimized for the large number of low value items. In this latter case simple control systems involving a minimum of human intervention are generally the most economical, even if buffer stocks must be held to maintain reliable supplies.

A simple *ABC* code is sufficient for most purposes. The code should be based on annual consumption value, rather than individual component value, and the break points should be found by Pareto analysis. In one company as an example, this analysis found the following distribution:

> Class *A*: 6% of the items, representing 52% of total value
> Class *B*: 43% of the items, representing 39% of total value
> Class *C*: 51% of the items, representing 9% of total value

Once the classes have been defined, the parts lists must be annotated by the cost office to show the appropriate class, *A*, *B* or *C* opposite each item. They can find the 'cost per piece' from their cost accounts and the 'quantities per year', from the parts lists and annual production programme. Multiplying the two gives the annual consumption value.

(c) Common and special parts and materials

The Production Controller also needs to know if each part and item of material is 'special' to one particular assembly on one particular parts list, or is 'common', being used on more than one assembly in the same parts list, or on more than one product. He needs this information to indicate where consolidation of orders will be required.

A simple method of showing this is to ring, or underline those items in the source code which are common, or in other words appear more than once in the parts lists. For example the following entries indicate that the ringed items require consolidation:

Part No.	Material	B	F	M	Value
21	BS	1	②	4	C
22	BS	①	—	⑥	C
23	Fd	2	③	⑤	A

(*d*) *Form of parts list*

A form of parts list which incorporates all these types of information is illustrated in Figure 6.1. This form is designed for a company with four

	Parts list		Product Code			Sheet No.		
	Part No.	Description	per set	Material		Value code	Source	Ordering system
				Form	Specification			

Figure 6.1. Parts list

main processing departments. The last column is ruled to show the type of ordering system to be used, and this is the next subject to be examined.

6.4 THE CHOICE OF ORDERING SYSTEM

Ideally all made parts and made material items should be controlled by period batch control. This will give minimum stocks, an even load of work, minimum obsolescence, maximum savings from family machining, and if the division into groups and families has been well planned, should also provide the simplest and most efficient method of ordering and control. The only exceptions will be items with very long throughput times. These will require special scheduling. In some cases, for example, it may be possible to allow two cycles in the standard ordering schedules, for a class of items with very long lead times, which are all made in the same group. In general however such items should be eliminated as far as possible by design, or method change, or by buying instead of making. Production flow analysis described in a later chapter, can be used to find these parts.

Period batch control is then the obvious choice for made parts and the choice of ordering system with Group Technology is therefore mainly concerned with purchased items.

(a) Purchased Class A parts, and special material items

It is highly desirable that purchased Class A value items, and any special material items should also be controlled by period batch control. In the first case this is desirable to reduce the investment in stocks. In the second case it is desirable because special materials are particularly liable to obsolescence.

The test in each case is: will the supplier deliver at cycle intervals, to the lead time dictated by the standard ordering schedule? If the answer is 'Yes', he can be given a long-term supply contract and be sent a 'call-off note' each cycle to indicate the quantities of each item to be delivered before assembly or processing starts for the cycle. As an example, if the standard schedule is as illustrated in Figure 5.3, suppliers of finished parts will have four weeks lead time to deliver the requirements for each cycle and suppliers of raw materials for machining will have two weeks lead time.

(b) Scheduled delivery based on annual programme

Where for some parts the supplier cannot deliver at the required frequency, or cannot supply to the required lead time, it is still possible to use scheduled delivery based on the annual programme, to keep stocks at a low level.

Requirement schedules can be calculated from the annual programme, based on a delivery frequency acceptable to the supplier, and the issue of schedules, say eight times a year, with a lead time which is also acceptable to the supplier. Buffer stocks in full material sets, will have to be held in this case to give flexibility, so that the actual requirements found from the series of short-term programmes can vary from the long-term forecast requirements calculated from the annual programme. It is desirable that the annual programme should be revised at regular intervals during the year for this purpose.

The current order state of items ordered by this method can be checked as each new cycle programme is issued, by the following simple calculation:

PRODUCT A	Cum: products to date from annual programme	200
	(+) Buffer stock in product sets	50
	Total provisioned	250
	(−) Cum: products short term programmes	217
	(=) Free sets	33

This method of ordering should be used where possible for all Class A value, and special material items, which cannot be included in the period batch control system. It can also be used efficiently for Class B purchased parts, or materials if the quantities are large enough to make scheduled delivery acceptable to the suppliers.

It is common with this ordering method to fix maximum and minimum control levels on the stock, to give warning if the schedule fails to meet real requirements. For this reason it is generally known as the Maxmin ordering system.

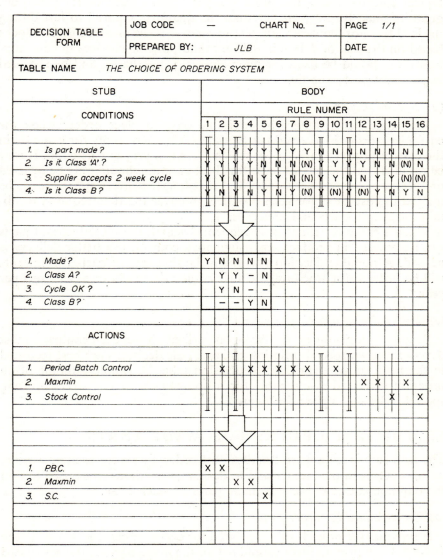

Figure 6.2. The choice of ordering system. Decision table

(c) Stock Control ordering

Stock control is an inefficient method for ordering made parts and for ordering any high value, or special parts which are liable to obsolescence. It can be used efficiently for Class *C* value purchased items however, particularly if they are common parts, which have a low risk of obsolescence.

The lead times must be specified by the buyer for all such items. A typical rule for fixing the order quantity might state that: 'The order quantity must be 50% greater than the quantity required to last during the lead time, or ten weeks supply, which ever is the greater'. Buffer stocks based on the risk of delays in delivery, and possible changes in consumption rate, should be fixed for main classes of purchases, and be specified as so many weeks supply.

(d) Special orders

For some items it may be advisable only to place orders when the customer's order is received for products. This may apply for example in the case of product variants for which there is a very low demand. It may be decided that the special parts for these variants should only be ordered on receipt of a customer's order and that longer delivery times should be quoted to customers for such products to cover the time required to obtain the special parts and materials.

When a product variant is in frequent demand, the special variant parts can be ordered in product sets using stock control, if a better delivery is needed. A possible decision rule might be that sets of parts for variants will be ordered for stock only if their annual demand exceeds six sets per year.

(e) The choice of ordering system

Basing its decisions on the factors described above, each company must develop its own special ordering policy. These decisions are best recorded in the form of an algorithm, or decision table. A simple example of an ordering system decision table for a company with no parts requiring special ordering, is given in Figure 6.2.

6.5 THE LIST ORDERS FOR MADE PARTS

The next step is to prepare standard 'list order' forms for each processing group existing in the factory and to design the methods to be used to find the requirement quantities for made parts for each cycle.

(a) The standard list order form

A separate list order form is required for every processing 'group' in the factory. Each printed form should list all the made parts in the associated 'family', divided into sections by material families and sub-divided into the tooling families for the machines on which their first operations are done.

A method for planning this analysis is described in the following chapter. A suitable list order form is illustrated in Figure 6.3.

	Item No.	Part No.	Description	Prod. req.	Spares	Scrap	Stock correction +	Stock correction −	Gross	Critical
	1									
	2									
	3									
	4									
	5									
	6									
	7									
	8									
	9									

LIST ORDER — Department: — Group: — Cycle No. — Due date — Sheet No.

Used to indicate parts with long throughput times

Figure 6.3. List order form

(b) *The 'Product group list' form*

To find the component and material requirement imposed by each short-term production programme, it is first necessary to divide each parts list into separate lists for every processing group involved in its manufacturing. These 'product group lists' are compiled by going through the parts list item by item, and adding each made part and made material item to the appropriate 'product group list' form. These PGLs are then printed.

Product: Gear box x 100 — Cycle 16 — Sheet No. 1/2
Dept. M/C shop — Group: 4 — Prog. qty 150

Part No.	Description	Per set	Production req.:			Item No. on List order
20732	Bearing housing	1	150			21
20739	Bearing housing	1	150			22
20762	End cover	2	300			106
20798	Oil seal housing	1	150			23
20718	Flange	1	150			79

PRODUCT GROUP LIST

Figure 6.4. Product group list

When a short-term programme is published, the components and materials required to meet it, are calculated separately for each product in turn, on its special set of 'product group lists'.

A typical 'product group list' is illustrated in Figure 6.4, which also shows the method used for 'explosion'. The column headed 'Item number' shows the position of each item on the standard 'list order form'.

(c) Transferring requirement quantities to 'list orders'

The next task is to transfer the programme requirement figures given in the 'product group lists' onto the single standard 'list order' form for each group. The 'product group lists' are first sorted into packs with the same group number, and the quantities are then transferred one by one, using the item numbers to find their correct positions on the list orders.

In the case of common parts, or materials, a separate item number will be allocated on the list order for each product, or assembly on which it is used, with a spare line after them for consolidation.

Any stock corrections required due to over- or under-production of parts, and any spare parts requirements will already have been entered on the list orders as they arose, during the previous cycle. The final step before issuing the list orders will be to add or subtract these corrections from the production requirement; add any additional requirements for spares sales, and add a scrap allowance to find the gross requirement.

The list orders for made materials will be prepared and issued first, because they have the shortest lead times.

6.6 PURCHASES ORDERED BY PERIOD BATCH CONTROL

A 'P.B.C. purchase list' is also prepared for all purchased items which are ordered under the period batch control system. The lists are made for each product separately, by abstraction from their parts lists in the same way as is used to produce the product group lists for made parts.

In this case there is no need to consolidate requirements onto a single list order for the Buying department. As soon as the short-term programme is fixed, the production requirement is calculated and any necessary stock corrections and additions for spares and scrap allowance are made directly on the P.B.C. purchase lists for each product. They are then all sent to the Buyer.

All the parts and material items on these lists will be ordered by call-off notes against long-term supply contracts. For the most part they will be high value special items and consolidation is unlikely to be a problem.

When the items arrive from the supplier, they will be sent directly to the quantity control point for issue to assembly, or in the case of materials, will be sent directly to the group where they are to be processed.

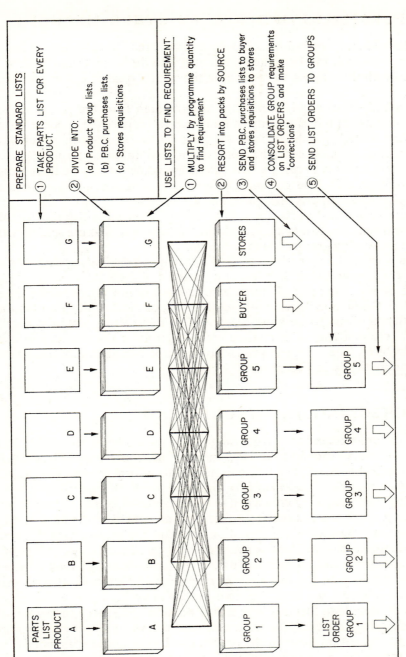

Figure 6.5. A production control system

PREPARE STANDARD LISTS

① TAKE PARTS LIST FOR EVERY PRODUCT.

② DIVIDE INTO:
(a) Product group lists.
(b) P.B.C. purchases lists.
(c) Stores requisitions

USE LISTS TO FIND REQUIREMENT

① MULTIPLY by programme quantity to find requirement

② RESORT into packs by SOURCE

③ SEND PBC. purchases lists to buyer and stores requisitions to stores

④ CONSOLIDATE GROUP requirements on LIST ORDERS and make 'corrections'

⑤ SEND LIST ORDERS TO GROUPS

PARTS LIST PRODUCT A

A B C D E F G

A B C D E F .G

GROUP 1 GROUP 2 GROUP 3 GROUP 4 GROUP 5 BUYER STORES

LIST ORDER GROUP 1 GROUP 2 GROUP 3 GROUP 4 GROUP 5

6.7 PURCHASES ORDERED BY OTHER METHODS

Purchased items ordered by scheduling against the annual programme, or by stock control, will be routed on arrival into the store. Some method is needed with these items, to requisition the correct quantities for issue each cycle.

Standard stores requisition forms are prepared from the parts lists, for each product, in the same way as that used to prepare the product group lists and P.B.C. purchase lists. As soon as the short-term production programme is published, the component and material requirement is calculated, and any necessary corrections are made directly on these stores requisition forms. The completed forms are then sent to the stores to authorize issue of parts and materials.

Issues of finished parts are sent to the quantity control point for onward transmission to assembly, and issues of raw materials are sent directly to the processing groups which use them.

The work can be greatly simplified by using a 'free issue system' for all Class C common parts. Stocks are maintained of these items in open bins in the assembly shop, and stores requisitions are not prepared for them. As Class C common items may represent 25% or more of the total number of different items to be controlled, and as these items would generally require consolidation, this method greatly simplifies the production control problem. The complete production control system is now illustrated diagrammatically in Figure 6.5.

6.8 CHECKING THE GROUP LOAD

Each list order issued to a processing group should be accompanied by a 'load summary' showing the load in machine hours imposed on every machine in the group. The foreman needs this information so that he can tell which are the critical machines and plan the work efficiently.

Using the method recommended in an earlier chapter, of treating setting time as a reduction in capacity rather than an increase in load, it is only necessary to show standard operation times on the load summary form.

A standard 'product load form' is first prepared for every product and every group used in its manufacture. Each form shows the load imposed by one product on the machines in one group. When a short-term programme is issued, the total load imposed by the programme is calculated on its product load form. It is generally possible to list the machines used in each group on the product load form always in the same standard sequence. The total loads in the groups can be calculated very simply, by summing across all the product load forms using a desk calculator and a peg board, as illustrated in Figure 6.6.

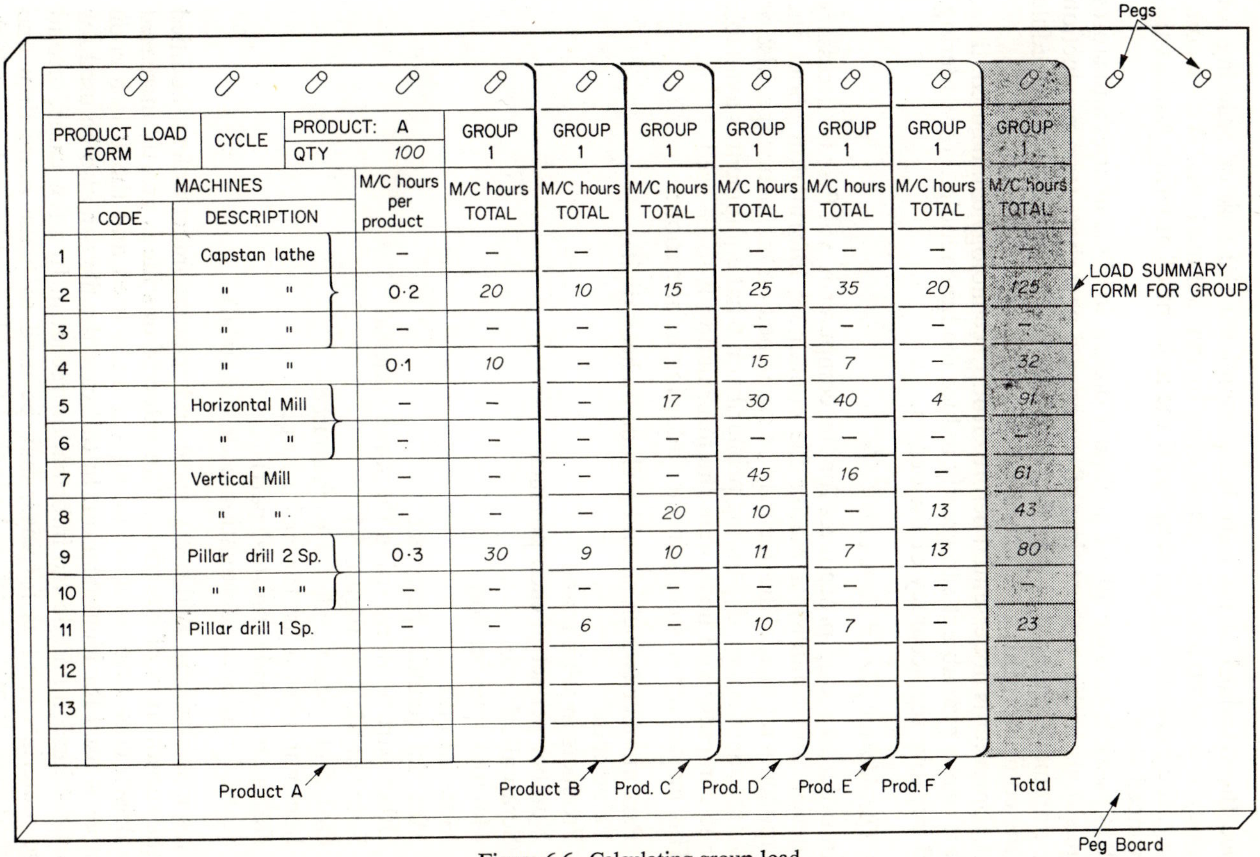

Figure 6.6. Calculating group load

6.9 ORDERING WITH A COMPUTER

Once the standard forms have been completed the task of ordering for each cycle is comparatively simple even by manual methods. With a computer, the job can be even simpler, if the amount of ordering justifies this advanced step.

It is possible to issue all the necessary orders, load summaries and stores requisitions within a short time of receiving a new short-term production programme. Depending upon the size of the programme and the schedule of the computer, this time may be as short as one or two hours.

A computer is not essential before Group Technology can be used, then, but if one is available it can greatly reduce the time required for ordering, and improve the accuracy of the orders.

(a) *The Master file or Component file*

In order to set up procedures for the computer it will first be necessary to design and establish a master file containing information about the components required. This file may be contained on magnetic tape, disc or other storage devices, depending primarily on what equipment is available on the computer and how often the information is to be used.

This master file will contain the following information:

1. Part number (which should include a check digit)
2. Value code
3. Products in which used
4. Number per set in each product
5. Scrap allowances
6. Material specification
7. Material unit
8. Material quantity per piece
9. Other part numbers using the same material
10. Source code (*see* Figure 6.1)
11. Ordering system code for each source
12. Item number on list for each source
13. Destination code (finished part)
14. Stores location or destination code (material)

This master file is used every cycle and remains intact unless modified by the substitution of new data. The value of this file is greatly increased if a Brisch classification and coding system is used and the Brisch code number is used for identification. In this case the file can also be used for variety reduction and design information retrieval. In a few cases, second stage materials such as forgings, may be used to make more than one finished part. It may therefore be logical to add an additional field which modifies item 8 above when necessary.

There are two additional files necessary in order to use the system. These may be prepared in several ways depending on the equipment and techniques used with the computer system employed. They include Key to magnetic tape, Key to disc, paper tape, punched cards, VDU terminals or other means. These additional files are the 'Cycle programme file' and the 'Corrections file'.

(b) The Cycle Programme File

A statement is prepared each cycle for each product in the new production programme. Each statement will contain:

1. The programme cycle number
2. The code number of the product
3. The number of products to be produced on the new programme
4. The number of products in stock

This file need not be retained after the run other than for re-run purposes if necessary

It may be possible to include other fields within the above file, such as the period sales programme, period stock plan, and programme restraints. If this is done it is possible to start with the sales programme and program the computer to produce the production programme.

(c) The Correction File

As part of the programme suite it will be necessary to include a correction file. This file will include the following parameters:

1. Part number
2. Any stock corrections (+ or −)
3. Additional parts required for spares

The correction file will be originated and continuously updated between the processing runs for successive cycles, as spares orders and necessary stock corrections are reported. This file will be used during the next cycle processing run. It need not be retained after the run other than for re-run purposes.

(d) The computer program for ordering

If the component master file is first sorted by groups using the source code (see Field 10 Component File), and then into 'list order item number' sequence (see Field 12 Component File), it is fairly simple to derive the order lists for each group.

A suitable method might run as follows: when ordering, each list is processed in turn. Starting with the first part on the list, the product code from the cycle programme file is matched to see if the part is needed for the cycle. If it is needed, the total production requirement is calculated. At the same time, the correction file is read and if any match occurs the proper adjustments are made to the requirement quantity. Also at this time any scrap allowance is calculated from the master file and is added in.

When these calculations are completed, the gross requirement is printed out, and the above process is repeated, until the first list order is complete. The process is then repeated for the remaining list orders.

Any unmatched corrections can be written to another output and be saved for the next cycle run.

(e) Load Checking with the Computer

Load checking requires one additional file, a product load file. One of these records is prepared for each product and for each processing group concerned in its manufacture. The following fields are contained within each record:

1. Product code
2. Group code
3. All machines in the group
4. The load in machine hours on each machine imposed by one product

To find the total load on the machines, this load file is used in conjunction with the cycle programme file. The general sequence of operations is as follows:

1. Calculate total load on each machine in the first group imposed by the first product.
2. Repeat for second product and subtotal by machine.
3. Repeat for remaining products.
4. Total for group.
5. Repeat for all other groups.

6.10 ORDERING FOR JOBBING PRODUCTION

The main characteristic of jobbing production is that the design is provided by the customer, or is made specially for the customer as part of the contract. With these types of contract it is impossible until the order is received to predict the quantities of materials and bought parts which will be needed. The lead time used to fix delivery dates must include sufficient time for obtaining supplies.

There are some types of jobbing production where there is a probability that orders will be repeated, but even in this case there is no certainty until the purchase contract is received and little possibility of forecasting when it will be received. Group Technology can still be used however, even with jobbing production, and gives most of the advantages obtainable with standard products.

(a) Group layout

Most jobbing factories specialize in a given range of products. They do this partly as a matter of policy and partly because the types of contract for which they can quote is limited by the types of processing plant which they possess.

The very small company is in effect one group. As the company grows it will generally be possible to divide the plant into a number of groups—each with its team of workers—and to divide the different types of item for which the company quotes into families so that all the items in any family can be completely processed in one special group.

The groups in large jobbing factories will tend to be larger than in companies making standard products and there will normally be fewer types of plant which exist in more than one group. Although it is comparatively simple to find a division into groups and families, it is more difficult with jobbing production than with standard products, to maintain an even balance of load between the groups.

(b) *Flow control*

With jobbing production a fixed cycle is again used. If the company makes assembled products, blank production programmes are prepared for all cycles for say six months ahead and any order accepted from a customer is entered on the programme for the cycle during which it must be delivered.

All orders for special parts and materials will be prepared as soon as possible after receipt of the customer's order. Orders for special purchased items will be sent to the buyer immediately, quoting the delivery date imposed by the standard schedule. The buyer will attempt to improve on this delivery if possible.

Orders for special made items will be entered on group list orders for each cycle. These will normally be issued to the standard cycle, although items from them may be transferred to earlier list orders, if necessary to correct a temporary imbalance of load. Cumulative load figures must be maintained for assembly and at least for the critical machines in each group. As soon as the capacity in any group is filled, and there is no further possibility of transferring work to earlier cycles, the programme and group list order concerned are 'sealed'.

Common parts and materials used in many different products will be ordered for stock. If they are very widely used and of high value, they can be ordered for scheduled delivery against a forecast based on a statistical projection of past usage. The remaining common parts and materials will generally be ordered by Stock Control.

6.11 SUMMARY

Most efficient production control systems use different methods for ordering different classes of material and parts. The choice of the best method for each item in every parts list depends on their type, annual usage value, whether they are common or special parts, and so on.

In general period batch control should be used for all made parts, and for high value purchases. Other methods are better for some classes of purchases.

The planning of the data processing system for period batch control and group layout takes some time, but once planned, the cyclical data processing operations can be carried out quickly even with manual methods.

7 Planning the Loading Sequence

7.1 INTRODUCTION

Production flow analysis finds the best division of the plant into groups and also finds which parts should be in the family of parts to be processed in each group. Period batch control in turn finds for each group, how many of each part should be produced each cycle, in order to meet the needs of the sales forecast and also to use the allocated processing capacity to the best advantage.

There is however one other factor which is important to the efficiency of a Group Technology application. This is the dispatching strategy, or the strategy used to determine the sequence of loading for the parts ordered each cycle, on the machines in a group. Luckily, experience has shown that a purely pragmatic approach can find a work schedule which makes Group Technology worth-while. In one factory the planning of the schedule was left to the working chargehands in each group. They succeeded in designing schedules which contributed to a 15% increase in capacity, in spite of a reduction in the ordering cycle from an average of twelve weeks to two weeks.

It seems likely however, that this level of results represents only a small proportion of the potential, and that Group Technology is a more important innovation than present experience can demonstrate. This chapter attempts to analyse the nature of the scheduling problem; to demonstrate the essential complexity of the material flow system, but at the same time to show how comparatively simple methods of analysis can be used to achieve viable solutions.

7.2 ADVANTAGES SOUGHT

Changes in the sequence of scheduling work onto the machines in a group, can lead to economies in production. Consider first the types of saving which can be obtained by improving the schedule, and the types of schedule change which must be made to achieve these gains.

(a) Savings in direct material

Big savings are possible in direct material usage and cost, by planning the scheduling sequence, so that all parts made from the same general materials are cut from these materials at the same time.

In a flame cutting section, cutting blanks from steel plate for example, of a thickness used to make many parts of different shapes and sizes, it may be possible to plan cutting to achieve 90% material utilization. Cutting numbers of each special blank from the same sheet, or plate, as is usually necessary with a stock control ordering system, might give a utilization of only 70%. The systematic use of off-cuts in this second case might increase material utilization to say 80%, but would involve extra costs for the storage and handling of the off-cuts.

Four main facts should be observed about these material savings:

1. They apply mainly to general materials such as bar, sheet, plate, and tube.

2. The savings are greatest if there are many different sizes of blanks in use, made from the same material.

3. The savings depend on the sequence of loading on the machines used to cut general materials into blanks.

4. Because blank cutting is generally an early operation, scheduling for maximum utilization will mainly affect first operations.

The savings obtainable in any company will depend on the proportion of general materials used, and on the degree of standardization of these materials. It is often possible to increase these savings by redesign of parts to use materials which would otherwise be scrapped as off-cuts, and by simplification to reduce the number of material varieties.

(b) Savings in setting time

Savings in setting time depend on the choice of a schedule which brings together for processing one after the other, all parts which can be made with the same tooling, at the same set-up. These tooling families may be different on all the machines in a group and the savings possible will vary widely for different types of machine, being greatest for machines with many tool positions and with high average setting times.

The criteria used to determine where the major effort should be made, may vary. Under conditions of high output it may be necessary to concentrate on the critically loaded machines, in order to reduce setting time losses and increase capacity and product output. Under conditions of under-load, it may be a better policy to concentrate on the machines where the biggest time savings can be made, in order to reduce labour cost.

(c) Savings in throughput time

The aim with Group Technology is to process a given load of work each cycle and to have it all completed by one common due-date. To achieve this aim it will be necessary to pay particular attention to those parts with the longest operation times and to use 'close planning' to reduce their throughput times. By starting following operations before the whole batch is completed at the previous operations, it is possible to include some parts in the families, even if the sum of their operation times is longer than the time allowed by the cycle. The need to schedule for minimum throughput times for the critical items, will provide an overriding limitation in these cases to the design of the schedule.

(d) Savings in machine idle time

The sequence in which jobs are loaded on the machines, will also affect the machine idle time. For example if jobs with long operation times on first operations, and short second operations are loaded first, the machines for second operations may stand idle for a time at the beginning of the cycle.

Because machine capacities are never in exact balance however, there will always be some machines in the group, which will inevitably have some idle time—'waiting for orders'. Priority can be given therefore, to planning a schedule which minimizes idle time on the heavily loaded machines.

It is necessary to ensure however, that the built-in idle time on lightly loaded machines is not exceeded. As an example of the danger, consider a key-seating machine used mainly for later operations, but only loaded to 20% of capacity. It might be possible that an otherwise optimum schedule would not complete early operations on the parts requiring key-seating until 85% of the cycle time had elapsed. The group would fail in this case to complete its task by due-date.

(e) Savings in operator idle time

The sequence of loading may also affect operator idle time, but this will only be a critical limitation on scheduling, if most of the operators can only operate one machine. Even though all operators may be working throughout the cycle, there may be some effective idle time if the schedule does not allow them to be used efficiently. For example, one operator may be able to operate three machines together, but he can only do this if the schedule finds work for all three machines at the same time.

(f) The optimum schedule

It will have been noted that the optimum schedule will vary according to the weight given to the different types of saving, and that the optimum sequence of loading will vary from machine to machine in the group.

The design of the optimum schedule is therefore extremely complex. It requires a deep understanding of the way in which changes in the schedule will affect savings and a clear statement of the criteria to be used in making decisions, together with an assessment of their relative weights. If this is achieved, however, relatively simple methods of analysis can be used to find a viable and near optimum solution.

7.3 DEFINITIONS

The meaning of a few special terms used in the analysis, must now be specified.

(a) Material family

A 'material family' is a list of parts all made from the same material. The production families allocated to each group can usually be broken down into a number of smaller material families. In the case of 'general materials', the material families will normally be based on material specification and size. In the case of special materials, material specification and size will still be important, but material form—forging, drop stamping, bar blank, casting, etc.—may also have to be considered.

(b) Tooling family

A tooling family is a list of parts all machined on the same machine at the same set-up. The parts processed on any machine in a group, can usually be broken down into a large number of tooling families. The tooling families on different machines will usually contain different lists of parts.

Because a change from one material specification to another—brass to cast iron, for example—generally increases setting times due to time consuming machine cleaning operations and tool changes, tooling families will normally be restricted to single types of material. Tooling families will therefore normally form parts of major material families.

It is not necessary that all the different tools used in the set-up for a particular tooling family, should all be used on every component in the family. The tools can be used in many different combinations and sequences for different parts.

(c) Critical component

A critical component is one which needs special attention to get it completed during the cycle. Generally critical components are those with many operations and long operation times. If made by conventional batch production methods, with which each operation is completed before the next is started, such components will tend to have very long throughput times. With group layout it is possible to give special preference to these parts, and to reduce their throughput times by close-planning.

(d) Critical machine

A critical machine is one which is loaded to near its maximum capacity. Special attention is necessary with such machines to minimize setting and idle time losses, and thus increase their capacity.

7.4 FINDING MATERIAL FAMILIES

The number of parts processed in one group will normally be relatively small. The material families can generally be found without difficulty, by manually sorting the route cards for all the parts in each production family. The sort is best made progressively:

1. First into separate packs for major material families, e.g. copper alloys, steel, cast iron, aluminium, etc., if necessary.

2. Second into sub-packs for minor material families by material form, e.g. Bar, tube, plate, castings, forgings, etc.

3. Third by size. This analysis is however only essential in the case of general materials.

The list of material families for the group should be printed, in two parts, one for general materials and the other for special materials. Inside each of these two parts, the list should be divided into major material families, each subdivided into minor material families, and—in the case of general materials—sub-sub-divided by size.

The list should now be annotated to show which of the material families can give major material savings. These special material families will all appear in the 'general material' part of the list, but they do not necessarily occur only in those families with large numbers of components. For example a large material family of thirty parts machined from 25mm dia. bar, may have very small potential savings if all parts are short and of approximately the same length. A small family of only three parts made from the same diameter bar, on the other hand, may give major savings if one is long and the other two are short. In this case it may be possible to make most of the short parts, from the 'short-ends' thrown out when machining the long parts.

7.5 FINDING THE TOOLING FAMILIES

The tooling families can again be found fairly easily by sorting the route cards. Because the tooling families are different for different machines, the machines in the group must be considered separately and in turn. One should start by examining the critical machines. It may not be necessary to find tooling families for lightly loaded machines.

The first step is to select from the production family all parts which have one or more operations on the particular machine being studied. By simple methods of analysis it is possible to divide these routes into packs, in such a way that there is a high probability that any tooling family will exist in only one pack. The analysis greatly reduces the area of search, but the final tooling families must generally be selected by eye.

The method of analysis may differ between processes and between machine types. The method described below is concerned mainly with metal cutting, but the approach is similar for other processes.

(a) 1st stage of analysis—by material

The first stage again is to divide the route cards for parts using the machine into packs by material. All tooling families are likely to exist wholly inside one major material family. There are three main reasons why this is so:

(*i*) When changing from one material to another the machine must normally be cleaned to prevent the mixing of swarf. This is in itself a major setting operation.

(*ii*) The cutting lubricant may have to be changed.

(*iii*) A change in materials generally involves a change in tooling. In metal turning for example, the cutting angles on tools and the speeds and feeds used, will be different for different metals.

In large processing shops it may be possible that different materials can be processed in different groups. In smaller shops they may have to share capacity.

(*b*) *2nd stage analysis—by work holding method*

For most processes the second factor which is likely to limit the choice of tooling family, is the method used to hold the work on the machine. On lathes, for example, the following list shows some of the possible methods:

1. Collets
2. Chucks
3. Between centres
4. Face plate
5. Spindle nose fixtures (special)

It is probable that all the parts in any tooling family will use only one of these methods, and sorting on this basis will therefore help to reduce the area of search.

In the case of the first two items, it is likely that the parts in any tooling family will all use only one size of collet, or chuck. Further division into sub-packs by size of collet or chuck, will still further reduce the area of search for tooling families.

(*c*) *3rd stage of analysis—by tools*

For many types of machine the first two stages of analysis, coupled with a final division into tooling families by eye, will be all that is necessary. Where there are still large numbers of parts in some of the packs, however, there will be advantages in adding one further stage of analysis.

Tooling families are by definition lists of parts which share a set-up containing the same tools. This final stage of analysis must therefore be based on tooling. The method applied in this case is called 'Tooling Family Analysis'. It uses a matrix and is similar to Group Analysis, described in Chapter 9 on Production Flow analysis. The parts are listed horizontally across the top of the chart, and the tools used are listed vertically up the side of the chart. The tooling families are found by re-arranging the sequence of listing both the parts and the tools. A simple example is shown in Figure 7.1.

Tool \ Part number	1	2	3	4	5	6	7	8	9	10	11	12	13	14	15	16	17	18	19	20	21	22	23
PART OFF	✓	✓	✓	✓	✓	✓	✓	✓	✓	✓	✓	✓	✓	✓	✓	✓	✓	✓	✓	✓	✓	✓	✓
FACE	✓	✓	✓	✓	✓	✓	✓	✓	✓	✓	✓	✓	✓	✓	✓	✓	✓	✓	✓	✓	✓	✓	✓
Rough turn	✓	✓	✓	✓	✓	✓	✓	✓	✓	✓	✓	✓	✓	✓	✓	✓	✓	✓	✓	✓		✓	✓
Centre	✓	✓	✓	✓	✓	✓	✓	✓	✓	✓	✓	✓			✓			✓	✓			✓	
Drill (1)	✓	✓	✓	✓	✓						✓	✓											
Drill (2)						✓	✓	✓	✓	✓													
Drill (3)											✓	✓			✓			✓	✓			✓	
Bore (1)	✓	✓									✓	✓											
Bore (2)						✓	✓	✓							✓				✓	✓				
Finish turn	✓	✓	✓			✓	✓				✓	✓	✓	✓	✓	✓	✓	✓	✓	✓		✓	✓
Chamfer			✓								✓	✓			✓						✓	✓	✓
Undercut (1)			✓														✓						
Undercut (2)																		✓		✓	✓		
Stop	✓	✓	✓	✓	✓	✓	✓	✓	✓	✓	✓	✓	✓	✓	✓	✓	✓	✓	✓	✓	✓	✓	✓

(a) Parts and tools used, listed in record sequence

Tool \ Part number	20	15	19	6	7	8	9	10	11	12	1	2	23	4	5	13	14	16	3	17	18	21	22
Part off	✓	✓	✓	✓	✓	✓	✓	✓	✓	✓	✓	✓	✓	✓	✓	✓	✓	✓	✓	✓	✓	✓	✓
Face	✓	✓	✓	✓	✓	✓	✓	✓	✓	✓	✓	✓	✓	✓	✓	✓	✓	✓	✓	✓	✓	✓	✓
1. STOP	✓	✓	✓	✓	✓	✓	✓	✓	✓	✓	✓	✓	✓	✓	✓	✓	✓	✓	✓	✓	✓	✓	✓
2. Centre	✓	✓	✓	✓	✓	✓	✓	✓	✓	✓	✓	✓	✓	✓	✓	✓			✓				
3. Rough turn	✓	✓	✓	✓	✓	✓	✓	✓	✓	✓	✓	✓	✓	✓	✓	✓	✓	✓	✓	✓	✓		✓
4. Finish turn	✓	✓	✓	✓	✓				✓	✓	✓	✓	✓			✓	✓	✓	✓	✓	✓		✓
5. Drill 2				✓	✓	✓	✓	✓															
6. Drill 3	✓	✓	✓						✓	✓		✓											
7. Bore 2	✓	✓	✓	✓	✓	✓	✓																
8. Chamfer	✓	✓							✓	✓		✓							✓			✓	✓
5. Drill 1									✓	✓	✓	✓		✓	✓	✓	✓		✓				
7. Bore 1									✓	✓	✓	✓											
6. Undercut 1																			✓	✓			
7. Undercut 2																					✓	✓	✓

(b) Sequence rearranged in tooling 'families' to minimize setting time

Figure 7.1. Tooling family analysis

(*d*) *Listing*

Once again the result of the analysis for each machine should be published, to assist in the preparation of schedules. The lists of components using each machine should be broken down into main classes by material; sub-classes by holding method, with a further division by size in some cases; and finally into sub-sub-classes by tooling families. These lists should be annotated to show which tooling families will give major savings in setting time. For some families on some machines, setting time reduction may be small, but the analysis may still be worth-while if it makes it possible to reduce the tooling investment.

7.6 SEQUENCE OF SCHEDULING PARTS IN A TOOLING FAMILY

With some processes there may be an optimum sequence in which the parts in a tooling family should be started. In general there are advantages in starting with the most complex part, or part which uses most of the tools. This will prove the accuracy of setting for most of the tools, and speed the work on the later simpler parts.

For other processes such as drilling for example, the sequence of loading for the parts in a tooling family is unlikely to be a significant factor. Where this sequence is important the fact should be noted on the tooling family list, and the parts in such tooling families should be listed in their best sequence.

7.7 SEQUENCE OF SCHEDULING TOOLING FAMILIES

With some processes again, the sequence in which different tooling families are started, may also affect savings. For example on a bar lathe, two tooling families may require different sizes of collet, but use the same tools. The setting time for the second tooling family can be reduced by scheduling them one after the other. Alternatively two tooling families may use the same collet size, but use different tooling of which say 70% is common. Once again some savings in setting time are possible by scheduling them one after the other.

With some types of machine the savings possible from tooling families may be small, but major savings can still be obtained by planning the sequence of loading to minimize setting time. An example is illustrated in Figure 7.2.

Again taking an example from an entirely different process: in colour printing, ink colour will affect the sequence. It is desirable to start with work requiring a light colour and change progressively to darker and darker colours, as this reduces the time required for cleaning during setting-up.

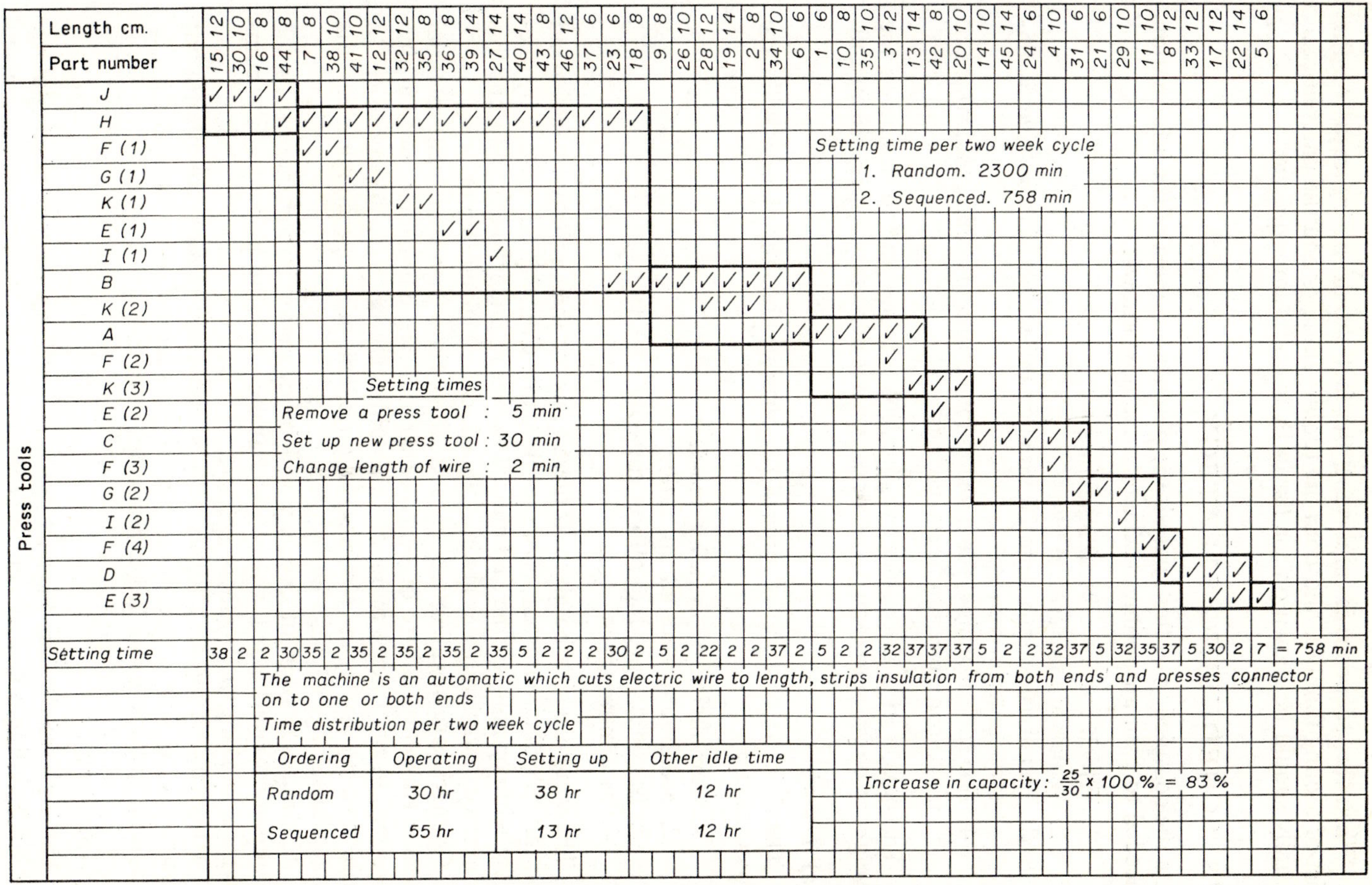

Length cm.
12 10 8 8 8 10 10 12 12 8 8 14 14 14 8 12 6 6 8 8 10 12 14 8 10 6 6 8 10 12 14 8 10 10 14 6 10 6 6 10 10 12 12 12 14 6
Part number
15 30 16 44 7 38 41 12 32 35 36 39 27 40 43 46 37 23 18 9 26 28 19 2 34 6 1 10 35 3 13 42 20 14 45 24 4 31 21 29 11 8 33 17 22 5
Press tools
J
H
F (1)
G (1)
K (1)
E (1)
I (1)
B
K (2)
A
F (2)
K (3)
E (2)
C
F (3)
G (2)
I (2)
F (4)
D
E (3)
Setting time per two week cycle
1. Random. 2300 min
2. Sequenced. 758 min
Setting times
Remove a press tool : 5 min
Set up new press tool : 30 min
Change length of wire : 2 min
Setting time
38 2 2 30 35 2 35 2 35 2 35 2 35 5 2 2 2 30 2 5 2 22 2 2 37 2 5 2 2 32 37 37 37 5 2 2 32 37 5 32 35 37 5 30 2 7 = 758 min
The machine is an automatic which cuts electric wire to length, strips insulation from both ends and presses connector on to one or both ends
Time distribution per two week cycle
Increase in capacity: 25/30 x 100 % = 83 %

Ordering	Operating	Setting up	Other idle time
Random	30 hr	38 hr	12 hr
Sequenced	55 hr	13 hr	12 hr

Figure 7.2. Sequence of loading and capacity

When this sequence is important, the fact should be indicated on the list of tooling families, and both the tooling families and the parts in each family should be shown on the list in their optimum sequence.

7.8 SCHEDULING STRATEGY

On the completion of this analysis the planner has most of the information needed to plan an optimum schedule. He now knows:

1. Which are the critical machines
2. Which are the critical parts
3. The division into material families and which of them give significant material savings
4. For each machine, the division into tooling families, and which of them can give significant savings

The next step is to consider the possible savings and to decide on the weight to be given to each. In other words it is necessary to prepare an aim.

(a) The aim

The following list shows some of the possible aims the planner will have to consider:

1. Completion of work by due-date
2. Maximum material utilization
3. Maximum product output capacity
4. Minimum setting cost

The weight which he gives to these aims, or their priority, will depend on the special circumstances of the company. Completion of work by due-date will normally be the first aim. However in under-load conditions this aim may be so simple to achieve, that it can be given low priority.

Changes in scheduling sequence, again, only brings significant material cost savings in the case of general materials. In companies using a high proportion of general materials, this aim may be given top priority. In others which mainly use castings, forgings, and other special materials, the material savings aim can be ignored.

The maximization of capacity will be of major importance when the company is overloaded with work, but may have no priority if the company is working well below capacity.

Minimum setting cost, finally, will be important in most conditions, but may have to take lower priority in some cases, if other factors such as material savings give a larger reduction in cost.

(b) Strategy

Having fixed the aim, the next step is to develop a strategy of scheduling, or a scheduling policy, which will achieve the aim. Assume that in a given factory there is a blank cutting department, cutting blanks from bar and plate, and a machine shop. The scheduling aims have been fixed as: completion by due-date; material savings; maximum capacity; and minimum setting cost, in that order. Each aim has over-riding priority over the one which follows it. A possible scheduling strategy in this instance might be written as follows.

(c) *The schedules*

It is assumed that Gantt charts are used for scheduling, similar to that illustrated in Figure 7.3, with the machines listed against each horizontal line, and with vertical divisions showing the cycle divided into hours. Two schedules are required, one for machining and one for blank cutting. The strategy of scheduling in this case might be:

1. *Machine shop schedule*. Find the critical parts. Schedule them to start first. Schedule them on all the machines they visit for completion by due-date.

2. *Blank cutting schedule*. Find material families containing critical parts. Schedule them for cutting first. Check that blanks will be cut in time to meet the machine shop schedule. If necessary split material families to achieve this, or increase the standard ordering schedule to give a greater lead time.

3. *Machine shop schedule*. Find critical machines. Find tooling families on these machines. Schedule the parts in these tooling families to give minimum setting time and maximum capacity on the critical machines.

4. *Machine shop schedule*. Find other tooling families on other machines, where significant savings in setting time are possible. As far as possible schedule the parts in these tooling families to obtain maximum savings and completion by due-date.

5. *Machine shop schedule*. Schedule the remaining parts to obtain completion by due-date. If necessary the tooling families already planned for machining together, must be split to achieve this over-riding aim.

6. *Blank cutting schedule*. Complete the blank cutting schedule. Cut all the blanks for each material family together. Plan the sequence of cutting material families to suit the machine shop schedule. Check that the schedule will provide blanks in time to meet the machine shop schedule. Normally there will be sufficient time overlap included in the period batch control standard schedule for the cycle, to make it possible to cut all blanks in their material families.

7. *Both schedules*. Check labour loads to ensure that no more machines are running at the same time, than there are operators to man them. Adjust the schedule if necessary. Normally the planner will have kept this need in mind when planning the schedule.

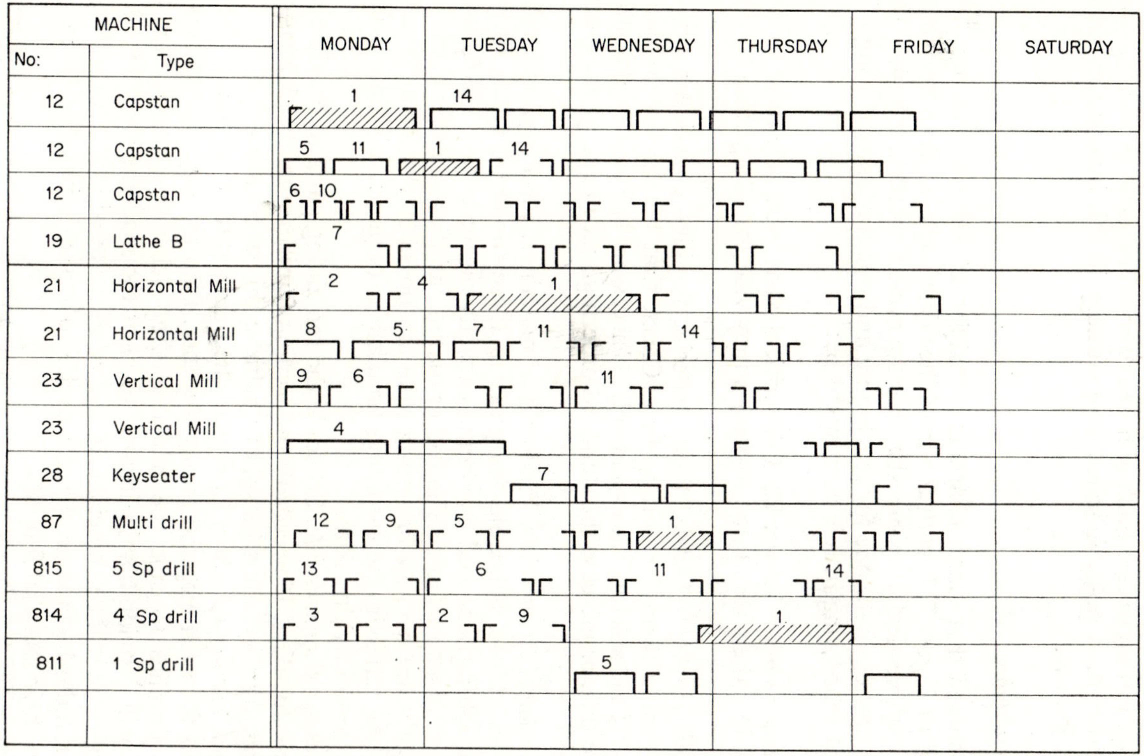

MACHINE		MONDAY	TUESDAY	WEDNESDAY	THURSDAY	FRIDAY	SATURDAY
No:	Type						
12	Capstan						
12	Capstan						
12	Capstan						
19	Lathe B						
21	Horizontal Mill						
21	Horizontal Mill						
23	Vertical Mill						
23	Vertical Mill						
28	Keyseater						
87	Multi drill						
815	5 Sp drill						
814	4 Sp drill						
811	1 Sp drill						

Note: The numbers on the chart are part numbers. Only a few are shown. Part No. 1 (cross hatched) is the critical part − Σ Op. times is max.

Figure 7.3. Gantt chart schedule

7.9 CYCLIC PLANNING

Where the company makes a few standard products, all of which are in continuous production the same components will generally be on order every cycle. The quantities of each item may vary however, due to differences in the product quantities specified in the production programme. In this instance it is generally possible to devise a standard schedule, which can be repeated every cycle. Even if the quantities ordered for different components, are different, from cycle to cycle, it has been found that a standard cycle can still be used efficiently (*see* Figure 3.6). This method was developed by Messrs. Brutsner and Erikson in Sweden and is named Cyclic Planning. It is used in a number of Swedish factories including the Volvo company, where the initial application was made.

7.10 THE LIST ORDER

It has been seen that the optimum sequence of loading may be different for every machine in the group, and that a strategy of scheduling must be used, which obtains the best compromise solution. One other problem remains. How best can the components be listed on the list order issued every cycle to each group?

The aim is to provide the maximum assistance to the foreman, or working chargehand in the group. Probably the best method is to divide the list order into sections for each machine used on first operations, and to show the parts in each of these sections in the sequence required by the optimum schedule. In this instance the list order shows the approximate sequence in which materials must arrive and the sequence in which each part must be started.

In the case of jobbing work, it is impractical to make such a deep analysis every cycle, but it is still possible with little effort to divide the list order into major material families and thus give the group foreman some guidance to the formation of tooling families.

7.11 SUMMARY

The sequence in which parts are loaded on machines has a significant effect on setting time, capacity, material cost, and idle time.

The reduction in setting time is particularly important to Group Technology, because it must more than compensate for the loss of capacity which would otherwise arise due to the change from long to short ordering cycles.

Simple methods of tooling analysis can be used to find the optimum sequence of loading, and these can be supported in the case of complex problems, by methods using matrix analysis.

8 Production Planning

8.1 INTRODUCTION

Production planning is the function of management concerned with planning, directing, and controlling the physical means to be used to produce the products or services provided by an enterprise. It deals with five main types of decision covering the choice of material form, of facilities, of processing methods, of handling and storage methods, and of layout.

Group Technology is a new strategy of management which is based largely on changes in production planning policy. This chapter examines the nature of these changes and their effect on the work of the production planner in an enterprise.

8.2 PRODUCTION PLANNING

A short description of the management function of production planning will serve to introduce the terms used in the chapter. As already specified, production planning is concerned with five main types of decision:

1. The choice of the material form with which component processing should start.
2. The choice of machines and other processing facilities.
3. The choice of the route, or series of processes and operations to produce each item.
4. The choice of handling and storage methods and equipment.
5. The choice of plant layout.

The first three are so closely related that they can be treated as one for present purposes under the title of the choice of processing method. The last two are also closely related, leaving two main types of decision:

1. Choice of method.
2. Choice of layout.

The decision made in production planning must of necessity be made progressively, starting with broad decisions which are then progressively elaborated. Three main levels of planning can be recognized. These are known as Factory planning, Process planning, and Operation planning. The types of decision made at each of these levels, in both method selection and layout, are illustrated in Figure 8.1.

Although planning must necessarily be progressive in the preparation of these plans, there is a continuous feed-back as the plans are developed leading to a gradual improvement of the total plan. For example one

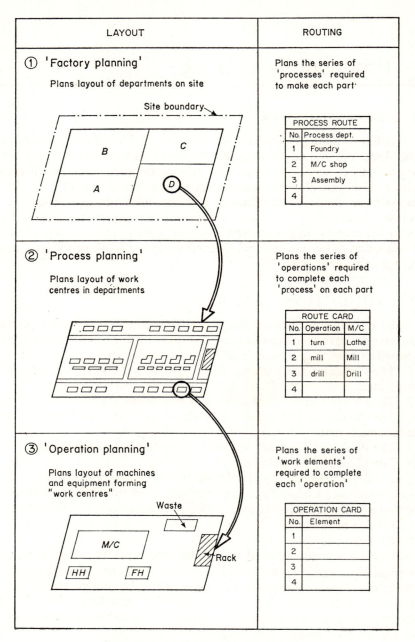

Figure 8.1. Levels of production planning

cannot usefully consider the plant layout of a machine shop under 'process planning', until 'factory planning' has decided that a machine shop is required and where it will be situated. Later work on the plant layout however, may indicate ways in which the earlier factory plan may be improved. The plan is developed in this way until no further improvement is possible, or there is no more time or money left for further planning.

8.3 PRODUCTION MANAGEMENT IN PRACTICE

In practice the choice of new facilities and of plant layout are infrequent activities. They are tasks of particular interest to top management and even if the Production Manager is deeply involved in the preparation of the plans, the final decision is normally made by a director. The choice of processing method on the other hand, is generally left very much to the Production Manager. In many companies this is so, because no one else in the management organization knows enough to dispute his judgements.

Each component and assembly drawing is considered in turn by the production planner, who first decides if it should be made or bought. For all made parts he then makes the following decisions:

1. What form of materials should be used
2. How the work should be split into operations
3. To which machine, or other work centre should each operation be allocated
4. What new tools and gauges must be supplied

These decisions are normally recorded on a 'route card', or 'operation layout' which shows all the operations required, numbered in their sequence of application, and also shows the machines on which they are to be done. The route card may also be used to record other data such as the type of container to be used and the standard times for operation and for setting.

The Production Manager is also responsible in many companies for 'work study' and in particular for 'work measurement'. He will probably have specialists working for him, who either measure or calculate the 'standard times' for each operation.

In practice today each different item to be made will usually be considered independently. The accepted criterion for a choice between alternatives is normally minimum direct cost. Subject to the need to achieve direct cost levels which seem reasonable to top management, the choice of method is left to the personal preferences of the individual planners. This freedom of choice may be limited by the fact that the traditional practice in the enterprise will normally be the most acceptable at floor level.

8.4. TRADITIONAL PRODUCTION PLANNING POLICY

Most enterprises today have a production planning policy, more often implicit than stated, which is based on sub-optimization. Generally each component is considered individually and only two criteria are given any real weight. These are minimum material cost and minimum operation time.

The first criterion tends to lead to the selection of a different material for each item produced. The second criterion tends to lead to an increase in the number of different routes between machines, and to complication of the material flow system.

(a) The selection of material form

If one considers each component as an entirely separate problem, it seems obvious that one should choose for every component the cheapest form of material which will meet the quality standards specified by the designer for that item. A simple example will demonstrate that this approach can lead to very uneconomical decisions. In a certain company a number of parts were made from a particular grade and thickness of steel plate (X). Due to the large size and awkward shapes of these components, material utilization was only 64%. The remainder was sold as scrap and after deducting disposal costs realized only 6% of its purchase cost.

A planner in this company was given a new component to plan. He found that a lower grade of steel than X was specified by the designer and using this grade of steel instead of X made an apparent saving in material cost of 4%. The planner accepted the material specified by the designer. As however the offcuts of material X would have been sufficient to make the total requirement of the new part, he actually chose a material form which inflated the possible direct material cost for the part by 1,500%. One can never find the optimum solution by looking at each item independently.

(b) The choice of method

Because each item is considered as an entirely separate and independent problem, decisions made with the criterion of minimum operation time can also increase total costs, even though they appear to reduce the direct costs, shown in the cost accounts.

For example the choice of one method rather than another may reduce operation times and the direct costs shown in the cost accounts, but induce a greater increase in production control and handling costs, due to the choice of machines for different operations which are a long way apart and in different departments. If handling and production control costs are treated as overhead expenses, this choice will appear to reduce costs, even though in fact it increases them.

It is comparatively simple to reduce operation times if one ignores all the other related variables. One can reduce them for example by using very large batch quantities, and by using automatic machines more appropriate to mass production quantities for small batches. Unfortunately there are no economic tricks by which one can avoid the realities of a situation and such methods inevitably increase total costs rather than reduce them.

(c) The choice of new facilities

The criterion of minimum operation time is also unrewarding if used as a guide to new investment. It may happen, for example, that the purchase of a particular new machine will reduce the direct costs of certain expensive components by 40%, and that this is the biggest reduction in the component direct costs which is obtainable. It may well, be however, that the same investment in some other machine which showed no reduction in component cost, would give a greater increase in enterprise profitability, if it eliminated a capacity bottleneck and made possible a significant increase in product output and sales.

(d) The material flow system

One cannot safely make any decision in production planning on an individual component basis. The sum of all the component choices of method and layout, determines the nature of the material flow system. The traditional methods of production planning, based on planning for each item independently, create an extremely complex material flow system. The present high overhead rates in industry are mainly due to the complexity of the material flow systems produced by this approach. A large proportion of the costs under such headings as accounting, costing, obsolescence, storekeeping, inventory control, progressing, and handling can be eliminated by simplifying the material flow system.

8.5 PRODUCTION PLANNING POLICY WITH GROUP TECHNOLOGY

Production planning policy with Group Technology is based on the assumption that thousands of sub-optimum solutions can never find a total optimum solution. This would be true even with perfect information. With the limited information which it is economically possible to accumulate in practice, the sub-optimization approach is even less reliable.

(a) The material flow system

Production planning with Group Technology first attempts to design an efficient material flow system and then limits the freedom of the planner to the extent that all his detailed decisions for individual components must be made so that they maintain this standard material flow system.

The main criterion for efficiency when planning a material flow system is simplicity. Simplification can be defined as the elimination of unnecessary variety. In the simplification of material flow systems the aim is to reduce the number of different routes followed by materials. The simplest system is the one with the smallest number of possible routes between groups, and inside the groups, between work centres.

Simplification of the material flow system is economically profitable because it reduces both costs and the investment. It reduces first of all the costs of storage, handling, and management controls. It also reduces the investment, particularly in stocks, tooling, and buildings, which is needed to sustain any given level of output. It may appear to be possible to make some minor savings by treating some components as special cases, but these exceptions are dangerous because they complicate the total system and reduce the much greater savings possible with a good general solution.

(b) Line and group layout

The key to the simplification of material flow systems, is first to use line flow wherever it is economically viable, and second to use group layout where line flow is impossible. Functional layout should be avoided because it inevitably produces a very complex material flow system, which requires heavy additional costs to make it work.

One can put this policy in different terms by saying that the basic policy is to use group layout, but that where the machines in a group have a common usage sequence they should be laid out in lines to obtain the additional advantages possible from line layout.

(c) Component planning

To maintain an efficient material flow system it is essential that any new components introduced for manufacture, should either fit into one of the existing groups, or provide sufficient load to warrant the formation of a new family and group. New components should never be considered as special independent problems, but rather as possible additions to existing production families, material families, and tooling families. The aim when planning new components is to increase total profitability rather than to achieve good conventional cost figures.

8.6 PLANNING THE NEW MATERIAL FLOW SYSTEM

The work of simplifying a material flow system can be considered under six main headings:

1. Analyse the existing material flow system and find the natural division into families and groups.

2. Analyse the machine loads and find the best division of common machines between groups.

3. Analyse the labour load and determine how many men to allocate to each group.

4. Plan the layout in groups.
5. Plan the new control systems.
6. Change the layout and the control system.

(a) Finding the families and groups

The best method of finding the families and groups for group layout, is to analyse the existing material flow system, find the natural division into groups and families, and then eliminate those exceptional routes which do not fit this pattern. The technique used to do this task is called 'Production Flow Analysis'. It is described in detail in Chapter 9.

(b) Determine the best distribution of plant and labour between the groups

Production flow analysis shows which types of machine must be installed in each group. To determine the numbers of each type that will be required in the groups, it is next necessary to find the loads imposed on the different types of machine in each group by the likely product demands of the market. The methods used to check loads and determine the best distribution of the existing plant and labour force are described in Chapter 10.

(c) Plant layout in the groups

Knowing the number of machines to be installed in each group and the number of men who will work in them, the next task is to plan the layout of the groups. Methods are described in Chapter 11.

(d) Control systems

The most important control system requiring changing with the introduction of group layout is the production control system. The type of flow control system necessary for efficient operation has already been described in Chapters 4 and 5. Other control systems which may need modification are the accounting, costing, and inspection systems.

(e) Introduce the changes

The final task is to introduce the planned changes. A possible method is described in Chapter 15. As that part of the Production Management job which deals with the introduction of the new material flow system is covered in other parts of the book, it need not be elaborated here.

8.7 PRODUCTION PLANNING FOR NEW COMPONENTS

Once the material flow system has been simplified and the groups and families are known, the planing of new component processing methods with Group Technology takes place in six main steps:

1. Allocate the component to the most suitable group.

2. Find the material family in which it fits and replan material cutting if appropriate

3. Prepare the route card.

4. Find the tooling families into which it fits and plan the provision of new tooling if any.

5. Find the standard operation time.

6. Check the load on the group.

(a) *Allocate to Group*

Each new component will normally be suitable for processing in one of the existing groups. This will only be impossible when some entirely new process is being introduced, or there is already an excessive load on the machines in the appropriate group. In these cases it will be necessary to consider the creation of a new group, the division of an existing large group, or the expansion of an existing small group.

(b) *Find the material family*

In the case of parts made from general materials, the next job is to find the material family into which it fits and to modify the material cutting plan for this material to obtain the best possible material utilization.

The planner will have a list of the parts in the family, sub-divided into material families. If for example the new drawing calls for a particular grade and thickness of steel plate, he will find from his list which other items are made from the same material and add the new part to the same material family. If the steel plate is flame-cut using a cutting drawing with an electronic tracing head, he will modify the cutting drawing to include the new part.

As far as possible each cutting drawing will be restricted to a single product. If they cover more than one product, changes in the product mix on successive programmes may cause excessive cutting of materials for some parts. One way of overcoming this problem is to designate any small blanks required in large numbers as 'fillers'. Separate drawings of these items can be attached to the product cutting drawings by the flame cutter during cutting, to use up spare material.

If the planner finds that the new component does not fit into any existing material family, but that there is a similar material in use for other parts, which might be used for the new one, he will refer the matter back to the designer.

(c) *Prepare the Route Card*

The planner will have a network flow diagram for each group showing all the routes between machines and the number of parts using each route (*see* Figure 11.4). He will attempt to plan a route for the component, which uses the machines in the group and maintains the preferred sequence of machine usage. In this way he will maintain the simplicity of the material flow system inside the group.

In some of the groups there may be preferred routes which he is developing with a view to the later formation of a line. For these he will have standard route forms. He will attempt to fit new parts into one of these standard routes before considering other solutions.

An insight into the nature of the problems can be gained by an examination of Figures 8.2 and 8.3. These illustrations are taken from a paper by J. Szadkovski.* They show 46 possible operations for machining a shaft. There are 1,296 feasible machining processes. Szadkovski points out that if a criterion is chosen—cost for example—and the costs for each operation are shown over their arrows, the shortest path through the network will indicate the optimum process. This path may be different for each different criterion and for a large number of different sub-groups of parts.

In all companies it will be found that not all the feasible solutions are considered during planning. The adoption of an often informal code of practice, will mean that the majority of the feasible solutions are not considered. This fact will be reflected in the composition of the groups formed by production flow analysis.

(d) Find the tooling families

For each of the principal machines in any group, the planner will have a list of parts using the machine, sub-divided into tooling families of parts which can all be produced with the same tooling at the same set-up. He will attempt to fit new parts into one of these tooling families.

In some cases the addition of the new part to a tooling family may necessitate the addition of some new tools to the tooling family tool list and modification of the set-up diagram. He will make these changes when required.

If the new part does not fit any existing tooling family, he will investigate the possibility of forming the nucleus for a new tooling family, with some other component in the family, which also does not belong to any existing tooling family.

(e) Find the standard operation times

Next the planner must find the standard times for the operations. Ideally, he or a specialist in work measurement in the department, will use one of the pre-determined motion time study systems to find these standard times. In many cases where the part fits into an existing tooling family, he can find the standard time very easily by modifying the calculation sheet for some other similar component. If the company has a classification and coding system, similar components can be found very quickly.

---

* SZADKOVSKI, J., 'An Approach to Machining Process Optimization', Int. J. Prod. Res., 1971, 9 (3).

i	j	Operation	Machine tool
1	2	Manufacture of rod	
1	6	Manufacture of forging	Hammer
1	7	Manufacture of forging	Rotary swaging
2	3	Cutting of rod	Circular saw
2	4	Cutting of rod	Band saw
2	5	Cutting of rod	Automatic cutting machine
4	8	Planing and centring	Semiautomatic planing and centring machine
4	10	Planing and centring	Centring and milling machine
4	9	Planing	Automatic milling machine
9	17	Centring	Automatic centring machine
6	11	like 4–8	
6	13	like 4–10	
6	12	like 4–9	
12	18	like 9–17	
7	14	like 4–8	
7	16	like 4–10	
7	15	like 4–9	
15	19	like 9–17	
17	20	Roughing	Multiple-tool semi-automatic lathe
17	23	Roughing and forming	Semi-automatic tracer-controlled lathe with program control
18	20	Roughing	Multiple-tool semi-automatic lathe
18	21	Roughing and forming	Multiple-spindle chucking machine
18	22	Roughing	Multiple-tool semi-automatic lathe
19	21	Roughing and forming	Multiple-spindle chucking machine
19	23	Roughing and forming	Tracer-controlled lathe
20	21	Forming	Multiple-tool semi-automatic lathe
20	24	Forming	Tracer-controlled lathe
22	21	Forming	Multiple-tool semi-automatic lathe
22	24	Forming	Tracer-controlled lathe
21	25	Rough grinding	Cylindrical grinding machine
24	25	like 21–25	
25	26	Machining of splines	Hobbing machine for splines
25	27	Machining of splines	Multiple-spindle milling machine for splines
25	28	Machining of splines	Broaching machine for splines
25	29	Machining of splines	Slothing machine for splines
27	30	Threading	CRI-DAN lathe
27	31	Threading	Milling machine for short thread
27	32	Threading	Lathe with threading head
31	33	Heat treatment	
33	34	Improvement of centre holes	Vertical grinding machine
34	35	Semi-finishing grinding	Cylindrical grinding machine Plunge-cut grinding
34	36	Semi-finishing grinding	Cylindrical grinding machine Traverse grinding
34	37	Semi-finishing grinding	Centreless grinding machine
35	38	Finishing grinder	Cylindrical grinding machine
36	38	Finishing grinder	Cylindrical grinding machine
37	38	Finishing grinder	Centreless grinding machine

Figure 8.2. Data for operations

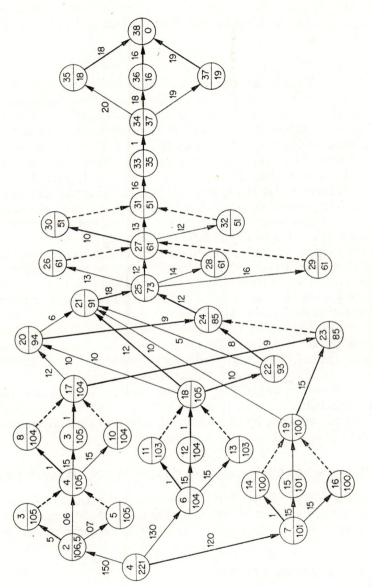

Figure 8.3. Operation network

He will see if the sum of the standard times for all operations is long. If this sum approaches the length of time available in the working cycle, he will note that the part is critical, or in other words has a critically long throughput time, when he adds it to the family list order (*see* Figure 6.3).

(*f*) Check the load

Finally the planner must check the effect of adding the new component on the work load in the group. He will have a test programme which provides a typical annual production programme for the purpose of load checking. He will also have an annual load summary form showing the load imposed by this programme on each machine in the group. Where production is at an even rate throughout the year, simple methods of calculation can be used to modify the load summary and check load against capacity. Where production is seasonal and complex changes have to be made involving several products, it may be necessary to check load against capacity for different periods of the year. This is still fairly simple using the method illustrated in Figure 6.6.

For the purpose of testing whether the existing group can accept a new part, in most cases he need only check the loads on the critical machines. He must also however from time to time, add the loads imposed by new parts onto the load summary for all machines, to provide accurate information for future decision making.

If the load on any machine is found to be excessive, he should consider ways in which the capacity of the group can be increased. Alternatively if the group is already large and production is growing, he may have to consider the desirability of splitting the existing group into two.

In some cases, particularly with simple parts, it may be possible to fit some components into more than one group. A shortage of capacity can sometimes be overcome by transferring these types of part from one group to another.

8.8   ORGANIZATION OF PRODUCTION PLANNING

The introduction of Group Technology may make it desirable to change the organization of the Production Planning department. The main change that may be needed, is from centralized to decentralized organization.

(*a*) Current organization practice

Production planning in most companies today is centralized both organizationally and geographically. There is usually a Production Planning department. the head of which reports to the Production Manager, or Production Director. There is usually one central Production Planning office.

In companies with several major processes, the production planners will generally specialize in different processes. For example one may specialize in machining, another in sheet metal work and another in foundry work. Certain types of work may be done by specialists, who provide a service to the planners. Examples are time study, standardization, and tool design. The Planning office will issue its plans in the form of route cards—which will be issued to the processing shop foremen—and tool requisitions and tool design drawings, which will be issued to the Tool room, or Buying department.

(b) Advantages of centralization

The main advantages of centralization are that it permits close control of the work by the chief planner, and that it makes it easier to use functional specialists efficiently. The large centralized production planning department can be organized for efficient data processing; there can be close supervision of the work of the planners, and co-ordination between different planners is facilitated. It is probable that as far as the efficiency of data processing is concerned, the centralized office will always be the best.

(c) Disadvantages of centralization

The main disadvantages of centralization is that it tends to isolate the planners from the men and machines, whose work they are required to plan. With centralized planning the planner tends to work mainly from recorded information rather than information gained directly by contact with the foremen in the processing shops and by observation of problems on the shop floor. In extreme cases this can lead to the preparation of plans which are unusable in practice, and to bad feelings between the planners and the processing shop foremen.

In some factories the processing shop foremen have authority to change routes to suit their special needs and the route cards bear little relation to the actual methods in use. It is difficult to see the advantages of running an efficiently managed planning office if the plans it produces cannot be or are not used.

(d) Decentralization

The alternative to centralized planning is decentralization. With this approach each major processing department has its own specialist planning office inside the department. Companies which have adopted this approach say that production planning is a service. The aim should be to optimize the service. There is no point in optimizing the data processing efficiency of the planning department at the expense of the efficiency of the service it offers.

The needs for consultation, communication, and co-ordination between the processing shop personnel and the planner are much more frequent and important to efficiency, than the need for consultation between the planners of different processes. It is better therefore if the planners are situated near the work centres for which they plan, rather than near each other. The limited amount of co-ordination necessary between planners can still be controlled by a chief planner in a small central office, which can also house any centralized services which are too small to warrant division.

(e) Production Planning and Group Technology

With Group Technology the case for decentralization is even stronger. With traditional forms of layout and of production planning, there will be some components which are made in several different departments. With group layout all the parts made in any department are completed inside one group in that department. In the first case it can be argued that centralization makes co-ordination easier. In the second case the planner for say a machine shop, has little or no need to confer with anyone outside the machine shop. Centralization only makes the job more difficult.

The job of production planning with Group Technology described earlier in the chapter, requires an intimate knowledge of the existing materials and methods in use and of the men and machines employed in the groups. The plans made for new components must be related to the plans previously made for earlier components and must improve the general operating efficiency of the group. Only a limited proportion of the information needed to do this job efficiently can be embodied economically in records. The planner also needs personal contact with the groups if he is to fully understand each group system as a whole, and gain the co-operation of its foreman and machine operators.

8.9 SUMMARY

The fundamental change in production planning which is needed with Group Technology, is the change from planning on an individual component basis to planning on a family basis. The term 'family planning' has other associations, but this is in fact what is required.

Production planning with Group Technology starts by designing an efficient material flow system and then restricts the freedom of choice of the planner to the limited extent necessary to maintain and improve this system.

In planning each new component the aim is to fit it as far as possible into the existing family-group structure, and to fit it also into an existing material family and tooling family.

9 Production Flow Analysis

9.1 INTRODUCTION

Production Flow Analysis is a technique used to simplify material flow systems and to find the families and groups for group layout. The technique is applied in four successive stages, as illustrated in Figure 9.1. The main information needed to use it is an accurate route card for every part produced.

The first stage called 'Factory Flow Analysis', studies the way in which materials flow between the different production processes in a factory. The lists of machines used to carry out each process are called 'Processing Units', or 'P.U.s'. Within limits imposed by the need to separate incompatible processes factory flow analysis combines P.U.s. doing processes on the same parts, into larger units called 'Major Groups'. The major groups found by this analysis contain the largest possible groups of compatible machines, which can complete all the parts in their 'major families' without intermediate visits to other major groups, or to outside contractors. This change simplifies the material flow system. Exceptional parts with routes which do not fit the new simplified material flow system between major groups are then examined and modified individually. The second stage is called 'Group Analysis'. It uses a matrix to divide all the parts assigned to a major group into smaller 'families' and all the machines into 'groups', in such a way that each family can be completely processed in one 'group'. The third stage is called 'Line Analysis'. It again uses network analysis to analyse the routes between the machines in a group, taken by the parts in its family, in order to find the best arrangement for plant layout. The fourth stage is called 'Tooling Analysis'. Again using a matrix, it finds the division of the parts processed on each machine into 'tooling families', and also finds their optimum sequence of loading.

The first of these stages—factory flow analysis—is essential in all except the simplest of companies. One cannot successfully introduce group layout in a processing department where 20% or more of the parts are routed to outside contractors, or to other departments for intermediate operations and then return to the department for further work to be done on them. This kind of complexity must be eliminated by factory flow analysis, before an attempt is made to find groups and families inside the departments. If the parts made in a department cannot be made completely without intermediate visits to other departments, it will be impossible to

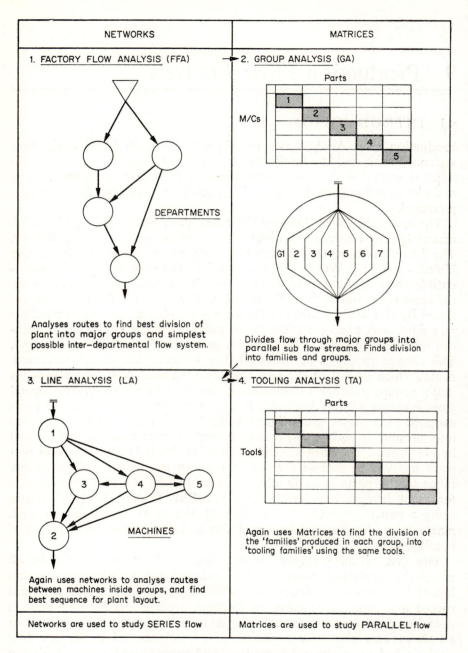

NETWORKS	MATRICES
1. FACTORY FLOW ANALYSIS (FFA)	2. GROUP ANALYSIS (GA)
Analyses routes to find best division of plant into major groups and simplest possible inter–departmental flow system.	Divides flow through major groups into parallel sub flow streams. Finds division into families and groups.
3. LINE ANALYSIS (LA)	4. TOOLING ANALYSIS (TA)
Again uses networks to analyse routes between machines inside groups, and find best sequence for plant layout.	Again uses Matrices to find the division of the 'families' produced in each group, into 'tooling families' using the same tools.
Networks are used to study SERIES flow	Matrices are used to study PARALLEL flow

Figure 9.1. Stages in production flow analysis

divide them into families which are completely processed in particular groups.

In small factories carrying out several different processes, the major groups found by factory flow analysis will be small and will themselves have the qualities of groups. In larger factories Group and Line Analysis provide a simple method for finding the further division into smaller groups and families inside these major groups, and the most efficient layout of the machines in each group. This chapter considers only the first two stages of production flow analysis and leaves line analysis and tooling analysis for examination in later chapters.

9.2 ROUTE CARDS

The main information needed for production flow analysis is contained in the component route cards. Before they are used they should be checked for completeness and accuracy. The main points to be checked are that:

(*a*) There should be a separate route card for every made component, and for every assembly requiring further processing after assembly.

(*b*) Each route card should show all the operations used to make the item.

(*c*) The machine types used for all operations must be shown.

(*d*) The routes should be an accurate record of the methods actually in use, or alternatively of methods which have been used and can still be used efficiently without buying additional tooling.

(*e*) Ideally the operation time per piece should be shown for each operation.

Each of these points will now be considered in detail.

(*a*) *Separate route card for every component and assembly*

Some companies do not produce route cards for simple parts such as those cut from plate for welded fabrications. In many factories these parts do not even have part numbers. All omissions of this type must be repaired before analysis. Any part which at any time has a separate identity must be given an individual part number and a route card. Any assembly or sub-assembly which requires further machine processing before incorporation in the product will also require a separate route card.

(*b*) *Comprehensive list of operations*

Ideally each component route card should show all operations from raw material issue to assembly, and each assembly route card should show all machine operations necessary to complete the assembly. Parts can be joined together to form assemblies in many ways, including fitted assembly, welded assembly, sewing, stapling, packaging together, and so on. Once a component joins others in an assembly it loses its original identity. The assembly becomes the unit to be controlled. It must in turn have its own identity number and route card showing any additional processing, unless it is itself the final assembly, or completed product.

The route cards should show major manual operations as well as the machine operations. These operations will include processes such as inspection, de-burring, cleaning, and perhaps others. Actually this information is not needed for factory flow analysis or group analysis unless special plant is used, but it is needed later for line analysis.

(c) The machine type for all operations

The route card should show the machine type on which every operation must be done. Ideally the machine type code should be so devised that if two machines have the same code number, any job loaded on one of them could equally well be done on the other. The code should also be designed to facilitate the rapid finding of alternative machines for exceptional operations.

Often companies have good plant codes for some processes, such as machining and very poor codes, or no codes at all, for other processes such as heat treatment and welding. It is best if these deficiencies can be repaired before analysis.

(d) The routes should accurately record the methods used

Routes are often changed in production in order to spread load, move a difficult job to a more accurate machine, or other similar reasons. Unless the company is very well managed the route cards tend to become out of date.

It is comparatively simple to improve their accuracy. Orders can be given to production planners and foremen that they must report all cases where they have already changed, or wish to change, the standard route. To ensure that this is done, control can often be excercised through the costing system. All cases where costs are accumulated at other machines than those on the route card, can be reported and be investigated. Similar controls can also be developed in some companies through the inspection records system.

If a computer is used for analysis, it can be programmed very simply to check the routes and throw out for investigation those which contain obvious errors. It can find for example parts which use machines not on the plant list; routes for parts not on the parts lists; missing routes; and the omission in any routes of plant numbers or standard times.

Although it is desirable to improve the accuracy of the route cards before production flow analysis, the technique will itself detect minor errors and inconsistencies. Assume that among the made parts there are 100 similar parts produced on five different machines in the same department and that there is an optimum sequence of machine usage. Variations from this sequence will have no effect on either factory flow analysis or group analysis. Group analysis is not concerned with usage sequence, it looks only for lists of parts and the combinations of machines used to make them. Factory flow analysis is only concerned with the sequence of visits to departments or major groups.

Again, assume that in addition to these 100 parts there are ten other parts which could be made on the same five machines. Assume that due to clerical error, or for some other reason, one operation on each has been allocated to some other machine. With production flow analysis these parts will appear in the same family, being tied to it by the other four machines, but will be shown as 'exceptions' requiring individual investigation, because they use 'exceptional' machines outside the group.

It will be seen that the level of consistency required in the routes is not high. It is sufficiently accurate if all the machine types which are necessary to make each part are shown on the route cards, and at least the majority of these are the best available or most commonly used for the purpose. However, the larger the number of inconsistencies which can be eliminated before analysis, the smaller will be the number of exceptions requiring special study and correction.

9.3 FACTORY FLOW ANALYSIS

The primary aim of factory flow analysis is to find a simple and therefore efficient material flow system between major groups. To achieve this aim, the following secondary aims are adopted, within the limits imposed by possibility:

(a) If processing in stages in successive major groups is desirable for economic reasons, for policy reasons, or due to incompatible processes, the number of successive stages should be kept to a minimum.

(b) Each component should be fully processed in one major group during a single visit. It should not leave the major group for intermediate operations and then return for finishing.

(c) Each machine type should exist as far as possible in one major group only.

(d) Major groups should have minimum valency, drawing materials from the fewest possible sources, and issuing them to the fewest possible destinations.

(e) Incompatible processes should be separated.

These aims are themselves incompatible and it is never possible to achieve them completely. They provide a useful guide however, to the type of compromise decision which will give the maximum simplification of the material flow system, with the minimum investment in new plant and tooling. Factory flow analysis is done in ten main steps, as follows:

1. Divide into processing units
2. Allocate plant to processing units

3. Determine 'Process Route Numbers' (PRNs)
4. Analyse by PRN
5. Draw basic flow chart
6. Simplify the basic flow chart and find the major groups
7. Determine which parts are exceptions
8. Eliminate exceptions
9. Check machine loads
10. Specify the standard inter-major group material flow system

These stages are described below:

1. *Divide into processing units (P.U.s) and allocate plant*

The way in which the processing plant is divided into P.U.s for analysis can affect the efficiency of factory flow analysis. Because most companies today are organized on a functional basis, the existing division into departments and sections will sometimes provide a suitable basis for analysis. There are, however, certain conditions which may make it desirable to modify the existing division, in order to simplify the analysis. The main conditions are:

(*a*) Facilities which may have to service several major groups should not be included as a part of one processing unit.

(*b*) Departments which carry out two or more incompatible processes should be divided into separate processing units for analysis.

(*c*) Providing that they are not incompatible, two departments may be combined to simplify the analysis, if one takes all or most of its input from the other.

(*a*) *Facilities which may service more than one department.* A typical example is a forge department which, in addition to the forging machines, is equipped with saws and flame cutting machines used to serve several departments with cut blanks. Unless the company is large it will generally be more economical to centralize blank cutting than to split it. Blank cutting should be separated—on paper—from the forge, to form two separate P.U.s, in this case before factory flow analysis. Other examples might be shot blasting, and barrelling machines used in a foundry to clean castings, and also used to clean forgings and steel blanks, and a heat treatment section to heat treat castings, forgings, and machined parts.

If such facilities are at present managed by only one of the user departments, they should be separated and treated as separate P.U.s for the purpose of analysis. Alternatively, if the machines used by each user department are different, they can be allocated each to its own user department before analysis.

(*b*) *Incompatible processes.* Examples of incompatible processes are:

(*i*) Metal founding and precision machining
(*ii*) Drop stamping and precision machining

(*iii*) Welding and electroplating or other wet processes

(*iv*) Heat treatment and any process on inflammable or explosive materials

The main reasons for separating such processes are concerned with safety, working conditions, technological specialization, and product quality. Another reason in the case of production flow analysis is that if major groups are formed containing incompatible processes, group analysis may find groups containing incompatible machines.

(*c*) *Allocate plant.* If the existing division into departments is used, the existing lists of plant in the departments give the information needed for analysis. If there are any departments which must be divided, their plant lists must also be divided.

If the existing division into departments is unsuitable, the factory plant list must be carefully analysed and divided into processing units containing similar and compatible machines.

(*d*) *Example of the division into processing units.* In a recent project, used as an example in this chapter, there were six processing departments in the factory. They were adopted as the processing units for analysis:

1. Blank production (sawn and flame cut blanks)
2. Sheet metal department
3. Forge
4. Welding department
5. Machine shop (including heat treatment)
6. Assembly department (including painting)
9. Sub-contractors. There was a small number of parts which were routed outside for intermediate operations, and then returned for finishing.

Blank production was centralized rather than divide the steel stocks, saws, and flame cutting machines between the four departments requiring steel blanks (departments 2, 3, 4, and 5). The number '9' was allocated to the facilities of outside sub-contractors.

There were three assembly processes: mechanical assembly in department '6'; welding assembly in department '4'; and sheet metal assembly in department '2'. Because nearly all the sheet metal assemblies were composed only of made sheet metal components, component processing and assembly were left combined in this case in one sheet metal department.

Heat treatment and machining were combined into one department, when it was discovered that heat treatment was only used for operations on machined parts. The combination of these two incompatible processes before analysis would not be recommended today. It only worked out in this case because group analysis later found only one group needing heat treatment. Painting and assembly were also combined, because no painting was done until the main assembly stage.

2. *Determine 'process route numbers' and analyse*

The process route number (PRN) is a code number formed by listing in correct sequence the code numbers for all the PUs visited by a part. Using the department numbers from the above example as the PUs, 156 is the PRN for a part which starts in department 1 (blanks), goes next to department 5 (machining), and then goes to department 6 (assembly).

The PRNs are found by drawing a thick line on the route card between

Route card		P.R.N.	156

PART DESCRIPTION	PART NO.
Pin	E.28271

MATERIAL
BLK M.S. bar 65 mm dia x 156 mm L.G.

10	20/ 227	30/ 508	40/ 413	50/ 233	60/ 907	VR
STO	HLN	MV	D8	HL7	SA	STO

10	STO	USING 65 mm dia BLK M.S. bar cut off 156 mm LG.			1
20	HLN	Load to chuck face and centre Steady with centre and finish turn 50·8 / 50·7 mm dia, form 30° chamfer reload and face to length. *Do not form groove.* Remove sharp corners.	90 00 16		
30	MV	Load to vice and mill flat	30 00 04		5
40	D8	Load to pin jig and drill 6 mm hole	20 00 03		
50	HL7	Load to chuck and form groove	30 00 04		
60	SA	Deburr	00 00 01½		
	STO	Final inspection			
					6

Figure 9.2. Route card divided by departments and coded

any two following operations done on machines allocated to different departments. The department numbers are then written at the right hand side of the route and these numbers are listed in sequence to form the PRN code number, as shown in Figure 9.2.

Process route numbers are added to all the route cards existing in the factory, and the number of different parts with each PRN is counted. The results achieved with the sample of routes used in the example are tabulated in the 'PRN Frequency Chart' shown in Figure 9.3. Because the research was based on a sample of routes, the number of components is small. Because the company used a system of routing in which each route card only covered movement from one store to another, including some which ended in a 'part finished store', there were several successive routes for some components. Not all these routes were in the sample and there

PRN frequency analysis

PRN						NO. ROUTES	PRN						NO. ROUTES
1						69	1	6					1
1	2					4	2						8
1	2	3	4			1	2	6					20
1	2	6				4	3						5
1	3					8	3	1	2	6			1
1	3	2				1	3	4					1
1	3	2	4			1	3	5	6				1
1	3	4				3	3	6					7
1	3	5	6			3	4						5
1	3	6				10	4	1	4	6			2
1	4					22	4	1	5	6			1
1	5					39	4	2	6				1
1	5	1	3	2	6	1	4	5	4	6			1
1	5	2				3	4	5	6				7
1	5	3	5	6		1	4	6					41
1	5	3	6			2	5						13
1	5	4				3	5	4					4
1	5	4	6			1	5	6					107
1	5	4	9	9	5 6	1	5	9	5	6			1
1	5	6				103	5	9	6				1
1	5	6	4			1	6						59
1	5	9	5	6		1	9	6	5	6			1

44 different PRNs, covering 569 different parts.

Figure 9.3. P.R.N. frequency chart

are therefore several routes ending in department numbers 1 and 3, which are not assembly departments. Most of these parts were later found to be parts for welded assemblies. It will be realized that if comprehensive route cards had been used, covering all operations up to assembly, every PRN would have ended with a '6', a '4', or a '2'.

It will be noted that forty-four PRNs covered the whole sample of 569 parts and that a small proportion of the PRNs covered a very high proportion of the number of different components.

3. *Draw basic flow chart*

A basic flow chart is now drawn to illustrate the material flow system. A circle is drawn for each department. Arrows are drawn between the circles

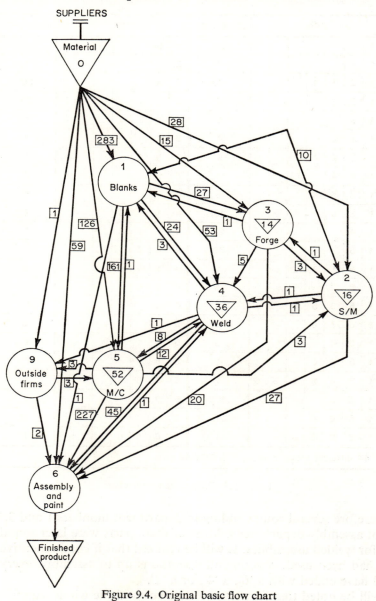

Figure 9.4. Original basic flow chart

to show all the material flow paths discovered when analysing the PRNs. The number of components using each flow path is determined from the PRN frequency chart and is also shown on the chart. For example, counting the number of parts covered by PRNs in which the number '3' follows the number '2', gives the number to be entered against the arrow leading from department 2 to department 3.

The basic flow chart from the example is shown in Figure 9.4. It illustrates very well the chaotic type of material flow system through which most engineering companies are trying to control material flow today. In this illustration the figures in rectangles show the number of parts which use each flow path and the numbers in triangles indicate the number of parts, whose routes finish in the indicated departments, and whose final destinations were unknown when the analysis was made.

4. *Simplify the Basic Flow Chart and find major groups*

The first step in simplification is to specify the restraints, or in other words to specify which processing units may not be joined together, due to incompatibility of process, economic reasons or company policy.

The restraints in this case were that, as most of the departments carried out incompatible processes, the only two which were considered suitable for joining together were the forge and welding departments. When it was found that most of the items made in the forge were used in welded assemblies, these two departments were joined to form a major group.

The final list of major groups was then the same as the list of departments, with the exception that departments 3 and 4 were joined to form one major group.

5. *Exceptions*

In the case used as an example the parts to be treated as exceptions— requiring re-routing to fit the majority pattern—were found by direct examination of the PRN frequency chart, Figure 9.3, and basic flow chart, Figure 9.4. This examination quickly showed that by eliminating, or simplifying the PRNs for only twenty-five parts (4·4% of the total), it was possible to achieve the very much simpler basic flow chart shown in Figure 9.5. Later, departments 3 and 4 were joined together.

The exceptions are all components with complex PRNs which do not fit the simplified basic flow chart. There are five main ways in which they can be eliminated:

(*a*) Re-routing operations from exceptional machines outside the major group to other machines already in the major group which are similar in type.

(*b*) Re-allocation of plant between major groups.

(*c*) Change of method.

(*d*) Change in design.

(*e*) Purchasing the part instead of making it.

In the example the majority of complex PRNs could be simplified to fit the simple basic flow chart in Figure 9.4. by methods (*a*) or (*b*) above.

Most practising production controllers will recognize these exceptions. They exist in many engineering companies under such names as 'special schedule parts', and 'special planning parts'. They are the critical path items

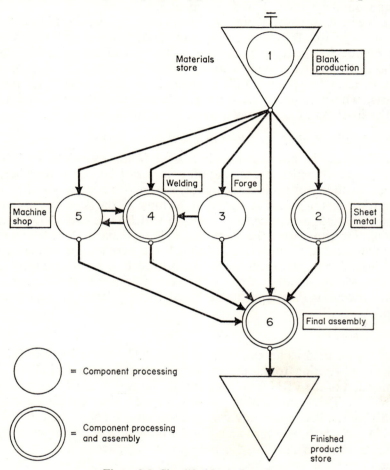

Figure 9.5. Simplified basic flow chart

which cannot be included in the normal production control system, because their routes are too complicated and their lead times are too long. These 5%, or less, of the parts may represent 20% or more of the work load on the production control department, and they will usually be responsible for the majority of delays and broken delivery promises. By finding these exceptions and eliminating them, factory flow analysis not only makes it possible to introduce group layout in the departments, but also makes a major contribution to productivity in its own right.

6. *Check machine loads*

At this stage of factory flow analysis it is possible to say what types of machines will be needed in each major group, but not how many. It is now necessary to check the machine loads on any machine types required in more than one department to determine how the machines of these types should be divided between the departments.

If a machine type is required in only one major group, the changes induced by factory flow analysis will have no major effect on capacity. If there was sufficient capacity before the change there will generally be more than enough after the change. Load checking in this case will only be necessary if new work has been planned for a machine during the elimination of exceptions. In the example, drilling machines were the only machines required in more than one major group and there was ample spare capacity to make this possible.

7. *Specify major groups and the flow system between them*

Having found the optimum material flow system between major groups it is necessary to issue specifications and instructions so that it can be maintained. The system can be specified by publishing the simplified basic flow chart. Initially it can also be specified by listing the machines installed in each major group and the parts made on them. These two lists can be varied in the future, however, without changing the flow system, providing that the changes do not introduce new flow paths on the basic flow chart, or overload a major group with work.

Instructions must be given that no new route cards may be issued, which introduce new flow paths not shown on the standard flow chart, and a control must be instituted to ensure that these instructions are followed. Once again the accounting system can be used to ensure that new complex routes are not introduced surreptitiously.

9.4 FACTORY FLOW ANALYSIS. A MORE COMPLEX EXAMPLE

The example just described is relatively simple. A measure of simplification was achieved before analysis, by consolidating: (1) heat treatment and machining, (2) sheet metal component processing and assembly, and (3) assembly and painting, into single processing units. It was then possible to find the exceptions by eye.

A more complex case will now be described. This is a study of the material flow in one of the Olivetti factories in Italy. In this factory there were nine departments:

1. First operation presses
2. Second operation presses
3. Automatic lathes

4. Supplementary processes—machined parts
5. Welding
6. Supplementary processes—pressed parts
7. Heat treatment
8. Electro-plating
9. Riveting

(a) The original flow system

There were 3308 parts produced and the PRN frequency chart showed 241 different process route numbers. The initial basic flow chart is illus-

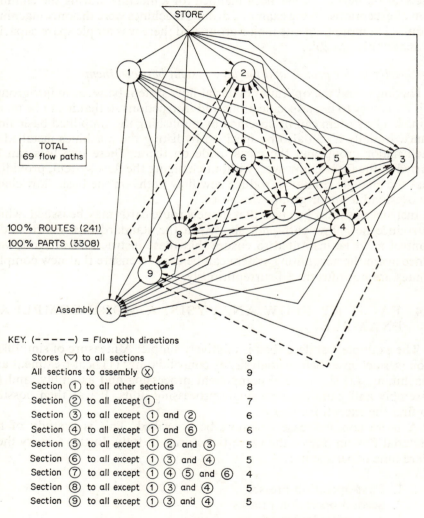

KEY. (– – – – –) = Flow both directions

Stores (▽) to all sections	9
All sections to assembly (X)	9
Section ① to all other sections	8
Section ② to all except ①	7
Section ③ to all except ① and ②	6
Section ④ to all except ① and ⑥	6
Section ⑤ to all except ① ② and ③	5
Section ⑥ to all except ① ③ and ④	5
Section ⑦ to all except ① ④ ⑤ and ⑥	4
Section ⑧ to all except ① ③ and ④	5
Section ⑨ to all except ① ③ and ④	5

TOTAL 69 flow paths

100% ROUTES (241)
100% PARTS (3308)

Figure 9.6 (a). Existing flow systems in Olivetti factory

trated in Figure 9.6(*a*). The flow system included 69 flow paths between departments. Thirty-two of these were accommodated in sixteen links with flow in both directions, or in other words with 'backflow'.

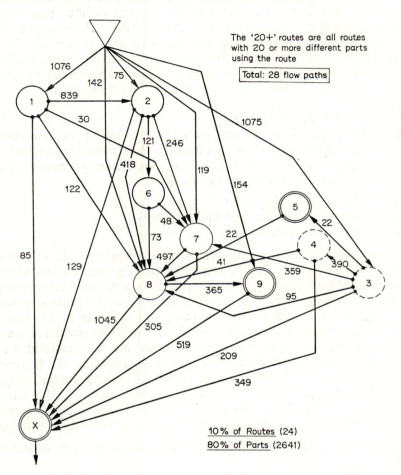

The '20+' routes are all routes with 20 or more different parts using the route

Total: 28 flow paths

10% of Routes (24)
80% of Parts (2641)

①		②		③		⑦		⑧		⑨		④	⑤	TOTAL	
IN	OUT	IN	OUT	IN	OUT	IN	OUT	IN	OUT	IN	OUT	IN	IN	IN	OUT
1076	839	839	129	1075	22	30	497	122	1045	154	519	390	22	1076	85
	122		418		390	246	305	142	365	365		OUT	OUT	142	129
	85	914	121		359	119	802	418	1410	519		349	22	75	1045
	30		246		95	359		73				41	⑥	119	305
	1076		246		209	48		497				390	IN	154	519
			914		1075	802		41					121	1075	349
								95					OUT	2641	209
								22					48		2641
								1410					73		
													121		

Figure 9.6 (*b*). The primary flow system

(b) Finding the primary flow system

The first step in simplification was to find the 'primary flow system'. The primary flow system is the system of routes between departments which covers the largest possible number of parts without backflow. It was found that if one considered only those PRNs with twenty or more parts, they included 80% of the parts, and used only 10% of the PRNs. The basic flow chart for these '20+' items is shown in Figure 9.6(b). It contains only 28 flow paths instead of 69 and all links between departments are uni-directional. It was accepted as the primary flow system.

(c) Simplification of flow system

All simplification is concerned with the elimination of unnecessary variety. The aim when simplifying a material flow system is to reduce the number of routes along which materials flow between major groups. There are only three ways in which this can be done:

1. Combine processing units
2. Re-allocate plant between major groups
3. Change component routes

The first two methods are illustrated diagrammatically in Figure 9.7. It will be seen that even very complex segments of a material flow network can be reduced by these means to very simple flow between larger groups. It is the policy of factory flow analysis to achieve the greatest possible measure of simplification by these means, and then use route changing for the small number of exceptions which do not fit the simplified system.

It will be obvious that the application of the first method would eventually obtain the 'simplest' flow system by reducing the factory to one major group. If this were possible it would indicate that a complete division into groups was possible with no restrictions on the allowed combinations of machines. This solution is however generally impossible due to 'restraints'. In the case described there were three main restraints:

1. Departments 1 or 2 should not be combined with department number 3

2. Plant from departments 7, 8 or 9 must not be installed in any other department

3. There must not be more than two stages of processing prior to assembly

A main aim in simplification is to find independent major groups. An independent major group is defined as one in which all the parts it processes only visit it once. If any part leaves for one or more intermediate operations and then returns for completion, the major group is no independent. The reason for this aim is obvious. If the major group is not independent it will be impossible to divide it later into smaller independent groups and families.

1. SIMPLIFICATION BY COMBINING DEPARTMENTS

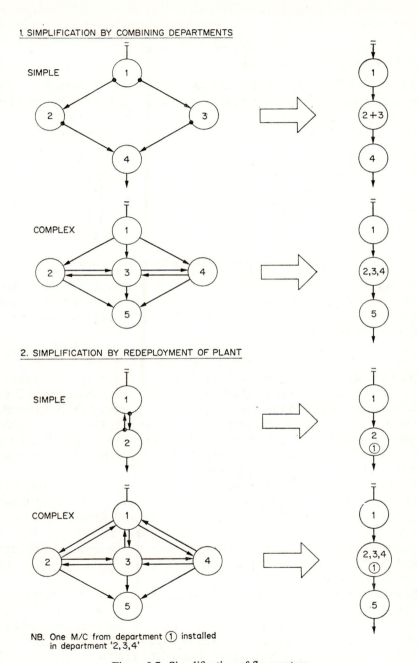

2. SIMPLIFICATION BY REDEPLOYMENT OF PLANT

NB. One M/C from department ① installed
in department '2,3,4'

Figure 9.7. Simplification of flow system

There are two conditions which ensure that there will be independent major groups:

1. There must be no 'loops' in the network
2. There must be no 'backflow'

Examples of these two defects are given in Figure 9.8. Actually it is still possible to have independent groups with loops and backflow, providing

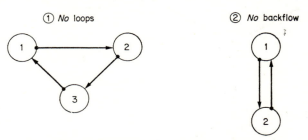

Figure 9.8. Conditions for homogeneous departments

that no part completes the whole loop, and no part visits any major group with a backflow link more than once. However, under these conditions single cycle flow control is very difficult, and loops and backflow must be excluded for this reason.

(d) Simplification of the flow system

The first step in simplification is to simplify the primary flow system. In the case illustrated in Figure 9.6(b), it was noted that department 2 only received materials from one other department, number 1, and department 6 only received materials from department number 2. They were combined to form a major group for 'press work'. Again it was noted that departments 4 and 5 only received materials from department 3. They were combined to form a major group for 'machining'.

When these major groups had been formed it was discovered that many of the PRNs with less than twenty parts per PRN, could now be accommodated, and that this number could be still further increased by moving one of the welding machines from the machining to the press department. The new material flow system achieved is illustrated in Figure 9.9(a). Only sixteen flow paths, instead of the original sixty-nine, now carry 90·5% of the parts.

The next stage was to combine departments 7, 8 and 9 to form a new 'finishing department'. This reduced the number of flow paths to eight, which carried 95·8% of the parts, leaving 4·2%, or 210 parts as exceptions. The network at this stage is illustrated in Figure 9.9(b).

Up to this stage the only machine type existing in more than one major group was 'welding machines' (five). It was found that with further re-allocation of the plant—in which a few machines would be taken from their main user departments and be installed in other departments—it would be possible to eliminate all but two of the exceptions. There is a possible choice here therefore, between maintaining each type of machine except the

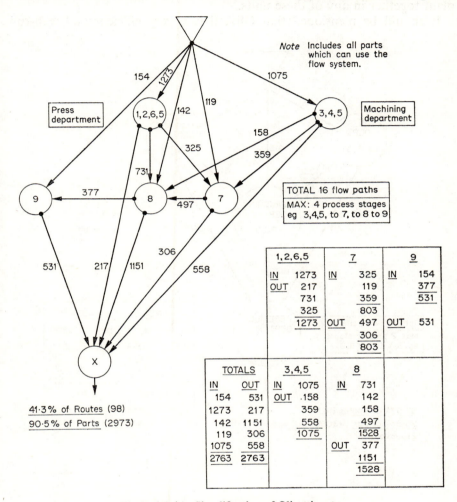

Note Includes all parts which can use the flow system.

TOTAL 16 flow paths
MAX: 4 process stages
eg 3,4,5, to 7, to 8 to 9

1,2,6,5		7		9	
IN	1273	IN	325	IN	154
OUT	217		119		377
	731		359		531
	325		803		
	1273	OUT	497	OUT	531
			306		
			803		

TOTALS		3,4,5		8	
IN	OUT	IN	1075	IN	731
154	531	OUT	.158		142
1273	217		359		158
142	1151		558		497
119	306		1075		1528
1075	558			OUT	377
2763	2763				1151
					1528

41·3% of Routes (98)
90·5% of Parts (2973)

Figure 9.9 (*a*). Simplification of Olivetti system

welders, in one department only and altering 4·2% (210) of the routes, or alternatively installing some types of machine in several departments and avoiding all except 2 route changes. The final solution of four 'major groups' will remain the same in both cases.

(e) The finishing department

At first sight heat treatment, electro-plating, and rivetting seem to be strange if not incompatible bed fellows. Analysis of the flow in this major group however, revealed a large element of line flow. Analysis is not yet complete, but it seems probable that this department will resolve into three groups and one line as illustrated in Figure 9.10 with no incompatible plant together in any of these units.

It should be mentioned that Olivetti is a very efficient and well-run

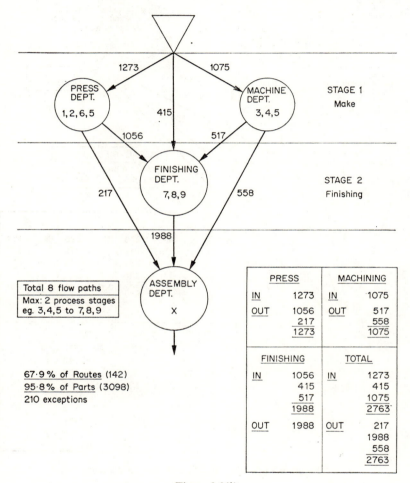

Figure 9.9(*b*)

company. The complex material flow system shown in Figure 9.6 is not unique to Olivetti, it is typical of what one can find in any company using functional layout and making products of similar complexity. It is a tribute to the persistence and ingenuity of human beings that we ever get any materials through such systems. The surprising thing is that only a very few advanced companies are considering the obvious solution of simplifying the material flow system.

1. FLOW BETWEEN 7, 8 and 9

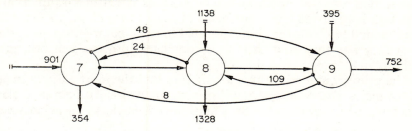

2. PROVIDE RIVETTING FACILITIES IN 7 and 8

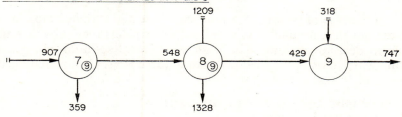

3. PROBABLE DIVISION INTO 3 GROUPS AND ONE LINE

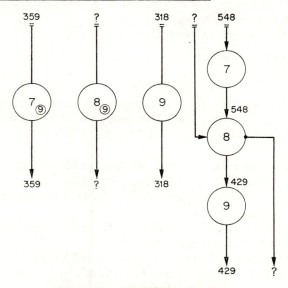

Figure 9.10. The finishing department

9.5 GROUP ANALYSIS

The second stage of production flow analysis is called Group Analysis. The task is to divide the components allocated to each major family into families and to divide the plant allocated to each major group into groups, in such a way that each 'family' is completely processed in one 'group' only.

The primary aim of group analysis is to find the most efficient division of the major groups into 'groups' of a required size. To help in achieving this aim, the following secondary aims are adopted. As far as possible:

1. Each part should be processed in one group only
2. Each machine type should exist in one group only

As in the case of factory flow analysis, these aims are incompatible and and are not fully attainable in practice. Nevertheless they provide a useful guide to decision making. The most economical solution will generally be that which most nearly follows both of these aims. Group analysis takes place in eight main steps as follows:

1. Renumber operations on route cards
2. Sort routes into packs
3. Draw pack-machine chart, or component-machine chart
4. Find families and groups
5. Check loads and allocate plant
6. Investigate and eliminate exceptions
7. Specify groups and families
8. Draw final flow system network

These steps are examined below:

(a) Renumber routes and sort into packs

For factory flow analysis it is only necessary to know the series of departments visited by each component. For group analysis it is now necessary to know which machines are visited by each component in each major group.

The operations done on any part are numbered consecutively starting with Operation 1 but with the following exceptions:

1. If a particular machine type is used for more than one operation on a component it is only numbered the first time.

2. Manual operations such as 'marking off', 'deburring', and inspection, are only numbered if special plant is provided.

This modified method of numbering provides all the information needed to find groups and families and simplifies analysis by reducing the number of operations.

All components which use the same machines in the same sequence are collected together in 'packs'. The sort is progressive, first into packs by machines for Operation 1. These packs are then divided into sub-packs according to the machines used for Operation 2. The process is continued until no further packs can be found. The method of sorting is illustrated in Figure 9.11. The number of packs can be further reduced by combining all packs which use the same combinations of machines. With the method of numbering recommended above however, the reduction in the number of packs by this means is unlikely to be significant. The sole and only

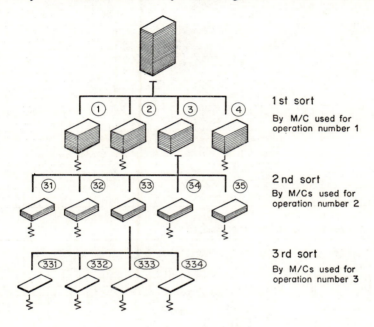

Sorting route cards into packs

Figure 9.11. Sorting into packs

purpose of this sorting operation is to simplify analysis by reducing a large number of components into a smaller number of packs of components with identical routes. The sort is not always necessary. With simple departments processing very few components, or with complex processes where most parts have different routes, there is little to be gained by sorting into packs. When a computer is used for analysis, the sort into packs is not always necessary but may be a useful method for reducing the data, in order to reduce memory capacity needs and run times.

(b) Draw pack machine chart and find families and groups

The method used for the next step is best illustrated by examples. Figure 9.12 shows a small sample from the initial component/machine chart for a machine shop and also shows how the families and groups were

(a) COMPONENT MACHINE CHART

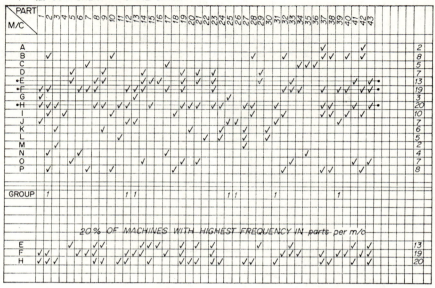

(b) DIVISION INTO GROUPS AND FAMILIES

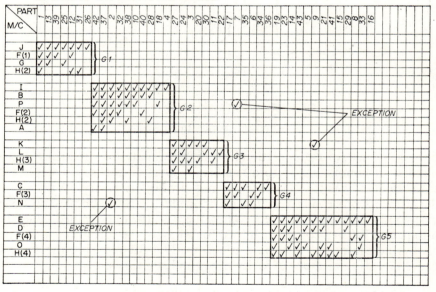

Figure 9.12. Group analysis

found by changing the sequence in which parts and machines were listed on the chart. The two charts are identical except that:

1. The sequences of listing for both parts and machines are different
2. Some machine types have been installed in more than one group

The method is first to calculate the usage frequency in parts per machine for all machines. The 10% of the machines with the highest usage frequency are not considered when forming groups due to the high risk that they will be needed in more than one group. They have been crossed out and rewritten below in Figure 9.12 (a). Groups are formed by examining the remaining entries. For example Part No. 1 uses machines J and G. Six other parts use the same machines and form Group 1. In this instance there are three exceptions requiring re-routing. Two types of machines were needed in more than one group: F and H.

A more complex example is illustrated in Figures 9.13 and 9.14, which show first an intermediate stage of manual analysis for a machine shop and second the final division into seven groups and families. In the earlier charts the machine types with the highest utilization frequency in parts per machine were listed first at the top of the sheet. This had the advantage of bringing together those machine types most likely to be required in more than one group.

Sixteen packs—5·7% of the parts—were exceptions requiring investigation. Seven machines out of the fifty (14%) were required in more than one group. However, it was found later that this number could be reduced to four, or 8%, by re-routing certain operations from, for example, one lathe type to another.

Group 4 in this instance had fifty-one parts in the sample and used twenty-five machines. On examination it will be seen that eight machines are very lightly loaded. The work from these machines could be rerouted to other machines of the same general type in the group and they were in fact redundant. This group produces all the gears and other complex components, including all items requiring heat treatment (FMC) and broaching. The group looks large on the chart because few components had the same routes and there were no packs with more than three parts. In actual fact this family was only the third in size. Both family No. 1 and family No. 2 contained more different parts.

(c) Check loads, allocate plant and specify groups and families

Once again for the purpose of finding the groups and families it is only essential to check the load on the types of plant required in more than one group. If there is sufficient capacity with functional layout for the types required in only one group there will be more than enough with group layout. Due to the increase in capacity caused by setting time reductions, apparent overloads of 10 to 15% can be accepted, when the load check is based on the average setting times found using functional layout.

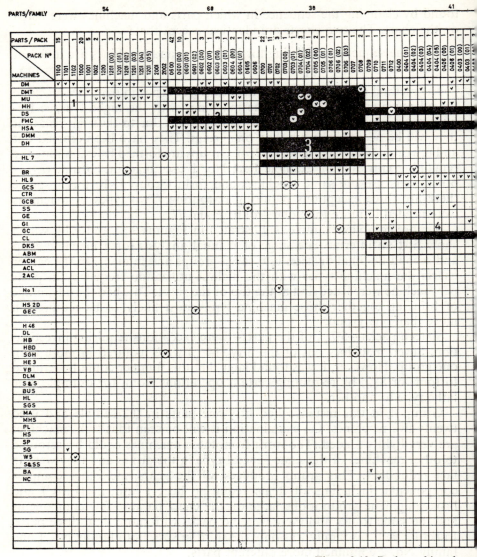

Figure 9.13. Pack-machine chart

Having checked and approved the allocation of plant to groups the next step is to eliminate the exceptions by:

1. Re-routing exceptional operations to machines inside the group
2. Change of method
3. Change of component design
4. Purchasing the component instead of making it
5. Further division of machines between groups

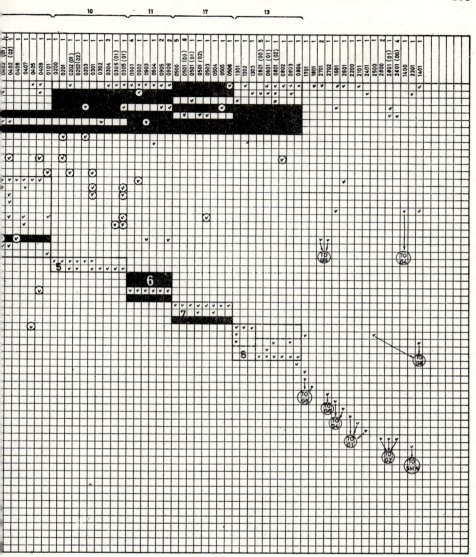

arly stage of analysis, machine shop

Further load checks may be necessary in the case of heavily loaded machines if new work is routed to them, during the elimination of exceptions.

The groups and families should be specified by listing the machines allocated to each group and the components allocated to each family. Finally when the groups and families have been formed, a full load check should be made and can then be made very easily, using the method illustrated in Figure 6.6.

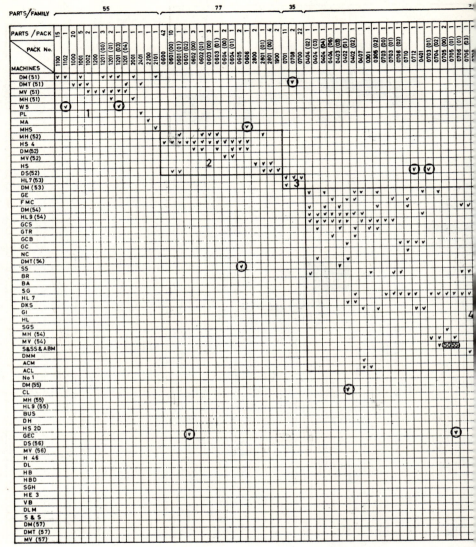

Figure 9.14. Pack-machine cha

(d) Final flow system network

When all departments have been divided into groups and families, a final flow system network diagram should be produced, showing the flow of materials between all the groups in the factory. This may reveal possibilities for the consolidation of groups found in different major groups, where one only feeds the other, and where the processes are not incompatible.

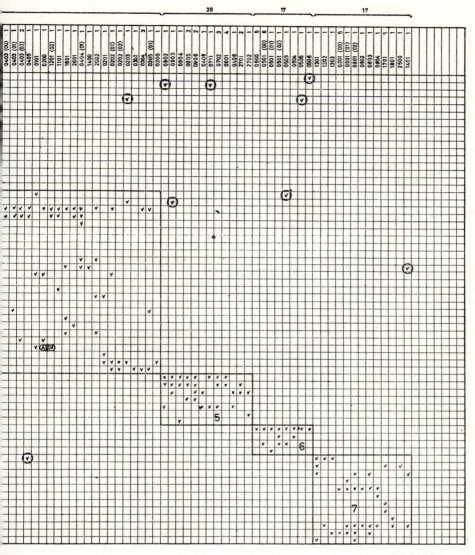

amilies and groups, machine shop

(e) Common operations

Group analysis is primarily a method for dividing a flow stream into a number of parallel streams. There may be occasions, however, when the matrix will indicate the desirability of a measure of series flow inside a department. If, for example, all first operations are done on the same machine, or group of machines, there may be advantages in forming a 'preparation group'. The same may apply to all last operations, where one

G

machine performs a common 'finishing operation' for two or more major groups. To obtain the advantages of Group Technology, however, intermediate common operations should ideally only be accepted as a temporary expedient. *See* Figure 9.15.

9.6 SAMPLES

It is possible to find the groups and families, as in the case of the example above, using only a sample of route cards, instead of all the route cards. In jobbing production, a sample taken from past orders is in fact the only possible way of finding the groups and families by group analysis.

The use of a sample greatly simplifies analysis, and in many cases will make it possible to use manual analysis, where this would be impossible if all the routes were used. The limit for manual analysis is probably 2000 fairly simple route cards. With a 20% sample, manual methods could be used therefore, in companies with 10,000 made parts.

The main deficiences in using a sample, are that a sample will not necessarily find all the plant, all the PRNs or all the exceptions, and it will not provide sufficient information for an accurate load check.

In the case of the plant, it is advisable to check the plant required for the sample against the plant list, and to add routes which include missing machines. There is no way of telling if any PRNs have been missed. It is likely however that if the sample has not found them, they will be of only minor importance and are probably routes which would be eliminated during simplification. The exceptions will not all be found with a sample. It will be necessary to introduce production planning procedures to check all orders during the early months of operation, and eliminate exceptions as they arise.

The main aim when choosing the sample is to obtain examples of all the different processing methods used in the factory and an accurate indication of the number of parts using each method. If the route cards are filed in different file sections for different products, or different processes, the numbers of route cards taken from each section should be proportional to the totals in those sections. The final choice of cards from each section can be based on random numbers, but it is probable that even random picking would be sufficiently accurate in most cases.

9.7 COMPUTERS

Only manual methods have been described so far, but it is obvious that production flow analysis is a technique which is ideal for the computer. It is probable that in the future, most computer companies will have applications programmes for the technique, and that any company with route cards will be able to use one of these package programmes to find its families and groups.

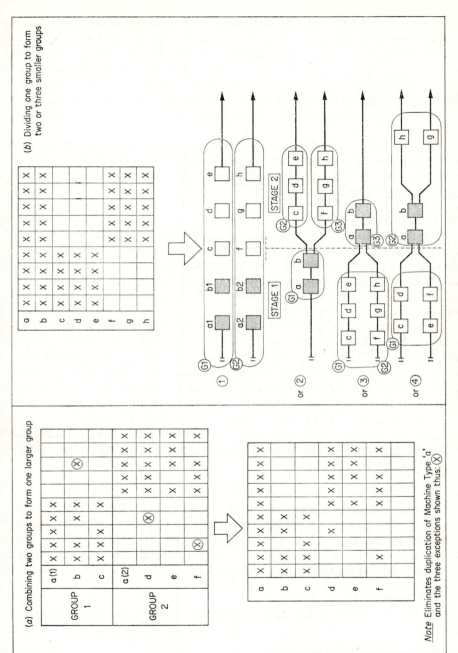

Figure 9.15. Combining and dividing groups

(a) Factory Flow Analysis

Finding the PRNs, and PRN frequency is a relatively simple job to programme. The simplification of the inter-departmental flow system can also be programmed. One method is indicated by the tabulation given in Figure 9.16. This repeats the information in the network at Figure 9.6(b). The simplification found in Figure 9.9(b) has again been discovered, in this case by marking up the tabulation. It shows the two obvious processing stages, and the obvious division of the first stage into two parallel departments.

If the computer is used to find the PRN frequency chart and the number of parts using each flow path, the remainder of the analysis is simple using manual methods. This is probably the simplest method of using the computer for factory flow analysis.

(b) Finding groups and families

Finding the division into groups and families is more difficult, but once again a tabular approach is a possibility as indicated in Figure 9.17. Marking up the tabulation finds the same division into groups and families as that found with the matrix in Figure 9.12. Unfortunately this method is unreliable if there are many machines and the print-out runs to over a hundred pages, as is sometimes the case.

Another computerized method called 'Component Flow Analysis', designed by El Essawy, has also been used successfully to find the groups and families for three factories, with others in course of implementation. This method uses the basic principles of production flow analysis, in that it analyses the information contained in route cards, but uses a different method to that described earlier in the chapter, to find the families and groups. Full details of this method have not yet been published.

There is also one computer application of Group Analysis being planned, using the approach described earlier in the chapter. The method used will now be briefly described.

(c) Group Analysis at Black and Decker

Implementation is a team effort led by Mr. B. G. Chapman for the company. The method and computer input and output specifications were prepared by the author, with assistance from Mr. J. D. Livingston of the Turin International Centre, and the systems analysis and programming were done by Mr. J. L. Hughes of Data Logic Ltd.

1. Data Bank

The factory concerned produces 1,390 made parts on 152 machines. The following data concerning each part was recorded on tape:

    (a) The operation numbers
    (b) The machine code numbers for each operation
    (c) The operation time per piece for each operation

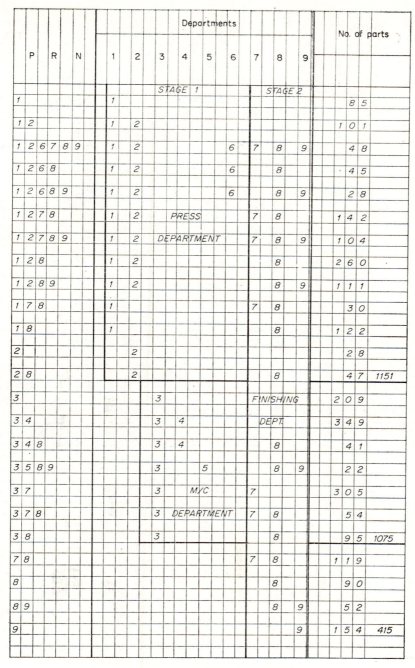

Figure 9.16. Tabular method. Factory flow analysis

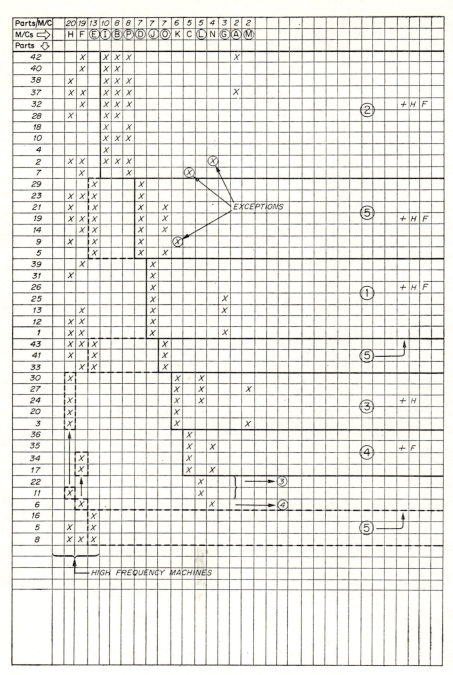

Figure 9.17. Tabular method. Group analysis

The process unit number, required for factory flow analysis, was derivable from the machine code numbers. A used-on record, showing how many of each part were used in each product, was already on tape.

2. *Data checking*

The route cards were checked and corrected first, by the planners with assistance from the cost office. The computer was then used to check the route data for:

(*a*) Machine numbers not in the current plant list
(*b*) Part numbers not now in production
(*c*) Missing machine numbers and operation times

This computer check proved its worth by finding over 100 minor errors and omissions, which were corrected.

3. *Sort into 'Sets'*

Instead of searching for 'packs', the computer was programmed to find 'sets', or lists of parts using the same combinations of machines. The data for analysis was reduced by this means, from 1390 parts to 755 sets. Apart from simplifying the analysis, this data will obviously have considerable value later, when looking for tooling families.

4. *Factory Flow Analysis*

This found a division into four major groups: an automatics department, a machining department, a press department, and a heat-treatment and finishing department. Group Analysis was done separately for each department in turn. Because many of the parts had intermediate heat treatment or finishing operations, some of these types of plant, which could be installed safely next to machine tools, were also allocated to machining and press departments.

5. *Machine usage frequency (F)*

The computer was used to find the usage frequency of each machine in each major group, or the number of different parts which it was used to process. The plant list was then printed out in usage frequency sequence.

6. *Group Analysis programme*

It is comparatively simple to find the groups and families by eye with a small sample. The mental processes used combine pattern recognition, the application of production know-how, and intuition. It has proved to be surprisingly difficult to find a method suitable for the computer, which will obtain the same result.

Fifteen different methods were tried before a reliable solution was obtained. The earlier methods were all based on the idea of a series of key machines, each used in high conjunction with several other machines to make a high proportion of the parts in their groups. Each group was formed before going on to the next one. These methods produced groups with far too many machines, low machine utilization and widely varying group size.

A random sample was then taken and a number of alternative methods were tested manually with the sample, before a viable solution was obtained.

The best method found so far will now be described. It is based on an entirely different principle to all the earlier methods tested, and is best described as 'Nuclear Synthesis'.

7. *Group formation by Nuclear Synthesis*

The earlier methods tested were all based on the idea that groups would form round important key machines, used in high conjunction with several other machines, to make many different parts. Unfortunately, however, such machines tend to be used with several different combinations of other machines. The new method emphasizes the importance of special machines used to make very few parts.

It was reasoned that there is a high probability that these low-usage machines will exist in only one group. It should be possible to form a large number of nuclei containing these machines; all the parts made with them and all other machines used to make them. These nuclei can then be combined with others using the same, or mostly the same, machines, to form any required number of groups.

In practice the following method was used:

Let F = number of parts using a machine (m/c)
f = number using a m/c in any one nucleus
Σf = cumulative number of parts which have used m/c, at any stage of analysis

To find the nuclei choose successively the machine for which $(F - \Sigma f)$ is minimum.

All the earlier nuclei contained one machine special to the nucleus. Those machines used to make very few parts, were as might be expected, those for which only one or two of the type existed. Bringing them together in one nucleus eliminated the risk that more would have to be bought. The later nuclei had to be based on machines with higher values of F, which had previously been used in other nuclei. The basis for selection here, is that there is a high probability that the machine for which $(F - \Sigma f)$ is minimum, will exist in only one more nucleus.

Figure 9.18 shows four of the nuclei formed by this method with the sample. It was decided that any nucleus in which the part using most machines, provided all the machines needed to make the others, was acceptable.

It will be seen that the first two nuclei are acceptable, even though there

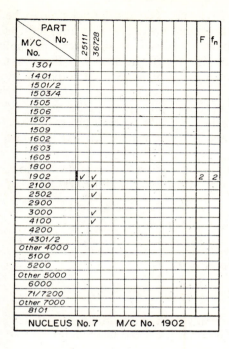

NUCLEUS No. 7   M/C No. 1902

M/C No. \ PART No.	25111	36728									F	fₙ
1301												
1401												
1501/2												
1503/4												
1505												
1506												
1507												
1509												
1602												
1603												
1605												
1800												
1902	√	√									2	2
2100		√										
2502		√										
2900												
3000		√										
4100		√										
4200												
4301/2												
Other 4000												
5100												
5200												
Other 5000												
6000												
71/7200												
Other 7000												
8101												

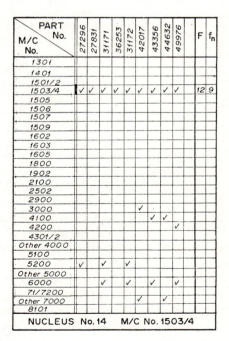

NUCLEUS No. 8   M/C No. 1602

M/C No. \ PART No.	27205	29006	33811	38700	46129						F	fₙ
1301												
1401												
1501/2												
1503/4												
1505												
1506												
1507												
1509												
1602	√	√	√	√	√						6	5
1603												
1605												
1800												
1902												
2100												
2502												
2900												
3000												
4100												
4200												
4301/2												
Other 4000												
5100	√	√		√								
5200	√			√								
Other 5000	√	√		√								
6000	√			√								
71/7200												
Other 7000												
8101												

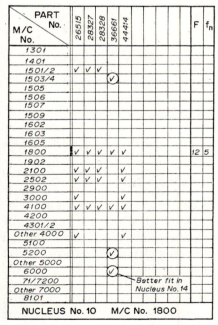

NUCLEUS No. 10   M/C No. 1800

M/C No. \ PART No.	26515	28327	28328	36661	44414						F	fₙ
1301												
1401												
1501/2	√	√	√									
1503/4				Ⓥ								
1505												
1506												
1507												
1509												
1602												
1603												
1605												
1800	√	√	√	√	√						12	5
1902												
2100	√	√	√		√							
2502	√	√	√		√							
2900												
3000	√				√							
4100	√	√	√	√	√							
4200												
4301/2												
Other 4000	√			√								
5100												
5200				Ⓥ								
Other 5000												
6000				Ⓥ								
71/7200												
Other 7000												
8101												

Better fit in Nucleus No. 14

NUCLEUS No. 14   M/C No. 1503/4

M/C No. \ PART No.	27296	27831	31171	36253	31172	42017	43356	44632	49976		F	fₙ
1301												
1401												
1501/2												
1503/4	√	√	√	√	√	√	√	√	√		12	9
1505												
1506												
1507												
1509												
1602												
1603												
1605												
1800												
1902												
2100												
2502												
2900												
3000						√						
4100							√	√				
4200									√			
4301/2												
Other 4000												
5100												
5200	√		√		√							
Other 5000												
6000			√		√		√	√				
71/7200												
Other 7000							√		√			
8101												

Figure 9.18 Nuclei

is poor machine conjunction in the first one. The third nucleus can be made acceptable by removing one exceptional part. The rule adopted for this correction was: Remove any part with two or more exceptional machines not used for any other parts. The fourth nucleus was the worst found. It contained two parts each using one machine not required by other parts in the nucleus.

It is interesting to note that the nuclei requiring the elimination of exceptional parts, or containing parts using single exceptional machines, all occurred at the middle of the range. The nuclei found first and last were all acceptable.

Twenty-four nuclei were formed. Sixteen were acceptable without modification. Five required the removal of an exceptional part. Four of

Group No.	Types of part in group
1	Hardened and ground shafts.
2	Gears.
3	Gear cases and other box-like parts made from castings.
4	Steel parts requiring only drilling and milling
5	Parts requiring both power press and machining operations.
6	Mainly bar lathe work.
7	Parts made on Herbert No. 4 with subsidiary operations.
8	Mixture, requiring mainly broaching, milling, drilling and some grinding.
9	Special line for mower parts.

Figure 9.19. Types of part in each group

these, plus three others, contained one or more parts using a single exceptional machine.

The nuclei were combined together, in a manner which, subject to certain special reservations, followed the general rule of progressively adding the one with least machines to the one with the next smallest number, which provided all the machines needed to make it, except for any special machines in the nucleus with fewest machines. Combination was continued until the required number of groups was formed. The final result contained nine groups. An examination of the parts in each group showed that the groups were reasonable and the method has been accepted as satisfactory. Perhaps the best proof of this is that we can find no way to improve the groups by eye. Figure 9.19 shows the types of part in each group.

A programme is now being prepared to use this method to find the nuclei from the total file of made components. These nuclei will then be tested manually for acceptability, to try different rules. Next, different rules for combination will also be tested manually. The load in machine hours will then be found for each machine in each group to check the capacity of the groups. It is expected that this work will lead to the development of a programme suitable for general use.

9.8 SIZE OF GROUP

In planning the number of groups it was decided to aim for groups of sociologically acceptable size, employing six to twelve workers.

The number of groups to be formed before stopping the combination of nuclei, will therefore be fixed in the following way:

Let E = total direct workers in a 'major group', on day shift
Q = desired number of 'groups'
$\therefore Q = E/9$

The number of machines in the groups will vary according to the value of Q, and the complexity of the parts in the families.

The group with most machines will probably make the parts in the nucleus using most machines.

If there are P different parts made in the factory, the most likely 'special' machines—existing in only one group—are those in which $F < P/Q$. All others are likely to exist in more than one group.

The number of special machines found by the analysis will also depend partly on the classification of machines by type. In the manual analysis of a sample, illustrated in Figure 9.19, only 11 out of 25 machine types were special to one group only. It is known, however, that the sample did not find all the machines with low values of F and the rather broad classification by machine type used for manual analysis, contains several other special machines with low values of F, embedded in the lathe, gear cutting, grinding, and drilling types. The proportion of special machines will be higher in the full analysis.

In the case of Black and Decker also, there are a number of machine 'lines' making special components and assemblies. The method of nuclear synthesis finds these lines as groups. As they employ fewer than six men in some cases, it may be decided to increase the value of Q, to allow for these smaller than normal units, and perhaps install them together in the same groups for control. Group 9 in Figure 9.19 is an example.

9.9 SUMMARY

Production Flow Analysis is a technique used to improve the material flow system of an enterprise. It is applied in four stages:
1. 'Factory Flow Analysis' (FFA) studies the flow of materials between

processing units, combines them to form major groups and finds the simplest possible flow system between these units.

2. 'Group Analysis' (GA) finds the combinations of machines known as 'Groups' and the lists of parts they produce, which are known as 'Families'.

3. 'Line Analysis' (LA) studies the flow of materials between machines inside groups.

4. 'Tooling Analysis' (TA) finds tooling families of parts, which use the same tooling in their set-ups, and also finds the optimum sequence of loading.

Production Flow Analysis is a technique which analyses the information given in route cards to find the answers to the above four problems.

There is a strong analogy between material flow systems and electronic circuits. The similarity is so great that we shall probably use Boolean algebra in the future to design efficient material flow systems, in much the same way as we now use it in electronics to design logical circuits.

All material flow systems, like electronic circuits, combine an element of series flow with an element of parallel flow. Production Flow Analysis provides a technique, or management tool which can be used to plan such systems. It uses network analysis to plan the series flow and matrices to plan parallel flow.

10 Loading

10.1 INTRODUCTION

One of the essential steps in production flow analysis is load checking. This is necessary, first when determining how many machines of a type required in more than one group should be allocated to each, and second, is helpful when planning how many men should work in any group.

In addition to these two types of load check, used in planning the initial introduction of Group Technology, load-checking is also necessary during operations. When the production programme for each new cycle is prepared, it must be checked to ensure that it does not impose a greater load on the machines in any group than the capacity which is available.

This chapter considers first the way in which group layout affects the processes of time study, and then considers these three questions of: how many machines per group?; how many men per group?; and how much work to issue per cycle?.

10.2 WORK MEASUREMENT

Loading is the task of comparing the work to be done, with the capacity available in a given period of time, to determine if the two are compatible. Depending on whether the work is manual work, or machine work, the comparison will be made in man-hours, or machine-hours.

To make loading possible, it is necessary to have some method of measuring the work content of all the jobs allocated to each work centre. It is necessary in other words, to know for every part in each family, how many machine-hours of work are needed to complete one part on each machine in the group.

(a) Time study

The oldest method of making these measurements is with a stop-watch. The job to be done is first divided into elements, or distinct parts each with a well-defined and easily recognized starting and finishing point. Measurement then proceeds as follows:

1. *Recorded element times.* The time required for an element is measured and recorded a reasonable number of times.

2. *Selected element times.* A single value is selected from these recorded times, using either the modal or averaging method.

3. *Basic operation time.* The selected element times are corrected for

sub-standard, or above normal performance by the machine operator employed during the study, using an approved rating scale. They are then added to find the basic operation time per component.

4. *Standard times* are then found by adding allowances to the basic operation time, for personal and other needs.

If the measurements are accurate and if rating and the addition of allowances are based on the same standards for all work, the standard time for a job should be the same, whoever does the work during the study, and whoever makes the time study.

With functional layout this method of measurement can be used without difficulty. One operator is chosen to do the job to be measured and he works continuously at the job until the study is finished. This is the normal way in which he would tackle the job even if he were not being timed. With group layout, the same standard time is still needed. To obtain an accurate measure with time study, the same method of timing must be used with the operator working continuously until the time study is finished. In this case, however, this method of working for time study is not always the same as that which would normally be used in the group, and time study will tend to interfere with normal group working.

When each operator works one machine the standard time per piece is the same for the operator in man hours as for the machine in machine hours. This is not the case if the operator works more than one machine. Because the machines are close together with group layout, there are additional opportunities for operators to work more than one machine, using the free time during the automatic part of the cycle for one of them to do other work on some other machine. These combinations of machine may vary however from cycle to cycle. With group layout the direct labour cost per part is difficult to measure and direct labour cost per group per cycle tends to be largely fixed cost.

The aim with Group Technology is to minimize the cost of the total batch of parts ordered for the cycle. This is not necessarily achieved by minimizing the operation times for each part. The number of man hours needed to complete a given total group load in machine hours, will vary with the skill used in scheduling the work on the machines. The level of efficiency reached at any moment, cannot be calculated on a man hours per part basis, but can only be measured accurately using random observation studies.

(b) Predetermined motion time standards

Although time study can still be used with group layout, albeit with some inconvenience, this type of layout increases the advantages to be gained by using pre-determined motion time standards. Among well-known and well-tried methods are M.T.M. (Methods Time Measurement); M.T.A. (Motion Time Analysis); B.M.T. (Basic Motion Time study); and the Work Factor system. These are proprietary systems which have been promoted by different consultants. Their main application is for manual operations. Each different company must generally create its own standards for cutting and other processing speeds, for use in the setting of standard times for machining operations. The speeds and feeds found in handbooks are generally lower than those which are obtainable in practice.

10.3 MACHINE CAPACITY

During loading, the work loads in machine hours found by work measurement are checked against the capacities of the machines in each group, which are also specified in machine hours.

(a) Types of machine capacity

The final category of machine capacity, which covers the machine hours usable for productive work, is known as 'standard machine running time'. The nature of this capacity is illustrated in Figure 10.1. The time distribution shown in this diagram is not exceptional. Only a small part of the maximum machine capacity, of 168 hours/week for any machine, is

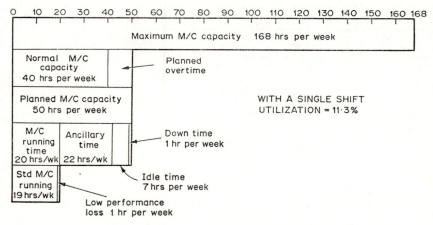

Note   The proportions of M/C running time, and ancillary time used above, are based on research findings by Professor Dudley of Birmingham University, in factories in the Midlands, and are applicable to functional layout

Figure 10.1. Machine capacity

normally available for useful work. This proportion depends partly on the number of shifts worked; partly on the processing methods chosen for each part; partly on the efficiency of setting; partly on the efficiency of production control, and partly on the efficiency of operation.

One important result of Group Technology is that it tends to reduce both setting time, which is a major part of ancillary time, and also idle time. Companies using Group Technology have claimed general increases in capacity for their machines of 15% and higher in spite of a general increase in batch frequency, due to the use of shorter cycles. However this increase will vary according to the type of machine, being greater for machines with normally high setting-up times, and with qualities which make it possible to reduce these times by applying the composite part and tooling family principles.

In addition to this general increase in capacity, it is also possible to plan for special larger increases for particular machines. By choosing the optimum sequence for scheduling work on these machines, by designing special tooling, and by selecting the operators with the highest performance ratings to run them, it is possible to obtain major increases in capacity for a small number of specially important machines.

(b) Group capacity

The capacity of the group as a whole must be measured in terms of the components, or product sets of components, which can be completed in a given time. This capacity depends mainly on the capacities of the most heavily loaded machines in the group. However, the distribution of load

COLUMN NUMBER:		1	2	3	4	5	6
MACHINE		Planned M/C capacity per cycle	Idle time No orders	Idle time Other causes	Ancillary time	Load running time	Columns 4 + 5
NUMBER	TYPE						
2067	Capstan	80	—	5	30	45	75
2092	"	80	—	5	30	45	75
2093	"	80	—	5	30	45	75
1961	V. Miller	80	10	5	30	35	65
1096	H. Miller	80	19	5	26	30	56
1732	"	80	19	5	26	30	56
2611	2 Sp. drill	80	28	5	12	35	47
2612	"	80	28	5	12 .	35	47
2573	4 Sp. drill	80	19 ·	5	16	40	56
567	Keyseater	80	52	8	10	10	20
M/C hrs	TOTALS	800	175	53	222	350	572

Figure 10.2. Group capacity

between the machines may vary in some cases, with changes in the distribution of different component types in the period order. Particularly with seasonal demand, the machines with the highest average usage may not be the same all the time.

Figure 10.2 shows a case where the most heavily loaded machine type in a group is used for all parts in the family. It shows the limiting case when the key machine is fully loaded and illustrates a typical condition of imbalance between capacities. This imbalance is only slightly affected by group layout and will be found equally prevalent with functional layout. Only a small proportion of the machines in most factories will require duplication in more than one group, and the majority of these will tend to be the simpler and cheaper types of machine, such as drills in machine shops, for which there is usually an excess of capacity.

It will be seen in the case illustrated that a 10% increase in group output would require a 10% increase in the capacity of only one machine type. Three methods are possible:

1. Operate the group to favour this machine type and increase its capacity by reducing setting time
2. Improve production methods on this machine type
3. Add one more machine of this type

Machines which are loaded below their capacity level will inevitably have some idle time, 'waiting for orders'. Note that for the case illustrated in Figure 10.1 the machine is fully loaded and the idle time of 7 hours per week is due to other causes than waiting for orders. If this were not so, there would be no point in working overtime.

Imbalance generally represents an unavoidable waste of capacity. It does however have one advantage. When checking the loads imposed by each new production programme during operations, a quick check can be made in most groups, by checking only the most heavily loaded machine. If that machine has enough capacity, it is almost certain that the remaining machines will have sufficient.

(c) Factory capacity

In the same way that group capacity is generally limited by one machine, factory capacity will generally be limited by one group. The change to group layout tends to make it very clear where are the real bottlenecks in a factory. Considerable increases in factory capacity can often be made, by adding one more machine of the most heavily loaded type in the most heavily loaded group. If the group must be increased to more than say fifteen workers, however, consideration should be given to dividing it. One British writer has likened the factory to the living body. The body grows by increasing the number of cells. If the cells grow they are diseased.*

10.4 HOW MANY MACHINES PER GROUP

Group analysis determines the division into families and groups and specifies the types of machine which must be provided in each group. The next problem is to determine how many machines of each type will be needed. There are two main cases to be considered: first the case of

* WILLIAMSON.

machines existing in only one group, and second the case of machines existing in more than one group.

(a) Type exists in only one group

Where a machine type is allocated to only one group, there is normally no problem. All machines of the type will be allocated to the group. If there was sufficient capacity before with functional layout, there should be more than enough capacity after the change to group layout. It is only if more work has been allocated to a machine during the elimination of exceptions, that a load check is necessary before forming the group. The load check in this instance should be based on a test production programme, which should:

1. Be as large as any programme which is likely to arise
2. Should not require more capacity than that which is available
3. Should contain an average distribution of product types

The number of machine hours required to produce this programme is calculated and is then compared with the standard machine running time. Depending on the type of machine, some overload can be allowed, due to the increase in capacity with group layout, caused by setting time reduction. If this figure is still exceeded, it may be necessary to replan some of the work, to take action to improve the productivity of the critical machine, or in the last resort, to buy new machines.

(b) Types of machine required in two or more groups

The loads must also be checked on all machines required in more than one group, to determine how many are needed in each. The same test programme should be used as that described above for the machine types

MACHINE		Standard	LOAD IN M/C HRS PER CYCLE AND M/Cs ALLOCATED										
TYPE	QTY	M/C running hrs/cycle	1		2		3		4		5 .		6	
XP 2 Sp. Drill	8	50	140	3	–	–	72	2	–	–	109	3	–	–
XQ 3 Sp. Drill	7	50	160	4	–	–	–	–	–	–	125	3	–	–
RD Radial	3	45	–	–	40	1	–	–	50	1	11	1	–	–
PZ H/Miller	3	40	–	–	19	1	–	–	–	–	–	–	55	2

Figure 10.3. Division of machine types between groups

which exist in only one group. Once again any additional loads allocated to a machine type, during the elimination of exceptions, must be taken into account.

Figure 10.3 shows the result of this analysis in the case of four machine types, each required in more than one group in a machine shop. In this instance there is an overload on the radial drill in Group 4. This overload might be eliminated in several ways:

1. Allocate only one radial drill (RD) to Group 4. Give this machine preference when planning the sequence of loading, in order to reduce setting time and increase its capacity
2. Same decision and use Method Study to reduce times
3. Allocate two radial drills to Group 4 and none to Group 5. Re-route some of the work in Group 5 on to the pillar drills, which are underloaded.
4. Combine Groups 4 and 5 to make one larger group
5. Buy one more machine

If it is decided to buy a new machine, it may be that a more suitable type can now be selected for one of the groups. Because group layout tends to bring together types of part requiring similar processes, it is probable that those drilled parts, for example, which are most suitable for multi-drilling, or for a numerically controlled drill, will exist mainly in one group.

With standard products made to the company's own designs, the distribution of machines between groups is unlikely to need changing once the best distribution has been found. It is only if there is a major change in the product range, the output, or the sales mix, that a change in group structure may be necessary. With a period batch control ordering system the same items will be ordered every cycle and the percentage distribution of load between machines will tend to be nearly the same every cycle, unless there are pronounced seasonal differences in product demand.

10.5 HOW MANY MEN PER GROUP

The number of direct workers per group will not normally be the same as the number of machines. It will vary from this number according to the following factors:

1. The automaticity of the machines
2. The distribution of load between machines
3. The layout of the machines
4. Labour relations

(a) Automaticity of the machines

If the machines installed in a group are automatically controlled, there will be possibilities for one worker to operate two or more of them. This practice is already widely used in the case of machines of the same type. Group layout largely retains this possibility—because most machine types will exist in only one group—and also adds the further possibility that automatic machines of different types may be operated by the same man.

The type of operating cycle will control how far it is possible to take advantage of automaticity. Figure 10.4 shows first the cycle for a capstan lathe and second the cycle for a chucking automatic. A large part of the cycle for the capstan lathe, including all the cutting time, is automatic. It is difficult to use this time, however, because the free time for the operator

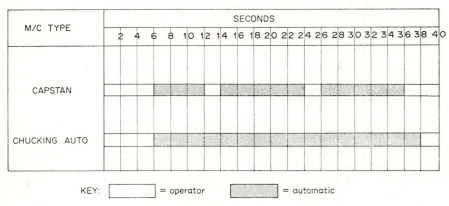

Figure 10.4. Different automatic cycles

comes intermittently in only small time quantities. In this case one operator must be assigned full time to operate one machine. The most that can be hoped is that he may have sufficient time in the cycle to either deburr, or inspect his own work. With the chucking automatic on the other hand, the operator only loads and unloads materials. He has a long free interval while the machine is working and he can operate three machines without difficulty.

(b) Distribution of load

If a machine is fully loaded, it will still be possible with group layout as with functional layout, to assign to it a permanent operator. In most groups there will be one or two machines which are fully loaded, but the remainder will normally be loaded for only a portion of the cycle period. Due to this underloading, fewer operators will be needed generally than the number of machines in the group. Figure 10.2 shows a typical case. There are 572 hours of machine running hours and ancillary time requiring labour, in the two weeks' cycle of 80 hours. Only the lightly loaded keyseater has an automatic cycle and eight setter-operators will be needed on day shift only, or seven with some overtime. If the first three machines had been chucking automatics, one man might have operated all three, thus saving 90 man-hours or one man. Only the running time cover would be reduced and there would be some increase in idle time due to machine 'interference'.

There is of course nothing new in this. In all machine shops, even with functional layout, there are always some machines which are underloaded and are not permanently manned. It is a common error to judge Group Technology by comparison with a hypothetical state of perfect capacity balance. The only valid comparison is with the existing balance.

(c) *The layout of the machines*

The layout of the machines forming the group can also affect the number of operators needed. This subject will be re-examined in the next chapter, but in brief, if two semi-automatic machines are placed next to each other, it may be possible for one worker to operate both of them at the same time even if they are of different types. If however they are at opposite ends of the group, this may be impossible.

(d) *Labour relations*

In the final resort, the number of operators per group is a question of negotiation. However valid the scientific basis for choosing a particular number of workers per group, the final decision in a democracy depends on what is acceptable to both the management and the workers. What is acceptable in turn will depend on the level of trust, or in other words on the state of labour relations existing in the organization.

The acceptable *quid pro quo* for a fundamental change in the method of working, will in most cases be a higher rate of pay. In some cases workers may also want the easier life which excess labour can apparently bring. They may be influenced in this choice by the fear that they, or their friends will become redundant. Management should at least know its own mind. It has more to gain from the former solution than the latter. In a factory filled with under-employed workers, everyone is un-productive. It is interesting to note that in Japan, where the factory employee is traditionally employed for life, if a new innovation makes some employees unnecessary, they are not generally left idle in the factory, but are given an alternate occupation in some other place.

(e) *The final choice for direct labour*

The final choice in any factory then, depends on negotiations. In preparation for such negotiations, management must know what is scientifically possible. This information should be freely disseminated to the workers and their union.

The main fear on the worker's side will be redundancy. A secondary fear will be that the rate of work will be increased. Bearing these facts in mind, the following is a reasonable basis for negotiation:

1. Determine by direct examination—considering automaticity, load distribution, and layout—how many men are necessary in each group to achieve the test programme.

2. Propose this establishment on a trial basis for say two months.

3. Offer a reasonable increase in pay for the change in duties.
4. Maintain average earnings during the trial period.

(f) Indirect labour

The choice of the number of indirect workers per group is only related indirectly to machine loading. Most groups will need a foreman, or working chargehand. Some groups may need a labourer for handling, cleaning, lubrication, deburring, and other simple jobs. Some groups may need one, or more skilled men for the pre-setting of tools, preventive maintenance inspections, quality control, and possibly in jobbing shops, for routing, tool planning, and marking out. The numbers of men required will depend on the type of component, the types of machine, and the work tolerances.

In general an attempt should be made to keep the groups homogeneous. It is normally better to assign someone to the group responsible for a range of duties, than it is to have large numbers of narrow functional specialists, without group loyalties, who do special parts of the work for many groups.

10.6 HOW MUCH WORK PER CYCLE

Long-term major changes in capacity can only be achieved by increasing the amount of plant in a factory. Medium-term capacity changes can be effected by varying the number of employees and in the short-term, capacity can only be varied by changing overtime hours, or by accepting idle time.

Long-term capacity is normally regulated in relation to a long-term programme, which may only be reviewed, say every three months. The aim is to maintain factory capacity at a level which matches the mean rate of product demand. Corporate planning and market research are techniques used to plan long-term growth. Medium- and short-term capacity on the other hand, are reconsidered at every cyclic programme meeting and are adjusted to match the latest forecasts. Management will generally be trying to balance the risk of loosing sales orders, with the costs of maintaining excess capacity. Normally they will aim at a steady rate of growth in the labour force, which as far as possible matches the general trend of growth in demand, in order to avoid the heavy costs of redundancy and later re-induction and training of new workers. Short-term changes in capacity are therefore mainly regulated by changing overtime hours.

(a) Loading with Period Batch Control

Having fixed the capacity level for the programme for a new cycle, the next job is to load sufficient work to use it. The tabulation in Figure 5.7 shows a simple example of how this might be done in the case of a factory making three products. If the mean capacity level has been correctly set in this case, any excess production for stock in one month will be absorbed in later months, when random seasonal changes in demand bring the requirement above the mean. If many products are made, more complex methods must be used as described in Chapter 6. If there are a few basic product ranges, as in shoes, socks, and wallpaper, for example— with a large number of variants of each—the quantities to be made of the ranges will be planned at the programme meeting. The distribution of these quantities between the variants will be determined by some such method as 'Stock ratio optimization', or STROP.

(b) *Determining the capacity available*

Some existing loading systems treat setting time as a fixed time per component batch and include setting time as an addition to load rather than as a reduction in capacity. With Group Technology this is impractical. In the early stages of introduction, each improvement in operating the new system will reduce setting times and make nonsense of any attempt to use a standard value per component for setting time. Later it will normally be more accurate and also cheaper to measure idle time and ancillary time by random observation studies, and use these figures to find the standard machine running time. With this method setting time is considered only once per machine when finding its capacity. If treated as load setting time additions must be made for every part using each machine every time it is produced.

(c) *Determining the load*

When checking the load during the process of planning the production programme, it is generally sufficient to consider only the one or two most heavily loaded machines. At this stage of planning one is only interested in feasibility. With standard products made to a company's own design, the same parts will be ordered every cycle. The most heavily loaded machines will therefore generally be the same every cycle.

To assist him in dispatching, the foreman in each group will also need a record of the load imposed by each short-term programme on all his machines. Figure 6.6 illustrates one method of obtaining this information. The standard forms show the load on each machine in the group imposed by one of each of the products produced. The total load is found by multiplying this product load by the number of products in the programme and summing for all products. The simplicity with which load figures can be obtained once the groups and families have been established, is another advantage of period batch control. This simplicity arises from the fact that all the load induced by any programme falls into one specific period of time. With a stock control system complicated load checking methods must be used, with balance of outstanding load records for each machine. An attempt must then be made to relate the total outstanding load on the machines to different time periods. The results are usually unsatisfactory.

(d) Loading with jobbing production

With jobbing production a single cycle ordering system can still be used. Capacities can be regulated by the same methods as those described above. As in the case of standard products, there will generally be one or two machines which will be the first to become overloaded. It is sufficient for programming purposes to consider the loads on these machines only. As new work is received, it is planned, and machine running times are estimated for the critical machine or machines. The work is then allocated to the next free short-term programme.

A programme load record is maintained, showing the load in machine hours allocated to the critical machines in each group. As soon as the available capacity is filled, the programme is closed, and new work is then allocated to the next programme, or to some later programme if the customer is asking for later delivery.

10.7 SUMMARY

Once flow control and group layout have been installed, it is simple—even with manual methods—to obtain accurate figures for the load imposed by any programme.

These load figures should only include operation times. Setting times per component are highly variable with loading sequence, and this fact makes standard component setting times completely misleading. Setting time is better treated as a reduction in group capacity, than as an addition to component loads. The amount of this reduction in capacity can be found by random observation studies.

Load checking is much more difficult during the planning of the groups and families, than it is after the groups and families are known. However, when planning the change from traditional methods to Group Technology, load checks are only essential for machines required in more than one group, or for machines to which many 'exceptions' have been re-routed.

When the natural division into groups and families has been found, it is easy to calculate the load per product in machine hours, on all the machines in each group, and also therefore to calculate the total load imposed by any programme.

With standard products the distribution of load between groups will vary with the type of group. Where groups are formed which make parts for particular products, the work load on the groups will vary with demand for the product. Where groups are formed which make parts for many products, the load will vary with total product output, but very little with changes in product mix.

With jobbing production the distribution of load between groups will depend on the types of orders received from customers.

11   Plant Layout in Groups

11.1   INTRODUCTION

Group analysis finds the different families of parts to be produced in the departments and also finds the associated groups of machines which will be used to make them. For each group there is a list of machines to be installed, and the problem now is to plan the layout of these machines in the space available for the department.

Plant layout is best tackled progressively, considering first what services must be provided for the department, second the relative positions to be taken by the groups and service centres, and third the layout of the machines in each group. Each of these stages of planning is examined below, with special reference to the particular needs of group layout.

Eventually the layout plan must be implemented. The problems of changing to the new layout are also examined at the end of the chapter.

11.2   SERVICES

In addition to the space required for productive machines in the groups in any department, space will also be needed for other services. Some of these are best arranged as common units to serve all groups, being installed inside the department in their own special sections. Other services are best divided and provided in each group. Group Technology obtains many of its advantages from the use of independent working groups. The second of these alternatives should therefore be given preference, where possible.

As an example of some of the services for which floor space may be needed in an engineering machine shop, consider the following list:

1. Superintendent's office
2. Foremen's desks
3. Tool grinding
4. Tool store and pre-setting
5. Raw material store
6. Finished work store
7. Inspection
8. Production planning
9. Maintenance
10. Battery charging (for trucks)
11. Fork truck parking
12. Swarf collection
13. Oil recovery
14. Notice boards
15. Lockers
16. Toilets
17. Heaters
18. Coolant mixing
19. Air compressor
20. Safety appliances

The best way of ensuring that provision is made for all necessary services, is to make a checklist such as this, and then to review every item to determine:

1. Is the service needed?
2. If yes, can it be provided most efficiently by sub-contracting?
3. If not, should it be a common service?
4. Should provision be made in every group?

When changing from functional layout to group layout, most of the items on the check list will cover services already provided in the department. There may be some additional items, however, which are only included because group layout introduces the possibility of decentralization. The problem in each case is to determine how the change to group layout will affect current practice. The services most likely to require a new approach are items (4) to (9) inclusive in the list above. Each will now be briefly examined.

(a) Tool store

In most present-day batch production and jobbing factories, the tool store is either part of a separate stores department, or is a centralized departmental service. It is usual to centralize the storage of all jigs, fixtures, and cutting tools and to issue them to the machines only when they are needed for use.

This method works well with large batch quantities. If the tools are only used two or three times a year in fact, this is probably the best way. With Group Technology, however, cycle times of two weeks, or even one week, are possible. With a standard product to a company's own design, the same tooling is needed every cycle. Centralization becomes economically unattractive, if all the tooling must be moved in and out of the store fifty times a year.

With the development of tooling families the same tooling will be used for many different parts and centralized storage becomes even less attractive. With group layout it is desirable that all jigs and fixtures in frequent use should be stored inside the groups, near the machines on which they are used. It will still probably be necessary to have a small central tool store, possibly for the factory as a whole, which stores consumable tools for replacement purposes and other infrequently used tooling as well.

(b) Raw material storage

It is desirable that all raw material delivered to the department should be stored inside the group where it will be used. This saves double handling to and from an inter-process store and its additional costs. The problem is to decide how much space to provide in the groups.

In the early stages of the development of group layout there are advantages in arranging that all the materials needed for each cycle are moved to the group before the cycle starts. In this way it is possible to build up confidence in the new system, and also to provide the best conditions for finding the optimum loading sequence. If this policy is followed, space should be provided for the maximum likely material requirement for one ordering cycle.

In some cases, where for example castings which are made in a foundry are later machined in a separate machine shop, it will be possible to operate efficiently with much lower stocks. By using the same sequence of loading work in both the foundry and the machine shop, it is possible to achieve a measure of continuous batch flow, without an intermediate casting store, and to operate with a very small stock of raw materials. In this instance it may only be necessary to provide storage space for four or five days' supply.

(c) Finished work

It should be possible to clear all finished work from the groups daily. The storage space required for this purpose in the groups, need not be more than that required for the maximum output of completed work, likely in one or two days.

(d) Inspection

Traditionally, in most factories inspection and quality control are the direct responsibility of a Chief Inspector. All inspection work done in the factory is normally done by a staff of inspectors who report directly to him.

With functional layout this type of organization has advantages. With this type of layout most parts are processed successively in a number of different processing sections under a number of different foremen. It is difficult to see the needs for some quality control restraints, when one only does a small part of the job. Under these conditions centralized inspection carries out the necessary function of co-ordinating quality control, throughout the departments and factory as a whole.

With group layout the need for this co-ordination is greatly reduced. Because most of the processes on each part are now done in one group, the foreman of each group has most of the factors affecting quality under his personal control. A strong case can be made for providing him with the necessary measuring equipment and for making him responsible for his own inspection and quality control. It is still possible to have a final inspection section which checks samples of the finished work from the groups.

This is not a new idea. For many years the British Aeronautical Inspection Directorate (AID) have delegated the responsibility for quality to the inspection departments of the companies which make materials, parts, and products for aircraft. There seems to be no reason why the same principle of delegated authority for quality, should not be equally successful inside companies. One can in fact find companies today in which there is still a Quality Control Manager responsible for policy and general control, but in which the responsibility for actual component quality and for all routine inspections, has been delegated to the group foremen.

This approach has been adopted by the Soc. Guilliet in France, which has one of the best Group Technology applications. They still have a centralized final inspection department, but all inter-operation inspection is delegated to the groups.

(e) Production Planning

In most companies today production planning is centralized in an office, separated both geographically and organizationally from the processing departments. When, as is common with functional layout, 90% of the parts are made in more than one processing section, this centralization is necessary for efficient co-ordination.

With Group Technology, however, the material flow system is simplified so that most parts are made in one department and one group only. Under these conditions it is possible to decentralize production planning, at least to some degree. A central production planning office will still be needed to co-ordinate policy and to obtain overall control. The planning of details of component method, however, can be delegated with advantage to the processing departments, which can each have their own specialist planners. In the case of jobbing work a case can be made particularly with simple products, for delegation of planning to the groups.

(f) Maintenance

Parts of maintenance might also be made a group responsibility with advantage. Minor preventive maintenance inspections, minor repairs, and lubrication are examples. General rules cannot be made, but at least in some companies such changes could lead to higher levels of servicability.

None of the six possibilities mentioned above—for tool storage, material storage, finished work storage, inspection, production planning, and maintenance—are essential changes, which must be introduced to achieve Group Technology in all factories. They are important, however, because they demonstrate the possibilities for new thinking which arise with the change to group layout. Many of our present practices are only reasonable with the present type of flow system imposed by functional layout. If we change the flow system, we will probably have to change many other firmly held beliefs as well.

11.3 LAYOUT BY GROUPS

Knowing the groups and services to be installed in the department, the next task is to plan the layout of these units in the area allotted to the department. There are three main jobs to be done: first, list the units to be accommodated; second, estimate their areas; and third, plan the layout.

(a) List units to be accommodated

The list of units to be accommodated will include all the groups found by group analysis, plus the services to be established outside the groups. Some of the services should be grouped together in sections for ease of control. Others, such as safety equipment, for example, must be dispersed throughout the department, but will still require space for their installation.

(b) Estimate areas

The best way to estimate the required area for each group is to use the trial layout method. Scale templates, or models of the plant to be installed in a group, are placed in any reasonable arrangement, on squared paper. A boundary line is drawn round them to form a square, or rectangle, and the area is measured. Too much time should not be wasted in arranging the machines during this area estimation stage. The area required for a perfect group arrangement will not vary greatly from that needed for a reasonable arrangement. If the areas allotted are on the high side, they will at least provide some room for future expansion. The final check is to total the areas allotted to each group and service and compare the total with the available area. As group layout normally requires less space than functional layout, there should be no unpleasant surprises.

(c) Plan the layout by groups

Plans are now made showing the relative positions in the department, for all the groups and service centres. Generally one starts by planning the gangways. As far as possible these should run in straight lines from principal doorways, and be parallel to the walls of the building. They should be well clear of building columns and other obstructive building features, such as stair wells and lift shafts.

The remaining area, after deducting the space needed for gangways, is available for groups and services. In choosing the positions for the groups, important considerations will be safety, the need to separate incompatible processes, materials handling convenience, and any economies possible in the supply system for electricity, compressed air, and other power services, by placing major user groups nearest to the source of supply.

In all instances where an existing functional layout is to be changed to group layout, it is necessary to examine the possibility of saving costs, by leaving machines which would be expensive to move, in their present positions. The cost of layout change depends mainly on three factors: the weight of the machines, the method of attaching them to the floor, and the method of coupling to power sources.

In the clothing industry which uses light machines, with no floor fixing and simple power-plug connection to the electricity supply, layout changing is very cheap. In modern factories in light and medium engineering,

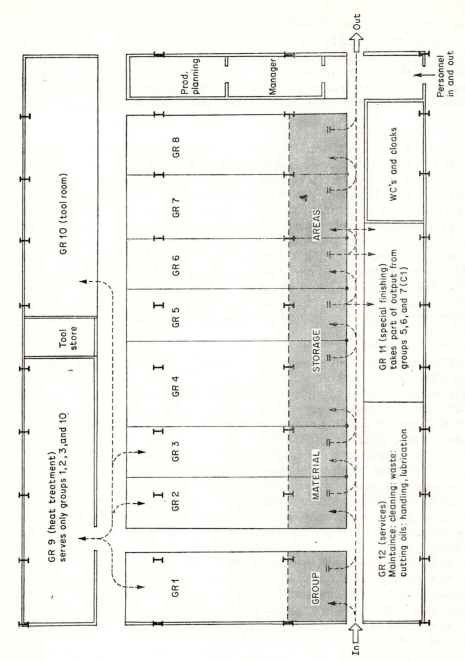

Figure 11.1. Section layout

with fairly light easily moved machines, held in position by glueing to the floor on felt pads, and using overhead buzz bars for power supply, layout change is again relatively cheap. It is only when the plant is very heavy, when it requires special foundation and pits, and when special conduited cables have to be run for power supply, that a layout change becomes expensive. Before planning the change from functional to group layout, a record should be made of all plant and equipment which would be costly to move, and an attempt should be made to plan a layout which leaves these items in their present positions.

Each group should be placed so that there is gangway access to the group for material delivery and for the despatch of finished work. It is not necessary with group layout for there to be gangway access to all machines in the group. Consideration should be given however to the problems of maintenance. Machines should be placed reasonably far apart, so that preventive maintenance inspections can be made safely while the machines are still running. As far as possible also, the machines should be placed so that any machine can be removed for overhaul, without moving other machines. There are advantages if the boundaries between groups run along lines of building columns, rather than have these columns in the middle of working areas.

Considerations of inter-group material flow seldom affect the choice of group position. Because groups are normally planned as independent units, there is no material flow between them. Very occasional exceptions to this rule can sometimes be accommodated. For instance, it may be possible for two adjacent groups to share the use of an expensive machine, which has a very low utilization rate, without losing the main advantages of group layout.

The departmental foreman's desk or office should be placed ideally so that he can see the whole workshop, he can see incoming and outgoing material consignments, and he has some control over the service sections. Figure 11.1 shows diagrammatically a section layout for group production, to show the type of information which it provides.

11.4 LINE ANALYSIS

The next task is to plan the layout of the machines and workshop equipment inside the spaces allocated to the groups. The main information needed to achieve this aim is concerned with the sequence in which the different components in the family use the machines in the group.

'Line analysis' is the third level of production flow analysis. By a further analysis of the information contained in the component route cards, it finds the best sequence in which to lay out the machines. In other words, it finds the relative machine positions which will give the nearest approximation to line flow.

Each group is considered separately and in turn. With simple groups containing very few machine types, full analysis is unnecessary. For more complex groups and families the analysis takes place in seven steps:

1. Renumber operations
2. Prepare machine operation number frequency chart for group
3. Adopt a single digit symbol for each machine
4. Determine Operation Route Nos. (ORN)
5. Analyse by ORN
6. Draw group flow network diagram
7. Simplify flow system

These steps will now be examined briefly in turn.

(a) Renumber all operations in sequence

For line analysis it is necessary to number all the operations. Each component processed in a department is given a separate series of operation numbers starting at Operation No. 1. All operations must be numbered including simple manual operations such as 'deburring' and 'inspection'. Separate numbers must also be used for all operations, even if the same machine type is used for more than one operation.

(b) Draw machine/operation number frequency chart

A machine/operation number frequency chart is now prepared for every group, showing the number of times each machine or other work centre is used for an operation numbered No. 1, No. 2 and so on. An example from a group in an engineering machine shop is illustrated in Figure 11.2.

(c) Adopt a single digit symbol for each work centre

The machines and other work centres listed in Figure 11.2 have been listed progressively by usage frequency, with those with a high utilization frequency for early operations at the top and those with a high utilization frequency for late operations at the bottom. Each machine and other work centre is given a single digit symbol for identification, consecutively in this same sequence. If there are less than ten machines in a group, numbers can be used. If more than ten work centres are involved, the twenty-six letters of the alphabet are more convenient.

(d) Determine ORN for each component and analyse

The operation route number (ORN) is found for every part in the family, by listing the symbols for the machines and other work centres, in the sequence in which they are used to make each component. The different ORNs discovered after examining all the route cards in the family, are listed in number (or letter) sequence. The number of times each ORN is used, is counted. An ORN frequency chart is then prepared like that

M/C NO.	MACHINE TYPE	1	2	3	4	5	6	7	8	9	Total	NOTES
2013	Capstan L.	80	5					①			86	Check 1 on 7
2014	" "	12	52								64	
2016	Turret "	3	32	27							62	
2194	Horiz. borer			61	19	2					82	
2198	Vert. borer		6	7	68						81	
3172	Pillar drill (1)				2	40		6			48	
3186	(2)					22					22	
3213	Horiz. mill.				6	27	46				79	
3219	Shaper					4	17	2			23	
	Totals.	95	95	95	95	95	63	9				

Table heading: Machine — operation no. frequency — M/C GROUP NO. 5 — OPERATION NUMBER

Analyses route cards to find how many parts
have operation number 1 on each machine; how
many have operation number 2 and so on.
Used as a guide for plant layout.

Figure 11.2. Machine operation number—frequency chart

illustrated in Figure 11.3, which deals with the group already illustrated in Figure 11.2.

(e) Draw the group network diagram and simplify

The flow network diagram is now drawn for the group using the data contained in the ORN frequency chart. For the first drawing of the network, a number of circles are drawn down the middle of the page. These are numbered from the top down, to represent the work centres in the group. Arrows are drawn between them to show all the flowpaths found in the previous analysis of ORN frequency.

This first network diagram is now redrawn to provide the simplest possible design of network with the minimum number of bent arrows and the minimum number of crossing lines. This second stage network for the case already illustrated in Figures 11.2 and 11.3, is shown in Figure 11.4. An examination of this network gives an immediate guide to the sequence in which the machines should be laid out, or in other words it leaves little doubt about which machines must be placed next to each other. This same diagram, however, also shows very quickly how the group flow system could be further simplified to improve its efficiency. A revised network,

H

ORN					No. of parts		ORN					No. of parts	
1					40		1	7				2	
1	1				1		1	7	6	8		1	
1	3	4			1	*	1	8				1	
1	3	7			1	*	2					2	*
1	4				10		2	4				3	*
1	4	6			1		2	4	6	8		1	*
1	5				2		2	4	8			1	*
1	5	8	3	7	1	*	3	4				1	*
1	6				3		4					1	*
1	6	7			1								

* ORNs later eliminated during simplification

Figure 11.3. ORN frequency chart

after a certain measure of simplification, is illustrated in Figure 11.5. By re-routing a small number of components, it would be possible to achieve a much simpler and more efficient material flow system.

It will be noted that line analysis is very similar to factory flow analysis. If a computer is used, the same programme can in fact be used for both techniques.

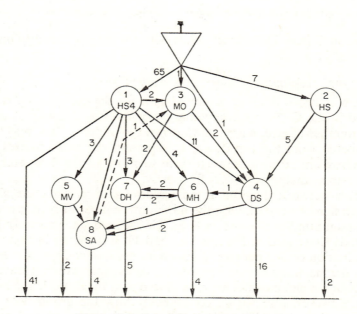

Figure 11.4. Group flow network diagram

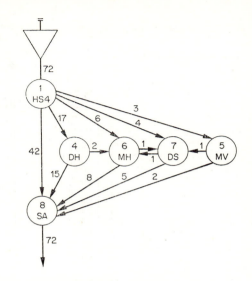

Figure 11.5. Simplified group flow network diagram

11.5 LAYOUT OF MACHINES IN GROUPS

Knowing the list of machines and equipment to be installed in the group, and knowing the ideal relative machine positions from the results achieved with line analysis, the next task is to plan the layout of the groups.

Two alternative layouts are shown in Figure 11.6 for the group already considered in the network diagram given in Figure 11.5. The first is a straight line layout and the second is commonly known as a 'U' layout. Both types may be required in the same department, depending on the shape of the building and the space available for the groups. Where there is an apparently even choice, the 'U' layout has advantages. Generally, handling distances are reduced; it needs less floor area; it tends to increase the possibilities for one operator to work two machines; and it is easier for the foreman to control material flow, when material receiving and issuing are both done from the same point. Contact between the members in a group is easier with a 'U' layout, than with a long straight 'line', and for this reason it is probable that the 'U' layout also has sociological advantages.

Two different methods of tooling storage are illustrated. In the first each machine type has its own special rack for tools. In the second case, tool storage is centralized inside the group. The first method is best when pre-setting is not used, and the tooling requires little attention between runs and is always used on the same machines. A sophisticated example of this type of storage for die-sets, with a roller track feed to the power press, has already been illustrated in Figure 2.3. The second method is

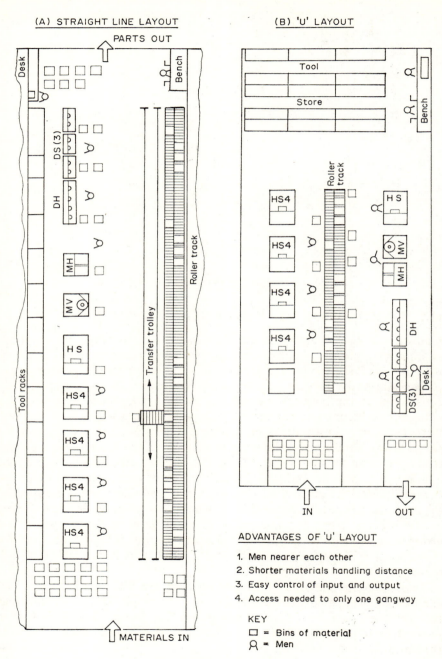

Figure 11.6. Layout of groups

best when pre-setting is used. In this case it is the setter doing the pre-setting who requires most of the tooling first, and the racks for tooling are best installed next to his bench and pre-setting fixtures.

In a small group such as the one just illustrated, there may be insufficient work to keep one setter fully occupied on pre-setting. The setter may have to double as inspector, or do other skilled work, such as minor tool maintenance, marking out, or machinery preventive maintenance inspections. Space and expense can be saved by centralizing all manual processes in one area, sharing benches, vices, and hand tools.

Where it has been decided that certain machines would cost too much to move, and the layout by groups has been planned to leave them in their present positions, the layout inside the groups will also be affected. In this case it will be necessary to accept a less than perfect solution, planning the rest of the layout to suit the positions of any unmoved machines.

11.6 LAYOUT OF LINES

The criterion for line layout is that—with perhaps a few minor exceptions —all components should use all the machines and should use them in the same sequence. Group analysis will normally find a range of groups, varying between a few in which most parts use the machines in the same usage sequence, and others in which there is considerable irregularity in usage sequence.

Groups in which there is a high level of common usage sequence, can usually be arranged for line layout. Large groups with irregular usage sequence may also contain some plant and components, which can be abstracted economically for line layout. The way in which these lines are laid out will depend mainly on the method used for balancing, and in particular on the methods used to balance machine capacities and operator loads. It should be remembered that line layout does not necessarily mean straight line layout. 'U' layout can be used for lines as well as for other types of group.

(a) Balancing machine capacities

All the stations in any line must produce at the same average output rate. However, no line has ever existed in which there was perfect machine capacity balance. There are always some machines which could produce at highest rates, but have been derated to balance the line. In the last expedient, we always derate the machine, or accept some idle time in its cycle in order to achieve the necessary exact balance. The job of balancing lines is restricted to achieving the best possible balance, prior to the final balancing by these means.

Assume that an approximate capacity balance has been obtained, by varying the numbers provided of each machine type, and by redeployment of work between operations. There are three main methods for balancing the outputs from each station on the line:

1. Standard line cycle
2. Component balancing
3. Total balancing

With standard line cycle, the output rate in pieces per minute is always the same from all stations, no matter which component from the line

PART NO.	QTY per week	STATION NO.				TOTAL
		1	2	3	4	
1	200	1·75 min (350 min)	1·20 min (240 min)	1·80 min (360 min)	1·50 min (300 min)	6·25 min
2	150	2·16 min (324 min)	2·72 min (408 min)	2·50 min (375 min)	2·16 min (324 min)	9·54 min
3	150	1·90 min (285 min)	2·30 min (345 min)	2·45 min (367 min)	1·86 min (279 min)	8·51 min
4	100	0·90 min (90 min)	2·10 min (210 min)	4·20 min (420 min)	2·00 min (200 min)	9·20 min
5	100	2·20 min (220 min)	2·00 min (200 min)	2·10 min (210 min)	2·50 min (250 min)	8·80 min
6	100	4·65 min (465 min)	4·20 min (420 min)	4·00 min (400 min)	4·50 min (450 min)	17·35 min
7	100	2·75 min (275 min)	2·40 min (240 min)	2·35 min (235 min)	2·00 min (200 min)	9·50 min
8	70	0·80 min (56 min)	0·90 min (63 min)	0·76 min (53 min)	0·95 min (66 min)	3·41 min
9	60	8·30 min (498 min)	9·50 min (570 min)	9·70 min (582 min)	10·20 min (612 min)	37·70 min
10	50	3·60 min (180 min)	3·10 min (155 min)	3·15 min (157 min)	4·00 min (200 min)	13·85 min

TYPE OF BALANCING	TOTAL MIN. REQUIRED PER WEEK AT STATIONS				CYCLE
	1	2	3	4	
Standard line cycle (SC)	11 016	11 016	11 016	11 016	10·20 See op. 4 part no. 9
Component balancing (CB)	3 423	3 423	3 423	3 423	Cycles times underlined above (†)
Total balancing (TB)	2 743 (Free 416)	2 851 (Free 308)	3 159 —	2 881 (Free 278)	——

(†) Note. Cycle times imposed by longest operation for each part.

Figure 11.7. Types of capacity balancing for lines

family is being produced. The cycle time in this case is determined by the longest operation time for any component which uses the line.

With component balancing, the output rate is different for each component. The cycle time in this case changes as each new component starts on the line. The time is determined by the longest operation time for any operation used to make a component in the family.

With total balancing, each machine in the line is allowed to run at its optimum rate. Some ebb and flow of stock between the stations is allowed. If there is any imbalance between the stations imposed by a given production programme, this is absorbed by allowing some machine idle time, or by derating, or in other words by reducing the speed of operation for machines which are underloaded.

The first two methods are important because they form the basis for most present day automatic material transfer systems. In principle, the most economical system for multi-component lines is total balancing. Some progress has already been made in designing automatic transfer systems based on total balancing. It is probable that most lines for families of parts in the future will follow this principle. Figure 11.7 shows the results achieved with each of these methods with a particular family of parts and demonstrates the special advantages of total balancing.

The main effect of the choice of method for line-balancing on layout, is that it affects the storage space which must be provided for work in progress. With standard line cycle and component balancing, no storage space is needed between operations. With total balancing some storage space must be provided. The amount of stock and therefore of space required, depends on the sequence of loading. However stock is only one of the factors which must be considered when planning the loading sequence. Throughput time, setting time, idle time, and direct material cost are others. At present there is no reliable scientific method for finding the optimum sequence of loading, and for finding the amount of storage space required between machines in totally balanced lines. Here is an interesting real life problem for operational research.

(b) Balancing operator loads

The balance of a line depends partly on the balancing of machine capacities and partly on the balancing of operator loads. With manually controlled machines and a state of perfect balance, machine load and operator load would be the same. However, because some machines have large parts of their operating cycles automatically controlled, and others have manually controlled cycles, and because machine capacities are never in perfect balance, this condition never arises in practice. It is necessary therefore to consider machine and operator balancing separately.

Operator load balance on lines can be improved in most cases, by arranging that the operator looks after more than one machine. There are two conditions which make this possible with line layout. First, it is possible if there are a number of underloaded machines close together, all of which do operations taking a short time, so that the operator can work more than one machine per cycle. Second it is possible if there are a number of machines close together, all of which have a large part of their cycles controlled automatically, leaving the operator free for other work.

11.7 INSTALLATION

Having designed the new layout, the final task is to install it. This is always a simpler job than it looks before one starts. It is one of those jobs which is nearly always economically successful, partly because a policy of occasional change is itself usually successful economically.

With the change from functional to group layout, the first problem is to decide whether to change the whole department all at once, or to make the move progressively. Probably the worst thing one can do is to find space, and plan and install one operating 'trial' group on its own, as a first move. This divides the department into two parts requiring different types of control system for efficient operation.

The best method, if it is possible, is to change each department in turn. Each departmental layout is changed all at one time, during a weekend, or during the annual holiday shut-down period. With careful pre-planning, with a good training programme before the change, and with some prior accumulation of finished part buffer stocks and material stocks, such an all-at-once method can be very successful.

Finally, if the changes required are too great to be possible completely in a single weekend, it is possible to make some of the major machine moves before the final changeover. Even if this means that for a period of time there will be functional layout with some machines dispersed from their controlling sections, this should not have any major effect on the efficiency level at present achieved. A major problem in this case is to find free space for the initial moves. A 'good housekeeping' exercise with particular attention to the removal of scrap and redundant plant, will often find the necessary space.

11.8 SUMMARY

The layout of the machines in a group can have an important effect on group efficiency.

When examining the layout by groups, many services—such as tool storage, quality control, production planning, and preventive maintenance —should be considered for inclusion in the groups, even though they are at present normally treated as specialist departments.

The technique of line analysis can be used to determine the arrangement of the machines inside each group, which will give the simplest material flow.

Considerations of material flow, safety, maintenance, and the mini-mizing of operation times, will be important criteria for the choice of the best layout. One other major aim should be to design a layout which provides the basis for a satisfying social relationship between the workers in the group.

12 Component Classification and Coding

12.1 INTRODUCTION

Nearly all the early applications of Group Technology were based on component classification and coding. Nearly all the pioneers in Group Technology were classification enthusiasts. Group Technology owes an enormous debt to classification and coding, which at the very least must be accepted as the midwife responsible for its delivery. Component classification and coding—although highly desirable in its own right—is however no longer essential for the initial stages of the introduction of Group Technology. Most of the savings of Group Technology can now be obtained without component classification and coding.

Component classification and coding was until recently the only known method of finding families. It was therefore an essential part of Group Technology. With the introduction of Production flow analysis, it is no longer needed for this purpose. Although the majority of experts still see classification and coding as an essential pre-requisite for Group Technology, it can now be argued that combining the two complicates both introductions, without serving any useful purpose to either of them.

This book adopts a middle view. It says that production flow analysis is a better method for finding families and groups than classification and coding. Companies without a component classification and coding system can therefore introduce Group Technology, without first incurring the expense and delay of introducing such a system. It says, however, that classification and coding is an important technique in it's own right; that it can make significant contributions to the later development of a Group Technology system, and that it should therefore be considered as a technique, or tool of particular importance to Group Technology.

12.2 DEFINITIONS

(a) Classification

Classification can be defined as either the division of a list of items into classes according to their differences, or as the combining of individual items into classes according to their similarities. The first definition takes an analytical view of the problem and the second a synthetic view.

Information can be classified in many different ways, according to different types of difference, or different types of similarity. For example, parts can be classified according to their shape, processing methods, value, type of product on which they are used, or—to use the general terminology of classification—they can be classified according to many different attributes.

(b) Coding

Coding can be defined as the assigning of symbols to classes, in such a way that the symbols convey information about the nature of the classes. The most common types of code, according to the digits used, are:

1. *Numerical* codes—all numbers
2. *Alphabetical* codes—all letters
3. *Alphanumeric* codes—mixed numbers and letters

Numerical codes have the advantages over alphabetical codes, that: there is a lower risk of reading errors; they are easy to handle with existing office machinery; and they have a wider utility, because the arabic numbers are understood in most countries, while there are many more different alphabets. Alphabetic codes on the other hand have the great advantage that each digit can have twenty-six different values, whereas with the decimal system there are only ten possible values per digit.

Codes can also be classified according to their mode of construction, into three main types:

1. *Monocodes*
2. *Polycodes*
3. *Mixed codes*

A *monocode* is a code in which each digit amplifies the information given in the previous digit. A well-known example is the Dewey decimal system, used in libraries throughout the world. A *polycode* is a code in which each digit is independent of all the other digits. Each digit in the code contains information in its own right, and does not directly qualify the information given by the other digits. A *mixed code* has some digits forming monocodes, but strings them together in the general arrangement of a polycode.

Monocodes are difficult to construct but provide a very deep analysis of the nature of the items classified. They are usually favoured for permanent information, which is unlikely to alter. Polycodes are easier to construct and to modify as needs change. Polycodes are generally preferred for impermanent information—such as cost, and annual requirement quantity—which is liable to change with time. Especially in the case of numerical codes, the ten values possible per digit only give a polycode very limited information storage capacity. Mixed codes, consisting of several small monocodes strung together like a polycode, can be used to increase the storage capacity.

Codes can also be classified according to their universality into:

1. *Universal codes*
2. *Tailor-made codes*

The Dewey decimal system, at least as far as its earlier digits are concerned, is a universal code. Tailor-made codes are codes which are specially designed to meet the needs of particular companies and particular problems.

The difficulty with universal codes when used for industrial purposes, is that much of their information carrying capacity is wasted. If the code is sufficiently deep to cover the needs of all companies, any individual company using it will find that there are some digits it cannot employ, because they are reserved for types of information it does not need. The main difficulty with the tailor-made codes on the other hand, is that they are expensive and take a long time to design and introduce.

12.3 AIMS OF CLASSIFICATION AND CODING

The aim of classification and coding is to provide a rapid and efficient method of information retrieval for decision making. In most companies today production decisions are still largely based on guess work. Questions such as the following cannot be answered accurately without a major investigation, and yet together they require types of information on which decisions ought to be based, which are made every day of the year.

1. What components are made with this type and size of material?
2. On which products is this component used?
3. Which components require a 2BA tapped hole?
4. Which other component is most similar to 'this' component and might be used instead?
5. Is there any tooling in the factory which could be used to make 'this' part?

The only economical solution to this type of information retrieval problem, which has yet been found, is classification and coding. The solution is clear, but there remains one problem. There is no limit to the amount of information which might be recorded and stored about components. The difficulty is to be selective and only store information which is necessary, either for well defined special purposes, or for routine operations. To be truly efficient, a code must be designed for the particular purpose for which it will be used.

One of the earliest and still the most important industrial classification and coding system, is that designed by the late E. G. Brisch and developed and widely applied by his partner J. Gombinski. The aim of this code was design simplification and information retrieval about designs. For these purposes it is the best code yet designed. With over twenty-five years of experience behind it and more than 300 applications, the Brisch classification system is well proven. It is described briefly below.

In recent years a large number of other codes have appeared, many of them based on the Brisch code. Some were primarily designed to find the families for group layout but also claimed the same advantages as Brisch classification in relation to variety reduction. Most of them have not been completely successful, partly because classification and coding of components is intrinsically a poor method for finding families and groups, for reasons described later in the chapter, and partly because they tended to fall between two stools, by trying to fill more than one major purpose.

There is a need in Group Technology for classification and coding systems for the following purposes:

1. Finding the components for composite parts
2. Finding the parts for material and tooling families
3. Finding the optimum sequence of loading

The problems of designing a code for these purposes are examined later in the chapter.

12.4 DESIGN SIMPLIFICATION

(a) Classification and coding for simplification

Simplification can be defined as the elimination of unnecessary variety. Any machine design can be examined at the five different levels: the product, assemblies, components, component design features, and materials. To reduce unnecessary variety at any of these levels, the first thing one must know, is which items are similar. Knowing the similar items, one can plan to eliminate some of the varieties, by substituting others which are nearly the same. The final step is to standardize the designs which remain, and to see that when items of these types are required in the future, these standard items are chosen rather than design new ones.

Any classification and coding system which is intended to bring similar items together for the purposes of variety reduction, will be concerned with such qualities as:

1. Shape, or function
2. Material qualities
3. Size

The shape of a part is a more positive identification than its function, which can only be described by name. Investigation in some engineering companies have found over 100 different names in use for identical items. For example in one company 111 different function describing names were used for plain single diameter pins, including pin, peg, dowel, stop, 'jack-leg plug' and 'man-handling bar knuckle jaw pin'. It is obvious in this case that a classification based on shape will be better for variety reduction than one based on function names.

Most complex products and assemblies on the other hand, are best classified by function. Some components can also be classified by function without ambiguity. For example a class containing 'worm wheels' is more accurately defined by this term, than would be possible by a progressive analysis based on shape features. According to J. Gombinski* the proportion of components which can be specified by function with advantage, varies enormously according to industry, from as little as 5%, to as much as 80%.

As far as materials and size are concerned, there are limits to the amount of detail which can be included in the component code. General materials will require their own special code for variety reduction. Normally, however, it would be unprofitable to add this relatively long code number, to the component codes of all items made from the material. Size is very difficult to specify in a component code. If arbitrary limits are set for size, for items of similar shape, there is a danger that almost identical items will have very different code numbers. It is also particularly difficult to specify size classes for irregular shapes. The best advice is that size should be among the last qualities to be coded in any code number.

(b) Brisch classification

The Brisch classification and coding system is based on four main rules:

1. It is a pure monocode
2. It is a numerical code of constant length
3. It is tailor-made to suit the special requirements of each company
4. It is based entirely on the permanent characteristics of the items classified

Classification starts with a sample survey in the company, to determine code capacity needs and special requirements. The first step is to design a classification plan, such as that illustrated in Figure 12.1. This plan fixes values for the first two digits.

Each main class shown in the classification plan is then expanded, as shown in the example in Figure 12.2. In this instance a 'surname' of five digits establishes the general class of an item, and a 'Christian name' of three digits, is sufficient to establish an exact identity for each particular item in the general class, providing only—as was the case in this instance—that not more than ten material specifications are possible for any shape, and there are not more than ninety-nine different sizes in each main class. Because the code number is unique for each item, it can be used with advantage as the identification symbol. Every component must have an

* GOMBINSKI, J. *The Brisch Classification and Group Technology*, Sept. 1969 Group Technology Seminar Proceedings, Turin International Centre.

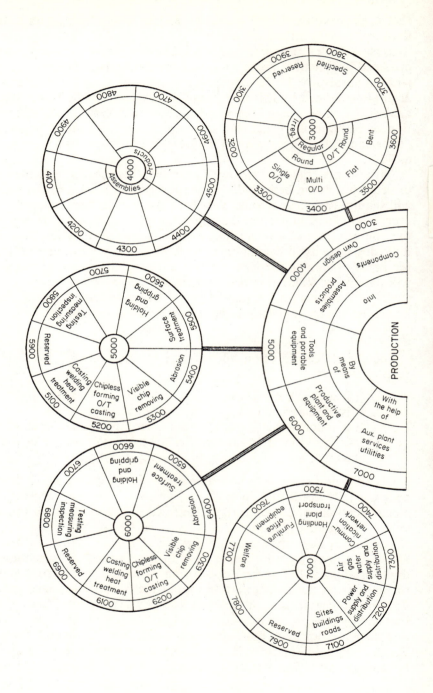

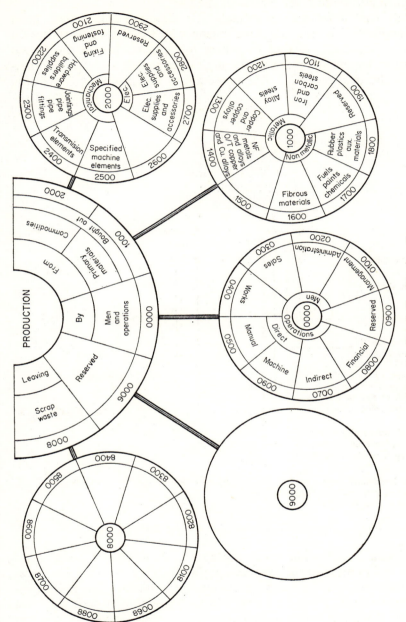

Figure 12.1. Brisch Classification plan

identification symbol, so if this is possible, it might just as well convey useful information about the nature of the part, as well as identify it.

A widely held belief among specialists in classification, is that 'fixed digital significance' is essential. One reason why the Brisch classification has been so successful, is that it ignores this convention. In the Brisch classification, for example, the second digit does not always represent material, as it did in Figure 12.2. The advantage of this flexibility, is that the

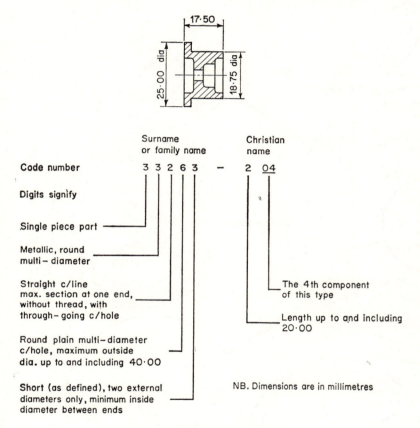

Figure 12.2. Expansion of a major class

most significant information can be chosen for classification for each main class, thus including in the code more significant data than is possible with 'fixed digital significance'. If a company produces 10,000 items it must inevitably have at least a five-digit identification symbol. Any code will need more digits. If with fixed digital significance one needs nine digits, one can probably manage with seven or eight digits without it.

In practice a photocopy is produced of the drawing for each item, which is reduced to a standard size. The prints for all items with the same surname are stored in the same file, or 'pocket'. When a designer requires a new part, he draws a rough sketch, codes it and then goes to the appropriate pocket to see if anything similar is available.

It might be more correct to say that this is what the designer ought to do. In practice, classification and coding systems only work efficiently in companies which have a strong enough management to see that they are used. Some designers resent classification and coding systems, on the grounds that they restrict their freedom of choice. It is difficult to see the advantages, however, of any system which repeatedly redesigns the same items over and over again. Art for art's sake is an expensive luxury in industrial design.

12.5 CLASSIFICATION AND CODING FOR FINDING FAMILIES

(a) Selection of information type for different problems

Coding systems for design simplification were based rightly, on such qualities as shape or function, material, and size. They were based on the assumption that if different items have the same values for each of these qualities, they are in fact identical. In this instance classification and coding goes direct to the heart of the problem, and is generally successful for that reason.

When looking for the families and groups for Group Technology, the only relevant information on which to base the division, is a list of the machine types used to make each item. Production flow analysis considers only this essential information. In this instance it uses the direct method to find the correct solution. The pundit may suggest that it would be better to use a list of the machines which ought to be used, rather than of those which are used. In practice, however, as was shown in a previous chapter, both approaches tend to find the same division into families and groups. Minor errors and inconsistencies in route cards cause them to be thrown out for investigation.

(b) Component classification is an indirect method of finding families

By contrast all the existing classification and coding systems designed for finding families, use an indirect approach. Many of the early systems were mainly shape and function systems like Brisch classification. Although it was never expressed in so many words, their use for finding families was based on the assumption that: 'if two parts have the same shape, they will be made on the same machines'.

Unfortunately this assumption is not true. For example, two parts may be identical in shape, but be made rightly, on entirely different machines, because: they differ greatly in size, or one has much closer manufacturing tolerances than the other, or because one is required in much greater quantities than the other, or because again, one has a special feature such as a keyway, which is not needed on the others.

Even if the parts are identical in all main respects, the assumption is still not necessarily true. In a given factory, for example, some items may be made on one machine up to the limit of its capacity, and the remainder be made on another second choice machine, because there is no more capacity on the ideal machine.

To overcome these problems, the latest classification and coding systems for finding families, include a great deal of additional information about design features, and also some production information, some of which is impermanent, requiring changing with, for example, changes in demand.

(c) Finding the groups

An important difference between production flow analysis and component classification and coding, for finding families, is that the first finds families and groups, and the second only provides a desk aid with which an intelligent engineer can find some families. In fact the difference goes even deeper. While production flow analysis does find the existing natural families and their associated groups, 'classification and coding' tends to create new families which did not exist before. When considering how they should be made, one has in turn to create new groups.

A change to Group Technology, which is based on classification and coding, is likely to be a more difficult and costly change for this reason than a change based on production flow analysis. For the same reason, a change to Group Technology, which is based on component classification, may require a larger investment in additional plant than one based on production flow analysis.

(d) Conclusion

The earliest classification and coding systems provided a desk aid, with which an intelligent engineer could find some viable families. The latest codes, which carry a great deal more information, are unlikely to be any more successful, because it is still impossible to code all the information needed for good planning, or to specify an exact relationship between component qualities and optimum processing methods. The best feasibility test is to ask 'Can the relationship be expressed in sufficiently simple logical statements, that it is possible to prepare a computer programme, which will work with component data and print out lists of families and their associated groups?' At present the answer is, 'no'.

Even if a solution is eventually found to this problem, it is unlikely that an indirect method of this complexity can hope to compete economically, with a simple direct method such as production flow analysis, which finds a complete division into both families and associated groups, at the same time.

12.6 CLASSIFICATION NEEDS OF GROUP TECHNOLOGY

Although it is not the right tool for finding families and groups, classification and coding has great advantages in its own right for information retrieval and variety reduction. There are also some problems in Group Technology which could benefit greatly from classification and coding. Four of these are:

1. Finding the components for composite parts
2. Finding the components for material and tooling families
3. Finding the optimum scheduling sequence
4. Tooling development

(a) Finding the components for composite parts

Up to the present, the main application for composite parts has been in lathe work. Parts which are suitable for a composite part, must be similar in shape. The best type of classification system for this task, is one based on shape. With the Brisch system for example, all parts capable of inclusion in one composite part, will be in the same pocket. It is a simple matter to find the suitable items by direct examination, and to eliminate the unsuitable items.

(b) Finding the components for tooling families

With other processes, parts generally come together into tooling families because:

1. They all have a similar feature and use the same tools
2. They can all be held on the machine by the same device
3. They are all made from the same material.

For example, in a group containing a hobbing machine, all gears of the same tooth form, tooth size, and number of teeth, which have the same bore, can probably be machined with the same tooling at the same basic set-up. This tooling family can probably be extended further, by the provision of quick-change sleeves, to allow the hobbing of identical gears with larger bores.

What is needed is a fairly elaborate classification of design features, and also a classification of tools which includes the methods for holding parts on machines. In addition to this, provision is needed for cross reference between these classes and the general component classification.

(c) Finding the optimum scheduling sequence

On some machines, finding the optimum scheduling sequence is a problem, first of bringing together all components from the same composite parts, and second of arranging the sequence in which these sub-families are tackled, so that the most complex items are done first, and each change to a new composite part, or individual part, involves a minimum of re-setting.

On other machines the solution is similar, but in this case it is the parts in the same tooling families which must be brought together even though they may be different in shape. In this instance it is parts made with the same tooling which must be brought together, and a classification of tools is needed.

Finally there are some machines where the optimum sequence of scheduling is that which brings together, for loading one after the other, components which are made from the same general materials. In all these cases, classification and coding can be a valuable aid.

(d) A possible solution

A possible solution would be to provide a classification and coding system based on the Brisch system, but including also a classification of design features, with its own monocode. Some system of cross reference would then be needed between the different parts of the code.

In this case the code would include detailed sub-codes for:

1. Materials
2. Products
3. Assemblies
4. Parts
5. Tools

as at present, and also one for design features:

6. Design features

The main cross references required for practical purposes, would be those between:

1. Materials and the parts which are made from them
2. Design features and the parts which contain them
3. Tools and the parts which are made with them
4. Parts and the assemblies in which they are used (a used-on record)
5. Assemblies and the products which contain them

Adding these cross references to the record would greatly extend the information retrieval possibilities of the code. One of the costly features of many present day computer systems, is that for each different purpose it is necessary to make a special study to assemble the input data. With classification and coding a large proportion of this data would be permanently available in the form of codes.

12.7 SUMMARY

Efficient classification and coding of the information about a company and its products, is a relatively new technique of major importance to industry.

Particularly now with the advent of the computer, efficient classification makes it possible to retrieve and analyse information in minutes, which would have taken months to retrieve in the past, even with a computer.

In saying that classification and coding is no longer a necessary pre-requisite for the introduction of Group Technology, it is not intended to denigrate the real worth of this technique. The only submission is that production flow analysis is a better technique for finding families and groups, and that companies which do not already have a classification and coding system need no longer wait for its introduction, before achieving the benefits of Group Technology.

13　Personnel and Group Technology

13.1　INTRODUCTION

The function of management which encompasses the hardest tasks in Group Technology is the personnel function. As with any major innovation, the real problem with Group Technology is to persuade people, at all levels, to accept the change. In comparison, the material flow and technological problems are relatively simple.

This chapter attempts three main tasks. First, it attempts to describe the nature of the change in working conditions and to show that Group Technology is a desirable change from the human point of view. Through the simplification of material flow, it simplifies the work of the manager and reduces the stress in the organization by reducing the amount of co-ordination with other managers which is necessary. Through job enlargement, the use of independent working groups, increased opportunities for participation in decision-making, and a closer association with the product, it provides greater job satisfaction and a happier working environment for the worker.

Second, this chapter describes some of the problems of training for Group Technology, and third, it attempts to show where the major conflicts are likely to arise, and to consider some of the ways in which they might be reduced.

13.2　GROUP TECHNOLOGY AND THE DIRECT WORKER

To understand the relationship between Group Technology and the working conditions of people in industry, it is necessary to consider the nature of the work tasks done, the methods of organization by which these tasks are assigned to different groups of workers, and the factors which affect the acceptability of different arrangements by the workers.

(a) Work tasks

All manual work tasks consist of a succession of basic work elements, or simple human motions. A succession of these elements done on the same machine or at the same work centre is known as an 'operation', and a succession of operations which completes an obvious major stage in processing—such as metal founding, forging, or machining, for example—is called a 'process'.

In the last resort the series of elements of work to be carried out by the workers is the same in Group Technology as it is with any other form of organization. The way in which they are combined into operations can be varied, however, as can also the number of times an operation is repeated, before changing to a new operation.

Complex operations consisting of many successive elements may take hours to complete, or in other words may have a very long 'cycle'. Simple operations consisting of few elements may have very short cycles of only a few seconds.

When the 'run quantities' of parts to be produced are very large, the worker may be required to go on repeating the same operation for years. When the run quantities are small, as in jobbing work, he may change operations four or more times per hour.

(b) Organization

For effective management, the workers and the machines they operate must be divided progressively into divisions, departments, and sections, the number of levels of organization depending on the size of the enterprise. These organizational units can be planned on the basis of process

Level of Organization	Division by process	Division by product
A. Division into departments or major groups	DEPARTMENTS 1. Assembly 2. Foundry 3. Forge 4. Sheet metal 5. Machining	MAJOR GROUPS 1. Major group 1 2. Major group 2 3. Major group 3 4. Major group 4 5. Major group 4
B. Division into sections or groups	SECTIONS e.g. Division of machining department 5.1 Turning 5.2 Milling 5.3 Drilling 5.4 Grinding 5.5 Gear cutting	GROUPS e.g. Division of major group No. 5 5.1 Group 1 5.2 Group 2 5.3 Group 3 5.4 Group 4 5.5 Group 5

N.B. A 'group' is a list of machines plus a team of workers. Each group completes its own special list of components known as its 'family'. Major groups are the largest possible groups of compatible machines.

Figure 13.1. Division by process or product

differences—as is most common today—or, on the basis of the product and its components, as in Group Technology.

Figure 13.1 shows the different units formed in a particular factory by each of these methods. Division at the first level finds departments. With division by process, most parts visit a number of different departments, sometimes visiting the same one several different times. With division by product into major families of parts, each part is completed in its own special major group during a single visit, unless it requires two major processes one after the other, such as metal founding and machining, for example, when it will be completed as a casting in the first department, before going on to the next one to be machined into a finished part.

Division at the second level finds 'sections', or 'groups'. Division by process first finds sections specializing in sub-processes. Most parts made in these departments visit two or more sections and only a few very simple parts are completed in one section only. Few parts go from one machine to another in the same section and there is little or no need for the workers in a section to co-operate in their work.

Division by product, on the other hand, further subdivides the machines in a major group into smaller groups, and sub-divides the parts made in the department into smaller families, each made in its own special group. In this instance all parts in a family are completed in its own group and the men work together as a team to complete a given number of different parts by one common due-date for each ordering cycle.

(c) Job satisfaction

It is impossible to specify exactly the conditions necessary for a satisfying job. Men differ in their needs and aspirations and job satisfaction is not subject to exact mechanical laws. There is, nevertheless, some evidence that the working conditions with Group Technology are more acceptable to human beings than those imposed by our present systems of production. There is also some evidence from sociological research and from practice, that the following factors contribute to the result:

1. Task complexity and cycle
2. Run quantity
3. Diversity of work
4. Group satisfaction
5. Product satisfaction
6. Participation

1. *Task complexity and cycle*. In spite of Adam Smith, there is evidence that human beings do not like repeating very simple tasks to a very short cycle, and that this type of division of labour does not provide the most economical production. A number of 'job enrichment' programmes in different companies have achieved increases in productivity by increasing the complexity of the operations done by workers.

An interesting example from the U.S.A., which has since been repeated in other factories in Europe, has been described by E. Heckshaw. He used individual audio-visual aids to teach illiterate Mexican girls to assemble very complex electronic assemblies, and achieved a substantial increase in output per worker over the previous method of line assembly with simple operations, due mainly to a large reduction in rejects and absenteeism, and to an increase in motivation and consequently production rates.

2. *Run quantity.* Changing to Group Technology in component processing departments, with the same processing methods, does not change the complexity of the work tasks. It does, however, reduce run quantities, and there is again some evidence that simple tasks are more acceptable if they do not have to be repeated too many times. The reduction in ordering cycles with Group Technology may be a contributory factor to improved job satisfaction.

3. *Diversity of work.* Another factor which may affect job satisfaction is the diversity of task which is possible. A man in a milling section may move from one milling machine to another during the course of his work, but all the tasks he does will be very similar. In a 'group', on the other hand, a worker who wants change will have the opportunity to learn to operate several different types of machines.

4. *Group satisfaction.* There is evidence that human beings have a strong need to 'belong' to a group, and to co-operate in the achievement of common goals. Some scientists see this need as originating in the need of our very early ancestors, to combine for survival into hunting groups.

In component processing, there is no doubt that groups support this need, much better than our present traditionally organized sections based on process specialization. The members of a group work together to complete a given load of work by a common due-date. The members of a section on the other hand work independently with different targets and have little need to co-operate in their work.

In assembly, too, there is evidence that group working, instead of line flow in a series of very simple operations, can increase both job satisfaction and productivity. Evidence of the revolt of workers against the mass production assembly line can be found in high rates of labour turnover, absenteeism, and quality control rejects. Chrysler in the U.S.A., for example, are reported to have a labour turnover of 45% per year and Volvo in Sweden to employ an excess labour force of 14% as a buffer against absenteeism.

A recent development is that companies as internationally reputable as Volvo, Saab, Philips, and Olivetti, have used group assembly in preference to line assembly in some of their factories, and have gained improvements in productivity, quality, and labour relations by so doing. It has been argued that these gains are only possible in mass production, where station job content is traditionally simple and cycles are very short. FIAT in Italy have recently increased the number of car assembly lines making the same car in one of their factories. Four lines were installed. This reduced the number of men on each line and increased the job content and cycle times at the stations on these lines both by a factor of four. It will be interesting to see how their results compare with those of Volvo and Saab.

5. *Product satisfaction.* Another factor in job satisfaction is the need to complete products to a significant and easily recognized stage of completion. Groups complete components and the people who work in them tend to get greater satisfaction for this reason than those who work in sections and never complete anything.

6. *Participation.* Finally a major need for job satisfaction is worker participation in decision making. Most of the effort in this direction in the past has been concerned with such subjects as works' committees and employee directors. For the majority of workers these types of representational participation are too indirect. What most men want is a bigger say in the day-to-day management of their own jobs.

With layout by process, the need for centralized co-ordination makes shop-floor participation very difficult without a drop in efficiency. With groups on the other hand, the main need for co-ordination with other groups is covered by the output plan to be completed by a given due-date. Provided that this target is met, day-to-day running can be delegated to the groups without loss of efficiency. There are already Group Technology applications where the men in the groups decide: who shall do which jobs; who can take a day off; and how shifts should be organized. There are other types of decision which might equally well be delegated.

7. *Job satisfaction and the worker.* The above factors in job satisfaction are those which are affected significantly by the introduction of Group Technology. It is not suggested that these are the only factors involved, or that a change to Group Technology will give an automatic improvement in job satisfaction and labour relations. What is suggested, is that Group Technology provides a working 'climate' in which it is easier to achieve good labour relations, than is possible with our present methods of industrial organization.

13.3 INDIRECT LABOUR

Leaving the direct workers and considering now the indirect workers, the position becomes more difficult. In general the number of jobs for skilled indirect workers such as draughtsmen, production planners, inspectors, and maintenance personnel, is not likely to be greatly affected. Some of the clerical and semi-skilled service occupations, on the other hand, are going to disappear and the numbers required for others are going to be greatly reduced.

The following are a few of the occupations where a reduction should be anticipated:

1. Storekeepers (particularly in inter-departmental stores)
2. Progress men
3. Production record clerks
4. Workshop dispatching clerks
5. Time keepers
6. Wages clerks
7. Accounting clerks
8. Typists
9. Move men

Some of the main savings of Group Technology arise due to the simplification of the material flow and related information flow systems, and the reduction in indirect labour which this makes possible. It is important that management should plan this reduction in labour force and not just wake up one morning to discover they have a redundancy problem.

In the first case, if one starts planning early enough, something can be done to reduce the gravity of the problem. The first step is to put an absolute ban on any new intake in the affected occupations. Normal wastage will help to reduce the extent of the problem, although it may bring other temporary problems in their place.

A second possibility is to extend the range of manufactured items. Some items may be found which are now purchased, although the plant needed to make them is available in the factory. Others may involve processes which have not previously been done. To be of any immediate use in avoiding redundancy, it is desirable that any new processes should be simple, so that unskilled labour can be quickly trained to do the jobs. The list of purchased items should be examined to find items, which are ordered in sufficiently large quantities to make manufacture economically feasible. Another way of reducing redundancy is to increase output. Group Technology will increase capacity and an increased sales effort may increase sales and find additional employment opportunities.

Finally a study should be made of all employees in the affected occupations. Some may be found who are skilled tradesmen who have been 'promoted' to white collar jobs, and can be persuaded to return to their trades when vacancies arise. Others may be found who can be retrained for other occupations with a more secure future.

Whatever is done to alleviate the problem, however, some companies which introduce Group Technology are going to have to face a redundancy programme. The Western World, partly due to a traditional distrust of paternalism, has chosen a system of industrial development based on the mobility of labour, coupled with government assistance to avoid major hardships. It does not always succeed in avoiding hardship and distress, but nor does paternalism, or communism, or tribalism, or any other social or political system for that matter.

13.4 GROUP TECHNOLOGY AND THE FOREMAN

The foreman's life is also changed with Group Technology. The first major change is that he stops being a specialist in one particular process and becomes instead a specialist in the production of certain types of component. Instead of being responsible for completing operations, he becomes responsible for the manufacture of whole components. Because he has all the means of processing under his control, he can be assigned the direct responsibility for both component quality and the completion of components by due-date.

Another major change is that he becomes much less dependent on other foremen. With functional layout he depends on other foremen and managers to supply him with part-worked materials of the right quality, in the right quantities, and at the right times. He depends on them also to lift and move the materials to and from the section, to check his work for quality, to tell him which jobs are urgent and so on. Generally he is competing for common services with other foremen. With group layout he is much more independent. His problems of co-operation are now largely contained inside his own group. His relationships with other foremen are easier because he is no longer competing with them for limited resources.

The technological responsibilities of the foreman are also expanded with group layout. A foreman who with functional layout needs to know only about lathes must acquire some knowledge about any other types of machine which will be installed in his group. This has not proved a difficulty in practice. Most men who rise to become foremen will have had experience with more than one machine type and much of the expertise required for one machine is transferable to others. For the foreman who knows nothing about a machine type he must now use for the first time, special courses will be better than leaving him to find out for himself.

Although it is perhaps not essential in the early stages of the introduction of Group Technology to consider them, there are also other possibilities for the technological enlargement of the foreman's job. There may be advantages in decentralizing: routine inter-operation inspection; minor tool maintenance; some of the preventive maintenance inspections; and the routing of new parts. In the past fifty years the prestige and authority of the foreman have been greatly reduced. In our blind acceptance of process specialization we have taken from the foremen many decisions which are better made by the man on the spot. With Group Technology there is an opportunity to change back.

In the long run, too, Group Technology will introduce major changes in the nature of the foreman's job. Traditionally most industrial organizations are autocratic. Most decisions are made by management and the foreman's main role is to communicate the decisions to his workers and see that they are carried out. With Group Technology the reduction in co-ordination needs between groups will inevitably lead to an increase in delegation of the responsibility for decision making to the groups. Some of these decisions will be made by the foreman, but there will also inevitably be a trend towards greater worker participation in decision making, and he may also therefore be subject to some decisions which are made democratically by the members of his group.

13.5 GROUP TECHNOLOGY AND SOCIOLOGY

Any major innovation will always cause stress, however desirable the end result. All the evidence so far, however, indicates that once the initial problems of adjustment have been overcome, Group Technology leads to better human relations and greater productivity. Most Group Technology applications report improved human relations and better team spirit. Some have backed these claims with more concrete measures of improved human relations, such as reduced absenteeism.

Sociologists and Psychologists have as yet done little research in Group Technology, and these assessments are not perhaps completely objective. This is a pity because a considerable amount of recent research in these fields supports the probability that Group Technology will have the observed effect.

Several research projects have pointed to the need for: independent work groups; an easily recognized task completion stage; the importance of rhythm and of working to a regular cycle; and of the need to base organization on the material flow system. Two works which illustrate the close correspondence between the findings of sociological research and Group Technology will now be described.

(a) Organization for minimum stress

A book was published in the U.S.A. in 1961 called 'The Measure of Management'. It was written by Eliot D. Chapple and Leonard R. Sayles. This book was based on research into the causes of dispute between foremen. It advocates an approach to industrial organization which is based on actual work flow. It points at the present predominance of functional organization and shows how this approach tends to break the responsibility for the control of work flow, and as a result to inflate the amount of co-ordination needed between managers; to induce stress in the individuals responsible for maintaining the flow, and to cause conflict between them.

'The Measure of Management' advocates an approach to organization which minimizes changes in responsibility along the material flow streams, and seeks by this means to minimize stress and conflict. In a sense the authors of this book are amongst the pioneers of Group Technology. Approaching the problems of factory organization from the point of view of the sociologist and psychologist, they came to the same conclusions as those reached for entirely different reasons by the production engineer and production controller advocates of Group Technology.

The division into groups in Group Technology follows the philosophy of 'The Measure of Management'. By dividing the organization into groups which specialize in the production of particular families of components, it reduces the need for co-ordination between sections and minimizes stress in the organization.

(b) Independent groups

One of the effects of Group Technology is that it creates independent groups of workers, who work together as a team with a common aim. Again there is evidence that this independence is important to the human being, and that it also leads to greater productivity. Some evidence in this case is contained in a book by A. K. Rice. This book called 'Productivity and Social Organisation' describes research carried out in a weaving shed in a textile company in Ahemabad in India.

At the start of the experiment the work was organized so that there were no independent working groups. Each of the traditional weaving trades was represented. The number of looms per worker was different for each trade. For example, weavers looked after twenty-four to thirty-two machines; battery fillers serviced forty-eight to fifty machines; gaters were responsible for eighty to one hundred and twelve machines. It will be seen that the labour in this factory worked independently. There were no teams, or independent groups of workers, working together with a common aim.

In the experiment, the looms were divided into four groups. The work done by each of the traditional trades, was studied. The work was then re-divided, in such a way, that each group could have its own team of workers, permanently assigned to the group and specializing in the production of a particular family of fabrics. There was a significant increase in productivity. This reorganization was undoubtedly one of the first applications of Group Technology.

13.6 TRAINING

The soundest basis for the introduction of Group Technology is an efficient training programme. This should be aimed at all levels in the organization, and should be based on readable handout material, competent lecturers, and good audio-visual aids.

(a) The Board

The first people to be trained, or should one say 'briefed', are the Board of Directors. One can say in fact that until they are convinced, it is a waste of time to go on. In theory it should be possible for a strong middle management to agree on a policy and implement most of the essential changes for Group Technology. In practice, however, the most successful applications so far, have been inspired, directed and controlled by some member of the Board of Directors, usually the Managing Director.

One suspects that Group Technology has made significant progress in the U.S.S.R. for a similar reason. The orders to introduce Group Technology came from the top, in a directive from the Supreme Praesidium of the U.S.S.R.

There are some beautiful examples of Group Layout from the technologist's point of view, introduced by production engineers on their own. Their only deficiency is that they have made only a small contribution to profitability. They never will make a major contribution until Group Technology is accepted as a total management change, and not just as the latest production gimmick.

A suitable training programme for directors might consist of a special one day seminar, with a few invited speakers. If possible someone should be found to contest the idea, even if he is employed specially as Devil's advocate, so that all possible objections are brought out early into the open.

Thereafter the directors should be encouraged to visit existing applications and to report back on what they find. Representatives of the board should be sent to attend current courses and seminars on the subject. Every readable reference should be studied and analysed.

Most Boards of Directors can be trusted to make reasonable policy decisions inside the terms of reference which they understand and are used to. The trouble with Group Technology is that it changes the restraints. Even the best Board of Directors cannot hope to make good decisions, if its members do not understand the system in which they are working.

(b) Management

All ranks of management will also need training, first in the general principles of the new approach and second in the special changes necessary in each function. Wide reading followed by seminars and discussion groups will meet the first of these needs. Visits should also be arranged if possible to see existing applications and key managers should be sent on courses and outside seminars.

The special training needs of functional specialists—such as accountants, personnel managers, marketing managers, and buyers—are very difficult to meet at present. Very little has been written on these special problems of Group Technology. It is desirable that at least a part of this training should be done in company with other specialists in the same field. This means training with specialists from other companies. The best people to organize such training in Britain would be the professional associations and institutes. No seminars have yet been run on these special problems of Group Technology, but no doubt the professional bodies would be glad to organize them, if there were a demand.

Management can also be trained by working on the design of the new systems that will have to be installed. Project work with real problems, is

I

one of the most effective training methods. The work to be done should be divided into self-contained projects, as described in the next chapter. Working groups should then be formed to tackle each problem. The restraints imposed by the need to produce a total integrated system, should be clearly defined, and there should be frequent co-ordination meetings, both formal and informal, to ensure that the different projects are compatible and harmonious.

(c) Foremen

The foremen again must first learn to understand the new conditions which they will face after the change to Group Technology, and second they may need extra training in any new processes and types of plant, with which they have not previously worked.

Consider first the processes; the type of training will depend on the complexity of the process. For simple processes the foreman can probably learn all he needs to know by reading the machine manual, and by talking to the foreman at present responsible for that plant. If the plant is of a type required in several groups, the foreman at present responsible for the process can be asked to give a demonstration and to answer questions. If the process is a complex one, using complicated plant, more formal training may be necessary. Some production machinery manufacturers run courses on their machines, or will arrange special instruction if requested. In Britain the Production Engineering Research Association and some technical colleges will also arrange courses.

As far as general familiarization is concerned, short lectures and long question and discussion periods can be used with advantage. It is important again with the foremen, that every possible objection should be openly discussed, before the actual change in layout.

The foremen should also be included in the project work in all cases which will affect their own future responsibilities. In particular they should be consulted about the layout of the machines in their group. As far as possible this layout should not be finalized without their agreement.

The foremen should also be involved in the finding of tooling families, in the choice of loading sequence, and in the manning of their groups. As soon as possible each foreman should be given the list of machines and personnel which will form his group and the list of parts which will form his family. Where a foreman will have several machines of the same general type, he should be encouraged to study the special qualities of each machine. He should also study the special skills and capabilities of the employees assigned to his group. Again he should be encouraged to find the end uses of the parts which his group will make and to discover the critical parts, which for quality reasons, or because they have long through-put times, will require special attention. He should familiarize himself with the special tooling available for each part.

Those companies which already have a component classification and coding system will have an advantage. It will be simpler for them to find the parts which form composite parts, and to find other types of tooling family as well. Even in this case, however, the foremen should be given the opportunity to study the findings and to suggest changes.

In companies which do not have a classification and coding system, a manual sort must be used of the route cards, the drawings or the components. A simple technique for sorting the parts in a family to find material and tooling families was described in a previous chapter. The initial effort should concentrate on the machine type which is most heavily loaded, and the foreman should be fully involved in the work.

(d) Operators

The machine operators should also be given the opportunity to familiarize themselves with the new system of work, and to learn any new skills they will need under the new system. With regard to familiarization, the issue of leaflets, poster displays, and special lectures can be used, and there should be ample opportunities for questions and discussions. Another method is to leave it to the foreman of each group, with or without some assistance from senior line management, to familiarize his own group. Special sessions should be arranged for shop stewards and union representatives, and their support should be actively solicited.

It may be necessary to teach additional skills to some of the operators. Wherever possible, this training should be based on trade tests, with some additional pay for each additional skill acquired.

13.7 CRITICAL CHANGES

In the following chapter, which considers the method of introducing Group Technology, an approach is recommended by which the total change is broken up into a number of small projects, each of which can stand on its own.

If this division into projects is carefully planned, each project will itself bring some benefit to the company and at the same time also contribute to the final aim. A surprisingly large number of these projects will have no direct effect on worker relations. The feeling of change in the air may itself be disturbing and all projects may generate some discontent in particular individuals, but only a small number of critical changes will have a general impact on the labour force as a whole. It is important that these critical change points should be recognized and that careful attention should be given to the way in which they are introduced.

The main critical change points are likely to be:

1. The introduction of period batch control
2. The introduction of group layout
3. Changes in the wages system

(a) *The Introduction of Period Batch Control*

The introduction of period batch control brings problems, because it changes working conditions. In the early days of the introduction, the need to balance the stock in product sets, may generate a greatly reduced and unbalanced load of work on the processing shops. Parts with large stocks may not be ordered for several months. Some workers may have nothing to do for long periods.

These problems of stock balancing are only temporary, but they can cause severe disruption while they last and they may lead to loss of earnings for some workers, and to disputes. One way of solving the problem is to introduce additional work. For example:

(i) *Pre-production batch for a new product.* If a new product is to be introduced in the near future, now would be a good time to make the pre-production batch.

(ii) *Increase the stock of spare parts.* The manufacture of spare parts in anticipation of future sales requirements can also help. It exchanges an excessive unbalanced investment in some direct materials for a temporary excessive investment in spares which can be run down over a longer period. It delays reduction of the investment but has the advantage that it reduces idle time losses for labour, while still allowing the balancing of the direct material.

(iii) *Increase assembly of finished products.* The load on the processing departments can again be increased by a temporary increase in assembly rate. This will reduce the period of time needed to balance the stocks. As in the case of spare parts, this method substitutes a temporary excessive investment in finished products for an excessive and unbalanced investment in parts, but again it helps to avoid labour idle time, and in many industries it will stimulate sales by reducing delivery times.

(b) *Batch quantities and Period Batch Control*

Another result of introducing period batch control is much more permanent in its effect. Generally the change will mean a reduction in processing batch quantities, or more precisely in run quantities. This change in some cases may tend to increase operation times per piece, but at the same time it will generally induce a greater compensating reduction in setting times. Under some traditional incentive schemes the change will reduce earnings, but with others earnings could increase.

One way to avoid disputes is to take this opportunity to eliminate an individual incentive scheme. It is desirable to change to a measured load of work per cycle and a group bonus system in any case, when group layout is introduced. Another way is to adopt a liberal attitude during the interim period, and allow the payment of average earnings, in cases where rates are contested on the grounds of reduced batch quantities.

(c) The introduction of Group Layout

The introduction of group layout brings problems, because it changes working conditions, because it is a change which may cause redundancy, particularly among the indirect workers, and because in many companies it will require a change in the payment system.

(i) *The change in working conditions.* The change in working conditions should not cause difficulties, providing it has been well planned and everyone knows what they have to do. It is important for morale that the change should be efficiently managed. In particular it is important that the new groups should not have to wait for materials particularly during the early periods after the change. This can be avoided by building up temporary stocks of raw materials, which may also be desirable for another reason.

If there is say, a casting store between a foundry and a machine shop, it is probable that the balancing of the stock when period batch control is introduced, will cause an even greater shortage of work in the foundry than in the machine shop. An increase in casting buffer stocks across the product range, will help reduce the impact of stock balancing and at the same time ease the later introduction of group layout.

After group layout has been successfully established, it should be possible to run down these stocks, eliminate the inter-process store, and establish direct material flow between the foundry and the machine shop.

(ii) *Redundancy.* No redundancy should arise due to the introduction of period batch control. The problem may arise, however, with the change to group layout. The avoidance of difficulties at this time depends on scrupulous fairness in the choice of those who must go, and the generous and sympathetic treatment of those selected to be redundant.

(iii) *Payment system.* The change from a financial incentive system to a daywork system with measured output, or a group bonus scheme should not present great difficulties, provided that average earnings are not reduced and rates of working are not affected, and can be shown to be the same.

13.8   OBTAINING POTENTIAL SAVINGS

Some of the savings from Group Technology come more automatically than others. For example, the introduction of group layout and period batch control will reduce stocks. Other savings are only potential savings until action is taken to achieve them. Amongst this latter category are included nearly all the savings in labour cost. Labour cost seldom reduces itself. Someone has to reduce it.

Redundancy amongst indirect workers is difficult to detect in most companies. The main problem will generally be a complete lack of any objective method for measuring output. Industry has always insisted on output standards for direct workers, but it is only in recent years that an attempt has been made to do the same thing for the indirect worker. One big company recently reduced indirect labour in an emergency by an arbitrary 15% in all departments, and found itself more efficient after the change than before. It is probable that the majority of manufacturing companies could do the same, but there are better methods of doing it.

Group Technology will accelerate the need for a reduction in indirect labour. There will be an inevitable trend towards an increase in the delegation of decision-making to the groups, leading to a reduction in the staff who now make most of these decisions. This change is desirable both socially—to increase the job satisfaction of the direct workers—and economically. Again a manager can control the work of more men in groups than he can in a traditional organization. We can expect a trend towards broader organization structures, with fewer levels of management, and therefore fewer managers and supervisors.

With the introduction of Group Technology the traditional excesses in indirect labour will be reduced by the elimination of the need for several of the existing occupations. One of the first steps when introducing Group Technology should be the establishment of methods for a gradual pruning of the organization. There are three main requirements:

1. A strong control of 'Establishments'
2. Systems analysis
3. The fixing of output standards

These requirements can be controlled by methods such as the following:

(a) Establishment committee

Each department and section in the enterprise should have a fixed Establishment, or authorized labour strength. This Establishment should be maintained under regular review. An Establishment Committee should meet regularly at say monthly intervals, to consider proposed changes, examine the records of actual strength and report on any excess.

The Committee should be encouraged to take an objective view of the problem, and to fix establishments at the levels required for efficient operation, irrespective of their present strengths. It should not generally be a part of the Committee's job to consider how to reduce any excess, this should be the director's responsibility.

(b) Systems analysis

The next requirement is to know what tasks are essential, and to plan the methods for doing them. The aim of the systems analyst is to design efficient methods for all necessary data processing and to integrate them into a total system, with the minimum duplication of effort.

One of the first tasks of the systems analyst will be to find and list the essential sub-systems. By so doing he will inevitably find tasks now being carried out, which are inessential, or of doubtful value. Later when he studies the sub-systems in detail he will again find data processing tasks, which are being done two or three different times in different departments. The reductions in establishment instituted by the Establishment Committee, should be based on the elimination of unnecessary and duplicated work found by the systems analyst.

(c) Output standards

The final requirement for control of the indirect labour, is some method for fixing output standards. A method which has been introduced recently in the U.S.A. and is now used by a growing number of firms in Britain, is called Group Capacity Assessment or G.C.A.

The aim of G.C.A. is to set standards for the number of orders which one group of men should be able to issue per week, the number of invoices which one group should be able to prepare per week, the number of drawings that one group of draughtsmen should be able to prepare per week and so on. All the well-known work measurement techniques can be used. It is recognized that many data processing jobs vary greatly in length from one job to the next. It is submitted, however, that standards can still be set on the basis of group output.

Redundancy of the indirect labour can sometimes be avoided by forming project groups to work on special problems. The final reduction in numbers is then achieved by natural wastage.

13.8 SUMMARY

In addition to its important economic advantages, Group Technology is also a desirable change from the human point of view. Through job enlargement, a closer association with the product, and a reduction in stress due to a reduction in co-ordination needs, Group Technology can provide greater job satisfaction and better labour relations.

This book has described Group Technology as a strategy of production management which takes over where line production is no longer applicable. Perhaps the most surprising development in Group production is that recently, companies as internationally famous as Philips, Volvo, and Saab have actually preferred group production—in cases where line production could have been used—for personnel relations and quality control reasons.

As with all major innovations, the introduction of the changes in working conditions due to Group Technology can cause trouble. Major difficulties can best be avoided by careful planning and training prior to the change, so that everyone involved knows what to expect.

14 Planning the Introduction of Group Technology

14.1 INTRODUCTION

Group Technology is a new approach to batch production, which involves a very complex series of related changes in management and technology. The only safe way to implement an innovation of this type is to divide it into a series of independent projects, each of which is capable of standing on its own. These projects are then tackled separately in a carefully planned sequence.

When divided into independent projects in this way, the introduction of a major innovation can be planned and controlled with precision, in relation to both the time schedule for the work—where CPA can be used to find the best schedule—and also to the budgets for cash, expenditure, and savings. In addition, if the work is held up for any reason, well-planned changes can stand on their own and will not need changing back even if there is a temporary hold-up in development. This chapter gives a brief outline of the way in which the introduction of Group Technology can be planned and controlled.

14.2 STRATEGY OF INTRODUCTION

Before starting to plan, the planner must have a clear idea of the strategy, or policy, he intends to follow. In general he has two main policy decisions to make:

1. Horizontal or vertical introduction
2. The general sequence of project introduction

(a) Horizontal or vertical introduction

The change to Group Technology will involve the completion of a number of major changes. Many of these have already been described in this book, including the change from stock control to flow control, the development of tooling families, and the introduction of group layout. There are two opposing schools of thought about how these changes should be introduced. They can be named the horizontal and vertical approaches and are illustrated in Figure 14.1.

With the horizontal approach, the first step is to plan and install one perfect group, together with its own special supporting systems and a full range of newly developed methods and tooling. When this first, or 'trial group', is running, further groups are planned and installed one after the other, until the total installation is complete. If the major system changes are listed across the top of a square, as shown in Figure 14.1, and if the groups to be formed are listed on the vertical axis, it will be seen that the horizontal approach attempts to take a succession of horizontal slices, completing each group together with a part at least of any necessary supporting changes, before going on to the next.

With the vertical approach each major system change is treated as a separate project and is tackled as a whole. Each project is introduced

	SYSTEM CHANGE PROJECTS										
Groups to be formed ↓	Group layout	Production control	Payment system	Costing system	Simplification	Variety reduction	Standardization	Tooling families	Tooling development	Method development	New plant
1											
2											
3											
4											
5											
6											
7											

The horizontal approach forms one group at a time
The vertical approach tackles one innovation at a time

Figure 14.1. Horizontal and vertical approaches to Group Technology

generally on a company wide basis—but occasionally on a departmental basis—as a series of sub-projects, one after the other. The different projects may be scheduled to overlap in time. Critical path analysis can be used to find the ideal schedule.

This book supports the vertical approach, on the following grounds:

1. With the horizontal approach no system change is completed until the last group is installed.

2. For a long period the shops must work with duplicate service systems, e.g. wages, production control, etc.

3. Most of the potential savings cannot be obtained until the last group is installed.

4. It is impossible to schedule and budget the work of installation with precision, when the groups are only discovered progressively.

With the vertical approach, projects are introduced completely and consolidated in turn. Each major, or key project is finished before going on to the next one. Savings are earned from an early stage in the introduction, and because planning is on a project basis, schedules and budgets can be prepared without difficulty, to form the basis of control.

(b) The general sequence of projects

The second main policy decision to be made concerns the general sequence in which the different projects should be carried out, which are necessary for the full development of Group Technology. Figure 14.2 gives a consolidated list of some of the changes considered necessary for Group Technology by a number of different writers on the subject. Assuming that all these changes are accepted as desirable, Figure 14.3 now illustrates two opposing views about the best sequence of introduction.

The first of these views advocates the earliest possible introduction of group layout and flow control, together with any other minor changes

---

1. *Classification and coding*—of products, components, and tools.

2. *Value analysis*—of products and components.

3. *Variety reduction*—of products, components, and materials.

4. *Standardization*—of products and components.

5. *Technological development*—of production methods.

6. *Flow control ordering*—in place of 'stock control'.

7. *Group layout*—in place of functional layout.

8. *Production flow analysis*—to find the groups and families for Group layout.

Figure 14.2. Changes claimed as necessary for Group Technology

which are essential if the new installation is to operate efficiently. The second view takes the opposite side and advocates extensive rationalization and technological development before changing the layout. In particular it considers that component classification and coding, variety reduction, simplification through value analysis, the planning and introduction of new processing methods, and tooling development, must all be completed, before it is possible to change the layout. This book rejects the second of these views, on the following grounds:

1. The changes in design, method, and tooling will need many years to complete, and will delay the introduction of Group Technology.

2. Only minor savings will be made before the changes in plant layout and production control system are completed.

3. Money must be found for a substantial initial increase in investment.

4. The combined result of new additional investment, giving an insignificant return for the several years before a complete group layout is achieved, will be years of reduced profitability.

The first view is preferred because the early introduction of flow control and group layout means that savings can be achieved from an early date and the capital for further development can be obtained mainly from the reduction in the stock investment.

If a stock control system of ordering has been used in the past, the stock

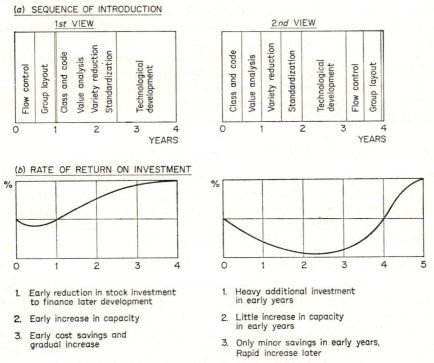

Figure 14.3. Alternative sequences of introduction

will not be in balanced product sets. One particular advantage of the early introduction of group layout and flow control ordering, is that it will gradually bring the stock back into balanced product sets. If one attempts to simplify the product range and reduce component variety before balancing the stock in product sets, there are bound to be big losses due to materials obsolescence. If flow control ordering is introduced early, most of these losses can be avoided.

A criticism which has been levelled at the early change of layout, is that 'it will tend to perpetuate existing bad practice'. The assumptions here are that in most companies existing production methods are badly planned, and that once the change has been made to group layout it will be difficult or impossible to improve it later. Neither assumption is generally correct. There are in fact big advantages to be gained by limiting technological change in the early stages, because:

1. Most of the desirable technological changes require a prior knowledge of the 'tooling families'.

2. It is easier to find and establish efficient 'tooling families' when the families and groups are already formed.

3. It is impossible, or at the least very difficult, to bring parts in the same tooling family together for processing one after the other, with conventional functional layout and a stock control ordering system. It is difficult therefore under these conditions, either to test the tooling families, or to obtain any savings from their use.

4. Technological development will be more soundly based and easier to introduce if the personnel are already used to group working.

5. It is better to continue with tried and proven processing methods during the early stages of introducing Group Technology rather than tackle two major revolutions at once.

14.3 PLANNING THE INTRODUCTION

Assume that a strategy has been adopted of vertical introduction, with the early installation of: short cycle period batch control; group layout; and a planned loading sequence. Assume also that it has been decided that some changes in the accounting methods, and in the incentive payment scheme are the main supporting changes required.

(a) Check existing systems

The first step in planning is to study the existing systems in the factory, to determine what features needed for Group Technology are already in existence. Four examples will show the type of information needed. If Pareto Analysis has already been used in the company and the parts are already classified by value, it will not be necessary to do it again and time will be saved during the installation. Again if the route cards are already maintained accurately, there will be no need to spend time rechecking them. Time will again be saved during installation.

If the company already has a period batch control system, there will be a big saving in the time needed for the installation of Group Technology. Even if it doesn't have a full period batch control system, however, it may be that certain parts of the existing production control system, can be incorporated in the new system without change. For example, if low value (Class *C*) items have already been abstracted from the main system, for separate simplified control with issue to free stores, this part of the system will not need changing.

If the company already have a component classification and coding system, it will save time when planning the division into tooling families and when searching for composite parts.

(b) Breaking the changes down into projects

Assume that the audit of existing methods has failed to find any features of importance to Group Technology. It has been decided that the main changes required in the first phase of development are:

1. Period batch control
2. Some simplification of the accounting methods
3. The substitution of a group incentive scheme for the existing individual incentives
4. Group layout
5. Some changes in purchasing methods
6. The introduction of a planned loading sequence in the groups

The next job is to divide these changes into separate projects, each of which can stand on its own. A list of such projects is given below for an engineering company with four main processing departments. The projects can be described briefly for this particular case, as follows:

1. *Establishment committee.* Form an Establishment Committee to examine the manning strengths necessary in each department at regular intervals, and to report regularly to the directors on redundancy problems as they arise.

2. *Pareto analysis.* Analyse all components by annual consumption value and classify them into *A* (high value), *B* (medium value) and *C* (low value) categories. Add these value class codes to the parts lists.

3. *Route cards.* Standardize the methods for the layout and preparation of route cards. Revise the machine type code and see that all items of plant are coded. Introduce methods to control and improve the accuracy of the route cards.

4. *Training.* Short courses in Group Technology. Train all levels of personnel, from the directors to the workers.

5. *Ordering class 'C' purchases.* Introduce a simple stock control ordering system for Class *C* purchased parts, with control of ordering in the stores and free issue to assembly.

6. *Ordering class 'B' purchases.* Introduce a scheduled delivery system, against annual supply contracts, based on a bi-monthly revised annual programme. Fix buffer stock levels to cover any probable deviation between this scheduled rate and the actual rate that will be imposed in the future by the flexible programming of period batch control. Institute a control system, to revise buffer stock levels as necessary.

7. *Factory flow analysis.* As soon as the route cards have been revised, carry out factory flow analysis. Plan a simplified inter-departmental, or inter-group material flow system between major groups. Find the

'exceptions' requiring elimination. Plan any redistribution of plant which is required.

8. *Simplify the inter-departmental flow system.* Eliminate the 'exceptions' found by factory flow analysis, by re-routing, redistribution of machines between departments, redesign of parts, changes of processing method, or by purchasing instead of making. Introduce controls to ensure that the simplified flow system is maintained.

9. *Introduce flexible programming.* Choose the initial cycle time for programming and ordering and plan the standard schedule for period batch control ordering. Design the forms and plan operating methods for the periodic programme meeting. Introduce the new programming method, but only use it initially to control assembly.

10. *Class A purchases.* Negotiate with the suppliers of Class *A* purchased items, for delivery against annual contracts, according to 'call-off' instructions, which will be issued at programme cycle intervals. If suppliers will not agree to this method for some parts treat these items in the same way as Class *B* purchases (6 above).

11. *Plan the period batch control ordering system.* Design the forms and plan the methods to be used for: 'exploding' the period production programmes into 'shop orders' for made parts; 'delivery call-off instructions' for Class *A* purchase deliveries; and stores requisitions for Class *B* parts purchased for stock. Prepare the manual and start training.

12. *Group analysis.* Use group analysis to find the families and groups for group layout. Find the exceptions requiring elimination.

13. *Plan new wages and accounting systems.* Plan new wages and accounting systems. Design forms. Negotiate change in wages system from individual piece work to group bonus. Train staff.

14. *Eliminate exceptions found in group analysis.* Study the routes for all exceptions found by group analysis and eliminate by re-routing, by changes in method, by redesign or by buying instead of making.

15. *Introduce period batch control.* Introduce the period batch control system planned earlier (11), for the ordering of all made parts, and for the control of delivery of all Class *A* purchased direct materials, which suppliers can be persuaded to deliver against cyclical call-off requests.

16. *Find tooling-families, inside all families in Department W.* Sort routes to find composite parts and other tooling families. Plan standard loading sequence. The initial aim should be to obtain without risk of failure a reduction in material cost and the reduction in setting time needed to make group production possible. The initial policy should therefore be to base this loading sequence primarily on bringing together parts which use the same materials, and parts which require similar set-ups.

17. *Use line analysis to plan the plant layout in Department W.* Use line analysis to plan the layout of machines in all groups in Department *W*, and to simplify the flow system inside these groups. At this initial stage the policy should be to achieve only that level of simplification which can

be obtained by re-routing inside the groups, without additional investment.

18. *Plan the manning of the groups.* Decide which foreman, or charge-hand will be in charge of each group. Decide how many operators are needed in each group and who they should be.

19. *Introduce group layout in Department W.* Move the machines into group layout. The choice of department for the first layout change may vary from factory to factory. In some companies it may be good policy to achieve the most difficult change first. In others it may be best to start with the easiest change.

20 to 23. *Repeat 16, 17, 18 and 19 for Department X.*
24 to 27. *Repeat 16, 17, 18 and 19 for Department Y.*
28 to 31. *Repeat 16, 17, 18 and 19 for Department Z.*

(c) *Estimate duration times*

After deciding on the best division into projects the next task is to estimate the duration times for each project in days. In each case it is necessary to assume that a specified number of people will be allocated to do the work, using specified methods and facilities. If later after finding the critical path it is decided that the time must be shortened, these provisions can be increased thus reducing the duration time. Alternatively if it is found later that a project is not on the critical path, the facilities and the number of people allotted to the project can be reduced.

(d) *Draw critical path network and find critical path*

Critical path analysis is useful for finding the best schedule for introduction. A network—using the projects listed above as activities—is shown in Figure 14.4. The estimated duration times are given on the network. The critical path in this case follows the sequence 1, 3, 4, 5, 6, 8, 10, 12, 14, 16, 17, 18, and has a total duration of 405 days, or 81 weeks.

The most difficult duration times to estimate are those which involve negotiations. The most difficult activity in this respect may be the change in the wage system. The most critical event as far as labour relations is concerned is event 10. When this event is reached, all the preparatory planning should be finished for the change to group layout in the first department. Most of the talking should be finished by this point, and if event 10 can be reached on time the final due-date should be achievable.

Two important activities are not included in the network, on the grounds that they need independent control. These are training and the work of the Establishments Committee. The training programme should certainly be related to the general introduction programme in that all training needs which are essential for the introduction, should be completed by the appropriate event dates. It should, however, be based on a longer view and should not stop when the initial introduction is complete. The work of the Establishments Committee should not be scheduled in advance. It

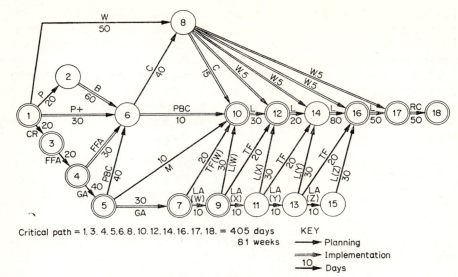

Critical path = 1. 3. 4. 5.6. 8. 10. 12. 14. 16. 17. 18. = 405 days
81 weeks

KEY

———▶ Planning
══▶ Implementation
10 ──▶ Days

Figure 14.4. C.P.A. network

1.2	Pareto analysis.
1.3	Correct routes and plant list.
1.6	Plan and introduce periodic programming.
1.8	Plan new wages system.
2.6	Revise buying methods.
3.4	Factory flow analysis (FFA).
4.5	Group analysis (GA).
4.6	Revise exceptional routes from FFA.
5.6	Plan 'period batch control' (PBC) method.
5.7	Revise exceptional routes from GA (*see* 4.5).
5.10	Plan manning of groups.
6.8	Plan changes in costing system.
6.10	Introduce PBC all made parts. 4 week cycle.
7.9	Line analysis (LA) for groups in Department W.
7.10	Tooling families for groups in Department W.
8.10	Introduce new costing and wages system.
8.12; 8.14; 8.16; 8.17	Change to group bonus in Departments W, X, Y, and Z.
9.10; 11.12; 13.14; 15.16	Plan layout in Departments W, X, Y, and Z.
9.12; 11.14; 13.16	Tooling families in Departments X, Y, and Z.
10.12; 12.14; 14.16; 16.17	Change layout in Departments W, X, Y, and Z.
17.18	Reduce PBC cycle to 2 weeks.

should exert more of a cybernetic control, watching changes in the requirement for labour and providing the information on which action is taken when necessary.

14.4 IMPLEMENTATION

Control of implementation should ideally be in the hands of the Managing Director. He will need an assistant working full time on the introduction, and he will delegate most of the work on the individual projects to the managers who will eventually make the changes and run the new systems. Without his central direction, however, it will be very difficult to obtain effective co-ordination between the different managers concerned.

There should be regular meetings for co-ordination, at which progress reports will be made on outstanding projects and at which plans will be made to overcome special difficulties. As each project becomes due for introduction, the Managing Director will call on the appropriate manager to report on what he is going to do, and answer questions from his colleagues.

The most important responsibility of the Managing Director will be to maintain good labour relations and morale. Apparently minor misconceptions and misunderstandings can easily wreck the project, if they are allowed to fester. He will need good channels of communication with all levels in the factory and with the trade unions, so that he is quickly informed about morale problems, and has a ready means by which he can correct misunderstandings as they arise.

14.5 SUMMARY

The secret of success in the introduction of Group Technology is to break the job down into a number of independent projects each of which can be introduced and can stand on its own.

Each project should be carefully planned, and be introduced only after training the involved personnel, and after briefing any others in the organization who may be affected by the change.

Planned in this way, it is possible to schedule and budget the introduction of Group Technology with precision, but still retain the option to stop development temporarily at any stage, if this becomes necessary.

15 Conclusions

Group Technology is a new philosophy of management which is based like line production on the simplification of material flow. Material flow systems like electrical and electronic circuits, consist of a mixture of series and parallel flow, as illustrated in Figure 15.1. Even in the simplest possible flow system there will generally be some series flow between departments to accommodate incompatible and common processes applied in sequence. Inside departments parallel flow through independent homogeneous groups will be the most common. Finally inside the groups the normal rule will again be series flow between the machines used for successive operations.

The form of the optimum material flow system is dictated by the nature of the products produced and of the processes used in their manufacture. It is not something new which must be created, but something which already exists and must be discovered. Production flow analysis provides a simple and reliable method for finding the best division into departments and groups, and the best arrangement for the plant in each group.

With a simple material flow system it is comparatively easy to regulate material flow so that parts are only made when they are needed to produce known or forecast requirements of finished products. The single cycle flow control systems used for this purpose have the added advantage that because they order large numbers of parts on the same days, they make it possible to schedule processing in tooling families, to give minimum setting time and thus obtain a significant increase in capacity. Because with group layout the machines used to make components are close together, throughput times are short and short cycles can be used for programming and ordering. This in turn shortens delivery times and provides a flexible system which can quickly follow changes in market demand.

A change from the traditional methods of functional layout and stock control, to group layout and flow control gives a major increase in profitability, because the same changes increase output capacity and reduce both costs and the investment needed per unit of output. These changes also simplify the later introduction and increase the savings possible, from rationalization and the technological development of processing methods.

Although group layout and flow control are the key changes, Group Technology is not solely a production management innovation. To obtain the full benefits, complementary changes must be made in organization

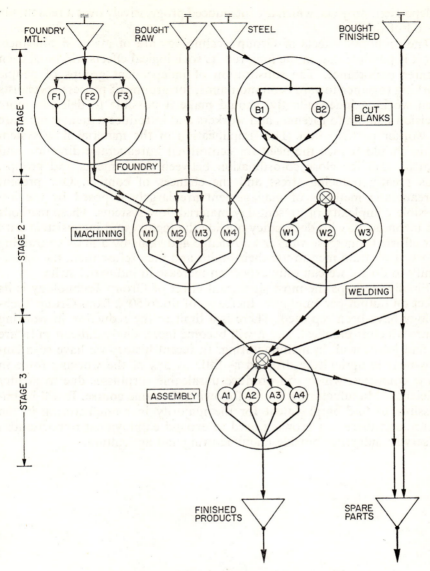

Figure 15.1. Flow between departments and groups

and policy, which affect all the other functions of management. Group Technology can therefore be completely successful only if there is total management involvement. The total introduction involves changes in nearly every management activity in the enterprise. In spite of the complexity of the innovation, however, introduction should still be possible in most enterprises, if the work is broken down into a large number of independent projects, which are introduced progressively over a reasonable period of time.

The economic effects of Group Technology are of major significance, but it is possible that in the long run its sociological effects will be of even greater importance. The substitution of independent groups of people working together towards common aims, for groups of process specialists each working independently, should make it possible to delegate more decision making to foremen and workers and introduce a greater measure of worker participation. The simplification of the material flow system again should reduce the need for centralized bureaucratic direction and control, and for close co-ordination between departments and groups, thus greatly reducing stress and the chances of conflict. Our present bureaucratic methods of management are largely imposed by the impossible complexity of present-day material flow systems. These methods are inconsistent with democracy outside the factory and inconsistent with our efforts to increase worker knowledge and skills by a massive training effort. If we train men to use their brains and then refuse them the opportunity to do so, we can only expect an increase in industrial strife.

Finally, perhaps the most significant effect of Group Technology is its effect on output per employee. Increases of up to 50% from Group Technology have been reported. There is a limit to the reduction in working hours which is practical, and it will become increasingly difficult in future to find jobs for all in manufacturing. In recent history we have seen employment in agriculture drop to as little as 5% of the working force in some countries, which still produce unsaleable surplusses due to greater efficiency. Manufacturing is now following the same course. It will be impossible to find employment for the majority in manufacturing in the future and there is a growing need to expand employment opportunities in service industries outside manufacturing and agriculture.

Index